Beachcomber

Also by Karen Robards
in Large Print:

Irresistible
Paradise County
Ghost Moon
Heartbreaker
Walking after Midnight
Desire in the Sun
Morning Song
Nobody's Angel

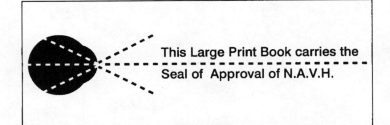

Beachcomber

Karen Robards

Thorndike Press • Waterville, Maine

Published in 2003 by arrangement with Atria Books, an imprint of Simon & Schuster, Inc.

Thorndike Press® Large Print Core.

The tree indicium is a trademark of Thorndike Press.

The text of this Large Print edition is unabridged.
Other aspects of the book may vary from the original edition.

Set in 16 pt. Plantin.

Printed in the United States on permanent paper.

Library of Congress Control Number: 2003110041
ISBN 0-7862-5654-0 (lg. print : hc : alk. paper)

This book is dedicated with love and appreciation to the memory of Mary Rose Miller, my children's honorary grandmother, who passed away on May 26, 2003.

It is also dedicated, as always, to my husband, Doug, and to my three sons, Peter, Christopher, and Jack, with all my love.

As the Founder/CEO of NAVH, the only national health agency solely devoted to those who, although not totally blind, have an eye disease which could lead to serious visual impairment, I am pleased to recognize Thorndike Press* as one of the leading publishers in the large print field.

Founded in 1954 in San Francisco to prepare large print textbooks for partially seeing children, NAVH became the pioneer and standard setting agency in the preparation of large type.

Today, those publishers who meet our standards carry the prestigious "Seal of Approval" indicating high quality large print. We are delighted that Thorndike Press is one of the publishers whose titles meet these standards. We are also pleased to recognize the significant contribution Thorndike Press is making in this important and growing field.

Lorraine H. Marchi, L.H.D.
Founder/CEO
NAVH

* Thorndike Press encompasses the following imprints: Thorndike, Wheeler, Walker and Large Print Press.

Prologue

Pretty girls in bikinis were everywhere, frolicking in the surf, walking up and down the beach, sprawled out on towels as far as the eye could see. It was the first Saturday in August, and Nags Head was sweltering and hopping at the same time. The sun was a fireball the size of an orange hanging low above the jagged skyline of hotels, condominiums, and private residences that stood like a backbone behind the creamy curve of the beach. The scent of suntan oil hung in the air. A raging boom box all but drowned out the hiss and growl of the ocean. Vacationers crammed the shore, all different ages and colors and sizes and shapes mixed up together, talking and laughing as they soaked up the last of the day's rays. Most of them were as invisible to him as he was to them. The girls were what stood out in vivid Technicolor. As his gaze moved from one to the other, lingering on a tall blonde here, caressing a curvy brunette there, his body tightened and tingled with a familiar anticipation. Just looking at them made him feel good all over. And why not? They were his favorite prey.

"Look out!"

A beach ball bonked him in the side of the head. It didn't hurt, but he blinked, startled, and glanced around. A college-age girl with long blond hair scraped back in a ponytail and generous assets barely contained by a tiny turquoise swimsuit grabbed the rebound.

"Sorry!" she offered with a grin.

"No problem," he said, but she was already running back to rejoin her friends. He played follow the bouncing ass until she dodged behind an old guy dragging a kayak out of the water. The beach ball arced over the old guy's head and was caught by another girl. A brunette. His eyes widened as she leaped into the air to grab the ball. The blonde was cute, a lively towhead with skin the color of crispy chicken, but it was the brunette who was something special.

She was taller than the blonde, and slimmer. A pink bandanna held her thick brown hair back from her face. It swung just free of her shoulders as she tossed the ball away. Her bikini was pink, too, cotton-candy pink, a shiny, stretchy fabric that his fingers suddenly itched to touch. He could almost feel the silkiness of it, the firm warmth of her skin beneath — the lovely unblemished skin that was as golden-smooth as melted caramel.

Watching her, his mouth watered. He clenched his teeth as the ache came over him, the hunger. His senses seemed to expand, take on a new acuity. He could smell the girl's musky scent, see obscure details such as the triangular dark mole in the crevice between her breasts and the small butterfly tattoo on her left hip, hear her mutter a fierce *damn it* as the ball skimmed over her head and knocked her bandanna loose.

She stopped playing to retie the bandanna. Her back was to him now, and his gaze drank in the sharp angle of her shoulder blades, the long sweep of her back, the curve of her ass.

"Liz, catch!" The blonde yelled, bounding back into his line of vision. The brunette turned toward the hurtling ball, caught it, and ran straight at him while three other girls chased her, shrieking with laughter.

Her breasts bounced like tennis balls when she ran.

At the last minute she sheared away, angling back toward the water. Laughing, the

9

other girls changed direction, too, and the ball once again flew through the air.

"I've got it!" A third girl in a yellow bikini, who was pear-shaped, with short, spiky black hair, caught the ball and pelted away with Liz and the pack in hot pursuit.

"Throw it, Terri!" Liz shrieked, and the pear-shaped girl threw the ball to her. Liz leaped to catch it, and her breasts almost bounced free of that teeny-tiny top.

The thick, hot throbbing between his legs was almost unbearable now. The need to possess her was so intense that he couldn't move. His eyelids drooped. His nostrils quivered as he inhaled more of her scent. Saliva filled his mouth, and he swallowed. He could almost taste the warm caramel on his tongue.

"Excuse me, do you know which way the Ramada Inn is?" a sandy-haired kid asked, stopping in front of him.

It took him a minute to process what the kid was asking. Then he shook his head without replying. The kid made a disgusted sound and moved on. While annoying, the interruption had served a useful purpose: it had cut like a knife through the thick haze of wanting that had him rooted to the spot. He caught himself, battling the beast back into submission, and deliberately took a breath to clear his head. He'd paused to stare at the girl, he realized, and that wasn't smart. He might attract attention and someone might remember him later, when she turned up missing.

"Oh, crap, it's in the water!"

Laughing, the girls splashed into the surf after the ball, which floated away on the waves. The thought of seeing that shiny pink bikini wet was tantalizing, but it was time to move on. He'd been standing there watching them for way too long. It required great effort, but he tore his gaze away and started walking. His heart was pounding. He was breathing way too fast. His feet felt as heavy as iron weights as he made his way across the hot sand. Skirting two little kids playing on a towel, he tamped his power down, deliberately drew back inside his shell, behind the protective coloring that kept anyone from seeing him, from recognizing the truth about who and what he was.

He became invisible again.

A safe forty yards away, he stopped in the shadow of a palmetto tree that grew right at the edge of the beach, just inside the grounds of the Quality Inn. Leaning back against the low stone wall that separated the motel from the sand, he rested his elbows on top of the wall, pushed his sunglasses back up his nose, and allowed his gaze to return to his quarry.

The hunt was on. He'd found the one he wanted. Now that he had her in his sights, the chances that she would manage to elude him were minimal. There was always an element of fate, of luck, in these things, but chance, as the saying went, generally favored the prepared mind. She was not prepared. In fact, she had no clue that she had been singled out. They never did. He had trolled these beaches before, so many times that he had the taking of young women down to a fine art. The Outer Banks teemed with potential victims: that was one reason he had chosen to move to the area. They were unwary, too, the girls, a little lax with their usual safety precautions, lulled into a false sense of security by the combined soporifics of surf, sand, and sun. Holy moly, they were on vacation, they seemed to think. What could possibly go wrong?

At the thought he allowed himself a small smile. Him, for one.

When Liz left with her friends, he followed, careful to stay back, to attract no attention, to blend in.

They didn't notice him. No one ever noticed him. Not until he wanted them to, that is. Then they noticed him, in a big way. Unfortunately, by that time it was usually too late — for them.

There were four of them, four pretty girls in four yummy flavors, each as tempting as a chocolate in a Valentine candy box, but Liz was the one he wanted. His blood hummed with anticipation as he trailed them through the lengthening shadows. It had been a while since he had allowed himself the luxury of a capture: he tried to limit himself, because he had learned the hard way that if he took too many too often people began to notice. Papers started spouting headlines like SERIAL KILLER ON THE LOOSE and the talking heads on TV yapped about the latest victims and how women could protect themselves and the girls started looking over their shoulders and jumping at anything that moved. Then pressure got put on the cops to find the killer.

They were too dumb to catch him but they could make his life difficult, which was why, a few years back, he had left his old stomping grounds behind and moved south. Said good-bye to girls in parkas and mittens and hello to babes in bikinis.

Good-bye to freezing his ass off and hello to balmy breezes. Good-bye to cops who were running details about the victims, the crimes, and the locations of the bodies through their computers in hopes of uncovering the one detail that would nail him and hello to cops who had no idea he even existed.

Best thing he'd ever done, moving. Look at him now: happy, excited, filled with the thrill of the chase. He was doing what he loved for the love of it again. The dark days of stress and worry and looking over his shoulder were behind him.

And he meant to keep it that way. Like dieting, all it took was the exercise of a little self-restraint.

The girls went through a small wrought-iron gate into the pool area of a hotel. He wasn't familiar enough with Nags Head to be able to identify which one it was from his particular viewing angle, but it didn't matter; as long as he managed to keep them in sight it was all good. Stopping in the shadow of a float-rental booth that had just closed for the night, he busied himself by shaking the sand out of his shoes as people trudged past without giving him a second glance. With the endless patience that always came over him when he was engaged in a hunt, he waited for Liz and her friends to move on, smiling a little as he listened to their chatter, watching as they rinsed off under the outside shower, savoring the knowledge of what was to come. When they started walking again, wrapped in towels now, he started walking too, careful to keep his distance. He followed them to the motel's stairwell and watched as they trooped up the cement stairs — it was the Windjammer, cheap, with long, open-air hallways in front of the rooms and lots of access from the outside — then crowded into a single room: 218.

"I'm starving," he heard one of the girls complain through the still-open door. "Can we please eat?"

"What about Taco — ?"

The door closed then, cutting off the rest of the conversation. But it didn't matter. He knew where they were staying. All he had to do now was watch and wait.

It took him five minutes to retrieve his camper, which was parked down the street. Forty-seven minutes later according to the dashboard clock, he watched Liz and her friends emerge from their room. Liz was in a halter and shorts that left her legs tantalizingly bare. It was late by then, ten-thirty, and by rights he should have been tired. But he wasn't. He never got tired when he was going after game. Instead, he felt energized, empowered, alive. At times like this he realized that the rest of his life was lived in shades of black and white. This — this hunting and taking — was the only time the world around him took on vibrant rainbow hues. It was exciting. It was intoxicating. It was liberating. It was, in fact, the only time he was truly himself.

The girls piled into a way-too-small Honda Civic and took off down Beach Road. His heart rate accelerated right along with the camper as he followed them, then watched through the Taco Bell's big glass windows as they ate. By the time they finished and parked on the strip to do some shopping at the T-shirt and seashell-jewelry stores, it was full dark. A moon as frosty yellow as a lemon drop was just starting its climb across the sky. He circled the block, getting a little electric thrill every time he spotted Liz browsing in one of the fluorescent-lit stores. When they popped into the Parrot Cay bar for drinks, he parked out front and waited. He wasn't in a hurry. In fact, he was enjoying himself. The picture he held in his mind was of himself as a lion creeping through the tall grass of a savannah toward a grazing gazelle. The lion was aware of everything, from the direction of the wind to the presence of other creatures that might sound a warning to the sharpness of its own hunger. The gazelle was aware of nothing but the sweetness of the grass.

Until the unwary creature wandered just a little too far away from the safety of the herd, which was how pretty little gazelles tended to meet their end. After about fifteen minutes Liz did exactly that. She came out of the bar alone, talking a mile a minute on a cell phone as she walked down the cement steps to the sidewalk. Either the noise inside, a desire for privacy, or the wish not to offend her neighbors had sent her right out under his nose.

And to think that, ordinarily, he hated cell phones.

It was close to midnight now, but the street was far from deserted. People came in and out of the bar; shoppers browsed the shops; cars drove past. Still, the sidewalk in front of the bar was dark and shadowy. And as she talked, she moved farther away from the door — and closer to him.

He couldn't stand it. She was too close, too tempting. Waiting for a better time

17

probably would be smarter, but it wouldn't be nearly as much fun.

His camper was parked at a meter about ten feet from where she was still jabbering away on that phone. His blood was rushing through his veins now. His muscles were tense, ready. His senses were on edge, alert, vibrating. He felt himself swelling, shrugging out of his everyday skin as he suddenly became as lethal as a high-voltage power line.

The beast was emerging, and it felt good.

Getting out of the camper, he headed toward her. She glanced at him, casually, as he drew close.

"Liz?" He quickened his step, greeting her like a long-lost friend delighted to run into her in this unexpected spot.

She frowned, breaking off in the middle of whatever she had been saying to look up at him questioningly. He saw that her parted lips were freshly glossed. They gleamed alluringly as they caught the soft neon glow of the bar sign overhead.

"Hi," he said almost tenderly as he reached her, and shoved his stun gun into her side. The sharp buzz always made him think of a mosquito zapper doing its thing. The acrid scent of burning slid up his nostrils like cocaine. His left arm was already around her in what was calculated to be a friendly-looking hug as she gasped and stiffened, then crumpled against him. Her phone hit the strip of grass beside the side-walk without a sound.

It took just seconds to bundle her into the back of the camper and close the door. He'd customized the vehicle to create the perfect holding chamber: there was no way out. Anyway, he had a good fifteen minutes before she would begin to stir, he knew from experience. That gave him plenty of time to get out of town. A quick glance around reassured him that no one was near; no one had seen. Her cell phone caught his eye: he didn't want to leave that behind. If it was found, her friends would immediately begin to worry. If it wasn't, they would most likely think that she had walked back down to the shops and start looking for her there.

"Liz?"

He was bent over, scooping up the phone. Straightening, he saw that one of Liz's friends — the pear-shaped one with the butch haircut whose name he vaguely remembered was Terri — was standing on the sidewalk only a few feet away, eye-balling him with an expression that was just a few more seconds' thought short of suspicion.

"What are you doing with that?" Her gaze glued to the phone now, she began to frown. A couple came out of the bar behind her, but beyond a casual glance paid them no attention; as soon as the pair hit the sidewalk they turned and headed, arm in arm, up the street. Nevertheless, he felt a stab of uncertainty, a sense that events were no longer entirely under his control. He hated the feeling and, by extension, hated her for causing it, for disturbing the flow of the moment, the excitement of the capture, the beautiful oneness he was feeling with all things strong and powerful and free.

"It was lying on the ground here," he said easily, glancing down at the phone in his hand. "Did you lose one?"

He held it out to her. His heart still pounded with excitement from his success with Liz. He was on edge, bursting with strength, bristling with energy. There was no tamping the power down. Not yet. It was too soon. He was afraid this girl would be able to read what was in his face, in his eyes, but there was nothing he could do but trust in his own luck and the concealing power of the darkness around them.

"My friend . . ." Brows firmly knit now, she stepped toward him, reaching for the phone. He already knew what he had to do.

"She's with me." The smile he gave her was really more of a snarl, and as she took the phone, the beast lunged at her. Her eyes widened as they made contact with his, but it was already too late. Catching her wrist, he yanked her against him and hit her with the stun gun. The little choked cry she gave just before she slumped over his encircling arm was scarcely louder than a cough. Picking her up, he looked around with the caginess of a wild animal to make sure they were still unobserved, then carried her the few steps to the camper and dumped her in beside Liz. Her head thumped against a metal tackle box he'd shoved back there a couple of days earlier. She would have a bump when she woke up, not that he cared. This one was ugly, he hadn't wanted her, but she'd forced herself on him and he would take her, too.

Maybe she could be a playmate for Liz.

At the thought, he felt a flicker of interest. He'd never taken two at once before.

Liz's phone lay on the sidewalk. Retrieving it, he walked around the front of his camper and climbed behind the wheel. Time to go; the longer he hung around, the greater the chance that someone might remember the camper when questions were asked. But he'd taken care to make sure that it was invisible, just like him. Neither of the girls seemed to have noticed it, just like they hadn't noticed him. Picturing their reaction when they woke up and made his acquaintance, his good humor was suddenly restored. He felt so good, in fact, that he caught himself whistling a happy tune as he drove out of town.

1

Two weeks later . . .

Sometimes in life, when one thing goes wrong it triggers another and another until disasters end up multiplying around you like horny rabbits. Unfortunately, Christy Petrino was getting the nasty suspicion that this just might be one of those times.

She was being followed as she walked along the moonlit beach. She knew it. Knew it with a certainty that made her heart pound and her breathing quicken and the tiny hairs on the back of her neck prickle to attention. *Someone was behind her.* She felt eyes on her, hostility directed at her, the intangible vibes of another presence, with a sense that was more trustworthy yet less dependably there than the usual five. Tonight, as it typically did when it hit her, this sixth sense of hers made a mockery of sight and sound, smell, touch, and taste. She'd learned in a hard school to trust it implicitly.

Please, God . . . Fear curled inside her

quicker than a coiling snake. Like any other good Catholic girl trembling on the brink of danger, she turned to a higher power for help even though it had been an embarrassingly long time since she had actually been inside a church. Hopefully, God wasn't keeping score.

I'll go to Mass this Sunday, I swear. I mean, I promise. Just let this be my imagination.

Clutching the slender can of Mace that was her next line of defense against the dangers that lurked in the night, she did her best to dismiss what her sixth sense was telling her even as she brought her other five senses to bear. The rush and hiss of the ocean as it lapped practically at her feet filled her ears. It drowned out all other sounds, not that it was likely that she would have heard any pursuing footsteps anyway, given the sound-deadening properties of the beach, she realized as her own steps faltered. Casting a compulsive glance over her shoulder, she saw nothing behind her but an empty seascape barely illuminated by dusky moonlight. Considering that it was after one in the morning and a drenching summer squall had done its bit to add to the suffocating humidity only an hour or so earlier, the fact that there was absolutely no one around could not be considered sinister: the family types that populated this particular stretch of Ocracoke's ocean frontage during August were doubtless all sound asleep inside their snug summer cottages. Except for those darkened cottages, set well back from the beach and barely visible over the rolling dunes, there was nothing to see but the lighthouse in the distance, willowy sea oats blowing in the rising wind that pushed a rippling line of whitecaps toward shore, and the pale narrow curve of the beach itself as it crooked like a bent finger out into the midnight blue of the Atlantic.

She was alone. *Of course* she was alone.

Letting out a sigh of relief, she cast her eyes skyward. *Thank you, God. I'll be there front row center on Sunday, I sw— promise.*

Then her pesky sixth sense reared its unwelcome head again.

"Are you being paranoid or what?" Christy muttered the question aloud. But accusing herself of paranoia didn't help. She started walking back to the house with — okay, she'd admit it — mounting fear.

She didn't like being afraid. Being afraid ticked her off. Growing up in Atlantic City, New Jersey, on the wrong side of I-5 in the less-than-aptly named neighborhood of Pleasantville, she'd learned early on that if you showed fear you were liable to get your butt kicked, or worse. A girl whose father was dead and whose mother worked all day and partied all night had to be able to take care of herself — and, in Christy's case, her two little sisters as well. She'd learned to be tough and she'd learned to be confident in her ability to handle anything life threw her way. Now, at twenty-seven, she was five feet seven inches tall, rendered fashionably slim and fit by dint of much effort, with medium brown hair that just brushed her shoulders, cocoa brown eyes, and a face that wasn't exactly beautiful but wouldn't send grown men screaming for the exits either. She was, in other words, all grown up, a lawyer — of all unbelievable things — with a life that until three days ago had been as close to perfect as she could make it.

Now it was blown to smithereens. And she was afraid.

"Wimp," she said under her breath as she walked on. There was nothing — well, probably nothing — to be afraid of. After all, she'd done what they wanted. She'd come here to the beach house on Ocracoke and stayed put, waiting for a phone call. When the call had finally come half an hour ago, she'd done exactly as she'd been

26

told: take the briefcase down the beach to the Crosswinds Hotel and put it in the backseat of a gray Maxima parked by the pool. What was in the briefcase she didn't know. Didn't want to know. All she wanted to do was get rid of it, which she had just done. In doing so, she'd purchased the keys to her prison.

It was over. She was free.

God, she hoped so. The truth was, if she was really, really lucky, and said her rosary fifteen times and buried a statue of St. Jude, patron saint of impossible causes, upside down in the surf, then maybe she would be free.

Or maybe not.

So call her a pessimist. Some people got visited by the blue bird of happiness. The bird that fluttered periodically through her life was more like the gray bird of doubt. Doubt that sunshine and roses were ever going to be a permanent fixture in the life of Christina Marie Petrino. Doubt that a pink Caddy with Happily Ever After written on it was ever going to pull into her own personal parking space. It was that doubt that kept suspicion percolating through her brain now, that made her imagine bogeymen in the shadows and threats in the whisper of the wind as she trudged back along the beach.

They had no reason to come after her. She had done nothing to them.

Except know too much.

Despite the humid warmth of the night, Christy shivered.

"Do this one thing for me," Uncle Vince had said. Remembering how she had been intercepted on the way to her mother's house and pushed into the backseat of a car where he'd been waiting, she swallowed. For the first time in her life, she'd been afraid of Uncle Vince, who'd been her mother's off-and-on boyfriend for the last fifteen years. Christy hadn't grown up in Pleasantville for nothing. She recognized a threat when she heard it. Uncle Vince had been a made man when Tony Soprano had been no more than a gleam in his daddy's eye, and his "request" had been on the order of one of those offers you didn't want to refuse.

But now she'd done what he'd asked, she reminded herself, walking faster now, in a hurry to get back inside the house even though she was (almost) sure there was no real reason to do what her instincts were screaming at her to do and get the heck off the beach. She'd delivered the briefcase. They knew now that she was loyal, that she wasn't going to go running to anybody, much less the cops. So she'd quit her job. Big deal. People did it all the time. So she'd said buh-bye to her fiancé. People did that, too. All over the world, employees quit and engaged couples broke up and nobody died. Just because Michael DePalma, who had been her boss at the up-and-coming Philadelphia law firm of DePalma and Lowery as well as her fiancé, had said *Don't you know you can't quit? After what Franky told you, do you really think they're going to let you just walk away?* did not mean that she was now first in line to get whacked.

Did it?

Maybe Uncle Vince, or somebody else, had decided that something more was needed in the way of ensuring her continued silence. Something permanent. Because she could still feel someone behind her in the dark. Watching her. Waiting. The picture that popped into her mind was of a hunter carefully stalking his prey.

The idea of herself as prey did nothing for Christy's blood pressure.

Drawing a deep breath, trying not to panic, Christy tightened her hold on the Mace can, and strained to identify shadowy shapes rendered spooky by darkness. *Oh God, what was that — and that — and that?* Her heart skipped a beat as she spotted possible threats. Only slowly did it resume a more even rhythm as she realized that the motionless rectangle that lay ahead of her that she'd first thought might be a man squatting in the surf was, on more careful inspection, a lounge chair left close by the water's edge; while the towering, swaying triangle — a man's head and shoulders? — rising menacingly over the top of a nearby dune was nothing more than a partially furled beach umbrella in its stand; and the round object — someone hunkered down? — just visible beside a patio fence was the protruding rear tire of a bicycle left trustingly outside.

Nothing but harmless, everyday, island-variety objects as far as the eye could see. As Christy told herself that, her alarm faded a little but refused to disappear entirely. The niggling sense of being watched, of another presence — of *danger* — was too strong to be routed by lack of visual confirmation. Wrapping her bare arms around herself, she continued to warily probe the darkness with every sense she could bring to bear. She stood very still, with the loose, ankle-length green gauze dress she had pulled on for her beach adventure blowing tight against her legs and her toes burrowing into the sand. Stars played peekaboo with drifting clouds overhead; a fingernail moon floated high in the black velvet sky; frothing with foam, waves slapped the sand, withdrew, and rolled in again, beach music with a never-ending rhythm that should have been comforting but under these disquieting circumstances was not. She listened and watched and breathed, tasting the salt tang on her lips as she wet them, smelling the briny ocean in the deep, lung-expanding breaths she deliberately drew in an effort to steady her jangled nerves.

"Okay, Christy, get a grip." Talking to herself was probably not a good sign. No, she realized glumly, it was *definitely* not a good sign. If she was getting a little crazy, she thought as she quickened her pace toward the small, single-story house that was now beckoning like an oasis, that should fall under the category of Just One More Big Surprise. She was up to her neck in disasters, and there was no telling where another one of those horny little rabbits was going to pop up next. Ordinarily she loved Ocracoke; she'd vacationed here at least half a dozen times in the past. Use of the beach house was an occasional perk of her mother's special friendship with Uncle Vince. But now this tiny beach community in North Carolina's Outer Banks was starting to feel like it had been ripped right out of the pages of a Stephen King novel. A vision of Blackbeard's ghost — the notorious pirate was said to haunt Ocracoke's beaches, his severed head tucked under his arm — shadowing her along the water's edge popped into her mind, raising goose bumps on her arms. Which was ridiculous, of course. Who believed in ghosts? Not she, but — the phrase that kept running through her head was, *something wicked this way comes.*

Dear God, I'll go to Mass every Sunday for the rest of my life if you'll just get me safely out of here.

She had to calm down and think this through.

If someone truly was behind her, if this terrifying sense of a hostile presence stalking her through the night was not just a product of overabundant imagination and overwrought nerves, then, clearly, it behooved her to get the heck off the beach. If she ran, anyone who happened to be back there would know she was on to them. If she walked, anyone who happened to be back there just might catch up.

That was the clincher. Yanking her skirt clear of her knees, she ran.

The sand was warm and gritty underfoot, dotted with puddles and strewn here and there with webs of stringy seaweed. Moonlight glinted on the clear blob of a jellyfish as it came tumbling toward her, rolling along on the outer edges of the inrushing tide. Fighting bubbling panic, gasping for breath, her heart beating a hundred miles a minute, her straining legs only wishing they could pump as fast, she pushed everything from her mind but the urgent need to *get off that beach*. The sound of the surf effectively deafened her; blowing strands of her hair whipping in front of her face all but blinded her. She couldn't hear so much as the slap of her own feet hitting the beach; she could barely see where she was going. But she could *feel* — and what she was feeling terrified her.

Her five senses be damned: at the moment only the sixth one mattered. And it was telling her that she was in imminent danger. There was someone behind her, giving chase — hunting her.

In the very act of casting what must have been the dozenth in a series of frightened glances over her shoulder, Christy tripped over something and went down.

She hit hard. Her knees gouged twin pits in the sand. Her palms thudded and sank. Her teeth clinked together with a force that sent pain shooting through the joint that connected her jaws. Salt spray hit her in the face as a large wave broke with particular enthusiasm just yards away.

Stunned to have been so abruptly catapulted onto all fours, she registered all that in an instant. She'd tripped. What had she tripped over? A piece of driftwood? What?

He's coming. Move.

Heart leaping as her own personal early warning system went off in spades, Christy obeyed, scrambling to her feet and at the same time instinctively glancing back to see what had felled her. Not that it mattered. Whoever was out there was closing in fast. She could sense him behind her, almost feel him. . . .

A slender arm, inert and pale as the sand itself, lay inches behind her feet. Realizing just what had tripped her, Christy was momentarily shocked into immobility. Then her widening gaze followed the limb down to the back of a head covered with a tangle of long, wet-looking dark hair, narrow shoulders and waist and hips, rounded buttocks, long legs. A woman lay there, sprawled facedown in the sand. She was wet, naked as far as Christy could tell, with one arm stretched out across the beach as if she had been trying to crawl toward the safety of the houses. She didn't move, didn't make a sound, didn't appear to so much as breathe.

She looked dead.

Then her hand moved, slender fingers closing convulsively on sand, and her body tensed as if she were trying without success to propel herself forward.

"Help . . . please . . ."

Had Christy really heard the muttered words? Or had she just imagined them? The pounding surf coupled with the frantic beating of her own pulse in her ears was surely enough to block out even much louder sounds. But . . .

"I'm here," Christy said as she crouched, touching the back of the woman's hand with equal parts caution and concern. As her fingertips made contact with cold, sand-encrusted skin, a swift rush of pity tightened her throat. *Poor thing, poor thing* . . .

The woman's fingers twitched as if in acknowledgment of her touch.

"La . . . law . . ."

There was no mistake: she really heard

the broken syllables, although this time they made no sense. The woman was not dead, but she seemed not far from it. Something terrible must have happened. Some kind of terrible accident.

"It's all ri—" Christy began, only to break off as her peripheral vision picked up on something moving. She glanced up, beyond the woman, to see a man perhaps three hundred yards away, slogging past the dunes that had concealed him up until that point, headed inexorably toward her, head down as he followed the footprints — *her footprints* — that even she could plainly see in the sand. Her pursuer! For vital seconds she had forgotten all about him. Terror stabbed through her now, swift and sharp as an arrow. Her heart leaped into her throat. He was little more than a bulky shape in the uncertain moonlight, but this was no ghost, no figment of her imagination. He was unmistakably there. Unmistakably real. The Mother of All Rabbits in a dark jogging suit with the moonlight glinting off something shiny in one hand.

A gun?

Even as she gaped at him, he lifted his head. It was impossible to see his face, his features, anything more than the sheer bulk of him. But she could feel his gaze on her, feel the menace rushing toward her as he looked at her and realized that she was looking back. For an instant, a dreadful, blood-freezing instant, they connected, hunter and prey zeroing in on each other through the imperfectly concealing darkness.

All thoughts of trying to help the woman were instantly forgotten as that sixth sense of hers went haywire, signaling bad news and screaming at her to *move!* Propelled by an acute attack of self-preservation, Christy leaped to her feet. Letting loose with a scream that could have been heard clear back in Atlantic City, she ran for her life.

2

"Shit. *Incoming.*"

That terse heads-up from Gary, boomed into the earpiece nestled way too close to Luke Rand's surprisingly tender eardrum, was all the warning he got as he slipped out through the patio door. Wincing, he was further auditorily assaulted by female shrieks coming from no very great distance away. Sliding the door shut, he looked around and saw Donnie Jr.'s hot little chickie scrambling across the dunes toward her house — and him — with the approximate grace of a hog on ice. Christina Marie Petrino — Christy to her family and friends, of which he was neither — was letting loose with fire-alarm caliber cries for help between pauses in which she appeared to be glancing over her shoulder. He hadn't noticed the shrill sounds before now, probably because before now he'd been busy inside her house. He barely had time to rip the earpiece from his ear and stuff it inside the pocket of his shorts before she slid down the last dune and came bounding right at him.

Time to think fast. Stand and bullshit, try to hide or run? Since he was caught on her tiny concrete patio, with her house behind him and a rickety privacy fence rising six feet high to his left and right, both running and hiding were pretty much out. To get out of there he'd have to head straight toward her. Considering the moonlight, there wasn't much hope that he could just blend in with the night and escape notice. As soon as she got a little bit closer, she was going to see him. Likewise, if he chose to move, the instant he stepped out of the narrow shadow cast by the overhanging eaves he would be visible. Since the name of the game here was *covert* operation, doing anything that might make her suspect that her house had been invaded while she'd been out was obviously not a good idea. The alternative was to hold his ground . . . no, advance . . . no, rush forward as if he were hurrying to her assistance, having used his keen powers of perception to discern from her cries for help that she was a damsel in distress.

And turn his bullshit generator on high.

As a plan it was cobbled together but it

would have to do. He was out of time. Because she'd seen him. There was no mistaking that. Her eyes found him as he stood motionless as a statue there amid her knee-high shrubbery. They widened with horror. Her mouth dropped open. Letting go of her long skirt so that it fell like a curtain over truly admirable legs, she skidded to a stop just feet away from the patio's edge and raised her hands defensively as though to ward him off.

"Hey there, what's the problem?" he asked in hearty good-guy mode, and, operating on the theory that the best defense was a good offense, strode out into the moonlight toward her.

Bad move. Backpedaling, she shrieked like she'd just come face-to-face with Son of Sam. Luke blinked, recoiling at the blast, then watched in bemused surprise as her foot caught on something and she abruptly sat in the sand, just missing planting her sexy little tush in a well-established fire ant hill. A small flashlight, a large cigarette lighter, something shiny and cylindrical that she'd been holding, flew out of her hand to land in the sea oats at the base of the nearest dune. She glanced behind her as if to see where the object had gone. Then her head snapped back around. Wide-eyed and clearly terrified, she looked up at him.

"Get away from me! Help! *Help!*"

"Hang on now . . ." He moved toward her with the clear intention of assisting her to her feet.

"Keep away!"

She frantically crab-walked backward, getting a little hung up in her loose dress but still managing to propel herself away from him at a pretty good clip. He couldn't help it: he succumbed to a flicker of purely male appreciation even as he watched her retreat. Her legs, long and slim and tanned, were phenomenal, as he remembered from his previous observations of her. They were also bared clear up past No Man's Land, which unfortunately for his continued appreciation of the view was covered by either shiny black panties or a shiny black bathing suit bottom. Her breasts — nice breasts, not too big but round and perky, constrained by either a flimsy bra or bathing suit top beneath the dress — jiggled like the real things. Her dark hair flowed down her back, her big dark eyes were wide as Frisbees, and her pointy-chinned, high-cheekboned face was turned up so that her delicate features caught the moonlight. Mob honey or not, she was a babe, and right at that particular moment she looked pretty darn cute scooting away from him on her backside. DePalma had good taste in women, he had to give the bastard that.

It was a damned shame she was going to end up in jail when this was all over.

"Look, it's okay. I'm not going to hurt you."

Holding up both hands palms out to demonstrate just how harmless he was, he smiled at her, going all out to exude good-neighbor helpfulness from every pore. She did not appear persuaded. Reaching the dune, she tried without success to move backward up the sandy slope that kept crumbling beneath her.

"Stay away!"

Disregarding that, he kept moving, stopping when his feet were just inches from her toes. He was confident that he looked innocuous enough, an average Joe on a beach vacation, nothing to alarm her at all in a smiling blond guy wearing ratty swim shorts and a partly buttoned madras shirt. Anyway, she'd been screaming before she'd come up over that dune, so whatever was freaking her out wasn't him. He smiled wider and was leaning over to help her to her feet when she let loose with another of those ear-splitting shrieks and threw a handful of sand in his face.

The stuff stung. Jerking upright, he shook his head, thanking his lucky stars he'd managed to close his eyes in time.

"Jesus," he said. "Chill, would you? It's okay. Everything's cool."

"Help! *Fire!*"

"Fire?"

That made no sense, but then it didn't really matter: the object was not to understand her, but to convince her of his harmlessness and get the hell out of Dodge. He tried smiling again and reextended his hand to her. She rewarded that gentlemanly gesture by kicking out at him like a pissed-off mule.

"Ow, shit!" She'd stiff-legged him! Pain shot through his leg as her heel connected with his kneecap. He grabbed his knee and hopped backward only to trip over the plastic chaise longue that he'd deftly managed to avoid during his two previous, infinitely more successful forays onto her patio.

This time it took him down. He hopped right into it, lost his balance, and crashed down on the footrest part. The cheap plastic collapsed beneath him with a resounding *crack!* His tailbone hit the ground with bruising force. Unable to stop the fall's momentum, he kept on going over, and the back of his head smacked concrete. To add insult to injury, the surviving part of the chair jackknifed over his head. Lying flat on his back on unforgiving concrete with sharp plastic shards digging into his butt and a plastic tent over his head, he quickly realized that seeing stars and looking ridiculous weren't his only problems.

"Don't move! Don't move!"

In the very act of pushing the chair off his head, he looked up to find one more sure sign that the situation was quickly deteriorating: an agitated woman dancing above him armed with a can of self-defense spray.

It was pointed right at him.

Shit. A faceful of Mace he did not need.

"Lady, I'm on your side," he yelped, both hands reaching for the sky in imitation of all the cornered bad guys in all the spaghetti westerns he had ever seen. "I'm just trying to help you. You don't want any help, that's fine by me. I'll just go away."

She still held the spray on him, arms extended, clutching the can with both hands like Dirty Harry with his .44, her finger clearly itchy on the trigger. But his words seemed to give her pause. At least she didn't immediately make like a skunk and spray.

"What are you doing on my patio?"

Good one.

"Looking for my cat." The excuse just popped into his head, probably because he'd seen a cat prowling out near the edge of her privacy fence when he'd come in.

"Looking for your cat?"

To say that she sounded skeptical was an understatement. Okay, so as an excuse that one kind of sucked.

But Luke nodded. "Marvin. I was looking for my cat Marvin. I saw him run under those bushes." He jerked a thumb sideways toward the bushes in question, the knee-high ones he'd been standing in when she'd spotted him. "I didn't even think about them being on somebody's patio. I just went after him. I didn't mean to trespass. I'm sorry."

She glanced at the bushes. While her attention was momentarily distracted Luke considered leaping up and grabbing the can, but the thought of the consequences if he wasn't quite quick enough dissuaded him. He knew Mace. He'd trained with it, he'd seen people hit with it, and he'd been hit with it himself. Twice. It wasn't an experience he cared to repeat.

"There's no cat under there."

"You probably scared him away with all that screaming. I'll be lucky if he's not clear on the other side of the island by now." Luke managed to sound suitably aggrieved. "What's with the sound effects, anyway? You hurt yourself or something?"

Her expression changed. Her face tightened, and she cast a hunted glance in the general direction of the ocean.

"There's a woman on the beach — she needs help right away — and a man. He —"

"You over there! Where's the fire?" It was a frail-old-woman kind of voice. Luke dared to glance away from the menacing can, and discovered a flashlight beam bouncing like a ball in the darkness just beyond the privacy fence. Clearly whoever was carrying it was approaching along the path through the dunes that connected this beach cottage to the one on its north side. He cringed inwardly. He knew who was hurrying to Christy's rescue, or at least he thought he did. Her name was Rosa Castellano, and she was the widow of one-time mob capo Anthony "Chub" Castellano. Eighty if she was a day, she lived in the house next door year-round now, courtesy of mob kingpin John DePalma, Donnie

Jr.'s father, who owned several properties along this stretch of beach. She basically spent her days tending the lush garden she'd cultivated in her front yard and watching the goings-on in the neighborhood. Luke had a feeling that not much got past her. He knew that he, personally, had not gotten past her. She'd been out in her yard when he and Gary had arrived that morning, and she had watched them suspiciously until they had disappeared into their rented house, which just happened to be next door to Christy Petrino's on the south side. It was owned by John DePalma too, and had been rented out for the summer, but they'd managed to wangle a kind of emergency sublease.

"Mrs. Castellano, is that you?" There was relief in Christy's voice. Luke glanced at her sharply. The fact that she knew Rosa Castellano was interesting, if not particularly surprising. Made men and their families had to retire somewhere, and the beaches of the eastern United States were becoming the place of choice. In fact, there were so many former associates of John DePalma in residence up and down the Outer Banks right now that a better name for it would have been New Jersey South.

"Yeah, of course it's me. Who were you

expecting, Madonna? Your mama called and told me you were here and asked me to keep an eye on you."

Mrs. Castellano came around the corner of the privacy fence as she spoke and stopped short to turn her flashlight on Luke. Its beam caught him full in the eyes. He squinted, and waved a feeble hello. Mrs. Castellano squinched up her eyes and frowned as if trying to place him in her memory.

"Could you go home and call for help?" Christy asked, still keeping him covered with the spray.

"I already called the fire department when I heard you yelling 'fire.' You need the cops, too? You shoulda said." Mrs. Castellano was a plump dumpling of a woman with sparse white hair, enough wrinkles to do a whole litter of shar-pei puppies proud, a sharp, beaklike nose above a tiny, pursed mouth, and an age-stooped back. Tonight she was wearing a knee-length robe zipped up over what was presumably a nightgown and mule-type slippers. She might look frail, she might sound frail, but Luke suspected she was about as frail as Ma Barker.

"Aunt Rosa, I *am* the cops, remember? I'm a deputy sheriff." A dark-haired man, late thirties, maybe five-ten, two hundred twenty solid pounds, appeared behind the woman, with what looked like a .40 caliber Glock in one hand. He was wearing dark pants and a white underwear-type T-shirt. Like his body, his blunt-featured face was broad and bulldog aggressive. What he basically looked like was a charter member of Thugs-R-Us. Or, alternatively, a cop, as he claimed.

"Oh, yeah, I keep forgetting." Mrs. Castellano shook her head, adding under her breath: "It just don't seem right, somehow, a Castellano turning deputy sheriff."

"Uh, I'll just get up now," Luke said, wincing slightly at the residual pain in his knee as he did so.

"Don't move!" Christy squeaked. Bristling with renewed suspicion and hostility, she re-aimed the Mace at him.

"Just chill, would you?" Luke said with disgust. He held up his hand in an effort to keep her more aggressive tendencies at bay.

"I got it covered," Castellano said to Christy in a soothing tone, and moved purposefully forward, his eyes on Luke and his pistol not quite in play but ready in his hand. "So what's the deal here? Where's the fire?"

"There's not any fire." Christy looked at Luke. "This guy —"

Before she could continue, Luke jumped in, still in clueless good-neighbor mode. "Hey, I heard her yelling and came to help her and she freaked."

"Freaked!" Christy shot him a hostile look, then glanced back at Castellano. "He was hiding in the bushes on my patio! He claimed he was looking for his cat."

"Cat?" Castellano turned hard eyes Luke's way. They were small and dark and mean, the kind you wouldn't want to run into if you were a punk kid up to no good. Or a guy with no better excuse for being on a woman's patio in the middle of the night than a nonexistent pet cat.

"Marvin," Luke said by way of confirmation. Hey, it was his story and he was sticking to it.

"Christy Petrino, meet my great-nephew Gordie Castellano. The deputy sheriff." Clearly oblivious to the turn the conversation had taken, Mrs. Castellano hobbled up to join the party. From her tone it was clear that matchmaking was on her mind.

"Pleased to meet you," Christy and Castellano said almost in unison. Now there was good, solid mafioso upbringing in action, Luke thought, observing the pair

50

of them through narrowed eyes. In the mob, crimes up to and including murder were commonplace, but the children were invariably taught to mind their manners. Then his gaze sharpened on Christy. Her brow was furrowed and her eyes were wary. This was an expression of distrust, and it was directed at Castellano. What was up with that? Was it her habitual attitude toward all members of the law enforcement community, or was it meant for this one in particular?

"There's a woman down on the beach . . ." There was an almost reluctant note in Christy's voice. She looked Castellano up and down, and her frown deepened. Yep, distrust was there in spades. The question was, why? Luke was willing to bet the rent that she'd been genuinely terrified of something from the moment he'd first spotted her coming over that dune until Ma Barker and the deputy had arrived. Why, then, wouldn't she welcome said deputy with open arms? Still looking at Castellano, she hesitated and added, "Uh, you didn't happen to just come up from the beach, did you?"

"Me?" Castellano shook his head. "Nah. I been watching TV with Aunt Rosa." He frowned at Christy. "A woman on the beach, you say? What about her?"

"There's something wrong with her. She's just lying there in the sand, and I think she's been hurt. She needs help. I — we should call an ambulance." The reluctant note was still there, which struck Luke as odd under the circumstances.

"What? Where?" Castellano's voice sharpened. Christy watched him, biting her lower lip for all she was worth.

"Toward the lighthouse."

The faint wail of a siren could be heard in the distance.

"That'll be the fire department," Mrs. Castellano said. She scowled at Christy. "Are they gonna be ticked off or what? Why were you yelling about a fire if there wasn't one?"

"Fire department, rescue squad, ambulance, here it's all the same thing," Castellano said impatiently. He looked at Christy. "How about we go on ahead and you show me where she is? Aunt Rosa can point the way to the guys when they get here."

"No! No." Shaking her head, Christy took a step backward. The siren was obviously louder now, closer. "They'll be here any minute, so it'd probably be better if we just waited for them."

She was afraid of Castellano, that much

was clear. Had they met before? From Christy's reactions, Luke didn't think so. But then, as he had reason to know, things were not always what they seemed.

"Yeah, you're probably right," Castellano said, watching her closely. "No point in taking a chance on them missing us in the dark."

"Look, it's been nice getting acquainted, but I can see I'm in the way here, so I'll just be going on about my business." Luke had to raise his voice now to be heard over the siren. A woman hurt on the beach was not his problem, and he was anxious to be gone before he had to explain himself to any more official types. The less attention he attracted, the better. He looked at Christy. "Sorry for the misunderstanding."

"Hold it." Castellano fixed those pit-bull eyes on him. His pistol was pointed down, but Luke had no doubt that could change in an instant. "Before you take off, how's about giving me a name and address? For starters."

Shit.

"Luke Randolph," Luke said easily, giving the name he had used to rent the cottage. It was uncomfortably close to his real one. He should have gone for something totally different. But then, when he'd used it, he'd never expected to find himself under the scrutiny of a curious deputy. If everything had gone the way it was supposed to, neither the deputy nor Christy Petrino would ever have noticed him. He would have been just one of hundreds of faceless vacationers spending the last few weeks of summer on this laid-back beach, and nothing more. But as luck would have it — and damn Gary anyway, he was going to give him hell when he saw him for that tardy heads-up — she'd caught him red-handed practically coming out of her house. Having been left holding the bag, so to speak, it was up to him to salvage the situation as best he could. Glancing at Christy, he opted for the truth — at least, a small part of the truth — and essayed a lopsided, hopefully charming, grin. "I'm your neighbor. Me and a buddy are renting the cottage next door."

Christy did not look charmed. Neither did she look convinced.

"That's true." Mrs. Castellano nodded. "I seen him move in. Him and some other guy, just this morning. Sonny and Nora Corbitt — they generally have the house next door to yours in August — won one of them last-minute Caribbean cruises, all expenses paid, and had to change their plans to take advantage, so their house came available just like that. Can you believe the luck? I ain't never won so much as a stick of gum in my life."

"He was on my patio," Christy said to Castellano, but her gaze met Luke's, and it was clear she remained suspicious of him. "I never saw a cat."

"So what happened? Did you hear him at a door or window? You think he was peeping in at you?" Castellano gave Luke another of those get-ready-to-take-the-perp-walk-you-creep looks.

"I . . . wasn't in the house. I couldn't sleep, so I went for a walk on the beach, and when I came back there he was, on my patio."

Liar, liar, pants on fire, Luke thought. He knew what she'd been up to on that beach.

Castellano's gaze shifted to Luke again.

"Hey, like I said, I was looking for my cat." Luke sounded so innocent he impressed himself. "He got out, and I don't like leaving him out nights, especially in a strange place." He glanced back at Christy then and tried to look penitent. "Sorry if I scared you."

"Well, lookee there, there's his cat." Mrs. Castellano pointed with the flashlight.

Like everyone else, Luke looked around

in surprise. Sure enough, she had a cat pinned in the light. Black and muscular, it was the one he'd seen sneaking around earlier. Oblivious to being observed, it was crouched in the tall grass at the foot of a nearby dune, tail twitching, ready to pounce, its attention solely focused on whatever it was apparently planning to have for a post-midnight snack.

"That your cat?" Castellano asked, looking back at Luke.

What were the chances of there being two cats wandering around in the vicinity of Christy Petrino's patio in the middle of the night? Slim and none. Luke mentally clasped the feral-looking feline to his bosom.

"Yeah," Luke said. "That's him. That's Marvin."

"Looks like he was telling the truth," Castellano said to Christy.

"I guess," she said, not sounding entirely convinced. But hey, there was the cat. Proof positive. What could she do?

Luke almost grinned. Sometimes things just worked out.

Flashing lights and a screaming siren unmistakably close now caused Luke to glance around. There was the fire truck, popping into view between houses as it raced along the narrow blacktop road that ran in front of this particular string of beachfront properties. As quickly as it appeared, it disappeared again. Christy's house blocked his view, but he distinctly heard the squeal of brakes. He might not be able to see what was happening, but he had little trouble picturing the scene: the truck screeching to a stop, firefighters leaping off, rushing over the postage-stamp-sized lawn toward the house. . . .

"Around back," Castellano yelled, hands cupped around his mouth. Only as Castellano's voice boomed through the sudden near-silence did Luke realize that at some point the siren had been turned off.

"Gordie, you scared the danged cat," Mrs. Castellano said. "Look at it go."

Luke watched as the cat leaped up the dune, bounding over the crest and vanishing into the night.

Yeah, sometimes things just worked out.

"Darn," he said, folding his arms over his chest just as a quartet of firefighters in full battle gear burst into view around the corner of Christy's house. At the same time, there was unexpected movement to his right. He glanced in that direction to discover a family with three or four kids coming toward them from the south, moving cautiously along the path that led through the dunes, drawn no doubt by all the commotion. A trio of teenage boys followed in the wake of the firefighters, having most likely chased the truck from town in search of whatever excitement they could find in this place where the lightning bugs and mosquitoes seemed to have pretty much cornered the market on nightlife. Behind the boys came two uniformed deputies, running to keep up.

Come one, come all, Luke thought with disgust. *Was there a hot time in the old town tonight or what?*

"Where's the fire?" one of the firefighters called.

"No fire." Castellano shook his head as they drew near. "That was a mistake. What we've got here is a woman reported injured on the beach." He turned to Christy. "You want to show us where now?"

She nodded and he took her arm. Luke watched with interest as she seemed to flinch, then pulled free and set off toward the beach without a backward look. Castellano stared after her with a gathering frown.

"You come, too," Castellano said over his shoulder to Luke as the whole group started over the dunes. "I got a few more questions I want to ask you."

Great. Now he would be on the radar screen of pretty much half the population, including the local fuzz and the woman he had under surveillance. But what none of them knew, and must not find out, was the truth about who he was and why he was there: FBI Special Agent Luke Rand, hot and heavy on the trail of Donnie Jr., aka Michael DePalma, who'd dropped out of sight two days earlier, right before a supposedly secret grand jury had returned a sealed indictment charging him with, among other things, racketeering and wire fraud. Keeping tabs on the bastard's girlfriend, who had headed south at about the same time with what sources in the know had claimed was a briefcase full of cash, had seemed like the shortest route to recovering their man.

Unfortunately, things weren't working out quite as planned. This little disaster was only the latest in a string of screwups. Plan A, which was keep out of sight, watch the chick, and wait for Donnie Jr. to show up, was officially a bust. Right about now seemed like a good time to go with Plan B — just as soon as he came up with it.

3

Holy Mary, Mother of God, pray for us now and at the hour of our death . . .

Sketching a quick sign of the cross over her chest, Christy turned away as the woman's body was lifted onto a stretcher. She wasn't fast enough. An arm, limp and pale, flopped off the side of the gurney, falling out from beneath the white sheet that was being drawn over the victim. Lifeless fingers dangled downward. The same arm that had first caught her eye on the beach? Christy didn't know — and couldn't bear to think about it. Dark liquid dripped from the flaccid fingers.

Blood.

As much as she wanted to, needed to, Christy could not tear her eyes away from the gruesome sight. A woman paramedic wearing white plastic gloves took hold of the wrist and returned the arm to the stretcher. Her movements were matter-of-fact as she loosened a strap securing the body, then refastened it to hold the arm in, too. The discreet covering was repositioned, and the body was at last out of view. Death had reduced the woman to an anonymous bundle, an object, a *thing* to be taken away.

A small dark stain appeared on the white cloth near where the hand had been tucked inside. Unable to tear her gaze away, Christy watched, mesmerized, as the stain slowly grew to the size of a baseball.

So much blood.

"She going to County Hospital?" asked a paunchy, bald, middle-aged man, who had arrived on the scene at the same time as the ambulance. Mrs. Castellano had identified him to Christy as Aaron Steinberg, the publisher *cum* primary reporter of Ocracoke's only local newspaper. Standing at the forefront of a shifting crowd of onlookers perhaps twelve feet away, Christy had no trouble hearing what was being said.

"Morgue," Gordie Castellano replied.

"Cause of death?"

"Can't say for sure till after the autopsy."

"Would it be safe to characterize it as a homicide?"

The white sheet had absorbed more of

the blood, and now the stain was about the size of a basketball. Christy's stomach roiled, and although neither she nor the speakers moved, the voices seemed to fade away. Shaken to the core, she closed her eyes and finally succeeded in blocking out the terrible scene, if not the thoughts that went with it. Guilt gnawed at her insides. If she had stayed with the woman, if she had gotten help to her faster, if, if, if . . .

It was too late for ifs. The woman was dead.

If she had stayed, she might be dead now, too.

Goose bumps prickled along her skin. The memory of that moment when she had looked up to find her pursuer bearing down on her was enough to make her heart start to pound like she'd just run for miles. Turning her back on the stretcher that was still being readied for transport, Christy took a deep, steadying breath and opened her eyes. She pulled her blowing hair back from her face with one hand, then stared determinedly out toward the horizon, where the star-studded night sky blended almost seamlessly into the black sea. Closer at hand, the reflection of the moon made squiggly white lines on the waves.

There was nothing she or anyone could do for the poor dead woman now. She had to concentrate all her energy on saving herself.

"You doin' okay?" the masculine voice, tinged with a southern drawl, coming as it did seemingly out of nowhere, made Christy jump. Glancing around, she saw that the speaker was her next-door neighbor, the guy with the lost cat, Luke something.

"I'm fine." Her brusque tone was meant to discourage further conversation.

During the hour or so they'd waited and watched on the beach, he'd stayed in her general vicinity but had said nothing to her. As far as she knew he'd said nothing to anyone, aside from a brief chat he'd had early on with Gordie Castellano. Now he was right behind her, standing far too close for her peace of mind under the circumstances. She stepped away from him dismissively and focused on the sea again.

"Finding her dead like that must have been real upsetting. You want to try to put it out of your mind." He was behind her again.

"She wasn't dead when I found her," Christy responded compulsively despite the fact that she didn't want to talk to him, didn't trust him, didn't much believe that he'd been looking for his lost cat on her patio. She had told her story over and over, to Gordie Castellano when he had questioned her, to the other deputies, to the paramedics, to the newspaper guy. Saying it aloud was an attempt to ease her conscience, she decided. She guessed she was hoping that if she told the story enough, she would find some sort of absolution for having abandoned the woman to her fate. "She was alive and talking. She said 'help me.' And — and something that started with *la* or *law.*"

She couldn't help it. Her voice shook as she finished.

A beat passed before he replied, in a slightly altered tone. "You did your best. You got help."

"Not fast enough." Christy shivered and crossed her arms over her chest. The wind blowing in from the ocean was stiff now, whipping up frothing waves like a whisk beating tall peaks in meringue. It sent the ends of her hair snapping back away from her face and picked up her skirt so that it streamed behind her, fluttering against his legs.

"You're shivering. You cold?"

"A little. It doesn't matter." Cold didn't

begin to cover it. Terrified, heartsick, disbelieving of this nightmare that somehow just seemed to keep on keeping on, was more like it. None of which she could say aloud.

"Yeah, it does matter. You've had a shock, you ought to try to keep warm." He moved, and a moment later something dropped over her shoulders. "Here."

Startled, she whipped around, but even before she saw him without it she had already realized what it was: his shirt. It was cotton, smelling faintly of something pleasant like suntan lotion or fabric softener, and warm from his body. It felt so good, so welcome, that for a moment she was almost tempted to keep it on. But under the best of conditions taking favors from strangers went against the grain with her. And this guy wasn't just a stranger, he was a *suspicious* stranger. Besides, if she didn't know better — which she didn't — she would be starting to suspect he was coming on to her.

Under the circumstances, that was something she really, truly, positively didn't need to deal with.

"Thanks," she said, shaking her head as she pulled his shirt off and held it out to him. "But no thanks. I'm not *that* cold."

"O—kay." His tone told her that he'd finally registered a rebuff. Accepting the shirt, he shrugged back into it. As he did so she narrowed her eyes against the reflected glow of the klieg lights that had been set up at the scene and took her first good look at him. He was about six-one and lean, handsome enough if you happened to like the blond surfer-dude type, which she didn't, with an angular, square-jawed face, eyes that were probably blue although in the uncertain light it was impossible to be sure, a long, slightly crooked nose, and a mobile, thin-lipped mouth. His hair was too long for her taste and curled in way-too-cute little ringlets around his ears and neck. His shoulders and arms and chest veered almost into hunk territory, being well-muscled despite his overall leanness, but they didn't quite make up for the sissy curls. He was deeply tanned, as if he had way too much free time to spend shirtless in the sun for a man who looked to be about thirty. As her personal taste ran toward men who were darker, brawnier, and altogether more macho-looking, she couldn't give him much more than a seven on her manly beauty scale. Given that he was wearing ancient-looking swim trunks that hung low on his hips and ended at his knees, and his hair looked like it had been finger-combed back from his forehead when wet, Christy assumed that sometime in the recent past he'd gone for a swim. In the ocean? Maybe, although some of the cottages had their own pool. Could he have been the guy on the beach? Watching him button his shirt up again, Christy weighed the possibility. She didn't think so. The timing was wrong, the vibes were wrong, and he was lean and blond whereas the man on the beach had been bulky and dark-haired.

Unless he'd been wearing some kind of cap. Unless the jogging suit he'd been wearing had been oversized. Unless he'd somehow managed to strip off the jogging suit before he got to her patio *and* beat her back there to boot. Unless the moonlight had played nasty little tricks on her eyes.

That was about four too many *unlesses* for her peace of mind.

"Whatever it was, I didn't do it." A slight, crooked smile turned up a corner of his mouth. There was the tiniest spark of satisfaction in his eyes as they met hers. Christy realized that she'd been staring, and he'd interpreted her attention as interest. Clearly the guy was used to women who were easily wowed. Her brows snapped together.

"You know, I don't think you have a clear view of the situation: I caught you skulking on my patio in the middle of the night. This does not make us friends. And I really don't feel like talking right now."

He held up both hands and rocked back on his heels. "Hey, no problem."

She turned her back on him pointedly, and resumed staring out to sea. To her annoyance, he continued to lurk behind her. Christy pursed her lips and determinedly ignored him. She would have left then and headed up to her cottage except for the humiliating fact that she was afraid to walk up through the dunes alone and Castellano had asked her to hang around in case he had some more questions for her. Not that there was anything more that she could tell him. He knew everything she did — or, at least, everything she was prepared to reveal.

The terrible thing was, the woman had been dead when their motley band of rescuers had reached her. As far as Christy could tell — and Castellano had insisted she take a good, close look — the woman hadn't moved since she'd left her except for the shifting of her previously outflung arm. When Christy had returned the woman's arm had been bent at the elbow and pulled in close to her body. Maybe she'd drawn it in from pain; maybe she'd been trying to crawl. Christy didn't know, and refused to allow herself to speculate. The major difference in the scene was that the area around the woman's torso was dark, black almost, stained in an uneven pattern that resembled nothing so much as the petals of a flower that had just blossomed.

Because of all the blood. Someone — Castellano? — had said that the beach was soaked with the woman's blood. Like ink on a paper towel, the blood was slowly being diffused through the sand.

There had been no sign of blood in the sand when she had knelt to touch that poor woman's cold but still-living hand. Christy could still picture the scene in her mind: the beach had been creamy pale. She could barely stand to think that all that blood had poured out of the woman's body from the time she had run away to the time she had returned with help.

If only she had been quicker. . . .

Castellano was headed her way again, the pocket-sized notebook he'd been using to jot down notes in hand. Although according to his great aunt he was officially off duty, he had more or less taken charge of the scene. While they'd all stood around waiting for the completion of the myriad tasks that the discovery of a dead person called for, Mrs. Castellano had confided in Christy that Gordie had been a homicide cop in Hoboken until six years ago, when on a visit to her and her sister, his grandmother, who was now deceased, God rest her soul, he had met and married an Ocracoke girl. The marriage was now kaput but Gordie was still here and so respected that he was in line to one day replace the sheriff, an amiable man in his sixties whom everybody called Bud. A hard-charging Yankee on a force of laidback southerners, Gordie, Mrs. Castellano bragged, got things done.

He also owned his own house, a nice ranch on Back Road, made a good living, and wanted kids.

"You say you saw a man." Castellano stopped beside her and flipped back a couple of pages in his notebook, checking out what he'd already written.

"Yes." Christy wet her lips.

"But you can't describe him."

"No." They'd been over this before.

"Was he tall? Short? Heavyset? Thin?

Any distinguishing features that you can remember at all?" He spoke with a tinge of impatience. Christy could feel him looking at her, but she refused to look back, keeping her eyes focused on the breaking waves instead. A needle of fear pricked her. Should she even have mentioned seeing a man? If the man had been sent by the mob and she talked about him to the sheriff's department, the consequences could be bad.

Words to live by: Nobody had ever earned a Sicilian necktie by keeping her mouth shut.

"It was dark. Basically all I saw was a shadow."

Castellano made a disgusted sound under his breath. Clearly not the answer he was looking for. Too bad. It was the best she was prepared to do. If she could have identified the guy positively, she might've taken a chance. But she couldn't. All she could do was give a vague description of his size and coloring. That wasn't enough to get anyone arrested — but it just might be enough to get her killed. Her heart skipped a beat at the thought.

"You say he had a gun."

"I said it *might* have been a gun. He was carrying something in his hand. I'm not sure what it was."

The nagging suspicion that it had been Castellano on the beach, Castellano tracking her by her footprints and then looking up to make that wordless but terrifying connection through the darkness, would not leave her. His build was right. The timing, as far as she had been able to work out, was doable. And he definitely had a gun.

Was he toying with her, feeling her out, testing her to find out what she had seen, what she would say? At the thought cold chills chased themselves up and down her spine.

"The victim spoke to you, is that correct?" From the corner of her eye she could see him consulting his notebook again.

"Y-yes."

"This is real important. You sure you heard her speak?"

"Yes. I'm sure." Christy glanced sideways at him. "Why is that so important?"

He hesitated, and looked up to meet her gaze. "Her throat was slit. So deeply that her vocal cords were severed. If she was talking to you, then it had to have happened after you left her."

It took an instant for that to hit.

"Oh my God." The woman *had* been murdered, then. It was a shock, but not really a surprise: Christy had sensed it from the time one of the firefighters had said the woman was dead. The man she had seen — he had to be the murderer. What were the chances that someone else could have materialized out of nowhere and killed her in the available amount of time? Not good. The menace she had sensed on the beach, the evil, the danger, had been vented on someone else. It had been directed at her, but she had escaped. The other woman had not.

The dead woman on the beach could have been her. It almost *had* been her.

Suddenly Christy felt dizzy. Her head swam. A curious ringing sounded in her ears. She closed her eyes and took an involuntary step backward, only to come up against something solid. Hands grasped her shoulders, steadying her.

"Hey, that was a little insensitive, don't you think?" Luke protested in his southern drawl. If Castellano replied, Christy didn't register it. She leaned back against her suspicious, annoying neighbor because if she hadn't she would have collapsed.

"Looks like they're wrapping things up." Mrs. Castellano, who'd been eagerly observing the proceedings from various vantage points, sounded almost disappointed as she joined them. Christy opened her eyes in time to see the stretcher being borne away, up the path through the dunes to where an ambulance waited to receive it. Yellow crime scene tape cordoned off the section of beach where the woman had lain. A police photographer was still inside the tape taking a few final pictures. His camera exploded in bright flashes against the inky ocean and a night sky that was being swallowed up by a fast-moving bank of clouds. The klieg lights that had been set up to illuminate the area were being shut down.

"Anything else you need to ask?" Luke asked. " 'Cause it looks like it's going to rain."

"That's it for now." Castellano closed the notebook. "Come on, Aunt Rosa, I'll walk you up to the house. Things are going to be hopping around here tomorrow, so I'm going to head on home to bed now."

The two of them started moving away.

"You ready to go?" Luke asked in her ear, tightening his hands on her arms. It was only then that Christy realized that she was still leaning back against him. Embarrassed, she straightened and pulled away with a nod, then hurried after the Castellanos. A moment later he fell in beside her as she walked with the Castellanos up the beach.

"You got her ID'd yet?" Mrs. Castellano asked her nephew.

"No, other than I'm pretty sure she's not a year-rounder. At least, if she is, I don't know her."

"Gordie! Hey, Gordie, wait up!"

Like the others, Christy glanced around to find Aaron Steinberg hurrying after them. Watching him move toward her with the moon at his back, it occurred to her that he, too, was about the same size and shape as her pursuer. The primary difference was that the moonlight gleamed off his bald head.

He could have worn a cap.

Her heart beat faster at the realization.

"Any possibility that this could be one of those college girls who disappeared on Nags Head a couple weeks ago?" Steinberg asked as he caught up.

Castellano shrugged. "There's no way to know until we get an ID."

"Correct me if I'm wrong, but just this year alone there's been something like five women gone missing along the Carolina coast. That's pretty interesting, don't you think?"

"I heard tell there's a serial killer on the loose," Mrs. Castellano said. "Wouldn't that be something? Now he's hit so close, maybe I should get out my gun."

A serial killer? Christy hadn't thought of that. The very idea was terrifying — but no more terrifying than the thought of being the victim of a mob hit, which was her newest, deepest fear. When it came right down to it, though, dead was dead. It was also a state she had no desire to experience firsthand.

"I took your gun, Aunt Rosa, remember? After you tried to clean it and shot a hole in the bedroom wall." Castellano sounded a little testy. He glanced at Steinberg. "You know, Aaron, people come and go around here for all kinds of reasons, and a serial killer's about as good for tourism as a shark attack. I wouldn't go speculating about anything like that in the paper, if I were you. Not unless you want to get strung up."

"Hmm." Steinberg shifted his attention to Christy. "Could you spell your last name for me? I wouldn't want to get it wrong."

"What do you mean, get it wrong? Get it wrong where?"

"I think he means in his newspaper," Luke said.

"Is that what you mean? Are you going to put my name in the newspaper?" Christy was appalled. Then panicked. Somehow, she was fairly certain that Uncle Vince and company weren't going to be thrilled with her if she ended up with her name plastered all over the news.

Steinberg beamed at her. "Dear, you found her. While taking a solitary, moonlit stroll along the beach. That's news."

"You know, this is just a thought, but putting her name in the paper might put her at risk. If there is a serial killer, I mean," Luke pointed out in a dispassionate tone.

Steinberg looked a tad sulky. "I suppose I could just call her 'a tourist.' "

"Yes, *please,*" Christy said.

"There's no serial killer." Castellano's voice was grim. "Five women missing in an area as populated as this is a *coincidence,* and that's all."

"Can I quote you on that, Gordie?" Steinberg asked with a glimmer of humor.

"Hell, no. This entire conversation's strictly off the record. Look, if you stop by tomorrow I'll give you what we've got on this one tonight, okay? Probably we'll find out that it's nothing more than a bad domestic."

"From your mouth to God's ears." Steinberg stopped walking, gave a farewell salute, and turned back toward the crime scene.

"Five missing women this year sounds like a lot," Luke said, with the air of someone making a disinterested observation.

Castellano snorted. "Not when you consider how many tourists we've got coming through here every year. All types, too, and they bring their problems with them. Drugs, public drunkenness, domestic violence, sexual assaults, you name it and we arrest 'em for it. Population's transient, too, which doesn't help." There was a pause, and Christy became aware that Castellano was looking at Luke in a considering way. "You mind telling me what you do for a living?"

Just then their little group reached the path that led up through the dunes to Mrs. Castellano's house. This was the long way around to get to Christy's cottage, but she wasn't about to break off and take the more direct route on her own — or with Luke, whose cottage lay just beyond hers, for an escort. There was, she felt, a certain safety in numbers.

"I'm a lawyer," he said.

"Oh yeah?"

Castellano seemed to find Luke's stated profession only mildly interesting. Christy, on the other hand, was immediately struck. Covertly, she gave Luke another once-over. He didn't look like a lawyer — but then, what did a lawyer look like? Short answer: *Not* a beach bum.

"We'll walk you the rest of the way," Castellano said when they reached the point where their paths diverged. Christy didn't argue — no way was she arguing about that — so the whole group turned toward her house.

"You need something, I'm next door," Luke said in her ear when they reached the edge of her patio.

Before Christy could reply, he raised a hand in farewell and continued on.

"What about your cat? Aren't you going to look for him?" Mrs. Castellano called after him.

"Probably home already," he called back, and kept walking until darkness swallowed him up.

"Any possibility he could be the man you saw on the beach?" Castellano asked.

"I don't think so. But like I said, all I really saw was a shadow, a dark shape."

Christy edged toward her door as she spoke. If the truth were told, she felt far more uncomfortable with Castellano than she did with Luke. Luke had been on her patio, true, and his stab at picking her up was not appreciated, but she was fairly confident that he hadn't been the man on the beach. She was far less confident when it came to Castellano. Only Mrs. Castellano's presence kept her from being truly frightened of him now. Wrapped in shadows, away from the klieg lights and the crowd on the beach, the bulky darkness of him looming so close made her stomach twist.

He could have been the man on the beach.

"I'd like to get a formal statement from you tomorrow, if you'll come down to the station," Castellano said. Christy was already halfway across the patio.

"I'll be there," she replied over her shoulder, faking a cooperativeness she did not feel, and reached the patio door. They watched until she was inside. Flipping on the outside light, she waved, called "good night," and slid the door shut.

And locked it. And drew the curtains. Then stood with her back pressed against it, eyes closed, chest tight.

It's over, she told herself. *You're safe. You're free.*

All she had to do was pack and get the hell off this island. But first she needed to calm down. Put the nightmare on the beach behind her. Rejoice in being once again snug inside her own living room.

Her own dark living room.

Hadn't she left a light on?

Christy's eyes popped open. Enough yellowish light filtered in around the edges of the curtains to allow her to see. Her gaze flew to the floor lamp beside the couch. Her heart gave a great leap in her chest. She had left it on. She knew she had. She was — *almost* — one hundred percent positive.

Maybe the bulb had burned out.

Christy barely had time to register that as a legitimate possibility when the phone rang. She jumped at the sudden shrill sound, then hesitated as she made an automatic move to answer.

Who could be calling her here? Only a few people knew where she was. And none of them would call at this hour.

It could be a wrong number. Or a crank call. Christy prayed that it was one or the other even as she flipped on the overhead light and started for the phone, which

81

rested on the tile-topped breakfast bar. Of course it was something like that.

But her sixth sense would not let her believe it.

Her sixth sense was signaling trouble again.

The phone was beginning its seventh ring when she finally got up enough nerve to pick up the receiver and put it to her ear.

"Hello?" she said.

4

Frowning thoughtfully, Luke let himself in to the small, ranch-style house that was his temporary home *cum* office. He was halfway across the lamp-lit living room before he noticed Gary, who had no business being in the house because he was supposed to be staking out the damned briefcase Christy Petrino had carted down to the beach a couple of hours earlier. Wearing headphones, Gary was waving frantically at him from Command Central, which was actually the tiny third bedroom.

Gary Freeman, Luke had decided early on in the course of their now three-day-old association, was his boss's revenge. All the late expense reports, the government-owned car Luke had wrecked and the other one he'd gotten blown up, the informant who'd disappeared with fifty thousand of the government's cash, obviously still rankled with Tom Boyce. Sticking him with Gary the Geek, as he was known to his fellow agents behind his back for, among other things, his computer expertise, had to be payback. It was the only way Luke could explain it. Right now, despite the heat, despite the beach, despite the fact that they were trying to run a middle-of-the-night surveillance operation, for God's sake, Gary was his usual Boy Scout–neat self. Picture Howdy Doody with Coke-bottle glasses and you basically had Gary. At the moment he wore well-pressed khaki slacks, a short-sleeved, button-down blue shirt that was tucked in and belted, polished leather dress shoes and dark socks. He was four years younger than Luke's own age of thirty-two, four inches shorter at five-nine and probably a good forty pounds lighter.

"Pick up," Gary mouthed urgently, pointing at his headphones as Luke walked into the bedroom.

Gary's potentially hair-mussing headphones could only mean one thing. Well, two, actually. One, the bug Luke had installed in Christy Petrino's phone actually worked. Two, she had a call.

A glance at the clock told him that it was twenty-two minutes past three a.m. Unless it was a telemarketer with a death wish, this call almost had to have something to do with her recent jaunt to the Crosswinds Hotel. Yee-ha. They were in business.

Sitting on the corner of the bed, he took the headphones Gary passed him and put them on.

". . . the hell did you do?" A voice squawked in his ear. The speaker was a man. Adult, blue-collar Jersey accent. Angry tone.

"Who is this?" There was a kind of wobble in Christy's voice. Was she scared? Yes, of course she was scared, Luke answered himself, deliberately clamping down on the quick spurt of concern he felt for her. She was many things, but she hadn't struck him as a fool, and she'd have to be a fool *not* to be scared now that she was swimming with the sharks.

The man continued in the same belligerent tone: "You don't worry about that. You worry about this. You go gettin' the cops involved, and we're not gonna be friends no more, understand?"

"I couldn't help it! A woman was killed. Tonight on the beach. That's why the cops were there. It didn't have anything to do with — the briefcase." She practically whispered the last two words, then paused, breathing so hard that Luke could hear it through the phone. Then her voice altered, grew stronger, indignant even. "Are you *watching* me?"

"Fuckin'-A, baby. Every move you make. Maybe you should want to remember that."

"I did what I was told."

A grunt. "Maybe. Except for you got the damned cops involved. That ain't the way we like it to go down, just so you know."

A beat passed.

"Is Uncle — is Vince there? Can I speak to him?"

A bark of unpleasant laughter. "Nah, Vince ain't here. Now you pay attention. Tomorrow you're gonna go visit the lighthouse. Around two. Make like a tourist. Somebody will get in touch. Understand?"

"No! No, I don't understand. I was only supposed to deliver the briefcase, and —"

"Be there." There was an unmistakable undertone of threat to that. Then the connection was broken as the man hung up.

Luke heard a sound that made him think Christy had sucked in her breath. Then she, too, hung up. He listened to the line go dead, then looked at Gary.

"We get a fix on that?"

Gary glanced at the computer screen in front of him. "Got a number." He hit a few keys, made a face. "One of those damned disposable cell phones. Not enough time to get a location fix. Sorry."

"Shit. Whoever it is, he's got to be fairly close by. How else would he know about what went down on the beach?"

Gary shrugged.

Luke pulled off the earphones, stood up, and moved past Gary to punch a button on the monitor, which, like the laptop Gary had been using, was set up on the small vanity. The vanity was cheap white wicker and flimsy, part of a matching suite that, like the rest of the furniture, had come with the rented house. The monitor flickered to life. Christy's kitchen and part of her living room appeared on the screen. The two cottages were nearly identical, fully furnished rentals with a combination kitchen/dining/living area, three minuscule bedrooms, two baths. She wasn't visible. He punched another button, and the tiny camera he'd installed at the same time as he'd bugged the phone panned the area. Ah, there she was. He hit the button and the camera stopped.

"She doesn't look too happy," Gary observed and then straightened the bedspread that Luke had mussed by sitting on it.

"She's got reason." Luke eyed the high-resolution image almost grimly. He'd concealed the camera in the clock above the refrigerator. She was standing in profile to it, head bent, facing the counter where the phone she'd just hung up rested. Rich brown hair fell forward over her face, veiling her features, but her body language spoke volumes. Her arms were crossed over her chest. The slender shoulders that had felt disturbingly fragile beneath his hands were slumped. She was breathing hard, visibly agitated. With that loose green dress hanging down to her ankles, she looked feminine, delicate, vulnerable.

Luke clamped down hard on another of those unwelcome spurts of concern. However downcast she looked, she was no innocent victim: her background was mob through and through. He'd done his homework: her dad Joseph had been a small-time hoodlum until he'd been shot dead in his own driveway when Christy was nine. Her mother Carmen worked in a cigarette factory and was mobster Vincent Amori's longtime girlfriend. Twenty-four-year-old sister Nicole was newly divorced from a hard luck wiseguy named Franky Hill and, with three kids under five, was basically a production line for a whole new generation of Future Mobsters of America. Twenty-one-year-old-sister Angela worked in a department store, ran with a tough crowd, and was a big-time party girl. Christy, a hard worker who had put herself through college and law school, came off at first look like the cuckoo in the nest. From everything he could discover, she'd kept her nose clean until she'd gotten involved with Donnie Jr., which was the Bureau's code name for Michael DePalma, both because he looked kind of like Donny Osmond on a real bad hair day and because he was the son of Don John DePalma. Christy had been on the Bureau's radar screen since she'd gone to work for Michael DePalma's law firm two years ago. At first Luke hadn't paid all that much attention to her. Then, as she'd started bedding the boss, he'd kept a closer eye on her. Now that Michael had flown the coop, Luke was convinced that she was the key to bringing him down.

The only problem was, he was starting to worry about her. And it didn't take a genius to figure out why. What was clouding his judgment on this issue was that she was a . . .

"Pretty woman," Gary steepled his hands beneath his chin and put into words exactly what Luke had been thinking.

"Yeah," Luke agreed, definitely not wanting to go there with Gary. "So what happened to the briefcase? Tell me it's somewhere you know it's going to stay put for a while."

Grimacing, Gary met his gaze. Without his brand-new partner having to utter so much as a word, Luke knew the score. He felt his blood pressure skyrocket. He'd already made the acquaintance of that expression — and it meant the news was not anything he wanted to hear.

"I lost it."

"You lost it?" By the skin of his teeth, Luke managed to keep his voice even. Fixing Gary with a narrow-eyed gaze that fell just short of being a glare, he fought for calm. *Ohhmm*, he thought, reaching deep down inside himself in search of the inner serenity he'd been assured was at his center in the yoga classes he'd recently attended as part of another surveillance effort. "How the — how could you lose it?"

"Well, see, you know how I was supposed to give you a heads-up when our girlfriend there started heading back home, then stay put and keep a lookout on the briefcase until you relieved me?"

Luke nodded, not trusting himself to speak. He was trying, but the on-ramp to the nirvana highway remained maddeningly out of reach.

"She delivered the briefcase, all right, put it in the gray Maxima just like she was told, then started walking back down the beach. As soon as she got out of sight I started to give you a holler, but the damned transmitter wouldn't work. It was dead as a doornail. I was afraid she was going to catch you in her house, but I didn't want to leave my post, so I didn't know what to do. I figured that the problem with the transmitter was probably dead batteries, but that didn't really help because I didn't have any fresh ones. Then I remembered I had a penlight in my pocket. Took Triple A, just like the transmitter. There was nobody in the car, the parking lot was dead, nothing happening anywhere. So I nipped into the men's room by the pool because it was the only place nearby that had lights and privacy, and I changed the batteries. I was only in there for a minute, I swear, and I didn't hear crap, but when I got back the car — was — gone." His voice faltered at the end, probably in response to Luke's expression.

"Gone?" Luke was starting to feel like a frigging parrot, but the enormity of the screwup was such that there were no words to do it justice. He'd checked the briefcase on one of his trips inside Christy's cottage. Catalogued and photographed its contents, from which he'd learned exactly nothing. The damned thing, which he'd expected to be full of money meant for Donnie Jr., was filled with old newspapers instead. Which meant, unless and until he was able to discern the significance of the newspapers, he still didn't have a clue as to exactly what was going down here. The next step, of course, was to follow the briefcase, see who picked it up — he couldn't get lucky enough to have it be Donnie Jr. himself — and where it went after that. Now they'd lost track of the briefcase.

"Yeah, gone. Poof. Just like that. Empty parking space."

Luke searched for his center again, but came up empty. Tranquillity Central might be in there somewhere, but he wasn't finding it. Or feeling it.

"So what did you do?" he asked carefully.

"First I thought — *shit*. Then I thought I better tell you. So I tried the transmitter again. Nada. The damned thing still didn't work. Then I realized that our girlfriend was going to get home soon and you still didn't know she was coming, so I started running down the beach — not the beach, exactly, but the path between the houses and the dunes — staying low because I didn't want our girlfriend to see me. The whole time I kept trying to see if I couldn't get the transmitter to work. Finally I smacked the damned thing and, boom, there it was, working. About that time our girlfriend started screaming and running up over the dunes. I sang out to you and hit the sand. She never even saw me."

Gary said that last part as if he expected congratulations. Luke fought off a vivid mental image of Ozzy Osbourne on stage biting off the head of a bat. Only Ozzy was wearing Luke's face, and Gary was the bat.

Abandoning the search for his center as a lost cause, Luke cast a cursory glance at the monitor — Christy was turning away from the counter, walking across the living room, switching on lamps — and let loose with a soft but heartfelt string of curses.

"It wasn't my fault!" Gary protested. "How did I know somebody was going to drive away in the car? The place was dead. There wasn't a soul around. The *ferries* are closed for the night. Where could anybody go? What were the chances?"

Luke swallowed several possible replies to focus on the big picture.

"You get the license plate number?" Already heading out of the room, Luke threw the question back over his shoulder.

"Yes, of course I got it." Gary pressed a key on the computer and rattled off the number. "What do you think, I'm an idiot or something?"

Clearly intended as a rhetorical question, that was probably best left unanswered, Luke decided.

"So?"

"The plate was reported stolen a month ago in Asheville." Standing in the bedroom doorway now, Gary watched as Luke jerked open the door that led from the kitchen to the garage. "Where are you going?"

"To look around, see if I can spot the car. Hell, this is an island. The ferries are closed for the night, like you said. Where could anybody go? You keep an eye on the monitor."

"Yeah, okay, but . . ."

Whatever followed that "but," Luke missed it. The door between the house and the garage was already closing behind him. He was driving a two-year-old Ford Explorer that belonged to the Bureau, and he backed it out of the garage and pulled onto the narrow road with careful speed. The rescue vehicles were gone now, and except for a few porch lights this part of the island was dark as a hole.

The way things were going, he was starting to feel like one of the Keystone Cops, Luke reflected savagely. His headlights speared a startled possum that froze for a second before scampering to safety in a stand of loblolly pines beside the road. Murphy's Law definitely applied to this case: Anything that could go wrong pretty much had. Agents tracking organized crime used to command the best of everything: hot cars, hot gadgets, and hot chicks. Now investigations like this were the Rodney Dangerfield of law enforcement: They got no respect. Preoccupied with the war on terrorism, the Bureau had parked home-grown enemies like the mob at the rear of the lot. Still, a low-level eye had been kept on the usual suspects, and enough information had been gathered to wangle an indictment against Donnie Jr. When he'd flown the coop, Luke had been called in. The fact that Luke had been enjoying the first week of a well-deserved three-week vacation hadn't mattered, either to Tom Boyce or himself. What had mattered was that he was way familiar with the players. In his first years with the Bureau's Philadelphia office he'd tracked them exclusively. Since then, he'd also had to focus on a variety of higher-priority cases, but his determination to bring down DePalma, his father, his friends, and associates had never waned.

That was the reason Boyce had tracked him down in Cayman Brac, where Luke had been scuba diving with friends. Upon hearing that Donnie Jr. had disappeared, Luke had immediately packed up his gear, abandoned his vacation, and grabbed a plane to Durham, North Carolina, from which he would travel on to Ocracoke Island, where, according to a snippet of cell phone conversation overheard by the Bureau's electronic ears, a large sum of money was being transported by courier for some unspecified purpose. The unlikely locale — Jersey was DePalma and company's usual turf, with satellite operations in New York and Philadelphia — that was nevertheless a known haunt of the DePalma family's, the amount of money involved, the urgency, the timing, all pointed to a rendezvous with Michael DePalma, in Luke's estimation. In Durham, at Boyce's request, the local office had provided him with a car, equipment, and a temporary partner in the person of

Gary. The car had been passable, the equipment something less than state-of-the-art, and Gary an absolute whiz with computers, as advertised, though unfortunately less than stellar at just about everything else. Just that morning they'd gotten into Ocracoke and moved into the cottage that had been emptied for them the day before by agents posing as sweepstakes operators. Next door, Christy Petrino was already in residence. Luke had been surprised — no, make that flabbergasted — to discover that the bagman whose activities they were tracking was none other than Donnie Jr.'s sexy lawyer girlfriend. But it had served to reinforce his gut feeling that Michael DePalma was the intended recipient of the money. Why else would they use her, unless Donnie Jr., who'd had to split fast, meant to pick up both girl and money at the same time?

But there were some problems with that theory, as he was discovering. Christy Petrino was scared. There was no mistaking that. By going with Plan B, which was to get close to her if possible and see what he could uncover by way of a few friendly chats, he'd seen her in a whole new light. As Donnie Jr.'s girlfriend, her image captured on dozens of videotapes, she'd seemed coolly confident, a brainy looker with her eye on the main chance. When he got up close and personal, she seemed — defenseless. Threatened. And, yes, face the truth, sexy as hell.

That last part worried him. He was afraid that it might be clouding his judgment. Because he was starting to wonder if Christy was here on Ocracoke of her own free will at all. The tone of that phone call, along with her demeanor and his instincts, had him wondering if she was being threatened or somehow coerced.

That was the thought he was mulling as he pulled into the parking lot of the Crosswinds Hotel. It was a small place, two-story frame, seventeen guest rooms with a pool out back. Laid-back family atmosphere. Luke knew, because he'd checked out just about everything and everyone on the damned island before he'd arrived.

The lot was pretty much full, which meant that it held about twenty cars total. The empty spot where the Maxima had been parked was easy to spot. Luke stopped across from it, got out, and, taking a flashlight from the back, checked out the space and the surrounding area, hoping to find something, an ATM receipt, a dropped business card, anything, that would provide some clue as to who had been in the car. All he found was a crushed coffee cup from Starbucks, which was one of Donnie Jr.'s favorite stops. Could have been anybody's, he knew, but he picked it up on the off chance that it might provide some kind of useful evidence if analyzed. Other than that, nothing. Not even so much as an oil slick. Tomorrow he would do some discreet investigating into the hotel's guests, but he was already fairly sure that the party he sought would not be among them. That would make it too simple. So far, nothing about this had been simple.

Getting back in the SUV, he spent about twenty minutes cruising around the island. The layout wasn't complicated: besides the long and twisty road that ran parallel to the shore, there were basically two main thoroughfares heading up through town. These were called, imaginatively, Back Street and Front Road, and at this time of night they were pretty much devoid of traffic. The problem was that this was high season in a veritable Mecca for tourists. There were cars everywhere, parked in driveways and hotel lots and campgrounds. Along streets. At the marina. Dozens of cars. Hundreds of cars. As far as he could tell, the one he sought was not among them. There were also lots of places, like garages and obscure dirt tracks and under tarps in backyards, where a car could be hidden from view. Finally he gave it up. His best bet was to stake out the ferries when they resumed operating at seven a.m. If he made sure they were both covered, he would at least know if the car left the island.

It was after four when Luke got back to the cottage and found Gary nodding off in the wicker chair. Luke poked him in the shoulder. Gary roused with a start.

"Anything?" Luke asked, nodding at the monitor, which was turned on but showed nothing more than a dark screen. There was only the one camera, and its range didn't extend into the bedrooms or bathroom. Coverage of the doors and central living area had been what Luke had been after, and that was what he was looking at now: clearly the house was dark.

"Nah. She turned out the lights and went to bed not long after you left." Gary yawned hugely. "You find anything?"

"Nope. At seven we start watching the ferries. I don't know about you, but I'm going to try to grab a couple hours' sleep."

"Yeah." Gary stood up, took off his glasses and rubbed his eyes. "What about her?" He nodded at the monitor.

"Got it covered."

"Great." Blinking like a sleepy owl, Gary muttered something that sounded like good night and headed for his bedroom. Luke thought regretfully about the queen-sized bed in the room he'd claimed for his own. But the surveillance equipment was in here, and just in case she should get another call or something during the night he wanted to be on hand. Luckily, he was a notoriously light sleeper. As long as he was in the same room as the monitor he could grab what sleep he could and still be confident of not missing anything.

A shower would have been a good thing, but he wasn't about to waste any of his precious two-plus hours on that. Stripping down, he turned the light off and fell into the twin bed naked. Turning onto his side, pulling the covers up around his shoulders, he cast one last bleary glance at the monitor. Not that he could see anything. Except for the tiny green light that reassured him that it was still on and functioning, it was as dark as the inside of the cottage. But, he reminded himself, there was audio feed as well, and if she breathed hard he would hear her.

As tired as he was, he only hoped she didn't.

5

Earlier he had followed Christy Petrino along the beach, taking his time, enjoying her rising fear. She'd been skittish, nervous no doubt about walking alone so late at night. With good reason, as he knew better than anyone. He'd kept her in his sights, jogging along, stopping when she did, in no hurry to do his thing. Now everything had changed: she had to die. Now. Tonight. The timing was wrong, the location was wrong, everything was wrong, but it couldn't be helped. She had seen him, down there on the beach as she'd crouched over Liz. She'd gotten a good, long look, just as he'd gotten a good, long look at her. To her, he was no longer invisible. Before she could remember where she had seen him prior to that little exchange of glances on the beach, before she could tell them something that might be used to bring him down, he was going to kill her.

The problem was, he was used to taking

women in a time and place of his choosing. It had been a long time since a kill had been forced on him like this. The change had rattled him; he'd lost his cool. He realized that as the slim pick he was just about to insert into the keyhole clattered against the metal lock on the front door of her cottage. Freezing as the sound died away, he paused to listen. Inside, the cottage remained dark and still. No light came on. There was no sign that she had heard. The sound had been barely audible, of course. His heightened senses had magnified it a thousand times.

It wasn't like him to be this jazzed up. Glancing down, he saw that his hands were shaking. His hands never shook. Too much adrenaline. He could hear his pulse racing, hear the pounding beat of his own blood in his ears. His muscles were tense, too tense, and he was breathing hard and fast. His grip on the pick was too tight.

Breaking into houses was not something that he did very often anymore. He'd been good at it, once, but his skills had grown rusty. Putting the pick between his teeth, he flexed his gloved hands, then tried again. The pick slid into the keyhole. Pressing deep, he manipulated the tip. Nothing.

He tried again.

He should have been in just like that, but the lock was surprisingly stubborn. The truth was, Liz's escape had unsettled him. How had she gotten out of her cage? None of them had ever escaped before. Not one.

He could worry later about how she'd done it, he told himself. For now, it should be enough to know that he had reclaimed her, punished her, silenced her. Forever. The look of utter terror in her eyes as he'd grabbed her hair and yanked her head back to deliver the coup de grâce flashed into his mind's eye. She'd tried to fight, tried to scream, but she was too weak and he was too fast. Her neck had been like butter; his knife had sliced right through. Her eyes, which had been staring into his, had widened, flickered, as she'd felt the blade. It was over in an instant. Her choked cry had turned into a liquid gurgle. The sharp smell of blood had filled his nostrils. Her eyes had been just starting to glaze over when he'd had to tear himself away. But even though the moment had been foreshortened, the pleasure had been intense. The triumph had been intense.

But because he'd had to stop to take care of Liz, Christy had gotten away. Not for long, though. There was still an hour or so left until dawn. He could still make things right. There was plenty of time.

He'd had to leave Liz's body on the beach; there'd been no time to do anything else. She was the first one of his that had been discovered since he'd moved south. It worried him that she had been found. Her body would yield clues to his identity, he knew. Bodies, like crime scenes, always did.

But clues were only as good as the people who interpreted them. And whatever they found would not be enough to identify him. Unless Christy pointed them in the right direction; then the clues might be enough to put him away.

The lock clicked open at last with a small metallic *snick* that seemed to echo like a gunshot in his ears. Restoring the pick to the tool belt at his waist, he glanced cautiously around. The night was dark and shadowy and alive with sounds: the whirring of insects, the piping of tree frogs, the distant hiss of the sea. The twin palmettos in the small front yard rustled as the brisk breeze ruffled their leaves. Closer at hand, tall shrubberies shielded the concrete stoop on which he stood. There was no one around. The help that had come too late for Liz was long gone, and the road in front of the house was deserted. The houses on either side were dark. Even their low-slung outlines were almost impossible to see, shrouded as they were in the blanket of night.

Turning the knob slowly, careful not to make any more noise than he had to, he let himself into the house. For a moment after he closed the door he stood motionless, letting his senses expand, taking the pulse of his surroundings. His eyes adjusted quickly. He was standing in the middle of the living area. A curtained patio door was straight ahead. A faint yellow glow lightened the edges of the curtains. She had the patio light on. He smirked a little at that. As if a light would stop him, or even slow him down.

The open kitchen was to his left. The bedrooms would be —

He heard a noise and looked sharply to his right.

It was the kind of sound a woman surprised by something might make: a cross between a gasp and a cry. He tensed, ready to jump her, scanning the darkness but coming up blank. Where was she? Had she seen him? Was she now backing away, trying to escape, trying to hide?

Frozen in place, he listened intently.

There were no retreating footsteps, no hushed breaths, nothing to indicate stealthy, panicked flight. After a minute or so of strained waiting, he heard something else: the faintest of incoherent murmurs. It was followed by the creak of a mattress and the rustle of bedclothes. Slowly he let out the breath he was holding. The sounds of a restless sleeper? Almost certainly. The cry? Maybe she was having a nightmare. And why not? She'd found Liz. And she'd seen him, down there on the beach. Was her subconscious replaying her fear, her horror, *her memories?* Was he starring on her mental movie screen even now? He lingered over the thought that he was the subject of her dreams and found that he was enjoying it. Even if this particular bad dream wasn't about him, he could just about guarantee her next one would be.

A small smile played around his mouth. *Guess what, Christy. Your worst nightmare is already right here in your house.*

His gaze fell on the phone. As a precaution, he'd cut the outside wires, but there was a good chance she had one of those damned cell phones. But using one that was not local was always tricky, in his experience, and hers would have been purchased in Philadelphia or possibly Atlantic

City. Not that he meant to give her the opportunity to use it.

Moving carefully as his eyes adjusted to the darkness, he crossed the living area to the arched doorway that led into a short, windowless hall. He knew it was short because he used the small flashlight he always kept on his tool belt to light his way as needed along the pitch-black passage. Quick flashes revealed chalky white walls. Beige carpeting. Two — three — four doors: three bedrooms and a bath. His footsteps made no sound as he crept toward the bedroom at the far end.

It was the only closed door. He knew she was behind it without even having to look in the other rooms. He could hear her turning over in bed, hear her uneasy murmurs, hear her breathing. He could smell soap and shampoo and woman.

Was she awake? The faintest of doubts caused him to frown. If she wasn't, she was a very noisy sleeper. He paused outside her door and pressed his ear to it. Everything he heard convinced him that she was asleep. He would creep up on her while she slumbered all unknowing, and hit her with his stun gun. Then she would be his.

At the thought, he felt himself starting to get excited. This kill had not been initiated by the beast, but the beast was growing interested. He could feel its rising tension, its anticipation. Christy Petrino was a young woman, attractive, of the physical type he liked. With Liz gone, she could be a playmate for Terri.

With that happy thought, he smiled at the closed bedroom door and reached for the knob. It was locked. Well, that was an easy problem to solve. He got out his pick again and, focusing his beam on the little hole in the center of the knob, slid it into the lock.

6

The dream started out as a pleasant one: she was in her own apartment in Philadelphia, in the cheerful yellow kitchen loading her supper dishes into the dishwasher. It was almost nine at night, she'd been home from work for about an hour, and she still had more work in her briefcase to finish before she went to bed. A quick knock on the door of her apartment sent her walking across the polished wood floor of the entry hall to look out the peephole. Her sister Nicole's ex-husband Franky was standing there. Franky had never been one of her favorite people even when he was married to Nicole, and he certainly wasn't now that it was all over, but he pounded with real urgency even as she stared at him through the peephole and she opened the door. He practically leaped in on top of her.

"They're after me! You gotta help me!" he begged, clutching her arms so hard it hurt. He was about her own age, a slight, handsome man with slicked-back dark hair and spaniel-brown eyes. Usually he was cocky to the point of obnoxiousness, but at that moment he was clearly terrified.

"Who's after you?" she asked, frowning.

And then he'd told her. . . .

That scene segued abruptly into another: she was crouched beside the girl on the beach, her own warm fingers pressed to cold, sandy skin. A croaked, desperate *"help me"* was just audible over the sound of the incoming tide. A man was jogging toward her, dark and menacing against the starlit sky. There was something about that bulky silhouette that struck terror deep into her soul. She jumped up, screaming. . . .

Christy awoke with a start. For a moment she lay unmoving, blinking in the semidarkness, not quite sure where she was. Her heart pounded. Her breathing was erratic. She felt — in jeopardy. In immediate, life-threatening jeopardy. Her sixth sense was practically doing calisthenics, going all out to get her juiced up. Her nerve endings were going wild as they were flooded with urgent messages to get up and run.

Then her gaze slid to the narrow slice of light that she could see shining around the edge of the not-quite-closed door of the en suite bathroom, and some of her terror began to recede. She remembered turning that light on before she crawled into bed, remembered positioning the door so that the light would not be enough to keep her awake, but would be enough to keep her from being plunged into pitch darkness as soon as she turned off the bedside lamp. Everything then came back to her in a rush. Of course, she was on Ocracoke Island, in the beach cottage, in the master bedroom, in the king-sized bed. Curled up in a tight little ball peeking fearfully out from beneath the covers.

With a great deal of relief, Christy realized that she'd had a nightmare. What a surprise. After the horror of what she had witnessed on the beach, after everything that she had been through recently, a nightmare was probably the least of the reactions she could expect. She'd been *traumatized*, damn it. It was unfair. It shouldn't have happened. She shouldn't *be* here. She wanted her life back. Her safe, peaceful, happy life.

Fat chance.

This was all the fault of her loser ex-brother-in-law Franky Hill, who didn't have enough sense to stay out of trouble and, more importantly, keep his big mouth shut. No, it was all Michael's fault, because —

She broke off in mid mental rant to stare, open-mouthed, at the bedroom door. Or, more particularly, at the knob. It was turning.

For the space of a heartbeat, she simply gaped at it, refusing to believe what her eyes were telling her.

The knob couldn't really be turning. Despite the sliver of light shining out around the bathroom door, the room was gray and shadowy enough for her to be mistaken. Plus, she wasn't fully awake. What she thought she was seeing was probably just some leftover remnant of nightmare.

Or not.

That was the thought that popped into her head as the knob started turning in the opposite direction.

Her heart leaped into her throat. The hair on the back of her neck spiked upright. She stopped breathing. Her eyes stayed glued to that shiny brass knob, and she watched with burgeoning horror as it continued turning slowly, stealthily, to the left.

No doubt about it: she was wide awake now and in full possession of every single one of her faculties. Unless this was some twisted, reality-show version of *Candid Camera* meets the *X-Files*, someone was outside her bedroom door trying to get in.

Thank God for the dresser she'd used to barricade the door. Wrestling it into place before she'd felt safe enough to turn in had left her sweaty and exhausted and feeling more than slightly stupid, but now her efforts with the unwieldy piece of furniture were paying off big-time. In fact, they just might save her life. Because if the knob was turning, clearly the cheap push-button lock had already been breached. Yes, she could see it, right there in the middle of the circle of brass, sticking up like an outie belly button. She swallowed as she faced the awful truth: the dresser was all that was keeping whoever was out there from being in here.

If she lived to be a hundred, she was never knocking paranoia again.

Even as she had the thought, she grabbed for her cell phone and the Mace, both of which she'd strategically positioned on the bedside table just in case, and rolled out of bed. Crouching like a runner at the starting line, she gave that twisting knob one more hunted look before catapulting for the bathroom. There was a window in

114

the bedroom, an old-fashioned double-hung that looked out over a vista of sand and sea oats and picket fence that separated her house from that of her cat-loving neighbor. Should she try to open it and climb out and run away? From what she remembered, it looked like it hadn't been opened in years. She was willing to bet her life that the darn thing was swollen or painted or nailed shut.

And she had the dreadful suspicion that her life was exactly what was at stake.

Choking back a bubbling series of blood-curdling screams that were doing their best to strong-arm their way out of her throat, she carefully, quietly closed the bathroom door and pressed down the same kind of worthless, push-button lock that had failed to protect her in the bedroom. Heart thudding, breathing hard, she backed away from the door until her back flattened against cold, smooth, circa 1950s green tile, and punched 911 into her phone. Alerting whoever was trying to get into her bedroom that she was aware of his presence by screaming her lungs out did not seem like a smart thing to do. Besides, if she screamed who would hear her? The cottage walls were concrete covered with stucco, designed in the pre–air-conditioner era to provide insulation against the sweltering heat. Making noise was something better left for the police when they arrived. The dresser wasn't *that* heavy. A few good shoves and a strong man would be in.

Remembering the big, burly figure she'd seen on the beach, Christy broke out in a cold sweat. She knew, absolutely *knew,* with a kind of instinctive certainty that she was never going to question again, that it was the man on the beach who was now outside her bedroom door. Clearly he was trying not to awaken her — and he also probably hadn't yet figured out what was keeping him out. When he did . . .

She thought of the poor dead woman with the slit throat, and started to shake.

"We're sorry, it's necessary to dial a one and the area code before accessing that number —"

Christy wrenched the phone away from her ear and stared down at it in disbelief. Of all the useless —

Thud. The dull sound came from the bedroom and it galvanized her. She knew what it was. He'd figured out that something was blocking the bedroom door and was trying to shoulder his way in.

Dear God, I'll go to Mass and confession every week for the rest of my life if you just help me out here.

On the theory that God helps those who help themselves, she dialed 911 again as she prayed, and at the same time glanced frantically around the windowless bathroom for anything that might be used to barricade the door. It was a small room, maybe seven by nine feet, with a black-and-white tile floor, green tile walls, and white fixtures. The sink was at one end, the tub was at the other, and the door and toilet both occupied the same wall. As far as containing something of substantial size that she could both move and use to block the door, she was pretty much shit out of luck. There was only a white wicker étagère . . .

Thud. Thud.

"If you'd like to make a call, please hang up and try again. If you need help —"

Arggh.

Her blood thundered in her ears. Her heart pumped in triple time. Mind racing, she dropped the worthless piece-of-junk phone on the green fuzzy rug that covered the toilet lid and grabbed the lone solid object — a glass-globed scented candle — off the étagère, placing it beside the phone. Then, she tipped the shelving unit over on its side, scattering the folded towels with

117

which it had been laden all over the floor. The étagère wasn't all that tall — maybe six feet, she guessed as she looked it over. But then, the bathroom wasn't all that wide . . .

In the blink of an eye, she had that étagère in place, flat on its back with its four rickety-looking little top legs braced against the door. Unfortunately, the top of the étagère missed reaching the opposite wall by about a foot.

Thud.

Christy swallowed.

He was in the bedroom.

She could hear his soft footsteps on the rug. They stopped, and she imagined him standing beside the bed. Imagined him figuring out that she was not concealed there amid the mounded covers. Imagined him looking up to find light glowing out from underneath the bathroom door.

Her pulse skyrocketed. She drew in a deep, shaky breath as she fought back incipient panic. Too late to turn off the telltale overhead light. Not that turning the light off would help particularly. The closet and the bathroom were the only two places she could reasonably be. Listening intently, she heard him cross to the closet, heard the rattle as the louvered doors were pushed open. Then she heard him coming back.

Fear turned her blood to ice. She was cold and clammy, breathing hard. Time to face facts one more time: the bathroom wasn't a sanctuary at all. It was a death trap.

Please, God. Please.

Her gaze lit on the wastebasket. She grabbed it and set it down between the bottom of the étagère and the opposite wall. Better, but no cigar. There were still a few inches of space remaining. She glanced around wildly.

More footsteps. Growing louder. Coming close. Then — hold your breath and wait for it — the doorknob moved. He had found her. He was just outside.

Her heart felt like it was going to pound through her chest. Her breathing came in quick, hard pants. A wave of dizziness assailed her. The room seemed to tilt.

Dear God, please don't let me hyperventilate and pass out now.

Snatching up her plastic toiletries kit from the back of the sink, she crammed it down between the étagère and wastebasket. At least the space was now filled. The wastebasket touched the wall; the étagère touched the door.

The million-dollar question was, would her makeshift barrier hold? She had a horrible, sinking feeling that she just might not want to find out the answer.

The knob moved again, rattled.

"Christy?"

The weirdly high-pitched voice made her skin crawl. Even more horrifying was the realization that he knew her name. She backed up until her spine and both hands were pressed flat against the wall.

"I know you're in there. Open the door."

A stray glance in the mirror told her that her face was white as death. Her eyes were huge, shiny black, terrified. Her lips were parted and colorless as she all but panted with fear.

Click. The button lock popped open.

For an instant, no longer, she was frozen in place, staring at the knob in horror. Then with a choked cry she lunged for the lock, pushed it in, and held it down hard, her heart jumping like a kid on a pogo stick as she focused on the unpainted wood panel right in front of her nose. The thought that he was there on the other side, just inches away, made her want to scream. But screaming was probably the worst thing she could do under the circumstances, she told herself. *Don't let him know you're scared!* What she needed to do was stay calm and think.

"I called the police on my cell phone. They're on their way!" she cried. It was a lie, but he had no way of knowing that. Her stomach cramped with fear as the knob jerked beneath her hands.

"You're going to be sorry you put me to this much trouble," the weird, high-pitched voice said.

Despite her best efforts the lock popped out again. He shoved the door hard and it moved, springing toward her without warning. Christy shrieked and stumbled back as the door hit the étagère, sending it scraping across the floor. She came up hard against the toilet as the wastebasket slammed into the wall with a metallic clang. An inch or so of space opened between the jamb and the door. Bathed in cold sweat, breathing like she had been running for miles, hanging on to the back of the toilet for support, Christy stared into that dark slit and felt as if she were looking into the jaws of hell.

It was dark in the bedroom, and the gap in the door was not wide enough for her to see his face. She could make out no individual feature, nothing more, really, than his approximate height. And yet . . . and yet . . .

"Hi, Christy."

She might not be able to see him, but he could see her. Oh God, he could see her. She took a quick, terrorized step to the left, out of his line of sight.

"I told you, the police are on their way! They'll be here any minute! They'll arrest you! You'd better leave right now!"

"How much you want to bet I can get to you before they get to me?"

He slammed against the door again. The wastebasket crashed into the wall. The étagère shook. The puny door shivered. To heck with staying calm: Christy screamed and dove for the Mace. But the barrier held. Clutching the can to her chest with both hands, dizzy with fear and horror, Christy grappled with the knowledge that she had maybe a matter of minutes before he broke through. Oh God, what to do? If he got through that door, she might be able to aim right for his eyes and disable him with the Mace. But that wasn't good enough to gamble her life on. Her frantic gaze lit on the phone. Snatching it up, she juggled it and the Mace and tried information — 411 — instead. It cost to use information. There were always operators on hand there.

His fingers slid through the opening. He was wearing black leather gloves. Christy watched, petrified with fear, as his hand closed around the edge of the door.

Ring.

"I'm coming in now, Christy. Then we're going to play."

Ring.

"The police are on their way! I've got the dispatcher on the phone right now! They'll be here any second!" She swallowed in a futile attempt to combat her suddenly dry throat. Then, lying as convincingly as she could, she yelled into the still-ringing phone, "This is 29 Ocean Road. I'm trapped in my bathroom with a man breaking down the door. I need help *now!*" Split second pause in which she pretended to listen. "They're almost here?" She looked toward the door. "Did you hear what I said? The police are almost here!"

His shoulder thudding into the door was his only reply. Screams ripped from her throat of their own volition as he slammed into the door again and again and again, in a series of quick, violent onslaughts. The wastebasket started to flatten. Shampoo leaked from the bottom of her toiletry kit. The flimsy wicker groaned. The barrier she'd thrown together was not going to hold much longer, she knew. Staring helplessly into the dark gap that he was slowly making wider, Christy caught the gleam of his eyes. A predator's cold and merciless eyes . . .

The gap was now about four inches wide. Still holding on to the edge of the door, he slid his bent arm inside. His shoulder was next . . .

Cold sweat drenched her as she realized that in the next few minutes she was probably going to die.

"No!" Christy howled. Dropping the phone, she leaped toward the opening, aimed the Mace and pressed the button. Spray shot through the gap in a thick white stream. The sizzling sound, the sharp acidic smell, made her think of liquid fire. "Take that, you asshole!"

He screamed, and his arm disappeared through the gap.

"Goddamn motherfucking *bitch!*"

Bingo. *Yes.*

Pumped now, driven by a terror-fueled rush of hormones, Christy dropped the empty can, threw her body against the door, slammed it closed, and pressed home the lock.

"I'm going to cut your fucking head off!"

Without warning the edge of a small hatchet ripped through the wood, its wickedly sharp tip slicing into the top of her shoulder. Screaming, she jumped back, clamping a hand to the wound. There was no pain; instead what she felt was shock, followed by a kind of icy numbness as she lifted her bloodied hand to stare with stunned disbelief at the blood welling up through the cut.

"Got ya!" He cackled with triumph. The wood creaked as the hatchet was yanked from view.

"Go *away!*" Christy yelled despairingly.

The door shook as he chopped at it again, then subjected it to what sounded like a full body slam. Forget being injured: her life was at stake. Christy flew back to hold the door, hold the lock. The hatchet hacked through the wood again, barely missing her face. Screaming with enough volume to take the roof off the house now, Christy dodged and held fast, reinforcing the étagère with her weight, holding down the lock with both hands. The spray had hit him, she knew it had, but it must have been a glancing blow that had angered rather than incapacitated him. She could hear him cursing, hear his harsh, rasping breaths. He wasn't bothering to try to unlock the door anymore; in his fury, he was trying to smash right through it.

Dear God, please save me. Please. I'll do anything . . .

Blood was running down her arm in crimson rivulets. She could feel its warmth, feel the slipperiness of the tile beneath her feet as dripping blood rendered the footing treacherous. The cut itself was at the very outer edge of her left shoulder, perhaps three inches long, a neat slice from a sharp blade that, fortunately, was unlikely to prove fatal. Still, glancing at it, she felt nausea roil in her stomach. Her knees threatened to turn to Jell-O. But she couldn't surrender to hysteria, couldn't collapse. Not now. If she did she was as good as dead.

"I'm going to carve you up, bitch. I'm going to make you beg."

His shoulder rammed the door, again and again and again. Heart pounding wildly, screams echoing off the tiled walls, Christy tried to hold the lock and the door. Then, finally, as he took the hatchet to it, she was forced to jump back out of the way. With the Mace gone, she was all but defenseless. Desperately, she looked around for the phone. It could be anywhere: beneath the towels that littered the floor, behind the toilet.

There was a loud *crack*, and the door

shot inward. Leaping back, she all but fell over the toilet.

He'd torn loose a hinge, Christy realized with horror. His hand shot through the gap that was inches wider this time to grip the edge of the door. The étagère shuddered as the door slammed furiously against it. The wicker groaned, and seemed to bend. This was it. The barrier was not going to hold —

Terror spurred her into action. Snatching up her curling iron from the back of the sink, she whacked his fingers with the metal rod. He cursed, and the hand vanished. But before she could slam the door closed again, he hit it hard. Jumping back, she slipped on her own blood and almost went down as the wastebasket crashed into the wall. There was a sharp *crack* as his foot came partway through the door. She could see the toe of a scuffed black work boot through the shards of wood.

"Help!" she screamed despairingly. "I need help!"

Faintly, as if from far away, she heard a muffled, rhythmic banging, *as if someone who wanted in very badly was beating on the patio door*. Probably it was no more than the drumming of her own pulse in her ears, but —

"Do you hear that? The police are here! They're here!" Shrieking out what she was almost positive was a lie, she scrambled for the door again. Not that she expected to hold him off for much longer; one or two more solid blows and he would be inside. But as she threw her body against the splintered panel she realized with disbelief that there was no resistance. She could actually almost close the door. He'd broken it so that it no longer fit properly in the frame, or she would have been able to close it all the way.

Was he gone? Impossible to believe that he could actually be gone. Or was it a trap? Was he lying in wait, hoping that she would open the door, ready to grab her if and when she did? Swallowing her screams, she put a cautious ear to the panel and listened intently.

The bedroom light came on. Christy blinked as light shone through the jagged holes the hatchet had left in the door.

"Christy?"

The knob turned beneath her hand, and the door thrust toward her again just as she was moving cautiously to peer out through the gap. Startled almost out of her wits, she screeched and jumped back. A hand curled around the edge of the door.

Only this time the hand was tanned skin. No glove.

Thank God, no glove.

"Christy, it's Luke. Are you okay?"

Luke. Breathing erratically, she looked warily through the gap and met his gaze. He was looking in at her just like the other man had done only moments before. There were differences though, wonderful, reassuring differences that she took several seconds to assimilate: his eyes were higher; his hand, even ungloved, seemed larger; his voice was different, deep, softly slurred, Southern. The light was on in the bedroom so that she could see him clearly. This was definitely her cat-loving neighbor.

"Oh my God," she said. As she processed the fact that she was not going to die tonight after all, her knees gave out, and she collapsed in a little heap on the floor.

"Damn it to hell and back. How badly are you hurt?" She could feel his gaze on her. The door rattled as he shook it impatiently. "Christy? Christy, let me in."

"Be careful. There's a man in the house. He tried to — kill me." She managed to get the warning out through teeth that would not stop chattering. She was so cold — freezing cold. And she was bleeding.

The cut stung now. There was blood everywhere, running down her arm in a crimson river, smeared on her hands and legs and feet, splattered all over the tile. Curling her legs up beside her, she clenched her teeth to try to control the sound they made and reached for a towel.

"He's gone. I've got a buddy with me, and he's looking around to make sure, but whoever did this took off when he heard us. You're safe now, I promise." His voice had gentled, had gone all soft and soothing as he watched her press the towel to her shoulder. He turned the knob, pushing at the door again. "Christy? Can you let me in?"

She was feeling slightly woozy, not quite on top of her game. Considering, she focused for a long moment on what she could see of him: untidy blond hair finger-combed back from his forehead, a slice of bronzed, handsome face complete with worried frown, large bare hand, muscular bare knee and calf ending in a sturdy ankle rising above a boat-sized white sneaker: this, clearly, was not her attacker. She was really, truly safe. Relief grew inside her like a huge, expanding bubble.

The knob rattled as he pressed against the door.

"Christy. Let me in."

It was an order this time, not a request. In her not-quite-all-there state, an order was what she needed. Drawing on the last reserves of her strength, Christy shifted and stretched a leg out to shove the wastebasket out of the way with her foot.

7

Luke pushed through the door, shot a lightning glance around, and hunkered down in front of her, his eyes filled with concern. They were blue, she registered absently. A bright, vivid, Carolina blue.

"Okay, let me see."

His hand closed over hers as she held the towel to the cut. Moving her hand out of the way, he gently lifted the stained towel and looked down at her bleeding shoulder. His lips thinned. Replacing the towel and her hand holding it, he met her gaze. Like his mouth, his eyes were harder than before.

"It's not that bad." His voice was still soft and reassuring even though his eyes were not. "You probably could use a couple of stitches, though. Are you hurt anywhere else?"

Christy shook her head. Now that the danger was past she was losing it, she realized with some chagrin. Her teeth were clenched so tightly that her jaws ached; if she unclenched them they would only chatter again. She was shivering, her breathing came shallow and fast, and she felt oddly boneless, like the jellyfish she had seen rolling in on the tide earlier. The memory made her stomach clench.

"You sure?"

He was looking her over carefully from stem to stern. It was only then that she remembered what she was wearing, or, rather, not wearing. Basically, she didn't have on much in the way of clothes. Bikini panties and a T-shirt were her customary sleeping attire. Tonight the panties were silky pink nylon. The T-shirt was a skimpy, thin-ribbed cotton tank, once neon green but now, thanks to numerous trips through the wash cycle, more of a squashed caterpillar shade. It molded itself to her breasts so that not the tiniest detail — like the reaction of her nipples to cold and shock — was left to the imagination. The sexiness of the non-outfit was mitigated by the fact that at the moment the garments, like the rest of her, were liberally adorned with blood.

"What happened?"

"I told you — he tried to kill me. He got in while I was asleep. He had a hatchet —"

She broke off, unable to continue. Just as she feared, her teeth chattered, making embarrassing little clicking sounds.

"Is that what happened to your shoulder? He attacked you with a hatchet?"

"He tried to chop through the door." She shuddered, then gathered her strength again to burst out with: "It was the man on the beach. The one who — killed that woman. He came after me." Another shudder racked her. "He would have killed me. If you hadn't come —"

"But I did come. He's gone and you're safe." He picked up another towel, folded it, and replaced the first towel with it. She automatically held the fresh towel in place, and he got to his feet. "You can tell me the rest on the way to the emergency room. Can you stand up?"

Christy gritted her teeth, nodded, and tried. But even with his hands gripping her elbows for support, she couldn't quite manage it under her own power. Her muscles simply would not cooperate. He ended up practically lifting her to her feet, and then she sagged against him as her knees gave way. She would have crumpled if his arms hadn't shot around her for support. He was warm and solid and smelled like suntan lotion and fabric softener, a scent that she remembered from before. She figured the source was probably his shirt. It was the same one he'd had on earlier, or at least she thought it was the same. Only now it was wrong side out, with no more than two of the buttons fastened and those in the wrong holes. His trunks were knee-length and faded blue, and she thought they were the same ones he'd been wearing earlier, too. From all appearances he had heard her screams, jumped out of bed, grabbed up the clothes he had discarded, and come running to her assistance.

One thing puzzled her: How could he have heard her screams through the thick cottage walls and over the ocean's constant background noise? If he'd been in his cottage asleep . . .

She frowned. "How did you know I was in trouble?"

His eyes flickered.

"Honey, you have a scream like a train whistle," he said, and scooped her up in his arms. Caught off guard, almost as surprised as she was embarrassed, Christy kept silent as he started walking toward the door with her. For all his surfer-dude looks, the guy was strong. The arms holding her were hard with muscle, and his chest was wide and firm. The faintest suggestion of five o'clock stubble darkened his jaw. The blond curls were misleading, Christy decided, resting her head against an impressively broad shoulder. They might be feminine, but the rest of him was definitely all man.

"I can walk," she protested feebly in an effort to keep herself from feeling like a total wuss, although even as she said it she realized she probably couldn't. She was shivering, light-headed, nauseated. Losing her cookies was not beyond the realm of possibility. If God was on the job, though, it would not be all over Luke.

He cut her a glance. "Get real."

Okay, he had a point. There was nothing for her to do but curl herself around the solid warmth of his body and concentrate on keeping her teeth from chattering as he carried her with no seeming effort into the now-well-lit bedroom.

"He got away, out the front door. At least, he couldn't have gone out the back or we would have —"

The strange voice made her start. Luke tightened his arms around her as a nerdy-looking guy with glasses stuck his head through the still partly blocked bedroom door. He broke off as his eyes fastened on Christy. From his expression she suddenly became all too conscious of how she looked: blood-soaked, barely decent, one arm looped awkwardly around Luke's neck and her long bare legs dangling over his arm.

"Whoa," the newcomer said, sounding taken aback.

Christy frowned. Some of the shock of the attack must be wearing off, she realized, because she was starting to feel uncomfortable about having strange men ogle her while she was wearing just a few scraps of cloth more than a tan and a smile.

"You look around outside?" Luke asked.

The newcomer nodded, his eyes still on Christy. Luke's brows twitched together, and he added in the wryest of tones: "Gary, meet Christy. Christy, Gary Freeman."

Gary's eyes jerked up to meet Luke's, and a couple of seconds of palpable nonverbal communication passed between them. Then Gary grimaced, jerked his head in acknowledgment of the introduction, and gave Christy another quick glance that went no lower than the towel on her shoulder.

"So what's with all the blood?" Gary asked, elaborately casual now.

"Bastard attacked her with a hatchet."

"Yowzers."

"Yeah," Luke said. "Coming through."

Gary quickly stepped inside the bedroom, leaving the passage clear into the hall, and frowned questioningly at the dresser sitting all cockeyed behind the door. He was wearing navy pajamas that looked like they were brand new, Christy saw as they passed him. His bare feet were thrust into shiny cordovan loafers complete with tassels.

"Is this thing here for a reason?" he asked, referring to the dresser, as Luke maneuvered her out the door and into the hall.

Admitting that she'd been too afraid to go to sleep without barricading herself in was embarrassing. But what else could she do?

"I blocked the door with it." If there was the tiniest note of defensiveness to that, it was because she couldn't help it.

"Did you?" Luke slanted a glance down at her. "Before you went to bed?"

"Hey, it probably saved my life. If he could have gotten into the bedroom without my hearing him, I would be dead." At the thought she started shivering again. "Did you lock the doors?" she added anxiously to Gary, who was following them down the hall. "He could come back. I don't think he has a gun, but —"

"He won't come back." Luke sounded so positive that Christy was comforted despite the fact that she knew he couldn't possibly *know* that. "What he was after was a woman alone. Believe me, now that he knows you've got company he's long gone."

"Anyway, I locked the front door," Gary said. "The patio door . . . well . . ."

"We had to break it to get in," Luke finished for him, and as they emerged from the hall into the lamp-lit living room Christy saw what he meant. The curtains covering the patio door were open, revealing the sickly yellow bug light that lit the patio and the opaqueness of the night beyond it. One of the doors was ajar, and the edge of a sheer fluttered wildly as the breeze from the ocean rushed in. Only jagged shards remained to cling to the edges of the door's silver frame. Long slivers of glass gleamed on the beige carpet. Luke walked by them into the kitchen area.

"Car keys?" Luke glanced down at her.

"By the phone." She nodded at her keys. The sight of the phone jogged her thought processes, which were still operating at approximately turtle speed. "I should call the police."

"Already did," Gary said. "They're on their way. Your phone's not working, by the way. I had to use my cell phone."

"He probably cut the wire." Luke scooped up her car keys and headed toward the garage door. He paused in front of it to look back at Gary. "Tell them that they can talk to her at the twenty-four-hour clinic on Front Street if they need to know something before she gets back. Yo, can you get the door?"

"Oh, yeah, sure." Gary hurried to assist.

"Wait," Christy said, her level of awareness just now catching up with the action. "I can't go anywhere like this. I need clothes, a robe, something. And my purse. My insurance card's in my purse."

Frowning, Luke met her gaze, then gave her a quick once-over, after which he seemed to see the force of her objection because he didn't argue.

"Where's your robe?"

"In the master bedroom closet."

"Okay." He glanced at Gary.

"Got it covered." Gary hurried away.

"Purse?"

"On that chair." Fighting the persistent

light-headedness that made her feel like she was going to pass out, Christy nodded at one of the four wrought-iron chairs that surrounded the small, glass-topped table in the middle of the kitchen. Her black leather purse hung from the back. Luke managed to snag the strap with his fingers. Then Gary was back with her robe.

"Here," Gary said, proffering the garment. It was deep red silk with quilted satin lapels and a sash, a Victoria's Secret special that she had always felt upped her sexiness quotient a couple of notches every time she put it on. If she'd been more herself, she would have felt self-conscious about having two strange men handle it. On the plus side, though, it probably wouldn't show bloodstains.

Keeping a careful grip on her, Luke set her on her feet and helped her get the robe up her good arm. Before she could even try to ease her injured arm into the sleeve, he bundled the rest of it around her, pulled the sash tight around her waist, slid her purse over his arm and picked her up again.

"Good to go now?"

Christy nodded. A few minutes later she was ensconced in the front passenger seat of her own white Toyota Camry being driven through the predawn darkness toward town, a little faster than she would have liked given the driving conditions. Besides being dark as pitch, it was raining again, a thunderous cloudburst of the sort that had cleared the beach earlier. Raindrops beat a brisk rat-a-tat on the roof, and the windshield wipers were on in full force. The smell of damp was strong even inside the car. A patrol car raced past them as they pulled out onto Silver Lake Road, its lights flashing but its siren off, as a nod no doubt to the peacefully sleeping citizenry. Probably headed toward her house, Christy surmised, unless there was a secondary crime wave going on in the vicinity.

"You doing okay?" Luke asked, looking over at her. They hadn't spoken since he'd put her into the car. The halogen lights ringing the marina glimmered softly in the distance, Christy saw as she turned her head toward him. Closer at hand, the establishments dotting the waterfront were dark. Besides the rhythmic swish of the windshield wipers, the only sounds were the hum of the defrost and the whoosh of the tires as they sped over wet pavement.

"I'm fine." What she actually felt was — cold. Woozy. In pain. And scared. Very, very scared. None of which she saw any reason to share with him. "You know, I think you probably saved my life tonight. Thank you."

"Just call me Johnny-on-the-spot."

She smiled a little at that, then frowned. "I wonder why my other neighbor, Mrs. Castellano, didn't hear me screaming or the patio door shattering and call the police?"

"Who knows? Maybe she's a heavy sleeper," Luke said.

"Maybe." Christy shivered.

"Did Marvin ever get home?"

A beat passed.

"Yeah, he got home before I did." He glanced her way and the corners of his mouth turned up slightly. "Hey, do you always stir up this much excitement everywhere you go?"

Christy grimaced and shook her head. "Ordinarily I live a very quiet, calm life. I'm a lawyer too, by the way."

His brows lifted. "You don't say? Now that I never would have guessed. You don't look like a lawyer."

"Neither do you." Her gaze slid over him. He really had a very nice profile, she decided, and the curls were growing on her. As was he. "Are you here on vacation?"

A glance glimmered her way. "Yeah. I drove down from Atlanta. You?"

"Yes." She looked out the windshield as he stopped at an intersection, then turned onto the main road that led into Ocracoke Village.

"You just got in today, didn't you?" The car picked up speed again. "You expecting anybody to join you? Husband? Boyfriend? Significant other?"

"No." No need to tell him that, having just dumped her fiancé for good and compelling reasons, there was no longer a man in her life. This guy might actually be very nice, but surviving was her focus at the moment. Hooking up was not.

"Taking some 'you' time, huh?"

"Something like that."

"Bad luck that you just happened to go for a midnight stroll on the beach tonight of all nights."

"Yeah." *Oh yeah.*

"About this guy who broke into your house — you said you think he's the same guy you saw on the beach?"

"Yes. I'm positive."

"What makes you so sure?"

Christy wet her lips. "They just — felt the same. Evil." There was no other word to describe the vibrations she'd gotten. Despite her robe, and the fact that he had the defroster on heat, she was suddenly shivering again. "And besides, they were about the same height and build and he knew my name and — and what are the chances that there could be two murderous lunatics out stalking the same small stretch of beach on the same night?"

"He knew your name?" Luke's voice sharpened, and he sent a glance sliding her way. "Are you saying he called you by name? In the house tonight?"

Just remembering made her feel dizzy. She nodded. "Yes."

"What exactly did he say?"

Oh, roiling nausea. "When he first spoke to me through the door he called me by name, in this weird kind of singsong voice. Then, later, he got the door opened enough to see me and he said, 'Hi, Christy.'"

"How do you think he knew your name?"

Actually, several possibilities came to mind, none of which she cared to share.

"I don't know."

Luke frowned thoughtfully, and Christy wondered with a little spurt of panic if in the course of their conversation she had somehow revealed too much. Uncle Vince had made it clear that if the organization thought she might spill the beans on what she knew, she was basically toast. On the other hand, she wasn't sure she wasn't a prime candidate to be toast anyway. The fact that her attacker had known her name was freaking her out, now that she thought about it. A hideous possibility had been niggling around in her mind ever since she'd stumbled across that poor woman earlier, and as she added the killer knowing her name to the mix it took on monstrous shape and form: what if the woman's murder had been a mistake? What if the killer had attacked the wrong person, down there on the beach? What if he'd been following her, Christy, meaning to kill her, and somehow gotten his wires crossed? What if the horror that had taken place on the beach had been a bungled hit directed at herself? And then this break-in had been an attempt to rectify the error? Among other things, that would certainly explain how her attacker had known her name.

Her blood ran cold at the thought.

"There's no one you can think of who might want to harm you?" Luke asked. His question was so in tune with what she was thinking that Christy started. It took a couple of seconds before she felt in control enough to reply.

"No," she lied. "There's no one like that."

"Maybe the guy's connected to something you have going on at work?"

Christy tried not to be too obvious about taking a deep breath. He was so on the money with his speculations that it was scary. "How could he be? To begin with, I work a long way from here — in Philadelphia. And I don't do the kind of work that gets people killed. I'm a corporate lawyer, not a defense attorney or a prosecutor."

Yes, but a corporate lawyer working for a firm that she'd just learned was basically a front for the mob. If Franky, the slimy little weasel, hadn't clued her in, she never would have gone hunting the truth, and she wouldn't be in this mess now. Damn Franky, anyway. She'd *told* Nicole that marrying him was a mistake. Her sister hadn't listened. Her sisters never listened. They screwed up, she cleaned up the mess. It was the story of her life.

"So what's your theory about what happened tonight?"

Christy hesitated. It was hard to sort out what she could say from what she was better off not revealing when she felt like her brain had gone on vacation and left the

147

rest of her behind. She closed her eyes and concentrated on remembering the image she had to convey if she had any hope of getting out of this with a whole skin: that she was the innocent victim of a crime and nothing more.

"I don't have a theory. How would I? All I know for sure is that a woman was murdered on the beach tonight, I found her, and then some crazy broke into my house and tried to kill me. It doesn't take a rocket scientist to figure out the two events must be connected."

She closed her eyes in an effort to end the conversation. He was obligingly quiet for a bit, apparently occupied with his own thoughts.

"Hell of a first day on vacation."

There was the faintest note of wry humor to that. Christy's eyes popped open and she glanced at him. His mouth turned up at the corners in the smallest of smiles.

"For you, too."

"Yeah."

The car slowed then, and Christy realized that they had reached the clinic. Good thing, because the towel was almost soaked through, and her shoulder was throbbing. A small, rectangular sign advertised Urgent Care Center, Open 24 Hours. Beside it, a convenience store was also still open. At nearly five a.m. on a rainy Sunday morning, neither appeared to be doing gangbuster business. There were a total of three cars in both parking lots.

"You are *not* carrying me in," Christy said as he parked in front of the clinic.

"Your call."

But she was still sitting in her seat, albeit with the door open and one leg out, by the time he came around the car. Her legs had the approximate tensile strength of limp spaghetti, she'd discovered. With the best will in the world, she was not going to make it inside the clinic under her own steam.

"No shoes," she said in sullen response to his inquiring look as he opened the door wider and ducked his head inside. It was still raining, though only lightly now, and raindrops glistened on his face and in his hair. His shirt was spattered around the shoulders. Beyond the car, she saw that the pavement was a torrent of muddy water that shone brown under the lights.

The corners of his mouth quirked up. "Definitely a problem," he agreed, sliding his arms around her.

Christy turned her face into his shoulder as he carried her into the clinic through the gentle rain.

8

It was almost dawn. He was back in his castle, his safe house, his hidey-hole. Back in the lair of the beast. And the beast was raging. Everything, *everything* tonight had gone wrong. Christy Petrino was still alive. He'd had to run for his life, not once but twice. And Liz had escaped.

How the hell had Liz escaped?

He would figure that out, but not now. For now, he had to concentrate on calming himself down. He was twitchy all over. His skin felt like it was splitting open. The beast felt almost too huge, too powerful, to be contained in his human body any longer. Its blood lust had been roused again, but this time it had been left unsatisfied. He had to slake it, and soon. If he went to work like this — and he had to go to work soon — someone might notice. Someone might see. Someone might guess.

What he was.

He was going to have to make do with

Terri. She was still in her cell; after punishing Liz, he'd rushed back here to make sure she hadn't gotten out as well. That would have created huge problems for him: he would have had to find her. Fast.

But that hadn't happened. Terri was still precisely where he needed her to be. Until now he hadn't had much use for her. With her butch haircut and flat chest and big ass, she wasn't up to his usual standards. He'd played with her a little, testing things out, but mostly he'd made her watch what he did to Liz. At first Terri had screamed and cried and begged him not to hurt her friend, but he'd broken her of that. He was good at breaking girls of bad habits. Three days after he'd taken her, he'd had Liz responding to the snap of his fingers. He'd do that for Terri, too.

And for Christy, when he brought her here, to play with her before he killed her. Now *she* was more his type. The fact that he'd made her acquaintance before supplied just that little extra fillip. That she'd squirted him with Mace and escaped him tonight would only add to the fun.

He was going to enjoy Christy Petrino.

On his way downstairs he turned on the overhead light. It was his way of letting the girls — oh, the *girl,* singular, now — know

151

that he was coming. Usually as soon as he did that he could hear their chains rattle as they scrambled up from the floor, hear their frightened breathing, hear them licking their lips and shuffling their feet nervously as they waited for him to appear. They'd learned not to cry out or scream. They'd learned that he was the master, and would be loved and obeyed — and feared.

He reached the bottom of the stairs and lifted his bag of toys from the hook on the wall. This level was specially outfitted with, among other things, four cells — not that he'd ever had four girls at the same time, but he believed in being prepared for all contingencies. There were two on each side, with the enclosed staircase and a utility closet serving as a partition in the middle. He'd kept Liz and Terri on separate sides so that they couldn't see each other unless he allowed it. It was one of those reward and punishment things that made his little hobby so much fun. He knew they called to each other when they were sure he was out, but he didn't mind that. The walls were thoroughly sound-proofed.

Liz's cell was on the left, but he refused to look at it for the moment. It would make him too angry, and he wasn't ready to kill Terri yet, not until he had her replacement in hand. But he already knew that the barred door of Liz's cell was locked, and the chain that he'd kept fastened around her ankle lay limply on the floor. It was still securely attached to the wall, and the shackle itself was locked as tight as the door.

How had she managed it? How? How? It occurred to him that in all likelihood Terri would know.

"Terri?" He felt his voice pitching higher as it tended to do when he got excited. "Terr-*eee*, are you ready to play?"

9

The sheriff's office was housed in an incongruously charming frame bungalow crouched close to Front Road right across from Howard's Pub. On either side of it were a busy Shell Oil station and the Curl-o-Rama, a hair salon. Christy parked along the live-oak-shaded street, which, like all of Ocracoke's roads, originally had been built for horses and buggies and didn't look like it had been widened since the horses left. Finding a spot was tricky, because the island, which had a winter population of approximately 900, was full to capacity with something in the nature of five thousand summer visitors. Christy knew, because she'd tried to book herself into a hotel for the remainder of her stay, which she hoped would be extremely short. Unfortunately, she had struck out. Everything from historic Blackbeard's Lodge to the new Hyatt was booked solid.

She would sleep in her car before she'd sleep in that cottage again. Even going back inside to gather up a change of clothes had been beyond her. Just thinking about it now made her break out in a cold sweat. She felt as if she were trapped in a house of mirrors, and every time she tried to escape she ran into a dead end. She was beginning to be afraid that there was no way out.

The scariest part of the whole thing was knowing that she was completely on her own. There was no one she could confide in, no one she could trust. To turn to her family was unthinkable: doing so would put them in mortal danger, too. Running to the authorities hovered at the back of her mind, but if she did, if she turned on the mob, she would have to hide out for the rest of her life. That went for her mother and sisters and Nicole's children as well. In a word, the situation was impossible. Better to sweat it out, to do as she was told until they were reassured that she wasn't a threat, and could be trusted to keep her mouth shut. The key was staying alive until that message got through.

Even her cat-loving neighbor had deserted her. Citing an impossible-to-reschedule appointment, Luke had disappeared soon after Sheriff Meyer "Bud" Schultz and one of his deputies had shown up at the clinic. His departure had left her feeling oddly bereft; it was embarrassing to realize that as long as he was around she'd felt safe. For all his surfer-boy looks, he'd taken charge last night with an effortlessness that, in retrospect, impressed her. He'd saved her life, calmed her fears and gotten her to the clinic with a cool efficiency that had resulted in a totally unfounded feeling that he was someone on whom she could depend. Then he'd taken off to, presumably, resume his interrupted vacation. She, on the other hand, was left to stew in the nightmare that was her life.

Not that she really regretted his leaving, of course. He was a chance-met stranger, a vacationing lawyer who had just happened to rent the cottage next door. There was no real help he could offer her. Feeling forsaken when he poked his head into the treatment room to say a quick good-bye was stupid. The sheriff had been with her when he'd left, asking her questions even while the doctor had been putting three stitches in her shoulder. In other words, she'd been in good hands. Afterward, the sheriff had made a phone call that had accomplished what she could not: he'd secured her a room at the Silver Lake Inn. A deputy had driven her to the hotel, where she had tried without much success to sleep for a few hours.

The sound of church bells had awakened her at noon, minutes ahead of the alarm clock. As she lay in bed listening to the pealing chimes, it occurred to her that she had missed Mass despite all the promises she'd made to God the night before. Wincing at the soreness in her shoulder as she headed groggily for the bathroom and a shower complete with a plastic bag jury-rigged on her shoulder to protect the wound, she'd sent an apology winging skyward, along with a thank-you for keeping her alive. She only hoped God didn't take offense at what was basically a *catch-you-later.*

It was now just after twelve-forty-five on one of the hottest, sultriest Sunday afternoons Christy had ever experienced, and she was headed to the sheriff's office at his request to look at some pictures of known violent offenders in the area. Not that it was going to do any good. As she'd told him and everyone else who would listen, at no time had she gotten a good enough look at the man to identify him from a picture or anything else.

And even if she could identify him, she would be afraid to, although she hadn't told the sheriff *that.*

Sleepy little Ocracoke Village was really amazingly crowded. The line of people waiting to get inside Howard's Pub for a late brunch snaked across the building's porch and down the steps to curl around the sidewalk. She went around it, then cut across the street, dodging a group of bicyclists who no doubt hoped that a spot of exercise would help them work off their own Sunday lunches. Two little girls still in their church dresses with their mother between them clasping their hands crossed the street in the opposite direction, hurrying past Christy as they sought to join the brunch line. Next door, the Shell station's parking lot was full of, among other things, a lot of oversized vehicles towing trailers hauling grown-up toys like ATV's and boats. Christy eyed them all grumpily. She, personally, was not having fun in this steamy vacation paradise. Her head ached, her shoulder throbbed, and she was spooked to her back teeth.

The blast of air-conditioning that greeted her as she pushed through the door into the sheriff's office was a relief. Even the gray-speckled linoleum floor and the institutional-green cinder block walls looked cool. She'd left the inn less than fifteen minutes ago and already she was wilting. Or maybe melting was a better word. She was, as they called it here in the South, glowing, which meant that her skin sported a fine sheen of sweat. Courtesy of the hotel gift shop, she was wearing a white bikini as underwear beneath a Day-Glo orange T-shirt decorated with dancing clams and white shorts, all of which the humidity had plastered to her skin. Her hair clung damply to the back of her neck, and she pushed it behind her ears impatiently. Even her feet in their strappy sandals seemed to be sweating.

To the left of the door, the receptionist's desk was empty. Behind it, through the open door of an office, she could see three men: Gordie Castellano, Sheriff Schultz, and Aaron Steinberg. The first two were in uniform, the third in plaid Bermuda shorts and a white polo. The sheriff, a beefy man of about sixty with flat Slavic features and a full head of white hair, was seated behind a metal desk. The other two were ranged on either side of it, and seemed to be arguing heatedly about some papers that were spread out in front of the sheriff.

". . . don't need this," Castellano stabbed a vehement finger down on the papers, glaring at Steinberg all the while. Sheriff

Schultz glanced up, saw Christy, and interrupted the men's argument by standing up.

"Well, Ms. Petrino, how ya feelin'? You get any sleep in your hotel?" He came around the desk toward her, smiling genially.

"Some." She produced a mechanical smile. His bluff heartiness was slightly grating on approximately four hours' sleep, but he'd gone out of his way to assist her earlier and she appreciated it. Of course, it didn't help that, like the other two men in the room, he fit the general physical description of her attacker. "Thanks again for getting me a room."

"Anytime."

"I hear you had another real bad experience last night." Steinberg looked her up and down, and his eyes widened. He turned excitedly to Castellano, who had nodded a greeting. "You see, I told you, this is real. Look at her. She fits the type. Dark hair, slim, twenties, attractive —"

"That is the biggest bunch of crap," Castellano said. His gaze swung to Christy, and to her discomfort he looked her over. This was her first look at him in a good light, and she saw that his black hair was cut military style and his blunt-featured face was not unattractive. He glanced back at Steinberg. "So she's slim and has dark hair. So are lots of women. So what?"

"I told you, she fits the type."

Castellano rolled his eyes and glanced at her. "Don't let him scare you to death. He's got serial killer on the brain."

"I don't know, Gordie, maybe Aaron is on to something." Sheriff Schultz took Christy by the arm and steered her toward his desk. "Of course, he could be adding two and two and getting five."

"What's this about being dark-haired and slim?" Christy discreetly pulled her arm from the sheriff's hold. As of last night, all stocky men officially gave her the creeps. He pulled an upright wooden chair into place for her in front of his desk, and she sat.

"That's the type he likes. The type he goes after. All of them, the girls who are missing, look alike." Now Steinberg thumped the papers on the desk, looking triumphantly at the other men. "Look at these pictures and tell me if Miss Petrino here doesn't fit the mold."

"You're serious, aren't you?" Christy's heart skipped a beat as she took a good, long look at the papers spread across the desk. From her vantage point they were upside down, but there was no mistaking that they were photographs of young women. Slim, attractive young women with dark hair. The heading on every one was a bold MISSING. Beneath the pictures was identifying information. From the look of the paper, the pictures had been printed out via a computer.

"Damn right, I'm serious," Steinberg said. Then, with a quick glance at Christy, he added, "Sorry about the language. Didn't mean to offend."

"This serial killer thing's got Aaron here pretty well het up," the sheriff added in a semiapologetic tone, meeting Christy's gaze. " 'Course, if it turns out to be true we'll all be het up."

"And I say it's nothing short of criminally stupid to go spreading rumors until we know for sure what we've got here, which we don't," Castellano growled. "Besides, it's not right to discuss this in front of Ms. Petrino, we're just scaring her."

"Rumors, schmumors. If that's coincidence I'll eat your truck." Steinberg made a sweeping gesture that encompassed the desktop. "There's eight of them. Eight over the last three years. Within a two-hundred-mile range up and down the coast. Five just this year here in the Outer Banks. Ms. Petrino should know about this because it concerns her own safety. It's a matter of public safety!"

"I hate to say it, Gordie, but there's a case for it." The sheriff shook his head. He picked up a picture. Christy saw that it was a head and shoulders shot of a pretty, college-age girl with long brown hair and a dreamy look in her eyes. "Take these last two: Elizabeth Ann Smolski and Terri Lynn Miller were juniors at the University of Georgia last year who came here two weeks ago for a long weekend on Nags Head and disappeared after going into a bar for a couple of drinks. Last night Elizabeth turned up dead on our beach, some seventy miles to the south of where she disappeared. You saw her body. You know what happened to her. And Terri's still missing." He picked up another picture and tapped it. This one was of a girl of similar age with short, spiky black hair — as far as Christy could tell, the only one with short hair in the bunch — and an infectious grin. "How do you explain that, if we don't have ourselves a serial killer?"

"He's going to say it was a domestic," Steinberg said in disgust.

"All I'm saying is that Elizabeth Smolski had just broken up with her boyfriend, it was a pretty messy split, and the boyfriend

163

was in Nags Head the day the girls disappeared, according to their friends," Castellano said. "We can't locate this guy. His friends, his family, his roommate — no one knows where he is."

"Elizabeth Smolski had bite marks all over her! She'd been kept alive for two weeks, during which time she was tortured and starved! Are you saying her boyfriend did that?" Steinberg thumped a fist on the desk, making the pictures — and Christy — jump.

"All I'm saying is that we better explore every other possibility before we start scaring people with stories about serial killers, 'cause if you go putting this in the paper the economy's going to go straight down the toilet." Castellano's face was tight with tension.

"What, do you think Elizabeth Smolski's boyfriend killed her, then a couple of hours later attacked Ms. Petrino in her house? I'd say that's a lot less likely than us having a serial killer in the area." Steinberg glared at Castellano, who glared back. Steinberg's gaze swung to Christy. "Or do you think these were two separate, unrelated attacks? Maybe Ms. Petrino has a murderous ex-boyfriend too?"

The suggestion, clearly intended to be

satirical, was so clearly within the realm of possibility, that for a moment Christy just sat there looking back at him, stunned. She'd never quite considered the matter in that light, but — *she did have a murderous ex-boyfriend.* From everything she'd been able to uncover, Michael's criminal involvement had been of the hands-off variety, but it had involved overseeing everything from prostitution to smuggling and distributing drugs and guns to ordering the killing of those who got in his way. The question was, had he ordered her to be killed? *Michael?* Was he behind what had happened last night? Christy had to bite the inside of her lip hard to keep from shuddering.

She'd been picturing herself as the victim of a faceless, organization-ordered hit. Now, suddenly, she wondered if the face behind it could be Michael's. Not that it mattered when it came right down to it: whoever had ordered it, a contract on her head was a really bad thing. She'd almost rather be worrying about a serial killer, she decided in despair. At least, if she went home, she'd lose the serial killer. A contract on her life was like having a terminal disease — it followed right along with her wherever she went, and, unless a miracle occurred, sooner or later she was going to wind up dying from it.

"Ms. Petrino?" Sheriff Schultz spoke, but they were all three looking at her now with varying degrees of frowns. Christy almost panicked, wondering what her expression might have given away.

"No, I can't say that I do," she replied, and was proud of how cool she sounded. "And besides, I didn't see much of him, but I saw enough to know that the killer isn't any boyfriend I've ever had. And I'm all but one hundred percent sure that the man on the beach and the man who attacked me are one and the same."

"See?" Steinberg's eyes gleamed triumphantly at Castellano.

"You just want to sell more papers," Castellano said disgustedly.

"All right, you two, let's agree to study this a little bit more before we do anything rash like put a story about a possible serial killer in the paper. Maybe the DNA results on Elizabeth Smolski will help us out when they come back. In the meantime, Ms. Petrino and I have business. Excuse us, would you?"

"Yeah, sure." Castellano glanced at Christy while Steinberg gathered up the pictures. "You staying at the cottage tonight?"

166

Not by the hair of her chinny-chin-chin. And why did he want to know? Her suspicion meter went up a notch where he was concerned.

"I got her a room at the Silver Lake," the sheriff told him. " 'Course, it's just for tonight." He turned to her. "Will you be staying with us any longer than that?"

"I don't know," she said, wishing he hadn't seen fit to share the name of her hotel. "My plans are kind of up in the air right now."

"Aunt Rosa has a couple of extra bedrooms."

"My wife and I have an extra bedroom, too, if you'd care to be our guest. And I know Elaine would surely love the company," the sheriff said.

"I'd chime in, but Bud here has a much nicer house. And Elaine can cook," Steinberg added with a wink.

Christy's gaze encompassed all three men. The thought that popped into her head when she considered spending the night in proximity to any one of them was, *No way.* She wasn't ready to trust any of them to that extent, not even the sheriff.

"Thanks. I'll keep it in mind," she said.

Castellano and Steinberg left the office, and she went through the mug shots

Sheriff Schultz had for her. Being alone with the sheriff was nerve-racking, and she looked at the photos quickly. Several of the men pictured were beefy and dark-haired. None of their faces looked familiar. Of course, the fact that she'd never actually seen a face might go some way toward explaining that.

"Well," he said in obvious disappointment when she got up to go. "It didn't hurt to look. Listen, I've been thinking: if you're concerned about your safety, I can probably spare a deputy to go around with you today. It's Sunday, and Sunday's usually kind of slow, except for the incidents last night, you know, but there's not really a whole lot we can do with it until we get some tests back."

A deputy as escort would be great, except for the fact that she was headed to a mob-ordered rendezvous.

Truly regretful, she managed a smile and shook her head. "I think I'm safe enough in broad daylight."

Sheriff Schultz frowned. "I think so, too, but you never know. You run into any trouble, you give me a call."

He pulled a business card out of his wallet and scribbled something on the back. Then he handed it to her.

"This is my number here in the office," he said, pointing to the front of the card. "This" — he turned the card over and ran his finger down the series of numbers he'd just written on the back — "is my home number. This is my cell phone. This is my pager. You call me anytime you feel like it, you hear?"

Christy nodded, accepted the card, and tucked it carefully into her purse. Then she said good-bye and left. It was still as hot and humid as a steambath outside and the street and sidewalk were still packed with cheerful vacationers, but Christy was all but oblivious to her surroundings now as she walked back to her car. She was still picking up vibes from Gordie Castellano that she could only characterize as *off*. But their significance was greatly reduced by the fact that she could also imagine both Aaron Steinberg and Sheriff Schultz himself in the role of her attacker. In fact, she thought semihysterically as she paused in the act of opening her car door to glance around at the happy-camper-filled street, about a quarter of the current population of Ocracoke seemed to fit the description. It freaked her out to realize, vibes notwithstanding, that her attacker could be anybody, anybody at all.

He could be watching me right now.

On that heartening note, Christy shivered and quickly slid inside her car. Once her bare thighs made contact with blistering navy leather, she yelped and forgot about her attacker for the moment as she hurriedly pulled a map out of the glove compartment and spread it beneath her legs. She started the car and, would-be murderer or no, rolled down the windows so that the pent-up heat could escape while the air-conditioning cranked up. But she didn't make a move to go anywhere. A quick glance at the dashboard clock told her that it was one-thirty. She had half an hour to spare and the lighthouse was perhaps ten minutes away.

She had a little time. Enough time to make a call. Existing in terror-filled limbo was not working for her, and she meant to do what she could to make it go away.

Heart pounding with nervousness, unsure of the wisdom of what she was about to do but unable to think of any better way of ensuring that she stayed alive, she pulled out her cell phone, which one of the deputies had thoughtfully returned to her at the clinic, rolled the windows up for privacy, and punched in Michael's number.

10

Christy felt almost sick to her stomach as she listened to the phone ring. Of course, the call was going to go through perfectly now that she wasn't really sure she wanted it to. Was that the way life worked or what?

The last time she had spoken to Michael had been to confront him with Franky's accusations, with the confirmation of those accusations that she had found while searching the office files, with her own new and terrible knowledge of what he was and what he'd done.

That's the way things work, Michael had said impatiently, with none of the shock or penitence she'd expected him to show. *That's the way things have always worked. Time to come out of your soap bubble, Christy, and shake hands with the real world.*

The edited version of her reply could pretty much be summed up like this: I didn't go to law school to be a crook, so go screw yourself.

She'd been a fool to think that Michael was legit, that the law firm was legit. She saw that now. She should have known that the apple wouldn't fall far from the tree.

"Welcome to the family," John DePalma had said at Christmas, when Michael had first told him they were engaged. Remembering the words now made Christy shake her head at her own naïveté.

How thick are you? she scolded herself with the mental equivalent of a palm clap to her forehead as the phone continued to ring. She'd lived in Atlantic City most of her life — and she knew all the stories about John DePalma. It shouldn't have been much of a stretch to figure out that he meant family with a capital F.

Maybe, instead of stupid, what she'd been was willfully blind. Half the population of Pleasantville was connected to the mob in one way or another. Heck, crime was practically a cottage industry, the ultimate entrepreneurial opportunity. Nearly every TV and computer and electronic gadget in the neighborhood where she'd grown up had been purchased from Nine-fingered Nick, the local fence. Everybody knew that the laundromat had a bookie operation in the basement and that at the Mickey Dee's on the corner of Fourth and

172

Main you could pick up a baggie of funny seasonings right along with your burger. But the bottom line was, she'd left Pleasantville behind for the white-collar suburbs of Philadelphia for a reason. If she'd wanted to be a criminal she would've stayed put — and she wouldn't have studied her butt off and worked two jobs and finished first college and then law school at The College of New Jersey, either.

What she'd wanted was the kind of success that didn't involve constantly worrying about doing a stretch of two-to-ten on the state's dime when things went wrong.

She'd thought that Michael — dark, handsome, macho Michael, ten years her senior, a man who wore thousand-dollar suits and had an appreciation for fine wines that, to tell the truth, struck her working-class palate as tasting like cough syrup — felt the same way. Despite who his father was. Despite having grown up in the shadow of the mob. She'd thought he'd had a bellyful of criminal types at a young age just as she had. Obviously, she'd thought wrong.

When he'd offered her a big salary right out of law school to come to work for him, she'd been thrilled to accept, thrilled at the chance to live in Philadelphia, which was just a short ride up the interstate from Atlantic City where her mother and sisters — as well as a number of Michael's relatives — still lived, thrilled to work for Michael, who had basically taken her, a fledgling lawyer, under his infinitely more sophisticated and knowledgeable wing. In the two years she'd worked at DePalma and Lowery, she'd had her own apartment in a nice high-rise in a nice section of town, a job that she loved, a great wardrobe, a great car, new and simpatico friends and, as the pièce de résistance, a blossoming relationship with Michael. When he'd proposed, over a romantic, candlelit dinner, she hadn't even had to think it over: she'd accepted with the mental version of a pump-fisted *yes*. For the next few months she'd been happier than she'd ever been in her life, as blissful as Cinderella when she'd first squeezed her toes into that had-to-hurt glass slipper.

Until Franky had shown up at her apartment like the proverbial serpent slithering into Eden. And told her that he'd fouled up an operation Michael's goons had sent him on, and he was afraid they were going to kill him.

Michael's voice answering the phone

snapped her out of her reverie. For the first couple of seconds, just the sound of that all-too-familiar voice made her feel dizzy. Her heart pounded. Her breathing suspended. Goose bumps popped up on her arms. Then she realized that what she was listening to was a message and not Michael himself, and she breathed again, slumping a little in the seat with relief. It was then that she finally knew it for sure: she wasn't in love with Michael anymore. What she felt toward him now was — fear.

". . . I'll get back to you as soon as I can. Thanks." *Beep.*

Christy took a deep breath. If she could just talk to him and explain . . . "It's Christy. It's important. Call me."

Disconnecting, she discovered that her hands were shaking.

She stared at the phone for a minute, then mustered her resolve and placed one more call.

"Yeah?" The voice at the other end was as familiar to her as Michael's.

"Uncle Vince? It's Christy."

His sharp intake of breath was clearly audible. "Jesus Christ, what are you doing calling me? I can't talk to you now. Shit's happening here, and —"

There was something in his tone that

told her he was getting ready to hang up.

"Somebody tried to kill me last night," she interrupted desperately. "Was it a hit? Did Michael — or somebody — put a contract out on me?"

There was the briefest of pauses.

"Jesus." She heard a sound that she thought was him swallowing. "No, of course not, there's nothing like that. I told you, if you do what you're told and keep your mouth shut you'll be okay."

"Look, I delivered the briefcase. You told me that was all I had to do. But I got another call last night and —"

"Not on the phone. Don't tell me over the phone." She could hear him breathing hard and fast. "Look, I'll check it out. The deal was, you deliver the briefcase and you're out. But maybe something's changed. Maybe they're feeling the heat down there like we are up here, and they got to do something different than they planned. You do what they tell you until I say different. I got to go now."

"Wait! The cottage was broken into — there's a lot of damage, the locks need to be changed . . ."

"Call Tony at Manelli Management. He'll fix it. And then stay off the fucking phone. Don't call Carmen and get her mixed up in this, whatever you do."

He hung up.

Don't call Carmen. Her mother. Christy took a deep breath and closed the phone. No, she wouldn't call her mom, her chain-smoking, hard-partying, mobster's moll of a mom, who, for all her shortcomings, loved her and her sisters fiercely. If her mother had any inkling that Christy was in danger, she'd raise enough hell with Vince to be heard all the way to Canada. Then she'd drive down here to Ocracoke. Then she'd raise more hell, till she very likely got herself, and Christy, killed. And maybe Nicole and Angie, too.

Calling her mom was undoubtedly a really bad idea. But she ached to do it nonetheless. When she had *real* trouble, heartbreaking trouble, world-shattering trouble, her mother was the person she automatically turned to.

Case in point: after confronting Michael, she'd done what any grown-up, self-sufficient woman does after dumping both job and fiancé in one fell swoop — called her mom. Not wanting to say too much until she'd had time to sort out all the implications of her discovery, she'd said only that she and Michael had had a fight. Come home and we'll talk, had been her mother's familiar prescription. But when Christy had done just that, driving straight down I-5 to Atlantic City, she'd gotten the biggest shock of all: goons had surrounded her car when she'd stopped at the intersection nearest her mother's house. They'd forced her out at gunpoint and thrust her into the backseat of a black BMW parked nearby, where Uncle Vince had been waiting. There he'd taken her on what he called a field trip, and in the process spelled out the facts of life for her. Christy's blood had run cold as she'd finally understood.

If she'd been thinking about going to a prosecutor friend of hers with what she knew — and she had indeed been considering just that — that little field trip with Uncle Vince had dissuaded her. Sick with horror, she'd agreed to do one "favor" for him, i.e., drive the briefcase he'd given her to Ocracoke and wait for a phone call telling her where she should deliver it, after which he had promised that as long as she kept her mouth shut she, and her family, would be left alone forever after. She'd thought she understood: he meant to compromise her by making her party to whatever criminal enterprise the briefcase was connected to, on the theory that after delivering it she couldn't go running to the cops whenever she felt like it without getting herself in trouble as well.

Among other negative consequences, a lawyer convicted of a felony could pretty much count on being disbarred. If she went to the cops after doing Uncle Vince's favor, all her years of hard work might well have been for nothing. Her prized education would go right down the tubes. She would be a criminal, too.

She understood that. And she had been willing to put her future on the line, to deliver the briefcase and be compromised. It was better, way better, than the alternative.

Which involved herself and her mother and sisters being dead.

Because Uncle Vince had made it clear: the threat if she didn't cooperate wasn't only to herself, but to her mom and Nicole and Angie, too.

When she'd finally gotten to talk to her mom that night, she'd told her only that she and Michael had broken up, she'd quit her job in consequence, and she was going on a little vacation to Ocracoke, where Uncle Vince had generously offered her the use of the beach cottage to recuperate.

Her mother had had no problem with that. Man trouble she understood.

An imperative rap almost in Christy's ear made her jump, and brought her sharply back to the present. Heart pounding, she whipped her head around so fast that her neck hurt. When she met Castellano's dark eyes she almost levitated through the sun roof before she managed to get herself under control. He'd knocked on her window. The street was full of people, and he was in his deputy's uniform. What were the chances that he was about to harm her?

Lowering the window, she nonetheless realized that she was breathing too fast and the look she gave him was more than a little wary.

"Is something wrong?" he asked, frowning as his gaze ran over as much of her as he could see. "You've been sitting there a long time."

"I was making a phone call." From somewhere Christy summoned up a small smile. "But thanks for checking on me."

"Good enough, then. Sorry to interrupt." Lifting a hand in farewell, he straightened away from the car. The sun was so bright where he was standing that she had to squint to see him — and what she saw chilled her to the bone. Glare reflecting off the polished surface of the car blurred his features so that he was scarcely more than a shape — and that shape was stocky and powerful and very, very similar to the one she'd seen on the beach.

But was it the same? Dear God, she wasn't sure.

Heart pounding, Christy raised the window.

Get a grip, she told herself fiercely as the glass rose between them. *Whether it was him or not, he can't do anything to me here.*

Still, she made haste to be on her way. Conscious of Castellano's gaze on her, pulse still not back to normal, Christy managed a wave and pulled out into the street. A glance at the clock told her that it was 1:52. If she didn't get a move on, she was going to be late.

Would Castellano be waiting for her at the lighthouse? Or someone else? The voice on the phone had said someone would be in touch. That could mean anyone.

The one thing she was sure of — well, fairly sure of — was that the voice on the phone had not belonged to Castellano.

The only thing to do, she told herself, was keep putting one foot in front of the other and see if she couldn't find some way out of this chamber of horrors before it killed her.

A glance in the rearview mirror told her

that he was standing stock-still on the sidewalk watching her drive away. Friendly concern or something more sinister? She didn't know. She couldn't tell. Heck, who knew anything anymore?

Turning various possibilities over in her mind, she drove past families in shorts and sandals pedaling along on their bikes, past picturesque buildings lavishly trimmed in gingerbread, past sleepy-looking horses pulling carriages full of tourists through the winding streets of Ocracoke Village, without really seeing any of it. The laid-back charm of the island was basically wasted on her; it was impossible to settle in to the nineteenth-century atmosphere when she was in a near-constant state of mortal fear. The antiques shops, the restaurants with their chalkboard signs that all seemed to advertise fresh seafood, the picture-postcard beauty of the harbor, where sailboats and houseboats and cabin cruisers of various sizes skimmed the waves on their way out to sea, were lost on her. When she found herself eyeballing the squat white lighthouse through her windshield, she was surprised to find herself already at her destination. Visitors were as thick as dandelions on an early summer lawn in the park surrounding the lighthouse, Christie saw as she parked. It occurred to her as she got out of the car that she didn't know who or what she was looking for.

Not that it mattered. She felt fairly confident that whoever or whatever it was would find her. The thought made her heart lurch.

Now that she was out of the car, the steamy heat planted itself on her like a big wet kiss. Christy felt herself glowing again before she had taken more than two steps across the gleaming black macadam. Her shorts hung no longer than mid-thigh, and her T-shirt was a thin cotton knit. She couldn't have been any hotter if she'd been wrapped in the ankle-length wool winter coat left behind in the closet of her apartment. Summoning up mental images of glaciers and penguins in an effort to beat the heat, Christy walked slowly through the parking lot and then across the grassy park to the white picket fence that kept tourists from actually touring the lighthouse, which, according to a brochure thrust into her hand by a helpful Park Services employee, dated back to 1823. With the dazzling azure of the cloudless sky and the deeper turquoise of the ocean for a backdrop, the lighthouse was still disappointingly prosaic in appearance. What popped into Christy's mind when she stood in front of it was that it looked like nothing so much as a saltshaker. A saltshaker standing in a scraggly patch of green grass.

Okay, so maybe her appreciation for the romance of history was a little lacking today.

But at least her sixth sense was working. She realized that as she felt the uncomfortable little prickle of awareness that told her someone was looking at her. Clutching the brochure as if it were her lifeline to the future, she glanced quickly around. Nothing and no one leaped out at her as the obvious source. But still, it was unmistakably there — this feeling of eyes boring into her back.

There were people everywhere she looked. None of them were paying the least attention to her.

She was breathing erratically, she realized, and her heart was doing a weird little tap dance in her chest. Glancing down, she saw that she'd shredded the brochure without realizing what she was doing. Fear had its own metallic taste, she'd learned over the last few days, and as she wet her dry lips she tasted it again in her mouth.

Restlessly she started walking, dumping the program into a waste can, following the line of the picket fence as it led toward the observation deck overlooking the sea. Near the observation deck were a small open-air snack bar, a museum devoted to Blackbeard, a souvenir shop largely featuring Blackbeard, and a set of stone steps leading down to the rock-strewn beach where a reenactment of Blackbeard's epic final battle was under way. Tourists milled about in small chattering clumps, taking pictures, posing with the lighthouse in the background, scarfing down hot dogs and soft pretzels and fries. The smells wafting past her nose made Christy feel queasy. The heat and lack of sleep combined to make her head pound. She hadn't eaten yet today, she realized, and guessed that was partly responsible for the churning of her stomach. The feeling that she was being watched persisted, but she could not locate the watcher. Casting quick glances around, she wandered through the park, doing her best to make like a tourist without really registering anything she saw, waiting for the tap on her shoulder or other ah-ha moment that would tell her that she had been contacted.

She did this for an hour and a half.

Nothing, except she was accidentally clobbered by a plastic sword, courtesy of a passel of shrieking kids in pirate hats engaged in what appeared to be a reenactment of the reenactment. Also, an elderly man asked her to take a picture of him and his family in front of the lighthouse, and approximately two dozen mosquitoes decided to dine out on her unprotected flesh. Calling the management company about the repairs to the cottage kept her occupied for all of five minutes, and then she was at loose ends again. Finally, she gave up scanning the assorted multitudes for some sort of sign and retreated to the snack bar, where she ordered a large Diet Coke and a small packet of aspirin. It was too hot and she was too nervous for anything else.

Sitting disconsolately at one of the metal tables, she swallowed the aspirin, drank the Coke, and read one of the ubiquitous brochures, which had been left behind by some other, apparently equally unappreciative, visitor.

In the midst of all that tiny print, the fact that jumped out at her was that on Sundays the lighthouse closed at five p.m.

A little more than an hour to go. Her fear having been blunted by the heat and the lack of action, Christy was not eager to move out from beneath the corrugated aluminum awning into the blaze of the sun again. If someone was looking for her, she wasn't that hard to find. No bloodhounds required. Her T-shirt was neon orange, for heaven's sake, and she was one of the few people wandering around alone.

What happened if no one got in touch? That was the thought that was starting to loom large in Christy's mind as she made a quick pit stop in the ladies' room. Did that mean that she was free to pack up and go home?

"You wish," was her reluctant conclusion. Through the mirror, she met the gaze of a woman washing her little girl's hands at the sink and realized that she had spoken aloud.

Ducking into a stall, she did her business and was fighting with the plastic dispenser over toilet paper when she happened to glance down, under the door.

What looked like a man's black work boot walked past. Even as she registered that with instant, skin-prickling horror, the door of the stall next to the one she was in opened with a near silent swish.

11

Having discreetly trailed Christy to the rest rooms, Luke took a calculated risk and ducked into the men's room for a lightning-quick visit of his own. He was just exiting, moving fast as he sought to get away from the dual entrances into a position where he could watch Christy emerge without being observed himself, when she catapulted out of the ladies' room at what looked like warp speed and literally ran smack into him.

Shit.

"Hey," he said, grabbing her elbows as she recoiled with a startled squeal. Having her fall flat on her hot little tush was not on today's agenda if he could help it; he felt bad enough about not having prevented the hurt she'd suffered last night. But he hadn't foreseen that someone would break into her cottage and try to take a hatchet to her. His expectations had been more along the lines of her boyfriend hooking up with her there. In the kind of lucky break that had been few and far between lately, the Starbucks cup had yielded pay dirt: a partial thumbprint belonging to Michael DePalma. There was still a slight possibility that he was wrong — the cup might have remained in the car after DePalma had exited it elsewhere, and been thrown out by one of his stooges — but Luke was willing to bet that Donnie Jr. was on the island.

"L-Luke."

For some unknown reason, she cut her eyes to his feet. Then her head snapped up, and her eyes met his. Even as he watched a whole kaleidoscope of emotions play across her face, he realized that those Bambi-sized eyes were dark with fear. His muscles tensed. So far, with this girl, the news had uniformly tended to be not good.

"What's up?"

Her lips trembled, and she cast a haunted glance over her shoulder.

"I think — I think he's in the bathroom. The man from last night."

She was shaking, clearly scared half to death. He glanced past her at the door through which she'd just exited.

"Wait here," he said sharply, and left her standing there while he strode into the ladies' room. No scandalized shrieks greeted him, which was a relief, but there was a reason for that: the rest room was empty. A quick check of the facilities confirmed that no one was hiding in a stall, and also revealed that there was a back door. Conscious of having left Christy outside alone, he turned on his heel and headed out the way he had entered. Just as he pulled the door open, a sixtyish woman started to walk in. She stopped dead, gaping at him.

"Sorry, wrong rest room," he muttered, exiting quickly while the woman stared indignantly after him.

Christy had backed up against the yellow-painted concrete wall that shielded the rest rooms from view. His gaze raked her, absorbing in the space of about a heartbeat how terrified she looked — and how sexy. Automatically he registered details: straight brown hair tucked behind her ears; skin damp from the heat; a worried line between her brows; soft pink lips parted to allow for quick, shallow breaths that also caused her chest to rise and fall in a way guaranteed to attract the attention of any man who liked women. Unwillingly he noticed how her T-shirt molded her full breasts and clung to her closely enough to reveal both the bandage on her shoulder and the round little nubs of her nipples jutting against the cloth; how her shorts made her truly gorgeous legs look about a mile long; how slim she was, and how pretty. He also saw that her face was white as a tube sock and her eyes near black with fear.

"Empty," he said in response to the tense look she greeted him with.

"It can't be."

"There's a back door. Come on."

In a hurry and unwilling to leave her behind, he caught her wrist and pulled her after him as he strode around the building to get a fix on anyone who might at that very moment be hastening guiltily away. She went with him without hesitation, and he got the impression that she was glad to no longer be alone. Glad of his company.

He felt a flare of protectiveness toward her. Whatever she had or hadn't done, she was definitely in over her head now.

"What are you doing?" she asked when he stopped in the lee of a Dumpster to shield his eyes from the sun and look carefully around. He wasn't sure how it had happened, but her fingers were twined with his now, satin-skinned fingers that reminded him irresistibly of how she had felt in his arms last night. Her bare legs had been satiny-smooth too, and her body had been warm and firm and way too feminine in that slithery red robe. . . .

Don't go there, he warned himself. What he needed to keep in mind was that in this game of cat and mouse he and Donnie Jr. were playing, her primary function was to serve as bait for the mouse.

"If he came out the back, we should still be able to spot him."

"He's not here." She said it as if she were positive.

Scanning the available suspects, he had to concede that she was almost certainly right. A gaggle of headphone-wearing teenage girls had their backs to them as they bebopped toward the snack bar. An elderly couple licking ice-cream cones stopped at one of the half-dozen picnic tables under the nearby trees and sat down to finish their treats. A delivery man wheeled a dolly loaded with boxes along the concrete sidewalk that led to the souvenir shop. At first glance, the delivery man seemed like a possibility, but he was a black guy and according to Christy her attacker had been white.

"Could he have gone into the men's room?" Christy was looking back at the building. Glancing around, Luke saw that there was a rear entrance to the men's room, too.

"I'll check."

Even as he disengaged his hand from hers, even as he went back inside the rest room to look for a bulky, dark-complected guy of medium height — her description of the psychopath from last night — Luke realized that he was almost certainly too late. If the guy had indeed followed Christy into the ladies' room, and if he had then come out the back and gone into the men's room, it was a sure bet that he was long gone. From the way she had been running, he would have known she'd spotted him. What he wouldn't have done was hang around waiting to be caught.

He was right. The only person in the rest room was a skinny teenager using the urinal. Luke stuck his head out the front door and cast a quick glance around, but saw nothing suspicious. Then he headed back out to rejoin Christy.

She was standing near the Dumpster with her arms crossed over her chest, glancing cautiously around.

"Nothing," he said as he walked up to her. "You want to call the sheriff?"

She seemed to hesitate, then shook her head. Then she looked up at him with something that seemed ominously close to suspicion.

"So what are you doing here?" she asked. He could feel her barriers going up, feel her mentally distancing herself from him, feel her wariness.

She wasn't dumb, this girl.

"Same thing you are, I guess. Checking out the lighthouse. Hey, a tourist has to do what a tourist has to do, right?" He gave her a smile that was, hopefully, both innocent and charming. It wasn't a great answer, but he couldn't tell her the truth: that after striking out with the ferries, this meeting at the lighthouse was the best lead he had left. He'd been watching her since she'd arrived, in hopes that someone — with luck, Donnie Jr. himself or someone who could lead them to him — would show up. But he'd missed the guy in the rest room — if indeed there had been a guy in the rest room and she hadn't just gotten freaked out — which made him antsy. What else might he have missed?

She didn't look totally convinced, which wasn't all that surprising. He wouldn't have bought that answer, either. He got her attention refocused in another direction by adding quickly, "So you want to tell me exactly what happened in the ladies' room?"

That did the trick. Christy's eyes flickered and she glanced around, looking scared all over again.

"I saw his boot — at least, a boot that could have been his. A black work boot with a scuffed toe. I was in a stall and I saw his boot walk by."

She shivered. Now Luke knew why she'd looked down at his feet as soon as she'd run into him. She'd been checking out his shoes, which were a pair of rubber flip-flops. Gray sweat pants hacked into knee-length shorts and a navy T-shirt with the slogan Divers Do It in the Deep completed his ensemble. Not exactly regulation Bureau attire, but he couldn't have looked more like a tourist if he'd tried.

"You sure?"

"That I saw a black work boot? Yes. That it was his . . ." She hesitated, clearly thinking it over. "No. Not one hundred percent sure. It looked like it could be."

"Hmm." That was the best response that occurred to him. His gaze swung around, and he rechecked the previous subjects for footwear. The delivery man was out of sight, but the old couple was definitely in the clear. One of the girls, though, was wearing black combat boots with her shorts.

"Could those be the boots you saw?" He nodded in the direction of the teen's shoes. Christy looked, and frowned.

"I guess it's possible," she said after a moment, but he could tell she wasn't convinced.

"You sure you don't want to call the sheriff?"

"What's the use? What would I say, that I saw a suspicious boot?"

At her weary tone, Luke looked at her sharply. Where they were standing, on a stretch of concrete sidewalk behind the brick building housing the rest rooms, the sun beat down on them unmercifully. It didn't bother him, possibly because he'd gotten used to being out in it for hours during the diving vacation he hadn't gotten to finish. But the blazing heat coupled with the situation she was in seemed to be sapping Christy's strength. Though a little of the color had returned to her face, she was still far too pale, and there were definite dark shadows beneath her long-lashed eyes. Of course, he'd had maybe an hour of sleep, and she couldn't have had much more. The difference was, he was used to it. Going without sleep was an all-too-frequent part of his job.

That inconvenient protectiveness she

seemed to effortlessly rouse in him surfaced again.

"You had lunch yet?"

She shook her head.

"Breakfast?"

She shook her head again.

"Anything to eat whatsoever?"

"A Diet Coke. And a couple of aspirin."

"How about I buy you an ice-cream cone?"

It was an impulsive suggestion, made basically because she looked like she could use a boost in her blood sugar as well as her spirits, but she hesitated before she answered as if considering what her reply should be. He could practically read the thoughts running through her mind: if someone was planning to make contact with her, then having him around was probably a bad thing. From his point of view, too, taking a chance on scaring the guy off was not wise, since following whoever contacted her was his current best hope for nabbing Donnie Jr. But she looked so tired and scared and alone, and yes, face the truth, so knock-your-socks-off sexy, that she kept throwing him off his game plan.

"Well?" His prompt was a little testy because he didn't like having to face the fact that he was sufficiently attracted to her to cause himself problems.

"Sure," she said, and smiled, a quick flash of radiance that lit up her face. To his dismay he felt his heart give a little kick.

"Come on, then."

That was downright grudging, and he was careful not to touch her as they headed toward the snack bar. She didn't talk, and he didn't either, because he was busy reminding himself that she was Donnie Jr.'s girlfriend, that she was in trouble up to her neck, and that he was probably going to end up arresting her right along with her boyfriend before this was all over. It didn't matter. Call him a sick fuck, but he couldn't get the way she'd looked last night in her sexy pink panties and skimpy top out of his head. And never mind the fact that she'd been covered in blood at the time.

"Flavor?" he asked with way more gruffness than the question called for when they reached the counter.

"Vanilla, single scoop, on a waffle cone," she said to the girl waiting on them. He ordered a double scoop of Rocky Road, paid, and then they headed toward the picnic tables, which were scattered beneath a stand of live oaks that provided an island of cooling shade in the middle of the sun-baked park. The old couple had left, but two middle-aged women sat at another table chatting and sipping soft drinks while they watched a group of kids running around in the grassy open space beyond the picnic area. With the lighthouse for a backdrop and nothing but sea and sky beyond that, it was an idyllic setting. Too bad he wasn't there to enjoy it.

"So how's the shoulder?" he asked, focusing on the bandage creating a small but discernible bulge in her T-shirt rather than looking at any other part of her, such as her ass, as she walked ahead of him.

Shrugging, she threw a glance over her shoulder at him. "I'll live."

They settled down at the table farthest from the playing children. A slight breeze brought the smell of the sea with it and seemed to bring the temperature down maybe a couple of degrees. Above their heads, silver-gray festoons of Spanish moss decorated the trees. Insects buzzed, birds chirped and children yelled, reminding him of why he was still firmly single despite the best efforts of several past girl-friends.

"How many stitches did you end up with?"

"Three. And a tetanus shot." She made a face as a rivulet of ice cream ran down onto her finger. He watched, unwillingly fascinated, as she lifted her hand, cone and all, to her mouth to lick it off. The sight of her tongue lapping up the melted ice cream sent his mind shooting off to places it didn't need to go. He dragged it back, and refocused on the task at hand, which was to pry out of her any relevant information he could.

"I'm surprised you're out doing the tourist thing after an injury like that. Shouldn't you still be in bed?"

Her eyes flicked down to her ice cream. "The sheriff wanted me to come by and look at mug shots. Since I was out anyway, I decided to visit the lighthouse." She met his gaze then and gave a little shrug. "Like you said, a tourist has to do what a tourist has to do."

Yeah.

"So you planning to cut your vacation short now?"

"I haven't really thought about it." She licked up another dribble of ice cream, then swirled her tongue around the glistening white top. "How did your appointment go?"

Appointment? For a moment, as his gaze

stayed riveted on that swirling tongue, her meaning did not register. Then he retrieved his mind from the gutter long enough to remember the lie he had told, and forced himself to concentrate. Oh yeah, the purported reason he'd abandoned her to the tender mercies of the doctor and sheriff that morning.

"Good," he said amiably, and took a bite of his own ice cream. "Sheriff have any theories about what's going on?"

"He was talking about a possible serial killer." She lapped at her ice cream, then met his gaze so suddenly that it was all he could do not to respond with a guilty start. "Look, do you mind if we don't talk about what happened? I'd really rather just try to forget about it for a little while if I could."

He translated that to mean that, like himself, she didn't wholly buy into the serial killer theory. The more he thought about it, the more he was beginning to wonder if she'd somehow managed to tick off the mob.

"No problem." He concentrated on eating his own cone, and watching her eat hers. No, that last part wasn't good. Catching himself in the act, he forced his gaze away. "So tell me something. What made you decide to come down to a place like Ocracoke all by your lonesome anyway?"

Her eyes flickered. A good liar she was not. He'd noticed that flicker before, and now that he was on to it he saw that she did it every time she was about to tell something less than the truth.

"I just felt like getting away."

"Boyfriend couldn't come with you?"

"What makes you think I have a boyfriend?"

He grinned. "A girl as pretty as you always has a boyfriend. Guaranteed. If not a husband. But you're not wearing a ring, so I'm assuming you're not married."

She wrinkled her nose at him, which he interpreted as her way of acknowledging the compliment, and licked the top off the cone. And swallowed. Luke had to direct a hasty look at the kids again to keep from getting a boner the size of a baseball bat.

Christ almighty, when was the last time he'd gotten laid?

"You're right, I'm not married. And for the record, I don't have a boyfriend. Not anymore."

"Oh yeah?" This was news, if she was telling the truth and from the lack of flickering eyes he thought she was. "Sounds like something upsetting happened."

His teeth crunched into his cone as he oh-so-casually waited for the answer. He was absolutely not going to watch what else she did to hers.

There it went. Her eyes flickered. "Not really. We just . . . broke up."

"Recently?" Okay, so looking no lower than her nose was not doable. Glancing down at his cone, he finished it off.

"Very recently."

News indeed. She nibbled on the edge of her cone, straight white teeth crunching through the sweet brown waffle. Her mouth would taste like ice-cream cone. . . . He mentally pulled himself up short: *Focus on the investigation, you jerk.*

"That explains it, then. Came down here to mend your broken heart, did you?"

She glanced down, and was silent for just long enough to confirm that the answer was no. "Something like that, I guess."

Despite his best intentions, watching her swirl her tongue deep into the cone as she went after what ice cream remained almost did him in. He did a quick cutaway to the kids, only to discover that they and their mothers had disappeared. He hadn't even noticed them leaving, which was nothing short of astonishing, considering how loud the little rugrats had been. But then, he'd been focusing on other things.

"This boyfriend — is he a lawyer?"

Her eyes narrowed at him. Thank God, she was almost done with her cone. Watching her pop the last bit into her mouth, it was all he could do not to let out a sigh of relief.

"What makes you think that?"

"You're a lawyer. It makes sense that your boyfriend might be one, too."

"You know, you ask a lot of questions."

"Hey, I'm interested."

"Is that what it is?" She wiped her fingers on a napkin, then planted both hands flat on the tabletop and looked up suddenly to meet his gaze with unmistakable challenge in her eyes. "All right, so let's have it: what are you *really* doing here?"

To say that she had taken him by surprise was an understatement. He considered it a testament to his training that his eyes didn't widen.

"Sitting at a picnic table talking to you?" he ventured with a lopsided smile in an effort to buy time.

Her lips thinned. "Not cute. And don't give me that stuff about being a tourist and wanting to look at the lighthouse, because I don't buy it. It's way too much of a coincidence that we're both here at the same time. And I'm not a big believer in coincidence anymore."

The bad news was, he'd always been a sucker for a babe with brains. The worse news was, he seemed to have found one.

"You got me." He grimaced, then gave her a deliberately guilty smile. "Okay, I admit it: I saw you in town earlier and followed you out here."

"You *followed* me here?" Her eyes were suddenly dark with suspicion and her spine appeared to have gone rigid. "Why?"

"Jeez, Louise, do I have to spell it out for you? I think you're cute, okay? I think you're hot. I followed you out here to ask you to dinner, but then it occurred to me that you might be planning to meet someone, so I kind of hung around to see."

"You followed me out here to ask me to dinner?" She was still suspicious, but she was giving his answer due consideration. Clearly the woman was no stranger to being pursued. He wasn't in the clear yet, he could tell, but he was getting there.

"Why not? You're unattached, I'm unattached, and we've both got to eat."

She eyed him. "Hmm."

"Is that a yes or a no?"

Her expression softened fractionally.

"You know, I'd really like to, but —"

"Then say yes. What else are you going to do? Eat all by yourself? Go back to your house and order in pizza?"

"I have a hotel room for the night."

"I could meet you in the dining room. You name the time."

"You don't even know what hotel."

"You could tell me. It'd be better than eating in your room all alone."

It was the thought of being alone that was getting to her. He could see it in her eyes. Not that he blamed her, not after last night.

"Christy?" he prompted. "What hotel?"

Their eyes met.

"The Silver Lake Inn." It was grudging capitulation, but hey, it worked. "But this isn't a date, you understand. It's just a friendly dinner."

"I understand absolutely, and I'll be there at — what? Six-thirty? Seven?"

"Seven." From the way she was eyeing him it was clear that she was already having second thoughts.

"Seven." At the look on her face he had to grin. "Don't worry, my mama taught me better than to pressure a girl for sex the first time I take her out." A beat passed. "I always wait until at least the second."

She laughed. He hadn't seen her laugh before. The two deep dimples that appeared in her cheeks were nearly as beguiling as the sudden sparkle in her eyes. His grin broadened in enjoyment of her amusement.

From somewhere close at hand came the muffled sound of a ringing phone.

Just like that she stopped laughing. Her eyes widened. The joy drained from her face as if a plug had been pulled on it. Watching, he felt himself tensing up, too.

"Excuse me." Snatching up her purse, she jumped to her feet and retreated, moving away from the table, fumbling around inside her purse all the while. She almost dropped her bag getting the phone out. Then she clumsily tucked the purse under her arm while at the same time flipping her phone open and positioning it so that she could talk.

He couldn't hear a word she said. She was out of earshot, leaning against the gigantic trunk of one of the centuries-old trees as she talked, and he was sure she was keeping her voice carefully low. He couldn't even read her lips, because she'd turned her back to him. Not that either of those circumstances troubled him particularly. Gary the Geek had lived up to his billing: he was indeed proving to be very, very good at one thing. Using some sort of computer alchemy, he'd managed to rig up a system to monitor every call she made or received over her cell phone.

Luke mentally saluted his partner as he waited for her to finish her conversation. It took him a moment to realize just exactly what he was doing to pass the time until she returned, and then he immediately redirected his gaze. But not before he had reconfirmed something that he had noted several times previously: Christy Petrino had one very nice ass.

When she came back to the table, her face was every bit as white as it had been when she'd first come barreling out of that rest room, and she was chewing on her lower lip.

"Bad news from home?" he asked, cocking an eyebrow at her.

For a fleeting instant, as their gazes met, her eyes were unguarded. He read fear and desperation in them, and felt his muscles tense in instant, involuntary response. He realized then that his mission had just expanded above and beyond bringing Donnie Jr. to justice: he also meant to keep Christy safe while he did it.

"Something like that." She smiled at

him, but it was a poor, strained effort, not like the glorious, dimpled grin she'd dazzled him with moments earlier. "Look, about dinner: I can't, okay? I've got to go."

Then without another word she turned her back on him and walked away.

Luke stayed right where he was and watched her go. When she was just about out of sight, he pulled the transmitter out of his pocket and spoke into it.

"Yo," he said to Gary, who was ensconced in the SUV in the parking lot. "She's headed your way. I've got to hang back here, so don't let her out of your sight."

12

Seen by moonlight, the Silver Lake Inn was one of the more romantic hotels on the island, a true tourists' delight. He stood outside it, around by the pool near a sweet spire bush that filled the air with a heady perfume, looking the low-slung, cedar-shake covered building over with appreciation. He wasn't alone, there were two couples in the hot tub and some kids still swimming in the pool even though it was nearly midnight, but they didn't bother him. He was in his invisible mode again; he blended in.

Christy was spending the night in room 322.

Her third-floor room posed a little difficulty, but nothing he couldn't overcome. Unfortunately, she wasn't in one of the rooms that came with a balcony. A balcony always simplified things. There were ways to gain access to a balcony. But since that option was lost to him, he had to make use of what he had. Enclosed hallways were good, especially as the night wore on. As a general rule, very few people were out and about a hotel after, say, three a.m.

And the Inn's clientele tended to be older couples or families with children, so that helped, too.

On the minus side were the security cameras. Almost all the hotels had them now. They were both a selling point to the tourists and a hedge against a lawsuit if anything bad happened on the premises. But the security cameras here, as in most places, had their limitations. Specifically, they thoroughly covered the lobby and the areas around the elevators, while panning only occasionally down the halls where the guest rooms were located. And they didn't cover the fire stairs.

He'd checked.

So avoiding the cameras was doable and the fire stairs were available for use in making a quick exit.

Where the difficulty arose was in getting into her room. Oh, the lock and chain were no problem. He'd be through them in a minute, tops. But he'd already discovered that she was a suspicious-natured bitch, given to barricading doors and arming herself with Mace. She should feel safe here in the bosom of this nice family hotel. But if she didn't, if she'd piled furniture against the door again, thus making it impossible for him to get to her quickly, the likelihood of her waking up and screaming or phoning for help was greatly increased.

Or, though it wasn't an option that he liked, he could always wait for tomorrow.

If he kept following her, sooner or later he would get a chance to grab her. He had almost taken her today. But she'd managed to elude him, not that it was going to make any difference in the end. Pretty little gazelles always wandered into the wrong place at the right time — for him — sooner or later. The problem was, he didn't have the luxury of devoting unlimited time to the hunt. Which took some of the fun out of it. After all, he didn't need her for a plaything. What he needed, urgently, was Christy Petrino dead.

Because sooner or later she was going to remember where she had seen him before. He remembered her perfectly. He could replay their encounter like a first-run movie in his head at will.

With that thought in mind, he swallowed the last dregs of the Yoohoo he'd been drinking, dropped the container into the trash and walked purposefully toward the hotel.

13

The next day dawned bright and beautiful, one more glorious day in paradise. Christy knew, because she was awake when the sun rose. Standing at her hotel room's big picture window watching the surf roll in on the deserted beach, she'd been in a perfect position to admire the glowing streamers of pink and purple and gold spinning across sky and sea. Not that she was in any frame of mind to enjoy the sight. Although she'd piled every movable piece of furniture in the hotel room against the door, sleep had eluded her. Every step in the hall outside, every sound of a door being opened or closed, every rattle of a window had brought her awake, her heart thumping a mile a minute.

But nothing had happened. No one had bothered her. She had been left alone.

Not that she allowed herself the luxury of imagining, for even so much as a minute, that it was over. Nothing had changed. She wasn't safe, and she wasn't free.

The phone call at the park had made that clear. All these hours later, every word of that conversation ran verbatim on an intermittent loop through her head.

"Hello?" she'd said, all too conscious that Luke was watching her. But she'd walked away, turned her back to him. She was positive that he couldn't overhear. When she'd run into him, literally, after fleeing from the bathroom, she'd never been so glad to see anybody in all her life. But at that moment she'd found herself wishing that she could just snap her fingers and have him disappear.

"What the hell do you think you're doing calling Amori? You think he's running this show? I'm running this show. You don't call nobody unless I tell you, you got that?"

"Who are you?" Weak-kneed, she'd leaned against the tree for support and forgotten all about Luke. How had this person known she'd called Uncle Vince? she wondered frantically. Had Uncle Vince told him? Or . . .

"The king of the fucking universe, okay? You hear what I'm telling you? No more calls to Amori."

"I hear you."

"You better hear me. This ain't no fucking game."

"Somebody tried to kill me last night. Was it you?" She was breathing hard.

There was the briefest of pauses. "If I'd tried to kill you, you'd be dead. Now listen up. There's been a change in plan. A delay. You'll be getting a delivery at the cottage in the next couple of days. Then I'll give you a call, tell you what to do with it. Around the same time as before: one a.m. You be there, understand?"

"No, I . . ." Panic had suffused her voice as she'd started to explain that she wouldn't, couldn't, stay in that cottage, on this island, anywhere within a hundred miles of this place, for another hour, much less a couple of days, that she was terrified that the man who had attacked her was going to come back and finish the job, that all she wanted was to get her life back and go home.

But she hadn't had a chance.

"Be there, or you *will* be dead," he'd said, and hung up.

Like the conversation, the voice itself was engraved on Christy's mind. She was sure that it belonged to the man who had called her twice before, once to tell her to take the briefcase down the beach to the Crosswinds Hotel and the other time to send her to the lighthouse; other than that, she was fairly certain she'd never heard it before in her life. But both times she had followed his instructions she had come into contact with her attacker. Or at least, she thought she had: it was possible that the boot in the ladies' room had not been his, that she had panicked and gotten things wrong. But she didn't think so. Her sixth sense had gone on red alert, screaming *run,* and so far her sixth sense had been right on the money. If she was right about the boot, then the caller was either setting her up for the kill or the attacker had to be in a position to observe at least some of her movements and had therefore known she was at the lighthouse. Or maybe, despite his denials, the caller *was* her attacker . . .

The bottom line was, she was faced with two possibilities: either last night had been a badly botched hit, or really unfortunate timing had made her the target of a serial killer.

Either way, somebody wanted her to die.

Checkout time was noon. Leaving the relative security of the hotel room was hard. Dressed in another gift shop special outfit, this time a cotton-candy pink T-shirt and black shorts, Christy scooped her few belongings into the plastic bag the clothes had come in, checked her cell phone one more time to see if Michael had returned her call yet (he hadn't), and took the elevator to the lobby to check out. When she finished, there was no further excuse for delay; she had to go. Stepping out of the air-conditioned lobby into the parking lot felt like walking into a solid wall of steamy heat. Instead of spontaneous combustion, she suffered spontaneous glow. Nevertheless, she shivered a little as she headed for her car. Walking quickly, glancing around suspiciously at everyone and everything that moved, she felt almost as if she had a target painted on her forehead. At risk didn't begin to cover it. The knowledge that someone wanted to kill her was unnerving. So much so that when she reached her car, she paused, keys in hand, before inserting them into the lock. Then, feeling a little foolish, glancing around to make sure she was unobserved, she crouched down to look under it for a bomb. Not that she had a clue what one looked like, but as far as she was concerned at this point anything out of the ordinary qualified. She found nothing suspicious beneath the car, and nothing suspicious under the hood or in the trunk either. What she did find in the trunk was the pistol her mother had given her when she'd first moved into her own apartment, still in its case. To Carmen, who had kept a pistol in her lingerie drawer and another one in her purse and a third one in the glove compartment of her car for as long as Christy could remember, a gun was a household necessity, like a microwave or an iron. To Christy, who despised guns, a gun was something to be stowed out of sight and forgotten about if possible.

Until now. Her heart beat a little faster as she opened the case and picked up the pistol. It was heavy. The metal was warm from the heat of the trunk and smooth in her hand. The sun glinted off the bright steel. Curling her finger around the grip, she waited for the familiar churning in her stomach that occurred whenever she touched one. Her stomach tightened, but didn't cramp into full-blown nausea as it had when she had last touched it, which had been when, at her mother's insistence, she'd put it into her trunk, supposedly to take out again when she reached her apartment and stow away in her own lingerie drawer. Over time, she'd forgotten all about the gun's existence; probably she'd thrown up some kind of mental block. She hated guns like some people hated spiders, but thanks to her early years in Pleasant-ville she knew how to use one. Her father had taught her.

But she wasn't going to think about that. Remembering served no purpose. The point was, she knew how to use the gun. If her life was at stake, if she had to shoot to defend herself, she could. And, she thought, remembering how Elizabeth Smolski had been slaughtered on the beach, remembering the glinting eyes looking in at her through the gap in the bathroom door, she would.

Oh, yes, she would.

The problem was, she had a gun but no bullets. It had been unloaded when her mother had given it to her, and the box of bullets that had been included had been lost long ago. As far as problems went, though, that one was easy enough to remedy. Tucking the pistol away inside her purse, feeling ridiculously like her mother as she did so, Christy slid into her car and headed off for Hardy's Sporting Goods, which she remembered seeing not far from the sheriff's office.

"You're about the twentieth woman I've sold bullets or some kind of weapon to today," the clerk said as he rang up her purchase. He was a grizzled man in his late fifties with a beer gut swinging pendulously over the belt of his navy slacks. The name tag on his maroon polo shirt identified him as Dave. "You must've read the story in the paper."

Christy felt a tingle of premonition. "What story in what paper?"

"The one about the serial killer." He handed over a brown bag with the bullets in it along with her change. Nodding to his left, he added, "We got a rack of 'em over there."

Christy looked, and saw a wire rack filled with a neat stack of newspapers near the exit. With a quick "thanks" she headed that way and picked up a paper, then pushed through the door and walked back out into the blazing heat.

There it was, all right, she saw as she crossed the parking lot, capped with a big, bold headline: is a serial killer stalking area beaches? Beneath the question were eight small photos in two neat rows. Christy didn't have any trouble recognizing them as the pictures she'd seen on Sheriff Schultz's desk the day before. Sliding behind the wheel of her car, she read the article before she did anything except turn on the air-conditioning.

Eight young women have vanished without a trace from beach towns in and around the Outer Banks over the last three years. On Saturday night, one was found dead on an Ocracoke Island beach. Elizabeth Ann Smolski, 21, of Athens, Georgia, was still alive when a tourist found her lying on the beach shortly after one a.m. She subsequently died of knife wounds before rescuers could reach her in what Sheriff Meyer Schultz has characterized as a particularly violent homicide. Terri Lynn Miller, 21, of Memphis, Tennessee, who disappeared with Smolski on August 2, has not been found. Neither have six other young women ranging in age from 18 to 25 who have been reported missing along a two-hundred-mile strip of coast that includes the Outer Banks. None of the missing women were local residents. Besides being visitors to the area, they share similar physical characteristics: all are described as attractive, with a slim build and dark hair. Except for Terri Lynn Miller, all wore their hair shoulder-length or longer. These similarities, coupled with the sheer number of disappearances and Smolski's murder, are causing some in the law-enforcement community to speculate that the area may be harboring a serial killer who stalks vacationers as they frolic on our beaches. Authorities are calling him the Beachcomber. . . .

There was more, but Christy's hands were shaking so badly that the words blurred as she tried to read them. Viewed all together, the pictured women did indeed look eerily alike. They could have been sisters, almost. The sad thing was, they were all smiling, all happy-looking, clearly having no inkling what the future held for them. Remembering Elizabeth Smolski's fate, Christy felt dizzy. She had to lean her head back against the seat and close her eyes. The paper dropped from her suddenly nerveless hands to slide into the passenger seat. A vivid memory of those few minutes on the beach, when the poor girl had begged for help — and she had run — was impossible to get out of her head. But if she hadn't run, she would undoubtedly have died, too, she reminded herself fiercely. And she still might.

But not if she could help it.

She'd be damned if she was going to go gently into that good night. Growing up in

Pleasantville had its minuses, but it also had one major plus: she'd learned to do whatever it took to survive.

The feeling that she was being observed seeped into her consciousness slowly. When she recognized the warning tingle for what it was, her eyes popped open and she sat up. Pulse racing, clutching the steering wheel with both hands, she glanced all around. Lots of cars, lots of people. No one who seemed to be paying the least attention to her.

But her heart pounded, and weird little prickles raced over her skin.

That was good enough for her. Taking a deep breath, she put the car into gear and pulled out of the lot. The small faces of the pictured women were still visible from the corner of her eye as she drove. It occurred to Christy that she might well have been one of them, might yet be one of them. Cold sweat broke out on her forehead and dampened her palms, making the steering wheel feel slippery as she gripped it.

Panicking would not help her, she told herself. Thinking might.

She'd planned to make her next stop the management company's office to pick up the keys for the new locks at the cottage. Instead, she headed back through Ocracoke Village to the Curl-o-Rama. Spelled out in print, the serial killer theory suddenly seemed as probable as a botched hit. If it were true, then the killer was probably targeting her because he feared she could identify him. Or maybe because she fit the physical description of the missing women.

That last was something she could change.

Marching into the Curl-o-Rama, Christy told the girl at the front desk what she wanted. Minutes later, draped in an enveloping black cape, she was tilted back over a shampoo bowl as a hairdresser named Claude went to work on her. Claude was tall and pudgy, dressed all in black, and wore his own hair in a neat ponytail at the nape of his neck. Under other circumstances, this would undoubtedly have given Christy pause. But these were desperate times, and they called for desperate measures.

Claude positioned the chair so that her back was to the mirror and refused to let her look as he put the finishing touches on her hair.

"This looks so *fabulous* on you," he said, running his hands through her newly shorn locks in what she guessed was an effort to give them that tousled look. "So young, so fresh, so new."

In the chair beside her, a middle-aged woman with her hair wrapped in neat little foil packets looked up from the magazine she'd been reading to eye Christy's head appraisingly.

"Your husband's sure gonna get a surprise."

"I'm not married."

"Oh, really? Well, I'm not surprised. Husbands hate it when their wives change their hair." Frowning, she looked Christy's hair over some more, then glanced at her own hairdresser, a plumpish blonde who was just coming back on the floor after taking a break. "You know, Linda, maybe I should get my hair cut like that."

"Henry'd kill you." Linda opened one of the little foil packets to check the color. "You're always saying how he likes your hair long."

"But it's a pain. And I've been wearing it this way since high school. And I'm forty-seven years old!"

"Sometimes it's good to do something different," Claude said, and spun Christy around so that she could look in the mirror. "The same old thing all the time can get boring." He was still busy smoothing stray ends into place as he met her gaze through the mirror. "So, sweetie, what do you think?"

Eyes widening, Christy stared at her reflection. She looked nothing at all like herself, was her first thought. Her hair was barely jaw length, scissored into feathery layers, and as blond as Marilyn Monroe's.

"It's definitely not boring," she said, still looking at herself. With her eyes and skin, that pale blond shade should not have worked. But, somehow, it did.

"That's what I want, not boring," the woman beside her said positively.

"Marilee . . ." Linda made it into a warning.

"I like it," said the receptionist, who had left her post at the front desk to get in on the act.

The entire place was now staring at Christy's hair.

"I can always take you dark again, if you want," Claude offered, his hands gently kneading the base of her neck. Clearly he took her continued examination of her reflection as an expression of doubt. Christy met his gaze through the mirror. He looked rapt.

"No." Christy didn't feel like being kneaded, and she didn't feel like being stared at, either. Claude's fascinated expression as he surveyed his handiwork was starting to give her the creeps. He was the right build for . . . No. She was not going to start seeing attackers under every bush. If she did, she'd go nuts. Shrugging out from under his hands, she stood up. "This is perfect. Just what I wanted."

Which was the literal truth, she reflected as she handed over her credit card, not without a twinge for the amount the transformation had cost her. What with the hotel room, the gift shop clothing spree, and other assorted purchases, she was getting dangerously close to her credit limit, she knew. It didn't help to reflect that, since she was now unemployed, her bank account had no prospects of being replenished anytime soon. But her financial health had to take a backseat to her *life*. And her life was what this expensive new hairstyle was meant to help protect.

Several hours later she still had trouble recognizing herself whenever she caught a glimpse of her own reflection in a shiny surface. But looking on the bright side, whoever was trying to kill her wasn't going to recognize her easily either.

Of course, the fact that she was going to have to stay at the cottage again might just be a dead — she winced at the word — giveaway.

But the voice on the phone had said, *Be there, or you* will *be dead.* Call it a hunch, but she didn't think he was kidding.

It was nearly six-thirty by the time she got up enough nerve to pull into the garage. She hadn't wanted to wait until later because the very idea of walking through the cottage after nightfall made her stomach churn and turned her knees to Jell-O. The thought of calling the sheriff to beg for the loan of a deputy to stay with her occurred to her, only to be reluctantly dismissed. She knew as well as anyone how the mob worked. Like kudzu, that scourge of the South, they could take over anything. Infiltrating a small town's sheriff's department would be a piece of cake — and Sheriff Schultz himself fit the description of her attacker. Besides, what if the sheriff appointed Castellano her guard dog? If she trusted the wrong person, she would basically be jumping out of the frying pan into the fire.

The bitter truth was that she was on her own.

Willing herself not to remember the damage a gun could cause, Christy fished the pistol — a .38 Colt Automatic — out of her purse and broke into a full-blown cold sweat as she loaded it. Outside, the heat and humidity were just shifting into the bearable range, while the sun still beamed benevolently from low in the western sky. Inside, the cottage was cool and dark and once again pristine. From the looks of it, Christy realized with some surprise as she walked quickly through the rooms with her now-loaded pistol clutched in both clammy hands, the attack might never have happened. The glass had been replaced in the patio door and the broken pieces removed from the carpet. The dresser was back in place beneath the mirror on the far wall of the master bedroom. The bathroom had been cleaned and a whole new door put on to replace the one that had been destroyed. Only the étagère was missing. Whoever the management company had sent over had done an incredible job. Even so, all she wanted to do was hurry up and get out of that house.

Which, of course, wasn't happening. Until she received and then handed off whatever it was her mystery caller had said would be delivered, she was more or less locked into the cottage. Under the circumstances, the obvious thing to do was make herself as safe as possible inside the house.

Forget Mace; if the guy came after her again, she was now armed with a gun. In addition to the new locks, thanks to her shopping spree at a local hardware store the front door was treated to one of those hanging alarms that wails at about a thousand decibels when the door is opened. It also had a rubber wedge shoved beneath it that, in theory, should make it impossible to open from the outside. The door that opened into the kitchen from the garage got similar treatment. The patio door was a little trickier, but she had found an alarm for it, too, as well as a brace made specifically to keep intruders from forcing it open. With all those protective devices in place, she felt safe enough to unload the few groceries she had bought. Then she opened the patio curtains wide to let in as much light as possible, and went to change clothes. After two days of wearing whatever she'd been able to scrounge up in the gift shop, it would be nice to be back in her own things.

Using the bathroom where she'd been attacked was definitely out. After taking the quickest shower on record — scenes from the movie *Psycho* kept running through her mind, which greatly expedited the proceedings — in the second bathroom, she toweled off, stepped into her own undies, and pulled on a lemon yellow T-shirt dress with a big pink rose on the front of it. Loose and knee-length, it was perfect for what she had in mind: an evening spent lazing around in front of the TV trying to figure out how to keep herself alive.

The dress, coupled with her new hair color, made her look like either a ray of sunshine or a bolt of lightning, Christy decided as she took a look at herself in the full-length mirror on the back of the bathroom door. Or a daffodil. Or a dandelion. What she did not look like was herself: a woman whose conservative style had been deliberately chosen to reflect both her profession and her seriousness about rising in it.

But being blond made her look — sexier. Yes, definitely sexier, and more fragile, and even a little ditzy, in a Reese Whitherspoon–adorable sort of way. And it made her eyes look bigger and her cheekbones higher. Or maybe that was the cut.

She only hoped that blondes really did have more fun. Or, at least, better luck. As a brunette she'd been striking out big-time.

Removing the wedge from beneath the

door, she lifted the alarm from the knob and then, gingerly, picked up the gun. The familiar tightening began in her stomach as the bad memories crowded in. Determinedly, she pushed them back. Then she gripped the weapon properly, unlocked the door and headed for the living room, where she put the gun down on the coffee table, curled up on the couch and mentally worked through her options one by one. After doing that for about fifteen minutes and coming to the conclusion that all of them basically sucked, she gave it up. Doing her best to fight off incipient panic, she went to stand in front of the patio door and looked out through the glass.

Purple thunderheads were starting to pile up far out over the ocean, which probably presaged another late storm, but in the meantime it was a gorgeous evening. She could just see the beach beyond the dunes. Open for business despite having been the site of a grisly murder only two nights before, it was still packed with people at — she glanced at the kitchen clock — 7:35. Another hour of daylight remained, and adults and children alike sunbathed, frolicked in the surf, and just walked up and down the sand as if nothing bad had ever happened there, or ever could happen there. For a moment Christy watched them enviously. What she wouldn't give to be one of them, here in this beautiful place, on vacation, happy and carefree. Or, at the very least, terror-free.

A movement in the shrubbery nearest the door caught her eye. Tensing, she eyed the swaying bushes with misgiving. The glossy greenery was so thick that it was impossible to see through, but it was only knee-high. Unless she was about to be attacked by a murder-minded midget, she could hold off on the cardiac arrest. Still, she watched the branches warily, and when something leaped out without warning she jumped.

It was a black cat. A big black cat. Luke's cat. Marvin, that was its name. She remembered in vivid detail the first time she had seen it.

In its mouth was a small gray bird struggling frantically to be free.

All thoughts of serial killers and hit men vanished in an instant. Christy shoved the brace aside, turned off the alarm, released the lock and pushed open the door. A salty sea breeze hit her in the face. Laughing voices and the rush of the ocean filled her ears.

"You! Drop that!" she yelled, clapping her hands sharply as she stepped out onto the patio.

The cat jumped just as she had done a moment earlier and cast a startled glance around at her. It was so surprised that it dropped the bird, which chirped in desperation as it tried to hop away.

"Scat!" Christy clapped her hands again, hoping to scare the cat away. Marvin gave her a contemptuous look and refocused on the fluttering bird. Crouching, its muscles rippling beneath its short coat, it clearly meant to reclaim its prey.

Christy pounced before it could.

"Bad cat," she scolded, straightening with the clearly unhappy feline in her arms. It was a big cat, heavy and muscular, weighing probably a solid twenty pounds, and it was making no attempt to hide its displeasure about being cheated out of its dinner. It squirmed, struggling to be free, but she, a cat lover from way back, already had it tucked securely under her arm with its front paws imprisoned in one hand. The bird, recovering from the shock that hopefully was all it had suffered, hopped a couple of times and then took wing. Watching it soar overhead, the cat lashed its tail and yowled.

"Oh, hush up." Christy scratched behind its ears. The gesture did not appear to mollify it. It was tense, growling, clearly indignant at having been interrupted at such a crucial juncture in its life. She could feel its back paws digging into her side, and shifted to dislodge them.

"Christy, is that you?" Mrs. Castellano hobbled into view around the edge of the privacy fence and stopped to look Christy over with a frown. Today she was wearing a long flowered muumuu and leaning on a cane. Her bare feet were stuffed into blue plastic drugstore sandals. Her bare ankles were thick as sausages above them. Her white hair was styled close to her head in neat pin curls. Behind her was her nephew, still stocky, still scary, still in uniform complete with holstered gun. He, too, frowned as he looked at her.

"Yes, it's me." Christy had to fight the urge to scuttle back inside the cottage and lock the door.

"You done something different with your hair?" Squinting at her as though to get a better look, Mrs. Castellano sounded puzzled.

"I decided to go blond."

"There you go. That's it." The old woman nodded with satisfaction, and stopped squinting. "Yeah, I can see why. It adds a little something — gives you some pizzazz. Don't you think so, Gordie?"

"The hair looks good." His gaze met Christy's.

"Thanks," she said, doing her best to keep her expression from revealing the cold little frisson of distrust that ran down her spine as she looked at him.

"We were grilling out on Aunt Rosa's patio and heard you yell," Castellano explained. "With your track record, we thought you might need some help."

"I was just saving a bird from my next-door neighbor's cat," Christy replied. He might be as innocent as a baby, but the bottom line was that he made her nervous. She didn't like the way he looked at her, she didn't like the way he looked, period, and she definitely felt uncomfortable in his presence. And at this point, that was good enough for her.

"You want to eat with us? We got steak," Mrs. Castellano said.

"Uh, thanks, but I think I better take this bad boy here home before he gets loose again. I was just going to grab my keys and head on over next door. We can't have him eating all the birds, now can we?"

Heart thudding, realizing that she was all

but babbling, Christy stepped back inside her open door for just long enough to grab her purse off the couch, watching Castellano through the glass all the while. If he'd made a move toward her, she would have fled screaming out the front door. But he didn't, so she didn't. Stepping back out onto the patio, making sure she had a good grip on Marvin, who was still clearly determined to return to his earlier pursuits, she slid the door shut behind her and heard the lock click into place.

"Well, I'll just be running along."

"You want to come over later, feel free." Castellano met her gaze and smiled. He was attractive in a blunt-featured, prize-fighter kind of way, but it was all Christy could do not to shiver at the thought that those smiling dark eyes might have been the ones that had looked at her through the gap in her bathroom door. "Aunt Rosa and me, we generally watch TV till around midnight."

"Or later," Mrs. Castellano chimed in.

"Thanks, I'll keep it in mind."

Edging around the pair of them with a smile and a nod, Christy barely managed not to break into a trot as she headed down the path that led to Luke's cottage.

She was halfway there before it occurred

to her that she was running to Luke because, since this nightmare had begun, the
only times she had felt safe were when she
was with him.

14

"She's on the move. She went out through her patio door," Gary yelled from Command Central, where he'd been monitoring the action in the cottage next door. Luke, who had spent the better part of the day trailing Christy around Ocracoke, was just walking into the master bedroom after taking a shower.

"*Shit.*" Cursing under his breath, Luke whipped his towel off and grabbed for the first clothes that came to hand. "Where the hell can she be going now?" Then, as an afterthought, "Did you say she went out the *patio* door?"

"That's what I said," Gary hollered back. "Wait, she came back in. She's picking up her purse. She's carrying something — No, she's closing the door. She's leaving again."

"She still packing heat?" Luke pulled on a pair of ancient jeans and reached for an even more ancient gray T-shirt.

"No. She left it on the coffee table. I'm

looking at it right now."

"She look like she was headed down to the beach? She have on a swimsuit or anything like that?" Luke jerked the T-shirt over his head and looked around for his shoes. Ah, there they were, over by the closet.

"Not that I could tell. Maybe under her clothes. You want me to go after her?"

"I got it covered. You keep on doing what you're doing."

What Gary was doing was taking every scrap of information that could be gleaned from the newspapers that had been in the briefcase Christy had put in the Maxima and running them through the computer. It was slow going, and so far had yielded exactly nothing except a recipe for gazpacho that Gary had tried and raved over, but Luke still had hopes of finding a destination, a code, a sentence, something that made sense of the delivery. Of course, it was possible that it had been no more than a test run, but . . .

He was hopping around on one foot putting on his second sneaker when he heard a knock at their own patio door.

For a split second Luke froze. It couldn't be. It had to be. What were the chances that it was anyone else?

"I got it," Gary called. As Luke heard footsteps heading through the living room, he was galvanized into action.

Knowing Gary, it was entirely possible that he'd forgotten to close the door to Command Central.

Gary had, indeed, forgotten. Luke reached the tiny third bedroom in the nick of time and closed the door to the sound of the patio door sliding open. A pair of quick strides took him into the living room. He arrived just in time to see Christy smile at Gary as she stepped inside. Luke's gaze slid over her — he'd already gone all goggle-eyed with the shock of her new hair color when she'd first emerged from the beauty salon as a blonde and was over it by now — to focus on the thing she held in her arms.

The *cat* she held in her arms.

"Your cat was on my patio again," she said, while Gary, behind her, looked on aghast. "He's a little upset because I made him lose the *bird* he'd just caught."

There was obvious reproof in the way she said "bird." Not that it bothered Luke. He didn't care if the damned cat caught every bird in the universe. What was worrying him was that she was giving every indication that she expected him to take the animal from her.

Luke managed to summon up an apologetic grimace even as he eyeballed the cat. The cat eyeballed him back. Its eyes were narrowed into malevolent slits. They glowed a deep, angry yellow. The thing was growling, its tail lashing, its back feet pushing against Christy's hip as it tried to get free. Clearly oblivious to her danger, Christy held on to it as she waited for him to relieve her of her burden.

Time seemed to stretch out endlessly, but in reality no more than a second or two could have passed before Luke faced up to the hideous reality of the situation. The thing was no more a pet than Christy was a linebacker for the Dallas Cowboys. It was a feral cat that had probably been a pet once but had been abandoned to fend for itself long since.

Now here it was, regarding him balefully, a huge, muscular, battle-scarred tom with one chewed ear and a bad attitude. It looked like a feline Mike Tyson.

It also looked royally ticked off.

"Thanks for bringing him home." Academy-Award–winning didn't begin to describe the caliber of his acting as he smiled and reached for the cat.

"I couldn't let him kill that bird." Relieved of her burden, Christy brushed off her arms and the front of her dress. Oh, joy. Fine black hairs fluttered toward the carpet. Behind her, Gary took aghast to a whole new level.

"Of course not," Luke said.

The cat was heavy. And mean. As soon as he took possession of it the thing hissed and tried to leap for the still-open patio door and freedom. He would gladly have let it go, except that releasing a supposedly loved pet back into the wild from whence it had just been so thoughtfully returned might seem, in her eyes, a trifle suspicious. Besides, Gary was closing the patio door.

"He gets like this when he's hungry," Luke said heartily, trying his best to sound normal, and turned away so that she could no longer see either the cat or his expression. "I'll just go feed him."

Bite me and you're toast, was his telepathic warning to the cat as he carried it off to his bedroom. It spat and tried to swarm up his chest by way of a reply.

"*Shit.*" The curse escaped before he could stop it. Trying to cover up his reaction even as he tore the animal's claws from his flesh and held it, struggling, away from his body, he added for the benefit of any listeners, "I just remembered we're out of litter."

"I'll put it on the grocery list," Gary called back gamely as Luke dumped the monster in his bedroom and quickly shut the door before it could escape. Damn it to hell and back anyway, who would have thought that she'd go and remember about the cat, much less catch it and bring it to him? He was probably going to need frigging rabies shots.

He made a quick pit stop in Gary's bathroom to wash the wounds, swiped his styptic pencil — Gary was the only person he knew who actually had one and used it — to staunch the blood, winced at the sting as the chemical penetrated his lacerated flesh, rubbed on antibiotic ointment, and headed back out to the living room.

With a forced smile on his face.

For this he was putting in for combat pay.

Christy was perched on a stool with her elbows resting on the breakfast bar watching Gary take the lasagna he'd promised Luke for supper out of the oven. Now that Luke was able to focus on something besides the cat, he noticed that she was wearing an oversized T-shirt in a sunny yellow that was only a couple of shades brighter than her new pale blond hair. The shirt fit her loosely but because she was sitting, the soft knit was pulled tight around her truly remarkable ass. Below it, her long, tanned and equally remarkable legs, were bare, like her feet.

He could see panty lines, he realized. A thong? Studying the faint outline, he mentally shook his head. Bikini panties, like the ones she'd been wearing —

He stopped that thought dead in its tracks, but not before he felt his pulse kick it up a notch.

"Sorry I took so long," Luke said. Christy turned to look at him. "But I thought I better give" — here he almost dropped the ball as he sought for and failed to remember the damned cat's supposed name — "him some supper."

"Yeah, he's, like, hypoglycemic or something. He gets cranky when he doesn't eat." Gary, who knew nothing of the whole cat saga, shot Luke a wildly inquiring glance that his Coke-bottle glasses magnified about a thousand times. Christy, fortunately, was still looking at Luke and didn't see.

"Gary invited me to stay for supper. Do you mind?" Christy sounded a little uncertain of her welcome. He guessed that her abrupt withdrawal of her acceptance of his dinner invitation the previous day was making her feel shy. That, or the fact that she had marched over here to express unhappiness about the behavior of "his" cat. Meeting her gaze — those long-lashed brown eyes looked downright seductive when paired with a fringe of champagne-colored hair, he discovered to his dismay — he felt his breathing quicken.

"Nah. Glad to have you."

"I told her we had more than enough for three," Gary put in, rattling crockery. Glad of the distraction, Luke nodded and glanced his way without really seeing him.

"I really appreciate it," Christy said.

"So what's with the hair?" Luke asked, leaning against the counter. He'd liked her hair the way it had been before, dark brown and on the long side, silky like her skin . . .

All right, don't go there. This choppy blond hairstyle that didn't turn him on was a positive happening in his life, if he just had the sense to see it that way.

She smiled at him and his groin tightened. *Oh, boy,* he thought. Blonde or brunette, she still had what it took to make him get hot. Which, given the circumstances, was not a good thing. Not good at all.

Her smile disappeared. "Remember what I was telling you about a possible serial killer? Well, there was an article about all the girls who might have been victims in the local paper today. Eight in the last three years, including the girl on the beach."

"I saw that," Gary said, balling up the foil he'd peeled from the casserole dish and tossing it into the trash. "When I was waiting in line at the grocery. They were all brunettes."

"Yeah," Christy said in a significant tone.

A beat passed.

"Are you telling me you did *that* to your hair hoping that if the guy who attacked you was a serial killer he'd lose interest now that you're a blonde?" Luke couldn't help it. He had to laugh. It was such a ridiculous, typically female, weirdly logical reaction to a terrifying situation that he was bemused and charmed and blown away by her ingenuity all at the same time.

Christy's brows twitched together ominously. Lord, had he made it sound like he didn't like her hair? In his experience, as far as women were concerned that was the verbal equivalent of waving a red cape at a bull.

"By the way, your hair looks great," he added hastily.

"Luke, you want to set the table?" Gary asked.

Glad to have the subject changed, Luke nodded and moved around the breakfast bar into the galley-style kitchen. The casserole dish containing the lasagna was steaming on the cutting board now, and Gary had the refrigerator door open and was reaching into it. Luke stepped around him to grab the plates. In their few days together they'd come to a meeting of the minds about food: Gary liked to cook and was good at it. Luke liked to eat and was good at it. Gary made the meals; Luke set the table and cleaned up after. It was almost like being married, Luke reflected, except that Gary, with his slicked-back red hair and thick glasses, his bony body and persnickety ways, wasn't exactly what he'd pictured the few times he had imagined himself with a wife.

"Can I do something? Like make a salad?" Christy asked, sliding off the barstool.

"Already done." Gary produced the salad from the depths of the refrigerator with a flourish, Luke finished setting the table, and in just a few minutes they were all three passing salad and lasagna around and chatting like old friends. From his place at the table Luke had an excellent view out through the patio doors. It was growing almost dark, huge gray thunderclouds were rolling in, and people were leaving the beach in droves. The wind had picked up. The sea oats swayed noticeably, and in the distance he could see whitecaps breaking.

"This is wonderful." Christy took a bite of lasagna. Luke watched the movement of her lips as they closed around the fork, realized what he was doing, and forced his eyes away. They lit on Gary, who served as a worthy antidote.

"Gary's a heck of a cook." Luke tipped his beer toward his partner.

"Thanks." Gary flushed a little. Christy looked from one to the other. Her dress tightened across her breasts as she moved. Nice round breasts . . .

Luke caught himself breathing a little faster, and took a swig of beer.

"So how do you two know each other?" Christy asked, and ate some more lasagna.

Luke refused to allow himself to watch her mouth again, and so ended up staring at the curve of her throat, watching the muscles move beneath the silky skin as she swallowed. He imagined what that skin would feel like beneath his lips. . . .

Christ, he needed a woman bad. A different woman. *Not this woman.*

"From work," he said, and concentrated on eating. He knew what she was getting at, had even thought it himself: he and Gary were unlikely-looking roomies. Of course, she'd never been meant to know that they *were* roomies. She'd never been meant to see them at all.

"Oh, are you a lawyer, too?"

This time, thank God, she turned those big brown eyes on Gary.

Gary choked on his lasagna.

"Yep," Luke answered for him, since Gary was busy turning red and coughing and reaching for his water. Lying was not exactly Gary's forte. After this investigation was over, Luke vowed to do less of it himself. For one thing, if he hadn't lied he wouldn't now be stuck with a bedroom full of ticked-off feral cat that he was going to have to deal with later. In the meantime, however, lying was necessary, and lying well was better than lying poorly. A man who lied well rarely got caught, and not getting caught was the key to a successful surveillance. "A good one, too. He and I," here he tried to look suitably modest, "got the week off and the use of this beach house as a reward for winning our last case."

Gary made a strangled sound and chugged more water.

"So far it hasn't been much of a reward, has it?" Christy grimaced. "More like a nightmare."

Ah, an opening. If he could just keep his mind off other potential uses for that sexy mouth than eating lasagna, he might be able to work in a little subtle interrogation.

"I'm surprised you're not hightailing it back to Philadelphia."

She looked at him, and a beat passed. She covered it well, but knowing what he knew about her he didn't have any trouble discerning that she was struggling to come up with a remotely plausible answer.

Any woman in her right mind, having just survived a murderous attack and facing an unknown degree of continued peril, would run for home as fast as she could. *If* she could. But it had become clear, from her little chats on the phone, that Christy couldn't just leave. She was being compelled to stay, compelled to act as an organization bagman. And her real fear was that she had been targeted, not by a serial killer with a taste for brunettes, but by a hit man.

The question was, why? Christy knew, but so far he didn't.

Finally she came out with an answer: "This is the first vacation I've had in years, and . . . and it was a really bad breakup."

"Your boyfriend still back in Philly?" Luke loaded the question with sympathy. None of the contacts he'd checked with knew anything about a breakup between her and Donnie Jr., but that didn't necessarily mean that Christy was lying.

"I don't know." She took a bite of lasagna.

"You think maybe he took off for some 'me' time too? Or maybe he's on his way down here to make up?" He watched her keenly, without, he hoped, giving the appearance of anything more than the normal amount of interest.

"I — I don't know." She looked unhappy.

"You haven't talked to him since you've been here?"

"I — no." She put down her fork, took a deep breath and glanced at Gary. "This was great, but I don't think I can eat another bite."

Her plate was still half full. His questions had clearly made her too uncomfortable to finish. Luke felt a stab of guilt, then reminded himself that he was just doing his job. And his job was to catch Michael DePalma.

"There's ice cream for dessert," Gary said, shooting Luke a disapproving glance that, despite being kept below Christy's radar, managed to convey Gary's obvious feeling that Luke was the bad guy here.

"No, thanks." Christy glanced up at the clock and seemed to hesitate. Following her gaze, Luke saw that it was getting on toward eleven. Time to shoo the bait back into the trap. The sooner Donnie Jr. was caught, the sooner they could all call it a day.

"If you're ready to go, I'll walk you home," he offered, and stood up. Christy looked up at him mutely. For a second he saw fear, raw and unmistakable, in her eyes. After what she'd been through he couldn't blame her. He felt like the biggest bastard alive for sending her back to spend the night on her own when she was obviously terrified, but there was no help for it. Whether they'd broken up or not, she was the best link to Donnie Jr. that they had. If the man was in the vicinity, and that fingerprint said that he was, he would be paying Christy a visit sooner or later. Guaranteed.

And, while she didn't know it, she no longer had any reason to fear sleeping in that cottage. He might be using her for bait, but he meant to do whatever it took to keep her alive while he did it.

"I —" She broke off on what seemed to be the verge of confessing her fear, swallowed whatever she'd been going to say, and stood up. "Thanks."

He could almost see her mentally squaring her shoulders. The urge to pull her into his arms, to offer comfort and protection, to reassure her that she was safe, that he and Gary and a whole bunch of electronic gadgets were watching over her night and day, came upon him sharp and strong as a hard elbow to the ribs.

Ruthlessly he crushed it. Catching Donnie Jr. had to be paramount.

"Thanks for the meal, Gary," Christy said on an almost wistful note as Luke slid the patio door open and ushered her firmly through it.

"Anytime," Gary replied. Looking at his partner over his shoulder, Luke realized that Gary was suffering from the same kind of atavistic guilt that was making

Luke himself feel so conflicted. Only Gary's expression made Luke think that in Gary's case the guilt was winning.

Chivalry might not be dead, but in this case it needed to be stifled.

Luke closed the patio door before Gary had time to do something stupid, like spill his guts. He'd be damned if either one of them was going to blow this investigation over a pair of big brown *save-me* eyes.

15

"It's — really dark," Christy said as they reached the end of the patio and turned onto the sandy path. She was walking close to him, her arm brushing his side. The night was, indeed, very dark, so dark that he could barely see her, and he was glad that she'd brought it to his attention. Looking up at the starless, moonless sky, feeling the rush of wind blowing in from the ocean, sensing the promise of rain in the heaviness of the air, kept him from thinking about the warmth of her, and the smoothness of her skin, and how near she was, and . . .

"It's going to storm," he said.

As if to confirm his words, a flicker of lightning far out to sea revealed a flash of angry purple clouds. A distant rumble of thunder followed. An earthy scent on the wind warned of approaching rain.

Christy shivered. With her arm pressed right up against his, he could feel the faint quiver that racked her body. The path was narrow, little more than a track through the dunes worn bare of sea oats by generations of tramping feet. If she was going to walk beside rather than in front of or behind him, she had to stay close. But not quite that close.

"I hate storms. There's been a storm every night."

"It's the rainy season."

"I hate the rainy season." There was a barely discernible quaver in her voice. "Beaches should be full of sun and sand and happy people, not rain and . . . and —"

She broke off, but it didn't matter. He knew what she couldn't quite say: fear and violence and murder.

Another flash of lightning, only closer at hand. A clap of thunder. Beside him, Christy jumped, and crowded closer yet. Her hand slid into his. Luke felt the quick entwining of her fingers with his, the warm press of her palm against his, with an acuteness sharp enough to worry him.

"It's coming in fast," she said, and shivered.

"The good news is, it never lasts long."

He made no move to free his hand. In fact, he tightened his grip, wrapping her smaller hand securely in his larger one. Because after all, he told himself, she was probably only reaching out to him as an instinctive means of keeping the dark at bay, and if holding his hand made her feel safer, what was the harm in offering her what little comfort he could?

Which was bullshit, and he knew it, and knew too that he wasn't about to let go of her hand anyway. They were almost to her cottage now. He could see the dense outline of it squatting against the pale sand. He would be walking away from her soon enough. He might as well hold her hand while he had the chance.

"You know, I didn't really walk over to your cottage tonight to bring Marvin back." Christy's voice was so soft now that it was barely audible over the sighing wind and the dull roar of the breaking waves.

Marvin, he registered, glad to be temporarily distracted from his troublesome reaction to her. *That* was the damned cat's supposed name.

"You didn't?"

"I came because I was scared."

The confession refocused his complete attention on her in a hurry. He knew her well enough now to know that admitting to fear or any kind of weakness or vulnerability was not something she normally did. She was turning to him at last, confiding in him as he had wanted, but it wasn't the kind of information he'd been hoping to get from her. What he'd been angling for was some kind of revelation that would lead him to Donnie Jr. Instead, this was an opening up of her emotions to him.

He didn't want that. He really did not want that.

"After what you've been through, anybody would be scared." His voice was rough around the edges, because they'd reached her patio now and he knew that in just a moment or two he was going to have to walk away and leave her inside, alone and afraid.

His gut twisted at the thought.

"I'm not scared when I'm with you."

Her voice was now the merest breath, but he heard it, felt the clutch of her fingers, felt her eyes looking up at him through the dark. She trusted him, and that knowledge hit him like a blow to the solar plexus. Glad that in the darkness she could not see the expression on his face, he stopped walking and stood stock-still, his hand tightening on hers as he sought for some response he could make that was still within the parameters of his duty, his job, his real reason for being in her life.

He came up empty.

"Luke." She let go of his hand, but only to slide around in front of him and flatten her hands on his chest. He could feel their gentle pressure on his rib cage as if they were burning through his T-shirt to his skin. He couldn't see her but he could sense her, feel the tickle of her hair as the wind blew it against his jaw, smell the elusive fragrance of her shampoo, hear the gentle rhythm of her breathing. "I don't want to be alone tonight."

Shit.

"Christy."

"Hmm?"

He was breathing hard, too hard, like he'd just tried for a four-minute mile. Way too hard for a guy who was getting ready to turn a woman down flat, he realized. Searching for the right words, the best thing to say, he gripped her waist, meaning to put her away from him, to put some space between them, to get some perspective on this while he still could. But it was too late. She was already leaning into him, her hands sliding up over his shoulders, her breasts round and soft as they pushed against his chest, her whole body flattening against his as she went up on tiptoe to press her lips to his mouth.

For a second or two, maybe more, he endured the torture meted out by those moist hot lips, endured the gentle pressure, the movements, the flick of her tongue against his mouth, while his breathing went haywire and his heart slammed against his chest and pure heat shot through his veins, through his muscles, making him instantly erect, setting him on fire.

Then he broke. Just like that he crumbled, caved, surrendered to a force far stronger than his own self-control.

"Christy."

It was a guttural growl, an admission of defeat. Wrapping his arms around her, he did what he'd been dying to do since he'd watched her eating ice cream in the park. He slid a hand beneath her hair to cradle the back of her head and slanted his mouth over hers and kissed her deeply. Licking into her mouth, tasting her sweet muskiness and feeling her shuddering response, he lost all sense of time, place, and circumstance. He wanted her. And she wanted him, too. And that was all he cared, or needed, to know.

Pulling her mouth from his, keeping her body close, she pressed sweet hot kisses along the line of his jaw. Gritting his teeth against the tantalizing onslaught, he held her tight and burned and wanted and all the while told himself to knock it off, let her go, step back and get the hell out of Dodge.

"Spend the night with me," she whispered against his skin.

Oh God, he wanted to. More than he could ever remember wanting anything in his life. He went a little crazy, groaning with need, reclaiming her mouth and kissing her with a slow hunger that gradually built to a burning crescendo. She kissed him back just as hotly, digging her nails into the back of his neck, snuggling her breasts against his chest. Turning with her so that her back was pressed up against the fence, aching with desire, he slid his thigh between her legs and covered her breast with his hand.

It felt so good, so warm and round, the world's oldest Viagra right there in his palm, and as he rubbed it her nipple jutted out.

No way was he going to be able to just walk away from this.

"God, I want you," he muttered, lifting his head on a mission to take that tantalizing piece of candy into his mouth, knowing that he was going down in flames here and no longer caring a bit. But before he could do anything she pulled his head back down to hers and stuck her tongue into his mouth instead.

"Jesus God."

She kissed like she meant it, like she wanted it, like a woman who had getting horizontal on her mind, and he kissed her back so thoroughly that the flames they generated basically incinerated his brain. His heart pounded like it was going to beat right through his chest. Another part of his anatomy threatened to burst out of his zipper. He rocked his thigh up higher between her legs, and the tiny sound of pleasure she made had him reaching for the hem of her dress.

He wanted her naked, like now.

Then lightning flashed, thunder boomed, and just like that it started to rain. And not a gentle rain, either. A torrent of lukewarm water spilled down on them, as if God had just popped a giant water balloon directly over their heads.

He was so far gone that it didn't bother him. After a single surprised glance up he was ready to continue on without missing a beat, and to hell with the storm. But she dragged her mouth from his and pushed at his shoulders.

"Let's go inside," she said. When he didn't immediately respond, she squirmed out of his arms and caught his hand to pull him after her toward the door.

The rain sluicing over him was at least some help in clearing his head.

Right. Good plan. Inside. A bed.

By the time she had the door unlocked and he followed her over the threshold, they were both as soaked as if they had taken a shower fully clothed. Wet as he was, the shock of the air-conditioning was severe. Severe enough to shock him back to semilucidity.

Not that he liked what his recovering intelligence said: Sleeping with Christy, his *bait,* was a really, really bad idea. The worst, for all kinds of reasons.

In short, he could not do this. Even if it killed him, and the way he was feeling right now it just might, he had to turn off his libido, turn her down, and walk away.

The light was on in the bathroom down the hall, providing plenty of illumination for him to see her by as she closed the patio door. Like himself, she was dripping wet. Her hair was plastered to her skull and her dress clung to her skin. Her eyes were wide and dark, her skin pale and shiny-wet, her lips slightly parted. She was still breathing too fast, and her nipples were hard round nubs that thrust prominently against her dress. As soaked as she was, she might as well have been naked. He could see everything: the exact size and shape of her breasts, the slender curve of her waist and hips, the indentation of her navel, the outline of her bra and panties, the slight protuberance that was the *yin* to his rock-hard *yang*.

She shivered and ran both hands over her wet hair to push the soggy strands off her face, then smiled a little nervously at him.

What he wanted to do was pull her back into his arms and kiss her senseless and strip off her clothes and his own and make love to her until they were both so hot that the rain evaporated from their bodies in a huge cloud of steam.

He might have done it, too, despite his slowly returning intelligence, had it not been for two things: one, the knowledge that Gary was on the job, watching their every move, listening to their every word, or sound, which was more relevant in this case as the action at least could be moved out of camera range; and, two, the uncomfortable suspicion that was growing by leaps and bounds now that he was getting enough brain wattage back to think it through that she was *using* him.

Or trying to.

Much as he hated to face the ego-deflating truth, it just didn't seem very likely that she'd come on to him like that because she'd suddenly developed an uncontrollable craving for his body. No, the more rational explanation was that she was after a little insurance that she would make it safely through the night.

In other words, she was ready, willing, and able to make a trade-off: protection for sex.

He was eyeing her a little grimly when she moved, walking toward him with a seductive sway, pressing up against him, sliding her arms around his waist.

Jesus Christ, that crash he was imagining was probably Gary falling out of his chair.

"I've got to go," he said, detaching her arms from around his waist and stepping deftly out of range.

"What?" She looked surprised, as well she might. He doubted that she'd ever had a guy turn her down before — not this hot little chickie.

"Yeah, I gotta get up early in the morning. Me and Gary, we're going fishing." His gaze lit on the pistol still lying on the coffee table, reminding him that she was, after all, truly afraid. He might be a little ticked at her; all right, he *was* a little ticked at her, but he could appreciate where she was coming from. Sort of. "If you want, I'll check the place out for you before I go."

"But . . ."

They were both dripping and freezing and too intent on their own separate agendas to do anything about it as she trailed after him while he walked quickly from room to room, turning on lights and conducting what was probably the quickest, least thorough search in history. No bogeyman, no surprise, he had this place rigged now so that a cockroach couldn't get into it without him knowing about it. The little witch was safer here than she would be locked inside a bank vault.

Of course, she didn't know that.

"Luke, *wait,*" she said urgently when they reached the living room again and he headed straight for the patio door. He turned to look at her, and she walked right up to him and wrapped her arms around his waist and pressed herself against him. She was looking a little bewildered, but she was game, snuggling her tits against him, looking up at him with those big brown eyes. "Don't you want to — to stay?"

Circe had nothing on this girl.

"Some other time, honey," he said, detaching himself. Then, with a terse "lock it after me," he let himself out the patio door.

As Luke had expected, Gary was agog. "You want to tell me what that was all about?" He emerged from Command Central as Luke stepped back inside their cottage and kicked off his soaked and sandy shoes. The supper dishes had been cleared and a vacuum cleaner, still plugged in, stood in the middle of the living room floor. Obviously, Gary had made good use of the available down time while Luke had walked Christy home. A look at Gary's smirk confirmed that Gary thought he had made even better use of his since he'd entered Christy's cottage.

"No." Luke was brutally direct as he headed for his bedroom, pulling his saturated shirt over his head and tossing it in the direction of the washing machine as he went. He could, of course, lie, or even spin a half-truth about her being scared into some kind of explanation, but he wasn't in the mood.

"Okay," Gary said, following him. "You know, she seems like a really nice girl. Maybe we ought to think about bringing her in, telling her we're here, offering her protection and some kind of deal if she cooperates with us."

"Yeah, and then if she runs to DePalma or Amori or one of her other mob connections with what she knows, what do we do? Nothing, that's what. We're screwed." Luke paused, his hand on the knob of his closed bedroom door, to shoot a frowning glance at Gary. "Anyway, aren't you supposed to be watching the monitor?"

Without waiting for an answer, Luke opened the door, and a black streak shot through, tearing across Luke's bare foot, flying past Gary, who fell back against the wall open-mouthed, and exploding into the living room.

"Ow! Shit! I forgot about the damned cat!"

Grabbing his injured foot, Luke hopped around in a tight little circle, foot stinging, swearing a blue streak, watching blood leak from a set of scratches that were an almost perfect match for the ones on his chest.

"Yowzers!" Gary was wide-eyed. "That's no cat, that's a frickin' wild animal!"

Having suffered no physical injury, Gary was much quicker to recover and get with the program. Shooting Luke an accusing look, he ran after the cat. In the living room, the animal was bouncing off the walls. Luke could hear it tearing around to the accompaniment of assorted crashing sounds, but he couldn't see it. Didn't want to see it. Still, a glimpse of Gary leaping through the kitchen wielding a dish towel in obvious pursuit of the cat made him smile despite his pain.

Yowl!

Scramble. Crash.

"Drop that steak, you — !"

The sounds of a raging battle made Luke's smile widen. Still, he was a professional. Far be it from him not to provide backup to a partner in distress.

He limped into the living room, took a good look at the crazed cat leaping over the breakfast bar with a trout-sized steak firmly clutched between its jaws, shifted his gaze to Gary snapping the dish towel into the empty space where the cat had been, pulled back the patio door, and jumped out of the way.

He'd done what he could. Now it was up to fate.

"Shoo! Shoo!" Gary yelled, wielding the dish towel so that it made another mean-sounding pop.

The cat, no fool, tore out the door and vanished into the night, steak and all.

A better man would undoubtedly feel guilty about having allowed a poor defenseless animal to be driven out into the pouring rain.

Luke slammed the patio door shut, and gave Gary a low five.

"So what was up with the cat?" Gary demanded, still panting, fists on hips, dish towel hanging forgotten from one hand. A glance around the room revealed the cat's path: crooked pictures, knocked over lamps, a broken glass.

"Long story," Luke said, already heading back to his bedroom to doctor his foot and lose the soggy jeans before he froze to death. "Don't ask."

"I am asking," Gary yelled. "It stole the steak I was marinating for breakfast tomorrow!"

That was the most passionate he'd ever heard Gary get. Luke glanced around at him with raised brows.

"Jesus, Gary," he said with a dawning grin. "Chill, man. I'll buy you another steak."

"I don't want another steak," Gary said, clearly seething as he stormed after Luke. "I want to know about the freaking cat!"

"Check the monitor, why don't you?" Luke recommended as he shut his bedroom door in Gary's face. He was still grinning as he padded toward the bathroom. It had just occurred to him that he was smelling something a little off, something that had nothing to do with wet jeans and hair and musty rental cottages, when he happened to glance at his bed.

What he saw froze him in his tracks.

"That damned cat took a dump on my bed!"

"Luke, Luke!" Gary pounded on the bedroom door. "Luke, get out here *now!*"

"What?" Contemplating the mess, Luke got sick to his stomach. He yanked open the door, glaring at Gary, in no mood to deal with hysterical rantings about a steak or a cat.

"I checked the monitor. She's leaving. She's packing up and leaving! Christy!" Gary said.

16

If they didn't have room at the Inn, then she was spending the night in the lobby. That was what Christy told herself as she rushed through the kitchen into the garage, flipped on the light, pressed the button on her key chain that popped the trunk, threw her small suitcase inside, slammed the lid and practically leaped behind the wheel. Locking the car doors, she turned on the motor before activating the garage door opener and to hell with the risks of being overcome by carbon monoxide, a danger that her mother was always preaching about in connection with starting cars in closed garages. She'd take her chances with carbon monoxide any day rather than leave herself vulnerable to attack by opening the garage door to the dangers that lurked in the night before she was ready to run over them.

She had to leave. She couldn't stand it. There'd been no delivery today, so she didn't have to hang around waiting for a one a.m. phone call, no matter what the guy on the phone had said. She didn't have to stay awake all night jumping at the slightest sound, cringing at every shifting shadow. She didn't have to deal with the pounding of her heart, the racing of her pulse, the fear-induced knot in the pit of her stomach that just kept getting bigger and bigger with every minute that passed. Not tonight. She could spend tonight elsewhere, and come back in the morning. Nothing — not even the cottage, not even the situation she was in — seemed quite as terrifying in the bright light of day.

As late as an hour ago, when she'd been eating dinner with Luke and Gary, she'd thought she was going to be able to tough this thing out. But as Luke had walked her home and the night had started closing in around her, as the wind had risen and the waves had crashed and the prospect of being all alone in the dark had loomed ever closer, she'd realized that she couldn't do it after all. Fear was a powerful motivator, as she had already learned. Fear was what had forced her to come down to Ocracoke in the first place. But the fear of what would happen if she didn't do precisely as she was told had turned out not to be quite as acute as the fear of being dead before morning.

What it had boiled down to as she had turned her choices over in her mind was basically a case of *possibly die now* versus *possibly die later*. Later had won out.

Even the cottage itself was starting to creep her out. Christy couldn't get over the weird feeling that someone was watching her even while she knew — hoped? prayed? — that she was alone inside.

It had occurred to her that maybe her attacker was hiding somewhere, in a closet, under a bed — Luke had not looked under the beds, she had realized after he had gone — behind the water heater, in a secret room that would open after she was asleep.

Not that she was planning to sleep. No how. No way. As she saw it, her best line of defense was the gun, and that only held true for as long as she was awake.

Even with the gun she couldn't help but imagine various bad things that *could* happen, which had left her feeling scared to death. So scared that it had taken her all of about fifteen minutes after Luke had left to decide to head for the Silver Lake Inn, and never mind the fact that they'd said earlier that they'd be full up for the rest of the week. Cancellations happened, and, if not, there was always the bar until its two a.m. closing, and then the lobby. She might not sleep, but at least she would be safe. She'd thought about calling just to see if they did have an unexpected vacancy, but she figured she was harder to turn away in person than over the phone. Besides, whether they did or not didn't really matter. No way was she spending the rest of the night alone. Lights and people were what she needed.

So she'd grabbed the bare essentials for the night and bolted.

Now rain pelted her car as she backed down the driveway, drumming on the roof with a brisk urgency that did not seem to have slacked off any from when the downpour had begun almost an hour before. Then she'd been soaked in a matter of seconds, and so had Luke. But thinking about just what they'd been doing when they'd gotten so completely wet brought humiliation with it, and so she did her best to push it out of her mind. Driving past Luke's cottage, though, she couldn't help but notice that the lights were still on. Under other circumstances, she would have pulled in there and shamelessly begged a bed for the night. But after what had happened between them, she would rather, by far, opt for a chair in the lobby of the Silver Lake Inn.

Had she really said *I don't want to be alone tonight* and kissed him like she was dying to take him to bed?

The short answer was, yes, she had. And she'd done it in cold blood, too, because she hadn't wanted to spend the night in that cottage alone.

Had he really turned into a virtual sex machine, pushing her up against the fence and kissing her like a man who had kissed far more than his fair share of women and caressing her breast and pressing his leg up between her thighs until he had actually managed to turn her on?

Yep, that too.

And then, when, to her complete and utter astonishment, he had finally gotten her as hot as he seemed to be himself, gotten her to the state where she was wanting his hand in her pants and his mouth on her breasts and a bed somewhere close by in the worst way, had he said, *I've got to go,* and, unbelievably, walked out on her because, he'd claimed, he had an early morning fishing trip scheduled with his pal Gary?

Oh yeah. There was no getting around that.

Christy didn't know precisely what had happened to change his mind between those first blistering minutes on the patio and that last freezing brush-off, but the end result she clearly recognized: she'd propositioned the guy, and he had said no.

Remembering, the discomfort factor was intense.

Luckily — or not — she had more important things to focus on at the moment than the recent apparent breakdown in her sex appeal.

Like staying alive.

There was a car behind her as she pulled out onto Silver Lake Road. She caught a glimpse of its headlights in the rearview mirror, and frowned. Not that there was any reason why there shouldn't be another car on the road, of course. It was getting on toward midnight, which was late for the local crowd, and it was pouring down rain, which should tend to discourage most of the tourists from getting out and about, but it was Monday and there were a few things open still, certainly at least one convenience store that she knew of, the bar at the Silver Lake Inn, the medical clinic, the marina . . .

She glanced in the rearview mirror again. All she could see of the car were its headlights, but that was enough to tell her that it was a good distance behind her, not close at all. There was absolutely no reason why it should make her nervous — but it did.

The impression she had that it was following her was probably nothing more than her usual rampant paranoia raising its nervous head one more time.

She hoped. No, she prayed.

A quick glance reassured her that she had easy access to her two-pronged self-defense system: the gun and her cell phone. Both were in her purse, along with a new can of Mace and, just for backup, an air horn with enough decibels to send any assailant running with his hands clapped over his ears at the touch of a button. Her purse was in the passenger seat. All she had to do was grab it, unzip the top, plunge her hand in, and she was basically a one-woman SWAT team.

Of course, the last time she had tried 911, the results had not been so good. She had since learned that there was an excellent reason for that: Ocracoke didn't have 911 service. The next time she needed help, she was calling, not stocky-bodied Sheriff Schultz, but the fire department. A self-defense instructor in a class she'd taken once had told his students always to yell *fire* instead of help if they were being attacked; people pay attention to that because a fire might affect them. The technique had worked well once, and she was counting on it to work again. So much so that she now had the fire department's number on speed dial.

So, see, she had no need to worry about the headlights that she could still see in her rearview mirror. Whatever happened, she was covered. Not that she expected anything would. She was in her car, driving straight to the hotel, where she was planning to park beneath the porte cochere in front of the entrance and run right in to the well-lit, well-manned lobby.

As she drove past the harbor with its semicircle of glowing halogen lights, it occurred to her that she might be able to see the other vehicle as it passed through the illuminated area.

She almost hit a telephone pole trying, and struck out to boot. It was too dark, and it was raining too hard, for her to see anything besides the headlights.

From Silver Lake Road she turned onto Cemetery Road, named for the British Cemetery that lay at its western tip and contained the remains of seamen from

HMS *Bedfordshire*, which was sunk by a German torpedo off the coast of Hatteras during World War II. During the day, this was one of the island's premier tourist attractions. So late on a rainy Monday, it was closed and the road was deserted. The Inn was located almost directly across from the cemetery, so she didn't have much farther to go, Christy comforted herself as she passed an RV park on the left and a condo development on the right and then plunged into the utter darkness of the piney woods that ran along either side of this stretch of road. Except for the sound of the rain and the swish of the windshield wipers, it was utterly quiet in the car. She had not realized how little developed this part of the road was, but then, she'd never driven along it in the dead of night before. There was nothing: no storefronts, no service stations, no houses . . .

In the rearview mirror she could still see headlights. She contemplated them for a second before, of necessity, switching her attention back to the road, which as far as she was concerned was no more now than a shiny, wet strip of blacktop that continually stretched out some twenty feet ahead of her. The beams of her headlights shone through silver ribbons of rain, and fat drops of water exploded on the pavement everywhere she looked.

It occurred to Christy that she was utterly alone. Except, she realized with another quick glance in the rearview mirror, for the vehicle attached to the other set of headlights.

Which were getting closer.

The hairs on the back of her neck rose with a little prickle.

Over nothing. A set of headlights in the dark.

What was there in that to make her palms start to sweat and her heart start to pound?

It was the silence, she decided. Along with the sense of isolation that went along with driving all alone through a dark, rainy night, the silence was what was getting to her. She reached down to turn on the radio. Nothing but static. Of course, it was programmed to pick up the stations broadcasting in and around Philly.

Just about the time she found a functioning channel and Elvis started to wail about being a hunk of burning love, the headlights appeared in her rearview mirror without her even having to look for them.

They were closer. A lot closer. In fact, they were right on her bumper. From their height, they belonged to a big vehicle, an SUV or a truck.

Christy frowned. Then she hit a bump and the song cut out. With a quick glance down, she checked the speedometer. She was doing thirty-five, which, given the weather and the road, was about as fast as she could safely go. But the headlights were staying close, too close for comfort. If she had to stop suddenly for any reason, he would bump her.

Through the rearview mirror she tried for a glimpse of the driver. Seeing past the glare of the headlights was impossible, of course. Seeing much of anything beyond the few feet of road in front of her was impossible. It was as if she and her car and the vehicle behind her were alone in an endless, rain-lashed dark tunnel.

Elvis, still burning, came back on without warning. The sudden burst of sound made Christy jump. With a savage jab, she turned the radio off.

The headlights were blinding her now. He was really following way too close. Gripping the steering wheel so tightly that she could feel the bumps on the hard plastic hoop gouging into her palms, Christy realized that she was breathing hard. That she was scared. That she was probably overreacting, but she was going to call the fire department to report seeing a blaze way out at the end of Cemetery Road. If this guy was tailgating her for a reason, she was going to do what she could to make sure that she never found out what it was. Whoever he was would soon find himself being pilloried by the bright beams of a fire truck. Which, because of the narrowness of the road, they would both have to pull to the side to let pass, and which she then meant to follow as if the hounds of hell were after her.

She was just reaching for her purse when the headlights behind her blinked. *Bright–normal. Bright–normal.* Okay, he wanted to pass. He was probably in a hurry to get to his destination, and she was going too slow to suit him. Typical male.

At the thought, she took a deep breath and tried to relax a little. Almost certainly that was what was happening here: she was being followed by nothing more sinister than a typical tailgating male.

Giving up on her plan to call the fire department for the moment, she wrapped both hands around the wheel and edged over a little to give him room to get by.

He pulled out from behind her and hit the gas. When the vehicle was almost opposite her, she glanced over and saw that it was a pickup truck. A white pickup truck with what looked like writing on the passenger door. Given the rain, and the darkness, and the split second she was able to actually look, the writing was impossible to read.

Those factors also prevented her from seeing whoever was behind the wheel. The truck apparently hit a puddle in the middle of the road, because suddenly it was kicking up water in great streams. Muddy water pelted the driver's-side window of her car. Thoughts of hydroplaning made her tense up until she was sitting bolt upright in the seat, and she eased up off the gas in an effort to slow down gradually. He maintained his speed, and in a matter of seconds they were running neck and neck.

The road really was narrow. The truck was too close. She had to concentrate on keeping the wheel steady —

The truck bumped her. Hard.

"No!" she yelled aloud, casting a single angry, terrified glance out the driver's-side window as her car bounced almost off the road. The right front wheel dipped onto the shoulder; the steering wheel jerked sharply under her hands. She could hear gravel flying up as she fought to get back on the pavement. Her heart leaped into her throat; her breathing suspended. When she felt a solid surface under all four wheels again, she wanted to weep with relief. As wet as it was, stomping the brakes would send her fishtailing into the trees, she feared. So she tried to gently, steadily, bear down on the brakes, knowing that she needed to slow down and calm down, thinking that the truck would shoot on past.

No such luck. Even as she got her car under control again, the white blur that was the truck veered close, and then *boom!* The sound of metal smashing into metal was as loud and terrifying as a gunshot.

"Stop it!" she screamed as her stomach knotted and her pulse pounded louder even than the rain in her ears. It was useless, she knew. The other driver could not hear her and would not stop if he could. *This is deliberate,* was the terrible thought that ran through her mind as the blow sent both of her right tires bumping onto the shoulder. Fighting not to crash, to return the car to the road once more, to get through this in one piece, she appealed for heavenly help in panicked bursts: *Please, God, please, God, please . . .*

Gravel hit the hood and side of her car

with the quick, staccato rhythm of machine-gun fire. Stomach lurching, Christy hung on to the wheel and steered for all she was worth. With a combination of luck and divine intervention, she managed to get back up on the road a second time. The terrifying gravel spray stopped.

A lightning glance showed her that the truck was still there, running a little ahead of her now but keeping pace. She slowed the car so she could stop and put it in reverse.

Boom!

The truck smashed into her again. Despite all her efforts, she was off the road, churning through gravel and then slithering over grass. Her headlights picked up a stand of thick-trunked live oaks. She was heading straight toward them. Screaming, she stood on the brake.

And went into a spin.

There was nothing she could do. The sound of screeching brakes and squealing tires filled the air. The wreck seemed to be happening in slow motion. For one blank, horrible moment Christy watched as flashes of white truck, shaggy green branches and gray tree trunks, muddy grass, and sparkling curtains of rain revolved in front of her windshield like a carousel of disaster, each caught as in a freeze-frame by the headlights. The car was completely off the road now, she realized dimly, pirouetting like an ice-skater in a death spiral.

It crashed with an ear-shattering *bang!*

Christy was thrown violently forward. At almost the same instant an explosion of white hit her in the face. For a moment she didn't comprehend what had happened; it felt like she'd been punched in the nose. She saw stars, felt a burst of pressure rather than pain and then a tingling.

She didn't realize she'd been screaming until she stopped.

The sudden dead silence was more terrifying than almost anything else.

Oh my God. She was in a car wreck.

How long it took her to register that she didn't know. It could not have been much more than a matter of seconds, because her air bag was still in the process of deflating when realization hit her. The windshield was cracked; beyond it rain, captured by the headlights, spilled across the hood in undulating sheets. Tiny purple spots floated across her field of vision. There was a terrible ringing sound in her ears. Her face felt tingly — weird.

Was she hurt? She was breathing. She

was able to move her legs, her arms. She was just lifting a hand to her face to check for blood when she remembered the white truck.

Terror hit her like a fist to the stomach. She'd been run off the road. On purpose.

Whoever had done it was almost certainly still nearby. Probably already running through the rain toward her car. When he reached her —

Christy had a vivid mental image of the obsidian eyes that had gleamed at her through the gap in her bathroom door; she remembered the high-pitched, almost gleeful voice, and the sickening feeling of the hatchet chopping into her flesh.

Who else could it be?

"I've got to get out of here!"

Panting with fear, she fumbled with her seat belt, managed to depress the button, opened her door, and rolled out into the rain. Torrents of water immediately pelted her, soaking through the shorts and T-shirt she was wearing, wetting her to the skin. The onslaught had the welcome effect of helping to clear her mind. Her legs were shaky; they felt about as sturdy as limp spaghetti, but terror kept her upright, propelled her away from the car. She couldn't run, her legs were too unsteady for that, but she could lurch, and lurch she did, her sandal-clad feet squelching through slippery mud.

A quick, hunted glance around revealed very little. It was too dark, and the rain obscured everything, even sound. All she could see were the twin paths of light that her still-functioning headlights cut through the darkness. They revealed that the car had fetched up against a tree in the stand of live oaks she had spotted before she'd hit the brakes. Fortunately, the car had hit on the passenger side.

There was no sign of the truck. No other lights. Could the driver simply have kept on going, content to have run her off the road?

You wish.

Her headlights pointed back the way she had come. She headed in the opposite direction, moving as quickly as she could, trying to remember how far it was to help, to the Inn, to the nearest house or campsite or service station . . .

Suddenly the darkness was so complete that it was impossible to see so much as her own feet as they stumbled over the ground. It took Christy a second for realization to strike. When it did, horror slid like a cold finger down her spine. Casting a terrified glance over her shoulder, she realized that her car's headlights had gone out.

Had been turned out.

He was here. He had parked his truck, turned out its lights, and come through the driving rain with one purpose: to find her.

To kill her, if she wasn't already dead in the wreck.

Christy faced that hideous near-certainty, faced the probability that it was her attacker back there by her car, looking for her, hunting her, meaning to finish what he had begun that night in her cabin, and her blood turned to ice. Her breath came in short, desperate pants. She bent almost double, moving as fast as she could away from the car, away from the road where he would surely look for her first. The mud grew deeper, sucking at her sandals, making each step an effort. The rain was a dull roar in her ears. It beat down on her head, her curved back, pounded the ground. It poured into her eyes and mouth. She could taste its earthiness, smell its scent, which made her think of fish.

Vainly she remembered her purse with its miniarsenal. In the shock of the wreck she'd forgotten all about it. It was still somewhere in the car. Should she try to circle back, try to get in the car and grab her gun, her phone?

Shielding her eyes from the downpour with an upraised hand, she glanced back. What she saw made her heart lurch. A narrow beam of light pierced the darkness, sweeping from side to side like a terrible eye. He had a flashlight; he was looking for her.

A scream bubbled up into her throat. She forced it back. Who was close enough to hear? No one, as far as she knew. Except him. A scream would only help him to find her. Her rubbery legs threatened to give way at any moment, but she forced herself onward, stumbling over the ground, knowing that she was fleeing for her life.

Headlights appeared out of the night, moving fast, heading in the opposite direction. From the fast but steady pace of the vehicle, she surmised that it was on the road. Its route was almost parallel to hers — until it rounded a curve and caught her full in its beams.

Stop! Please stop! Please!

She didn't dare yell the words aloud, but she stumbled toward the car as fast as her unsteady legs would take her, waving frantically with both arms over her head in the universal signal of distress. The beams rushed on without checking; the driver either hadn't seen her or had elected not to stop. Neck swiveling, numb with disappointment, she tracked it with her gaze: in seconds the taillights were no brighter than fireflies in the distance. Then they were gone, swallowed up by darkness and rain.

But there was still a light. A small round beam, like that of a laser pointer except white, was focused on her arm. As she stared down at it with first puzzlement and then disbelief, it swept over her from head to foot.

Christy realized what it was with a flash of horror.

The beam from her pursuer's flashlight. He'd spotted her.

Now that the need for concealment was past, she screamed, a shattering shriek that was lost in the roaring rain, and started to run. Slipping and sliding in the mud, screaming with every bit of lung power she possessed, she stumbled toward where she now knew the road was, hoping for another car, hoping for someone, anyone other than the monster who was chasing her through the dark, to appear.

The rain fell with a dull roar that brought its own kind of sensory deprivation with it. It seemed to wrap itself around everything, absorbing sounds, blocking her vision. Glancing desperately around, she wouldn't have known where he was had it not been for the bobbing beam of that tiny flashlight.

He was running now, too. She could tell by the way the flashlight joggled up and down, by how fast it was approaching. Lunging toward the road, gasping for breath, she felt as if she were trapped in one of those slow-motion nightmares in which no matter how hard she tried, she could not get up any speed. Her lungs ached as she fought to fill them with the dense, moisture-laden air. Her legs quivered and threatened to give out; her feet felt heavier with every step as her sandals grew increasingly weighted down with mud.

She wasn't going to make it. She knew it, even though she struggled on, refusing to give up, to accept the inevitable. In seconds she sensed rather than saw him closing on her, sensed rather than heard the heavy splash of his feet as he bounded along only steps behind. Her heart thudded like a trapped bird's; adrenaline gave her legs renewed strength. Serial killer or hit man: it didn't matter. What mattered was that when he caught her he was going to kill her. A burst of desperate speed sent her catapulting forward. Even with the slippery mud, even with the weight of her sandals and her limp legs, she managed to run as fast as she ever had in her life. But still he caught up to her as she had known he eventually would. A warm, fleshy hand wrapped around her upper arm.

Christy shrieked, managed to jerk free, and stumbled on.

A hard shove between her shoulder blades sent her hurtling to her knees. As quickly as she hit the drenched, muddy ground she knew that she was in big trouble, but it was already too late. Icy panic raced down her spine. Her stomach clenched.

With a quick jerk he grabbed a handful of hair and yanked her head back. For just an instant his body looming over her blocked the rain from her face. He was still only a shape, a figure from a horror movie, big and dark, emanating evil in waves. She could smell a sharp, acrid odor that she thought must be her own fear. Terror closed like a fist around her throat, sent cold sweat pouring over her in waves.

She was so frightened now that she couldn't even scream.

A vision of Elizabeth Smolski swam before her mind's eye. Was this how the poor girl had felt, in the seconds after Christy had run away, in the seconds before he had slit her throat and left her to die?

Had she, too, prayed?

"Hi, Christy," he crooned, in that terrible high-pitched voice that had been haunting her dreams. She heard it with nightmarish clarity over her pounding heart, over the rasp of his breathing, over the roar of the rain. Even as she registered this final confirmation that it was indeed him, the man who had attacked her in the cottage, even as she gathered herself together, prepared to fight, to scream, to do what she could to survive, he shoved something hard and cold into her neck.

No.

The pain was sudden and sharp and terrifying. Then it was — gone. She felt nothing. Nothing at all. Darkness rolled over her like an incoming tide, and she fell away into oblivion.

17

She wasn't heavy, but her limp body was awkward, especially now that it was wet with rain and slippery with mud. Strong as he was, he had to struggle to lift her, and even when he got her over his shoulder it was difficult to keep her in place.

Damn the rain anyway, it was complicating everything.

For one thing, he was in his work truck, not his camper. He hadn't really thought he'd be able to take her, not tonight, so he wasn't as prepared as he might have been.

But just as he had known she would, the pretty little gazelle had finally ventured within reach. He'd been patient, even though he didn't really have time for patience. He'd been following her, waiting for his chance, knowing that sooner or later it would come. His chance always came.

When her car had come swooping out of the garage, he'd been caught by surprise, though, he had to admit. He'd thought she was fixed there for the night, and he'd just decided that urgent as the need to take her was, he didn't want to chance another break-in. What she'd bought that day had been a factor; if she was buying bullets, she had to have a gun. No way was he risking getting himself shot. Now that she was on guard, it would be better to try to take her unawares, sometime when she was out and about.

Like tonight.

With one arm clamped around her body to hold her in place, he trudged toward her car, his head bent against the downpour. The field was a sea of mud. It sucked at his feet, making walking difficult. He tried to hurry, because it was always possible that someone would come along and catch him in their headlights, or see her car smashed against the tree. But he didn't have his usual strength. The beast was asleep, and he was on his own.

It was because of her hair. He hated it. It was ugly. It turned him off. What she had done to herself amounted to a desecration. Even Terri was more attractive to him now. More attractive to the beast.

Which was probably just as well.

They knew he was here. Which meant that, as much as he liked his tropical paradise, he was going to have to leave. To stay in the game he required fresh pastures and anonymity.

The newspaper article about him had been a wake-up call. He'd picked one up at the hardware store and read it, and even before he'd finished he'd known that he was finished in the Outer Banks. He was going to have to pack up and get out. They'd be hunting him again, the cops, coming after him with their computers and their DNA bases and their profilers. It was déjà vu all over again.

It was too bad, because he liked it here. Beach babes were his thing, he'd discovered. A girl in a bikini held no surprises. What you saw was what you got.

He liked that they'd given him a name, too: the Beachcomber. That was pretty cool, like the Zodiac or the Green River Killer or Son of Sam. Not every serial killer got a handle. It gave him a certain cachet.

If his old man had been alive, he would have been proud.

But his old man had been stupid, and now he was dead.

He, on the other hand, intended to live a long and productive life. But in order to do that, he was going to have to find a new hunting ground. And get rid of Christy Petrino, the one witness who could identify him.

But now he'd done that. She and her car were going to disappear tonight, never to be seen again. He'd hang around for a little while, a couple of weeks maybe, so that his departure didn't raise any red flags, and then he'd disappear, too.

Only unlike Christy, he'd still be alive and doing his thing somewhere else.

At the thought, he smiled. Then as he reached her car and slid her off his shoulder, he had a thought: maybe he should head for California.

They had beaches, and he'd always liked that Beach Boys song about California girls.

18

Luke lay still in the dark, cramped space, trying to work out where he was and what had happened. He remembered watching Christy: having changed her wet clothes for shorts, a T-shirt, and sandals, she had been rushing from room to room, cramming things into a suitcase, clearly getting ready to leave the safe confines of the cottage. For where? That was the million-dollar question. He remembered frowning blackly at the monitor as he'd tried to work that out. Was she meeting someone? She had received no calls. . . .

Didn't matter, had been his thought. Wherever she went, he was going to have to follow her. He was dead tired, ticked off, turned on, and facing the prospect of cleaning cat crap off his bed, but no matter: whither the man-trap next door went, he went, too. Lucky he'd filled the Explorer up with gas while she'd been busy wreaking havoc on her hair. Lucky too that

301

he'd outfitted her Camry with a homing device just in case she should try something stupid, like taking off for an unknown destination in the middle of a dark and stormy night. Such a night was, as he knew from experience, one of the very worst times to try to tail someone in a vehicle. He'd have to hang back, way back, or risk having her pick up his headlights in her mirror. As spooked as she was, that wasn't something she was likely to overlook. And given how little traffic tended to hit the streets in the wee hours on Ocracoke, he'd be doubly hard to miss. The homing device, which he'd installed more as a prudent backup than out of any real expectation of needing it, was going to prove to be a godsend tonight.

"Check the signal for the homing device," he'd called to Gary as he'd yanked on a shirt and dry jeans.

"Not picking it up." Luke remembered Gary saying that, and remembered cursing in response.

Then the rest of it came back to him in a rush. After glances at the various monitoring devices Gary had set up had confirmed that the homing device really, truly was not coming through and that Christy was still packing, he had taken advantage

302

of the brief window of time he had calculated he still had before she headed out to try to figure out what was wrong with the transmitter. Armed with a flashlight, he'd sprinted through the rain to her garage, slipped inside — he now had keys to her cottage *and* her car, so slipping inside had been as easy as unlocking the overhead door and ducking beneath it — and popped her trunk. The homing device was in the spare wheel well. He had leaned in, lifted the carpet, shined the flashlight into the cavity in search of the ugly little black plastic bug — and heard the door that connected the kitchen to the garage open.

Yipes. In the split second he'd had to consider Christy's reaction when she flipped on the overhead light and discovered him in her garage, he'd rolled into the trunk, which offered the only hope of concealment in the otherwise bare garage. By the time the garage light had come on as predicted, he'd had the trunk closed all but the tiniest little bit. Then he'd heard the click that had told him that she was using the button on her key ring to unlock her trunk.

Shit, like the total pain in the ass the woman had proved to be, she probably aimed to stow her suitcase in the trunk.

With something on the order of *explain this* running through his mind, he'd rolled to the back and pulled the carpet up over himself as best he could and tried to make himself as inconspicuous as possible, no easy task when his knees were practically under his chin and dust was shooting up his nose from the dislodged carpet, making him need to sneeze in the worst way.

If she looked into the trunk, she was going to think that her carpet was about nine months pregnant, which was something that he, himself, if he observed such a phenomenon in his own trunk, would instantly check out. Fortunately, she apparently didn't look. The suitcase whacked into his knee, his knee smacked his nose, and the trunk slammed closed.

Just like that, he and the suitcase and the carpet and the dust were alone in the dark. The car rocketed backward down the driveway, slammed to a shuddering halt and then headed in the opposite direction in a way guaranteed to make him carsick before many minutes had passed. Eyes watering, cursing under his breath, legs already starting to cramp up from just the thought that he couldn't straighten them out, he gave vent to a mighty sneeze that snuck up on him while he wasn't paying attention. Then he froze as it occurred to him that it was loud enough to have reached her ears. But she kept on driving without so much as touching the brake, so after a moment or two he was able to count himself safe. Hopefully the rain that was drumming like a crazed bongo player all over the car would cover up any sounds — like another sneeze, which he felt coming on — he might inadvertently make.

He'd been in tighter spots, more dangerous spots, more uncomfortable spots, no doubt about that. But from the moment he'd registered that Christy had, unknowingly, locked him in her trunk while he was supposed to be keeping her under surveillance, he hadn't been able to think of a single more ridiculous one.

The good news was, he wasn't going to lose her anytime soon. The bad news was, when she reached her destination he was going to have to somehow spring himself from the trunk and find a phone to use to call Gary, while managing to keep an eye on Christy at the same time.

Getting out of the trunk, while difficult, was doable. He could use the little multipurpose tool on his key ring to spring the lock, he didn't doubt, though it might take several minutes more than he had to spare if he didn't want to lose track of Christy. If that didn't work, he could probably kick his way out through the backseat. Or shoot his way out, if it came to that.

But, damn! He'd left his gun in the Explorer's glove compartment along with his cell phone, because as far as keeping Christy under surveillance was concerned, the Explorer had been his method of transportation of choice.

The trunk of her car had never even entered his head as an option.

Gary was going to have a field day with this. At the thought of how fast the tale was going to find its way up through the Bureau's ranks, Luke winced. He'd live it down, though, he knew — on a cold day in hell.

Having braced himself as well as he could against the bumps and sways and done his best not to think about what felt like the blazing speed at which they were moving, he'd just had a lapse in his positive thinking and was reflecting on what a scary driver Christy was when — *crash!* — the car had been hit by another vehicle. They went off the road, and all of a sudden he was bouncing around like a pebble in a wind machine.

The last thing he remembered was

fetching up with a mighty *wham* against something solid. That recollection brought realization with it: there'd been a wreck. Suddenly alert, he sniffed the air. No gas fumes. No smoke. Thank God, there didn't seem to be any fire.

Now that he knew what had happened, he realized that he must have blacked out on impact. Quickly he took stock of his situation: he was still in the trunk, curved around her small suitcase, his head aching in a way that reinforced his impression that it had taken a good solid blow when they'd hit. The car wasn't moving. Except for the never-say-die rain, there was no sound.

Christy.

Prickles of alarm had him lifting his head and tensing as he listened intently. Where was she? Had she been hurt in the wreck?

Damn the woman anyway, she was more trouble than his last ten girlfriends and his last ten surveillance jobs combined.

He didn't hear a thing other than rain, which was not, in his opinion, a good sign. He pictured her draped unconscious over the steering wheel, broken and bleeding, and felt a surge of fear so strong that it was probably going to bother him when he had time to think about the implications. At the moment, though, he didn't have that kind of time.

He had to get out of the damned trunk.

Being trapped in such cramped quarters had one advantage, he quickly realized. By feeling around in the dark, he was able to locate his flashlight in a matter of seconds. Finding his Weatherman tool was even easier: he could feel it stabbing into his ass, which was pressed hard against the back of the trunk. He was just fishing it out of his pocket when a *thump* not far above his ear announced the presence of someone — or something — else in the vicinity. Christy? Was she up and about? The sound had resulted from someone or something bumping the trunk lid right over his head.

Another *thump*, this time just above the left taillight, made him fairly certain that the sound hadn't come from something like a falling branch. He was almost sure it was Christy — who else could it be? — moving down the length of the car, leaning or falling against it as she went.

The good news was, she wasn't dead or injured to the point of immobility. The bad news was, if she was moving normally she wouldn't have been bumping so heavily into the car.

Maybe she was still woozy from the wreck.

On that semicomforting thought, Luke hesitated, weighing two possible responses to the situation: he could disclose his presence with a yell, or he could stay quiet, wait for Christy to go away, disable the interior light that would be a dead giveaway if there was a witness within miles when the trunk opened, and then get out of the trunk on his own and try to figure out what was what.

With a lightning vision of Christy's face if she should discover him locked in her trunk, he opted to keep his mouth shut and hang tight.

The cricketlike chirp of the button on her key ring that opened the trunk being depressed hit him about the same way the sound of a gun being cocked next to his head would have. Eyes widening, he froze.

For whatever the hell screwy reason, Christy was trying to get into her trunk. Fortunately for him, the automatic trunk release apparently wasn't working properly. Which gave him time to pull up the carpet and roll beneath it again as the tiny but unmistakable clink of metal scraping against metal told him that she had given up on the button and was sliding her key into the lock.

The trunk opened, the interior light came on, and for a moment Luke held his breath as rain and wind rushed in. He smelled the damp, felt the cool night air curl beneath the carpet, got a face full of dust, clamped his nose tight against the threatening sneeze, and braced himself for possible discovery.

And racked his brain for an excuse: *I just happened to be in the vicinity* . . .

He heard a thud and felt the bounce of the shocks as something heavy was deposited almost on top of him. A moment later the trunk closed with a solid *thunk* that made the whole car shake.

The darkness was once again absolute. He no longer had any room to move. Whatever was now in the trunk was lying partially on top of him and took up most of the remaining space. It smelled of earth, he realized as he struggled out from beneath the carpet. It was a heavy, inert object that — he touched it experimentally — was soaking wet. And resilient. And curved . . .

And had hair. Dripping hair that was perhaps six to eight inches long. What had been lying on top of him was part of a shoulder and an outflung arm. Pushing it over, his hand first touched and then closed around a narrow wrist, then slid down to find a soft palm and slender fingers.

His breathing suspended.

Christy. The horrible premonition became a certainty as his hand moved over her face. With a certain amount of grimness he realized that, just like the silkiness of her skin, the shape of her features was branded on his brain now: rounded forehead, high cheekbones, delicate nose, pointed chin. Getting so familiar with his bait that he could recognize her face by touch in pitch darkness had never been part of his game plan. But the game had gone wrong from the start, and now, like it or not, all he could do was play the cards remaining in his hand. And the plain truth was, he had the hots for her big time. Knowing that he could have had her, that for whatever reason she'd been more than willing, that he was the one who had walked away, was driving him nuts. Under different circumstances he would have walked barefoot over hot coals to get to her bed, but the circumstances weren't different. Staying close — but not too close — to her was his job, damn it. Still, she wasn't just bait anymore to him. She was

Christy, sexy and smart and vulnerable and scared. Even more than he wanted to capture Michael DePalma, he realized, he wanted to keep Christy safe. So far, he seemed to be doing a piss-poor job of both.

Her lips were parted, those soft, seductive lips that had all but driven him out of his mind not much more than an hour before, but he could detect no air passing through them. Cold fear clamped like a fist around his heart. With desperate haste, his fingers slid to the soft hollow beneath her ear. She was alive, he registered with relief. Unconscious, but alive. Her pulse was beating, faint but detectable.

One thing was sure: she had not ended up in the trunk as a result of any accident.

Taking a deep breath, surprised at how fast his own pulse was racing, Luke fumbled for and located the flashlight and was just about to turn it on Christy when a strange metallic grating noise from up near the front of the car stopped him cold.

What in hell was that?

The short answer was, nothing good.

Heart thudding, senses so attuned to what was happening outside the car that he was almost positive that he could hear the slosh of footsteps as someone moved around in the rain, Luke lay very still, listening. Clearly, the someone who had put Christy into the trunk had not gone away. It was almost certainly the same someone who had broken into her cottage and buried a hatchet in her shoulder. He would be willing to bet a large portion of his yearly salary that that someone was connected with Michael DePalma. Rage, primitive in its strength and intensity, surged through him, warming his blood, tightening his muscles. Women were disposable to Donnie Jr., as he had already learned. But the bastard wasn't going to dispose of Christy. Not if he could help it.

The problem was, at this juncture he might not be able to do a whole hell of a lot to help it. Locked in the trunk as they were, he and Christy were sitting ducks. A couple of bullets fired through the lid, and they were done. Or a lit rag shoved into the gas line. Or . . .

The possibilities were many and varied. The bottom line was, thanks to his own damned carelessness the two of them were now easy to kill. The one thing that was in their favor was that whoever this bastard was, he clearly had no idea that there was anyone in the trunk besides Christy. That being the case, the best thing he could do was be quiet and await an opportunity.

Now that he'd had a chance to think the situation through, Luke realized that he didn't dare use the flashlight for fear that its glow might show through the cracks. Moving as little as possible so as to make no noise that might attract the bastard's attention to the trunk, listening carefully to the grating sound that continued to mystify him, he carefully felt Christy's skull, her neck, her arms and legs and torso, checking for blood or any obvious injuries or wounds.

He didn't find anything, but that didn't mean she wasn't grievously hurt. She could be dying right there beside him and he wouldn't know.

At the thought, he broke into a cold sweat.

The grating sound stopped.

Instantly refocusing, Luke concentrated all his attention on what was going on outside the car. He could hear an assortment of just-loud-enough-to-be-heard-over-the-rain sounds, but precisely what they were or what they portended he had no idea. One thing, though, he knew with icy certainty: the object of this exercise was to kill Christy. Just what form the attempt would take he had no clue. He only hoped that he wasn't about to find out.

A thud almost directly over his head made him tense up. Trying to get enough purchase for his feet so that, if the trunk opened, he could immediately go on the attack, he hit the suitcase, shoving it a couple of inches along the wall. The sharp scraping sound it made paralyzed him. Had it been loud enough to have been heard by someone outside? There was no way to tell; he could no longer hear anything except rain. Nothing thumped. Nothing moved. Was someone out there listening, perhaps suspecting that Christy was conscious and moving? Was a weapon even now being trained on the trunk? If so, there wasn't a thing he could do.

It was a damnable realization.

Heart thumping, listening so intently now that he barely dared to breathe, he waited for a gunshot, for the trunk to spring open as the bastard decided to investigate, for something.

But the next sound he heard came from the front of the car. There was a muffled rattle of metal on metal, a jerk, and then the front end was hoisted into the air until it reached a near-forty-degree angle. He slid into Christy's inert form before he could catch himself, squashing her against the bottom of the trunk. She made a pitiful little sound that was somewhere between a whimper and a moan.

Had he hurt her? Was she in pain? The thought that she might be hurt and in pain made him wild.

"Christy?" It was a husky whisper.

No answer.

Cursing under his breath, Luke pushed himself off her, shoved the suitcase out of the way, then maneuvered his arms around her and tried to roll. In the close confines of the trunk, this was no easy task, but at last he managed to reverse their positions so that he was wedged in at the bottom of the trunk and she, still heavily unconscious, lay against him. She was cold to the touch, wet and limp as a rag doll. He wrapped his arms around her, trying to warm her, trying to protect her from as much of the merciless jolting as he could. In the process he, too, got soaked through. His hands moved over her again, carefully feeling the back of her neck, sliding the length of her spine, moving over her ass, her thighs. No obvious injuries. No warm stickiness that might be blood.

Thank God.

The car lurched slowly forward, bumping over the ground.

The blow to the head he'd suffered must be making him a little slow on the uptake, Luke decided. Because it was suddenly crystal clear what was happening: the grating sound he'd heard had been a chain being wrapped around the front axle. Add that to the weird angle and the uneven forward motion, and it didn't require any great feat of brainpower to figure out that the car was being towed.

And not by Triple A.

Jesus, that was bad, and it got worse the more he thought about it. There were cliffs on the island, tall rocky cliffs leaning out over the ocean, over Pamlico Sound. At this time of night, the tide was coming in. It would be an easy thing to drop a car over a cliff. By morning, it would be gone without a trace. There was a scrap yard, too, at the island's northern end; crushing a car into a cube the size of a cereal box was a time-honored mob method for eliminating the people inside.

Okay, first order of business: get out of the damned car.

"Christy." Pushing aside the sodden strands of her hair, Luke spoke softly into her ear. No response.

The car lurched wildly, and bounced and then the ride suddenly got a whole lot smoother. They also picked up speed. From this, Luke deduced that they were now traveling on pavement.

Wherever they were headed, they were getting closer to their destination by the minute.

"Christy."

Rubbing her cold, limp arms, he willed her to regain consciousness. He didn't know what their destination was, but he did know he didn't want to find out. They had to get out of the trunk, and the sooner the better. Preferably now, while the going was relatively good. Once the car stopped and whatever was going to happen started happening, the situation was probably going to get a whole lot hairier fast.

"Christy, wake up."

If he had to, he could probably spring the trunk, drop with her to the ground, then throw her dead weight over his shoulder and make tracks for the nearest phone, he calculated. Christy wasn't heavy, certainly not so heavy that he couldn't carry her to safety. The difficulty arose in getting her out of the trunk without either of them getting hurt. A limp body was notoriously difficult to handle, and dropping from the open trunk of a tilted, moving vehicle with her in his arms would be tricky, to say the least. Not that it wasn't doable, but it would be a lot easier on both of them if she was conscious and cooperating.

But whether she was conscious or not, he was going to have to make a move soon. At the speed they were now traveling, they were going to get wherever they were going way too fast for patience to be an option.

"Christy, I need you to wake up." His tone urgent now, he lightly smacked both cheeks. He was rewarded by a deep, shuddering indrawing of her breath, and then a kind of incoherent murmur. Inwardly cursing the darkness because he couldn't see, literally, his hand in front of his face, he felt something brush his cheek which, given their respective positions, he thought — hoped — might be her hair. Was her head moving?

"Christy, can you hear me?"

She responded with another of those incoherent little murmurs.

"Christy, it's Luke. I need you to wake up right now."

She stirred against him.

"L— Luke?"

Her voice was weak, a mere thread of sound, but he'd never been so glad to hear anything in his life. Luke let out a breath that he hadn't realized he had been holding.

"Yeah. Look, do you feel any pain anywhere?"

"Pain?"

Unsurprisingly, she sounded more than a little disoriented. But she was conscious and moving, and that was the main thing. He could feel her weight shifting, feel the nudge of her knees as she sought and failed to find room to stretch out her legs. Her head was resting on his chest, and he could feel the tilting of her chin as, he thought, she tried to look up at him, fruitlessly because of how dark it was. He was now every bit as wet as she was, thanks to the puddle that had dripped off her and that he was now lying in, but where their bodies touched, instead of him having grown cold, she seemed to have absorbed some of his warmth.

"Where are we?" She was clearly groggy.

"In the trunk of your car. Christy, listen to me: are you hurt?"

He could hear her breathing, feel the rise and fall of her chest against his. A beat passed. Her body tensed in his arms.

"Oh my God, he ran me off the road! The white truck — he bumped me on purpose. And then . . . and then when I wrecked, he chased me." Her voice was thin and shrill and agitated. "He pushed me down in the mud and" — she shuddered — "he shoved something into my neck. I thought he was going to cut my throat like . . . like . . ."

"Shh." She was breathing hard, shaking. Luke tightened his hold on her, cradling her against him. He was lying almost on his back with his legs bent at the knee, while she was draped across his chest with her legs curled up on top of him. His legs really were beginning to cramp now. He tried to stretch them out, to ease them, but there simply wasn't enough room. Grimacing, he ignored the twinges that warned of coming severe pain. "You can tell me all this later, okay? What we need to do now is get out of here as fast as we can. Can you take a quick inventory and tell me if you're hurt anywhere, please?"

He waited, arms wrapped around her, feeling the weight of her against him, listening to her breathing. It was too fast, too shallow, uneven. She lifted a hand to the side of her neck, felt it, and shuddered again.

"I . . . don't think so." She shifted and let her hand drop so that it was once again resting on his chest. Her voice quavered.

"He's still here, isn't he? That man. He's got us trapped in the trunk of my car." A beat passed as she seemed to struggle to take in the rest of the situation. "We're moving. What's happening?"

"As far as I can figure out, he knocked you unconscious, dumped you in the trunk and now he's towing the car somewhere."

"Oh God." She shivered violently. Stark fear laced her voice. "He's going to kill us."

"That seems to be the plan. Do you have any idea what kind of weapons he has? Does he have a gun?"

Christy took a deep, shuddering breath. "I don't know. I didn't see a gun. He . . . stuck something in my neck. I — now I think it might have been a stun gun."

That would explain both her unconsciousness and the lack of an obvious injury.

"Sounds right."

"Luke." There was something in the tone of her voice that warned him what was coming. "How did he get you?"

At the moment, he didn't have time to think fast.

"Tell you later," he said. "What we need to do right now is concentrate on getting out of here."

The car changed position, providing a

welcome distraction. A big jolt, followed by a slower pace and a seriously bumpy ride, made Luke think they'd gone off the road again. Not a good thing. Adrenaline surged through his veins as he realized that their journey was most likely nearing its end. He felt for his Weatherman, which he had returned to his pocket before repositioning Christy. He didn't have to search for the flashlight. He could feel it wedged uncomfortably against his thigh.

Time to go.

He kept his voice deliberately matter-of-fact. "Look, here's the plan: while he's busy towing the car to wherever, we're going to break out of the trunk and run like hell. Okay?"

A beat passed. Luke was just wondering if what he had said had sunk in when Christy said, "Okay."

It didn't take a psychic to figure out that she was still wondering how the hell he had wound up in the trunk with her. Well, a plausible lie would no doubt come easier when he wasn't preoccupied with keeping them both alive.

"Can you scoot off me a little, do you think?"

"I'll . . . try." She shifted, easing her weight away from him as best she could. It was a nice effort, but the small space and the angle at which the car was tilted kept the results from being impressive.

With both Weatherman and flashlight in hand now, Luke struggled to change positions so that he could get at the lock. It wasn't easy with a hundred twenty pounds or so of woman pressing down on top of him and no room for his legs, but the urgency of the situation was such that he managed to get his body wedged around so that he was facing the right way at last. She was now basically crouched on his back. It occurred to Luke that his task would be made infinitely easier if she held the flashlight while he worked the tiny Weatherman screwdriver. Once again he weighed the possibility that the faint glow might be able to be seen beyond the trunk. That would be good news if the driver of another vehicle should spot it and wonder at it enough to call for help; on the other hand it would be bad news if the killer should spot the light, say, through his rearview mirror, deduce from it that something was up with his victim and decide to check.

Forget the light. The risk wasn't worth it. Yet.

"What are you doing?" Christy asked after a moment, apparently unable to make sense of the sounds of him trying and so far failing to open the lock.

"Doing my best to pop the lock so we can get the hell out of here."

"Why not just use the trunk release?"

"You have a trunk release?" He felt like smacking his forehead with his palm.

"My mother made me get one installed in case I ever got kidnapped and someone locked me in my trunk. She's got a thing about things like that." Christy sounded marginally more together. He could feel her moving, feel her knees pressing down into his back as she apparently reached up behind her. "It's right up . . . *here*."

19

"Wait." Luke's voice was sharp. So sharp that Christy, who was in a major hurry to exit the premises, stopped short in the very act of wrapping her fingers around the lever.

"What?"

"Just hang on a minute, would you?"

"You're not ready to go?"

"Nope. Shh."

Shh, huh? She was dizzy, nauseated, and not, she was well aware, quite at the top of her game either mentally or physically. But the urgency of the situation was crystal clear to her nonetheless. She was alive, and she wanted to stay that way. Getting out of the trunk before her attacker could return for her was key. She'd never thought that she would live to be grateful for her mother's tendency to see the dark cloud in every silver lining, but she was. The trunk release really might, as her mother had insisted when she'd nagged her into getting it installed, save her life one day. Like today.

But only if she used it. She wanted to yank that puppy in the worst way. Before, claustrophobia had always been an abstract concept. But she was starting to feel as if she were suffocating. She could barely move, barely breathe. Luke's big body took up almost all the available space. Curled into what was basically a fetal position against his back, she was starting to gasp for breath. Was she on the verge of a panic attack? she wondered desperately. She'd never had one, but she'd seen them, and if ever there was an occasion for her to become personally acquainted with what one felt like, this would be it. What little air there was in the trunk was stale and smelled of mold. To make matters worse, her neck was stiff and sore, her entire right side felt like it was being rubbed raw as she was jostled up and down over the scratchy carpet, and the hard plastic edge of her suitcase stabbed painfully into her spine with every bump. The car rocked from side to side and bounced up and down at the same time, which was making her want to lose her lasagna. But the physical discomfort she was suffering was nothing compared to her fear. She was so terrified she could taste it. The sharp vinegary tang that rose up from the back of her throat like bile was nothing but pure terror reflux, she knew.

"What are you *doing?*" she hissed after what felt like an eternity had passed. She could sense him moving, feel the muscles in his back bunching, hear a series of strange little sounds that sounded vaguely mechanical, but what it all added up to she had no clue.

"Shh."

"Listen, I don't mean to rush you or anything, but you've got about a second and then I'm out of here, with you or without you." If there was more than a touch of sarcasm underlying that, then so be it.

"Shh."

Christy swallowed an urge to tell him to take that *shh* and shove it. Whatever he was doing, it couldn't be important enough to keep them where they were so much as a moment longer. There was no time to waste. Even as woozy as she still felt, she knew that. They had to get out of the trunk before her attacker could do whatever it was he was planning to do to her. She didn't know precisely what that was, but she did know what the end result was supposed to be.

At the thought of how very close she'd already come to dying, her breathing quickened to the point where the thought of having a panic attack had to take a backseat to the worry that she might be going to hyperventilate.

"Luke. . . ."

"There." Luke grunted with obvious satisfaction. Then, to her, "I cut some wires so that the interior light won't come on when we open the trunk."

"Oh." Okay, so maybe that *had* been worth waiting for. She took a deep, cleansing breath, trying to force out both fear and excess carbon dioxide. "Good idea."

"Yeah. Listen. I'm going to count to three, then you're going to hit the trunk release. When the trunk opens we're going to jump. Roll when you hit, stay low, then run for whatever cover's available. If for some reason I'm not right with you, don't wait for me."

"Yes, okay." No worries there, mate. Her one thought was that once she hit the ground she wasn't going to stop running until she was clear back home in Philadelphia.

"One. Two. Three."

Christy yanked the trunk release. There was a click, but the trunk didn't open. Panic knotted her stomach, tightened the already achy muscles in her throat.

"I said *three*."

"It didn't open," she said, her voice reedy.

"Shit." She could feel him shifting position. "I heard it unlock. Something probably got damaged in the wreck. Okay, hang on."

She felt his body surge upward, heard a thump as he apparently shoved hard against the lid above their heads. Just like that the trunk popped open. The lid swung up, then down, then bobbed with every bump. The rain had finally stopped, but the smell of damp was suddenly strong — and welcome, oh so welcome. Just like the warm rush of air that now blew through their little space, it symbolized freedom.

"Ready? Jump."

Tumble was more the word for what Christy did. With his hand locked around her wrist, Luke leaped, and, since her legs had proved surprisingly weak on the push off, she was more or less yanked out behind him. She fell like a brick and hit hard, landing on her hands and knees in inches-deep mud that at least served to cushion the fall. Little droplets of mud splattered up over her even as the shock of the landing shot through her shoulders and hips. She ignored the pain in favor of a quick, terrified glance over her shoulder. It told her that the truck, with her car attached like a laboriously wagging tail, continued on, its headlights cutting twin swaths through the darkness, its taillights staring back at her like small, baleful red eyes.

"You were supposed to roll." Luke's hand had dropped away from her wrist during the fall, and she had lost track of him as she landed. But he was beside her now, crouching in the mud, his head close to hers, his arm draping across her back. She felt surprisingly sick and dizzy, and the urge to flee had been supplanted by the need to collapse. For the merest instant she let her head droop against his broad shoulder. The humiliation she had suffered at his hands earlier had been pushed to the back of her mind, to be revisited when and if circumstances improved. She could see no more of him now than a dark shape, and she could not by the most convoluted stretch of her imagination figure out how he had wound up in her trunk, but she was suddenly overwhelmingly glad he was there.

"I forgot."

"You okay?"

"Yes."

"Then let's go."

His arm tightened, urging her forward. Summoning every last bit of strength she possessed, Christy scrambled with him toward the piney woods that lined either side of the narrow dirt track they'd landed on. That old saw about the spirit being willing but the flesh being weak seemed to definitely apply in her case, she discovered. Her muscles were as unreliable as cheap paper plates and her bones seemed to be nonexistent.

Up ahead, taillights flared. She and Luke were beneath the trees, sliding down a shallow, muddy slope that cut away from the track, when she caught the sudden bright flash out of the corner of her eye.

"Shit," Luke said, having apparently seen the same thing. His hand clasped hers now. Even as his grip tightened almost painfully, Christy processed what that brilliant little burst of red meant.

The truck had stopped. The flare had been the brake lights coming on.

Did the killer somehow know they were gone? Had he seen something? Had he seen them? At the thought, Christy's heart gave a great leap in her chest.

"Run," Luke growled in her ear, and took off.

Oh, yeah.

She didn't say it aloud. She couldn't. She didn't have enough breath. There was one good thing about abject terror, as she had already discovered: it could be counted on to provide a burst of energy when it was most needed. A moment ago, she would have thought that leaping through the undergrowth like a champion hurdler was beyond her. But she was doing it, and the way she felt at the moment she could keep on doing it all night. From somewhere in the vicinity of the truck, she heard a muffled thud, as if from something — like the trunk lid — being slammed down in frustration. Several scared glances over her shoulder later, she saw that the taillights were once again glowing a soft, steady red, with none of the brash brightness that signaled applied brakes. The only problem was, the dull red circles seemed to be growing larger rather than smaller.

Christy realized with a sinking sensation in the pit of her stomach that the truck was backing up.

He'd checked the trunk. He knew they were gone. She knew it with a kind of hideous certainty that defied logical explanation.

"Luke, Luke . . ." She tugged on his hand to warn him. Head lowered against the droplets their passage was dislodging from the trees, he was hauling her after him in their mad dash through the undergrowth.

"What?" He slowed, glancing around. Not that he could see her any better than she could see him. With the canopy blocking most of the night sky, it was even darker under the trees than it was out in the open. But she could see the shape of him, see the dark oval that was his head, the square of his shoulders, the gleam of his eyes.

"Look." She didn't have to specify at what. From the way his hand tightened on hers, she knew that he realized the significance of those enlarging lights just as well as she did. Thank goodness they were far enough away now where the chance of them being overtaken was — she prayed — small.

The brake lights flared again. Christy wasn't sure, but it seemed to her that the truck was stopping approximately in the place where they'd jumped out.

"Luke. . . ."

"Keep moving."

She *was* moving, just at a slower pace than before. Her legs were starting to remember how weak they felt, and her lungs were aching as a way of protesting her decision to run like a bat out of hell and breathe at the same time.

"What the hell's that?" There was a definite frown in Luke's voice.

Looking back up the slope they'd just traversed, through the tree trunks and drooping branches and tangled undergrowth, Christy saw the brilliant white beam of light making a broad sweep through the woods closest to the track. It hit her then that they'd probably made a pretty big hole in the undergrowth as they'd torn through it. Big enough to track them by? *Obvious* enough to track them by?

She discovered that she really didn't want to know the answer to that.

"He's hunting us," she said in a hollow voice.

"Yeah." Hand tightening on hers, he picked up the pace again.

Panting with terror and exertion, Christy ducked her head against the cascading droplets and ran, slip-sliding on the carpet of muddy, slimy pine needles and God knew what else underfoot, dodging around trees, clambering over fallen logs and other obstructions. Heart pounding, legs and lungs aching, she hung on to Luke's hand as if it were a lifeline in a raging sea.

They'd gone far enough and fast enough that the flashlight was no longer visible, if indeed he was still using it. The thought that he might have turned it off, that he might be right on their heels and they would never know until he sprang, sent cold chills down Christy's spine. Glancing over her shoulder proved useless; she could see nothing but the very nearest trees, and them only as shapes. The sound of her own breathing was loud in her ears; loud enough, she feared, to block out any signs of pursuit.

But she was sure, in her heart of hearts, that he was still pursuing them. From the way Luke was moving, he thought so, too. He was as relentless as an automaton, no longer running but moving at a fast, steady pace. She got a stitch in her side, and her legs grew more and more rubbery and her breathing more and more labored, but still she managed to keep up.

Her attacker had caught her once. Miraculously, she had survived that encounter. If he caught her again . . .

The thought, and the hideous images that went along with it, made her go cold all over. It also gave her the strength, and will, to go on.

With her practically scooting on her backside, they made it down another steep slope into a ravine, forded a small stream that coursed swiftly through its center, and clambered back up the other side. By that time Christy had figured out that they must be somewhere in the dense maritime forest that covered a good portion of the northern third of the island, but they'd run so far and so fast that she could not have told which way the road was, much less which direction to take to reach Ocracoke Village or any other place where they might reasonably expect to find help. All she knew was that the forest, a protected wilderness preserve where only the most gung-ho hikers and campers ever ventured, stretched on for something like forty miles.

At their current pace, even if they were traveling directly from point A to point B, which they weren't, it would take them a day or two to walk out. For the next few hours at least, her attacker could hunt them at his leisure.

That thought made her good to go for at least another couple of miles.

Finally her legs gave out and she could go no farther. She was so exhausted she could hardly stand. Pulling her hand from Luke's, she sat on a fallen log, breathing hard, willing her jellied muscles to toughen up even as she cast wary but fruitless looks into the surrounding darkness. A gleam of green down near the forest floor startled her; her heart leaped into her throat before she realized that what she was seeing was eyes. Several pairs of eyes.

Creature eyes. Wild, nocturnal creature eyes. Having such creatures nearby was better than having the green gleam auger the arrival on the scene of her attacker, definitely. However, it could not actually be considered good.

She only hoped that whatever was looking at her wasn't some kind of carnivore.

"What's up?" Luke retraced his steps to hunker down in front of her. She couldn't see his features, but she got the impression that he was frowning at her.

"This forest . . . goes on for miles." Her breathing was obviously labored.

"So?"

"I need a break."

"We'll take a break when we're safe somewhere."

"We need a plan."

"We've got a plan."

"Want to fill me in?"

"Run like hell." She couldn't be sure, of

course, but from the sound of his voice he was smiling.

"Oh, good plan." Okay, so she wasn't too tired to indulge in a little sarcasm.

"Hey, it's working so far."

"Until he catches us."

"Regular little optimist, aren't you?" There was that smile in his voice again. If she hadn't been exhausted to the point of near catatonia, aching in every muscle, joint, and major organ, and terrified out of her mind to boot, she might have found that hint of suppressed humor charming. As it was, she didn't.

"You know, just for the record, there really is a bad guy back there who really, really, really wants to kill us," she said.

"I'm aware."

"We've done the run-like-hell thing. Now we need to start thinking this through."

"I'm all ears."

Christy frowned. So much for a brilliant contribution from her partner in terrified flight. That meant it was all up to her. Was that the story of her life, or what? Usually, though, she managed to come through. Unfortunately, right now she was so tired she could barely form a coherent thought.

"Okay." She did her best with what brainpower she could summon. "Maybe we should try to find the road. You know, flag somebody down?"

"Yeah, we could definitely try that. When it's light. Like tomorrow. For now, even if we could find the road, which is doubtful, and even if there was any traffic on it, which is equally doubtful, flagging somebody down would be too dangerous. We wouldn't be able to tell if it was him or not until he stopped, and then it might be too late. Even if he didn't use it on you, I wouldn't want to bet my life that he doesn't have a gun."

Good point.

Christy didn't say it aloud. Instead she gritted her teeth, turned a deaf ear to her protesting body parts, and stood up. He stood up with her.

"So what's the plan?" He recaptured her hand.

"For want of an alternative, I'm going with run like hell," she said wryly. Run was an exaggeration, of course. Stumble was just about all she was capable of at the moment. If she hadn't already locked her knees in place, they would have collapsed beneath her.

"That's my girl." This time she was sure he was smiling. He carried her hand to his lips and pressed his mouth to her knuckles.

"If it will make you feel any better, I'm really good at navigating by the stars."

That did make her feel better — for about two seconds. Then she glanced up. "We can't see any stars!"

"There's that," Luke said, and chuckled. "Okay, so how about we go with water always runs toward the sea? See that stream over there? How about we follow that?"

Christy looked. Sure enough, just close enough to be visible she saw the merest glimmer of a shiny black surface snaking across the forest floor.

Staring at it, she frowned. Her gaze swung back to him.

"*Does* water always run toward the sea?"

She saw the quick gleam of his teeth through the darkness.

"There's one way to find out."

Still holding the hand he had kissed, he turned and started moving again through the tangled thicket that covered the forest floor. Somewhat less than reassured, Christy followed. But her knuckles still tingled from the touch of his mouth, and her thoughts had been given a whole new and entirely more pleasant direction. For a few blissful seconds she forgot all about her surroundings as she recalled in vivid detail just exactly how she knew that he was a really hot kisser.

Even if he had turned her down moments after she'd made the initial discovery.

Okay, there went the bliss, popped on contact with reality just like a soap bubble.

So give the man an A on foreplay and an F on follow-through, she told herself savagely. And put the whole humiliating episode out of your mind.

They kept going until she was staggering, until her legs were quivering and her feet felt like lead and she was absolutely, positively, sure that she would collapse with every step she took. Finally he stopped and dropped her hand.

"Luke?" She vaguely missed the warm comfort of his grip. Realizing that she'd been left alone in the dark perked her up — a little. A very little. Actually, after the first niggle of alarm she pretty much reverted to the apathy that had dulled her senses for the last couple of miles. Her new basic attitude was, if her attacker caught up, so be it. She was so exhausted that she didn't even feel afraid at the prospect. At least if she were dead she would no longer have to move.

His hushed voice seemed to come from several yards away. "Hear that? I think it might be the sea."

Now that she was actively listening, Christy definitely heard a kind of roar. Unfortunately, she was pretty sure it was only her poor overworked pulse drumming in her ears. Squinting in the general direction of Luke's voice, she thought she saw him moving through the trees.

She was just starting to stagger toward him when someone grabbed her arm.

20

He'd found them.

Heart in throat, Christy levitated about three feet in the air, yanking her arm free. She would have screamed like a steam whistle, too, but unfortunately her throat had closed up so tight from fear that the only sound that emerged was a terrified squeak.

"Be quiet," a voice whispered, and the hand touched her arm again. Christy jerked her arm free, looked desperately around, and started backing away.

More figures flitted through the trees, surrounding her, dark shapes closing in —

Oh my God, he'd multiplied. Serial killer times six. No, seven.

"L— Luke," she choked out, still with considerably less volume than the situation required. The figures were closer now, crowding in on all sides, making eerie little shushing sounds as they ringed her.

"Keep still," one of the figures breathed.

"You'll scare them."

Them who? Christie wondered wildly, as visions of the X-files danced in her head. This was definitely not her attacker, but that did not necessarily mean the situation was good. Had they stumbled upon a satanic cult? A coven of witches? An alien landing? *Survivor Forest?*

"Wh— who are you?" Christy got out as Luke heard or saw enough to make him realize that something was wrong and came loping back through the trees.

"We're here for the turtles," came the whisper, at the same time as a louder, sharper, "I think we've got eggs!" had the group dispersing faster than mist in the sun.

"What the hell is this?" Luke reached her seconds after the group surged past him on urgent, silent feet.

"No clue, but they think they've got eggs," she whispered with semi-hysterical humor. Whatever these extremely odd people were up to, they at least did not seem intent on causing her or Luke bodily harm, which made them top of the trees in her book.

"Let's see if they can help us. They're bound to have a car. Or a cell phone." Luke caught her hand, dragging her ruth-

lessly after him when her tired legs threatened to balk. Only the dazzling thought
that help was at hand enabled her to keep
up.

The group was crouched behind a tangle
of bushes and vines at the very edge of the
trees. Christy looked past them to discover
that the thick woods gave way to a narrow
beach that sloped down toward the ocean.
Beneath the trees, it was so dark that she
could barely see. Beyond them the sand
was a creamy curve sandwiched between
the charcoal shadows of the forest and the
gleaming onyx sea.

"Listen, we need help," Luke said,
crouching down behind the group. Christy,
with some vague feeling that being the
tallest living creature in the vicinity might
not be a good thing, crouched too.

"Shh, you'll scare them." The testy whisper was thrown over the speaker's shoulder. He was male, but that was about all
Christy could tell about him.

"Them who?" Luke sounded impatient,
but he had obligingly dropped his voice to
a whisper.

"The turtles. Could you be quiet, please?
We've been waiting here for three days to
witness this."

"Yes, do be still," another voice seconded in an irritated whisper.

Having been thus thoroughly chastened, Luke fell silent. Christy could feel his seething impatience in the tension of his body, but it was clear that at the moment nothing short of a shout was going to distract this group from their purpose. And, while Christy was not opposed to a shout on general principles, interrupting such concentrated focus at a crucial moment might not endear them to their newfound fellow humans. That it might also attract the attention of the human they most wanted to avoid was the deciding factor. On the theory that being near more people was better than being near fewer people, Christy inched so close to the huddled group that she could practically inhale their carbon dioxide. They all seemed to be riveted on the beach. Looking past them, Christy tried to fathom exactly what was going on.

For a moment she saw nothing but pale beach and surging sea and night sky occasionally illuminated by the moon and a few stars. Then she spotted what looked like a dark circle in the sand. It was about the size of a hula hoop, and as Christy watched, it moved, shifting, seeming to settle itself. Then, farther down the beach, she saw another.

"Look, this is an emergency." Patience was apparently not one of Luke's virtues.

One of the group made an exasperated sound and turned around.

"If you must talk, come back here," he whispered, and, still crouching, led them away from the group. At what he apparently judged was a safe distance, he straightened. Luke and Christy, who had followed, straightened too. They were well back from the beach now, but not so far away that Christy couldn't see the creamy stripe of the sand through the trees. With the rain gone, the forest was suddenly alive with the sounds of insects and tree frogs and various other night creatures. Glancing around distrustfully, she pressed close to Luke and slid her hand into his.

"If we could just use a phone, we'll get out of your way," Luke said, his hand squeezing hers comfortingly.

"A phone? There are no phones out here. This is a protected conservation area, and . . ."

"A cell phone," Luke specified.

"We don't have cell phones. We're here watching the turtles."

Christy could practically hear Luke grinding his teeth.

"There's someone chasing us," she burst out, careful to keep her voice down on the off-chance that said someone should be within earshot. "If he catches us he'll kill us. He wrecked my car and locked us in my trunk and . . ."

"We need to borrow a car," Luke interrupted firmly.

"We don't have a car. We hiked out here. We're a *conservation group* here to watch for turtles laying eggs. We've been camped here for three days observing this beach, and it's happening *right now*. And I'm missing it."

He sounded so anguished that Christy felt compelled to apologize. "I'm sorry."

"Where are we?" Luke asked. "Is there anywhere around where we could find a phone? Or help?"

"The nearest place I know of is the convenience store at the ferry dock, and that's to the west. Probably take you four, maybe five hours to get there on foot. You need to go back the way you came, through the forest." He pointed.

Christy shuddered at the thought, and pressed closer to Luke.

"Where does the beach go? Can we hike out along the beach?" Luke asked, his voice tight with barely concealed impatience.

"It doesn't go anywhere. This is just a little protected cove with a little protected strip of sand *where the turtles come.*"

"Christy . . ." Luke's hand tightened on hers. She knew what was coming.

"Can't we just stay with them? Just till morning?" she asked. The thought of trudging back through the forest made her want to collapse where she stood. It also scared her silly. Her attacker was probably still searching for them. If he found them in the forest she and Luke would be on their own. At least if he found them here there were other people around.

"We just have the one tent. There's no room." Their would-be benefactor's voice turned grudging. "I could let you have a couple of blankets, and maybe some food. But you have to be quiet and stay out of the way."

"That would be great," Christy said fervently.

Luke was silent for a couple of beats. Then he said, "Yeah. Great."

"Good. Fine. This way." He turned and headed off through the trees. They followed. A tent had been pitched at the edge of the beach a couple of hundred yards down from where the group was observing the turtles.

"Shh," their benefactor warned, and went inside the tent. He was back within minutes, thrusting a bundle into Luke's arms. "I wish I could be more help, but . . ." He was clearly anxious to get back to his turtle watching.

"This is fine. Thanks."

"If you're going to sleep on the beach, go *that* way." He pointed away from the turtles. "We'll be here all night. If you have trouble, give us a shout."

Then he was gone, hurrying to rejoin the others.

"Come on." Luke started walking in the opposite direction, and Christy followed. They skirted the edge of the beach, staying close to the trees but walking on sand. She could still see no more than shapes, but visibility was marginally better now that they were out of the trees. A salty smelling breeze blew in from the sea, ruffling Christy's hair, making her aware that her clothes were still wet from the rain. The pounding of the surf had replaced the animal chorus, which in Christy's opinion was a good trade. Moonlight broke through the clouds intermittently.

"Not too far away," Christy said, catching Luke's arm. The idea of being able to give seven other people a shout if the need arose made her feel a little better. Then she thought of something, and her hand fell away from his arm as she stopped in her tracks. "Oh my God, what if he finds us and kills them too?"

"Unless he's packing a machine gun, that's going to be hard to do. Anyway, whoever this guy is, he doesn't want mass casualties. Both times he's come after you, you've been alone."

That was true. Christy nodded, relieved. At least, sort of relieved.

Luke finally stopped in the lee of a pair of waist-high rocks a couple of dozen yards farther on. They jutted up out of the sand like dark teeth, forming a kind of crude V, with the apex pointing toward the trees. He squatted, putting the bundle down in the sand. Christy didn't so much squat as collapse onto her knees. She was just drawing a deep breath when she heard a click, and the faintest of glows suddenly illuminated their small area. Her eyes went wide. She glanced quickly at Luke, who was just inches away checking out the contents of the bundle. His hair was damp and the ends curled in cute little ringlets around his ears and neck, a soggy, mud-splattered gray T-shirt clung to his shoulders, making them look about a yard wide, and faded jeans that were equally soggy and muddy molded the powerful muscles of his thighs. His jaw was set, there was a smudge of mud on one bronzed cheekbone, and a network of fine lines around his eyes gave silent testimony to just how tired he was. She also saw that the bundle consisted of what looked like two blankets, both beige; a couple of bottles of water; and a pack of peanut butter crackers.

More to the point, though, she saw as she sought the source of the illumination, he was holding a small flashlight in one hand. His other hand covered the lens so that only a tiny fraction of the light it would normally emit escaped through his fingers.

Under the circumstances, even a smidgen of light was too much for her. Luke might think their attacker was nowhere in the vicinity, but there was no point in giving him the opportunity to be proved wrong.

"Turn it off! He might see!"

Luke looked around at her and snorted. "Honey, believe me, you should be more worried about scaring the turtles. Tracking us at night over the kind of terrain we covered would be almost impossible."

"From your mouth to God's ears,"

Christy muttered.

"We're safe enough for now. I think."

On that reassuring note, he shifted his grip on the flashlight so that the hand holding it also covered the lens, and turned the flashlight on her.

"Hold still a minute."

He took hold of her chin and turned her face to one side. Christy realized that he was looking at the place where the object had been shoved into her neck. Whatever he saw, he didn't like. His eyes narrowed and his lips compressed.

"Yep, stun gun," he said, and released her chin.

Christy compulsively reached up to rub the tender chord in question. Meanwhile, his gaze moved over the rest of her with an almost clinical detachment. She ran self-conscious fingers through her hair, pushing the damp strands back from her forehead and tucking them behind her ears. A glance down at herself revealed that her wet white T-shirt and navy shorts clung to her like a second skin, her bare legs and arms were scratched and dirty, and her sandals were caked with mud and sand.

Not that, under the circumstances, she should care a particle about what she looked like, she told herself sternly, but the annoying part was that she did. And face the truth: the reason she cared was because of Luke. His blond surfer-dude looks had grown on her to the point where she now found him distractingly handsome, and her pride required that he should think she was hot, too. It rankled to remember that the last time they'd gotten this good a look at each other, she'd been begging him to sleep with her. It rankled more to recall what his response had been.

Basically, *Thanks, but no thanks.*

If she hadn't been so tired, the memory would have been humiliating in the extreme. But she wasn't just tired, she was exhausted, so exhausted that collapsing flat on her face in the sand had seemed like a real possibility just a few minutes ago. The exhaustion factor reduced her humiliation to no more than an uncomfortable niggle. Anyway, the memory didn't seem to be troubling him, so she did her best to push it out of her mind.

"What happened to your eye?" There was a hard edge to his voice as his gaze fixed on her left eye.

"My eye?" Christy quickly lifted a hand to the eye in question. The flesh around it felt slightly swollen and tender, now that she was paying attention. It said a lot for the trials she'd endured over the last couple of hours that she was just this moment getting around to noticing. "What's wrong with my eye?"

"You've got a bruise right here." He gently rubbed his thumb over the tender area.

"Oh, it must have been the air bag." Christy tried not to find that feather-light touch disturbing. "When the car crashed it went off and hit me in the face."

His hand dropped.

"You'll be lucky if you don't have a black eye tomorrow."

"I'll be lucky if I'm not dead tomorrow," she said glumly. "And that goes for you, too."

Something about that made him smile. The sudden twinkle in his blue eyes made her heart skip a beat. *Okay, so he's a hunk. Get over it.*

"There goes that optimistic streak of yours again."

"Yeah, well, pessimists live longer."

She yawned in a deliberate attempt to distract herself from how much she was starting to like him. Unexpectedly, the yawn turned into the real thing. She lifted a hand to her mouth too late, then sat there blinking at him in surprise through lashes that suddenly felt as heavy as anvils.

He grinned, and passed her the flashlight.

"Here, hold this for a minute, would you? Block most of the light with your hand."

Luke kept his grip on it until her hand replaced his over the lens, then stood up. He looked very tall with her kneeling at his feet and the sea and the sky forming a dark backdrop behind him, and she was just absorbing that fact when he unfurled the blanket in his hands and gave it a shake.

"Here, help me spread this out, would you?"

She had to turn the flashlight off to comply. No way was she leaving it to shine at full blast, no matter what he said.

As it turned out, the darkness was only a slight inconvenience when it came to spreading out the blanket. It was made of Polartec, she discovered when she touched it, and in short order they had it stretched out so that it covered an area about the size of a double bed. They were both crouched on the sand at the foot of the blanket when they were finished.

"So, you want to get naked?" Luke spoke out of the darkness beside her just as Christy started to unfasten her sandals.

"*What?*" She could barely see him, of course, but she sank back on her haunches and glared at the dark shape of him nevertheless. Given their recent history, the question was both loaded and tactless. Earlier, she had been ready, willing and able to get naked, and he knew it.

"We're both wet. If we try to sleep in our clothes, it's going to be a long, clammy night."

"You know what? There are worse things than clammy."

"Like pneumonia?"

"It's too warm out for us to get pneumonia from sleeping in wet clothes."

"So as far as you're concerned naked's out."

"Definitely." There, that was at least a scrap of redemption for her wounded pride.

"Okay, so keep your underwear on." The barest hint of a teasing grin was there in his tone. He moved and, to her dismay, Christy saw his arms move and heard the swish of — she was almost sure — clothing slithering over skin.

"What are you doing?" Indignation laced her voice.

"What do you want, a play-by-play? I just took off my shirt. Now I'm taking off my shoes. When I get them off, my socks are coming off, and then I'm going to take off my jeans."

"I thought we weren't going to do naked!" The thought of him sitting there beside her without his shirt was annoyingly disturbing. She had a brief but vivid mental picture of just how hot he looked shirtless, then banished it from her mind. No way was she letting herself go there. "I'm keeping my underwear on. They're not that wet, anyway."

"Well, I'm not. Sleeping in my underwear, I mean," she clarified hurriedly.

"You do what you want. But we're going to have to wear these clothes tomorrow, and they have a lot better chance of drying out a little if we hang them up so they can get some air. Anyway, if we lie down on the blanket wet, we're going to end up sleeping on a wet blanket, which is never good."

"What if he finds us and you're in your underwear?"

"Believe me, being in my underwear is not going to stop me from doing anything I would do with my clothes on."

Christy saw him move, and heard his zipper being lowered. Ridiculously, her heart skipped a beat. Ignoring the mindless thing, she sought for some way to express her dismay.

"Look, I'm just not comfortable with this."

"What, are you worried that I'm getting ready to jump your bones?"

"No!"

"Good, 'cause I'm not."

That blunt statement caused her to stiffen. Deflating her opinion of her own sex appeal was getting to be a real specialty of his.

"Look," he added in a long-suffering tone as he stood up and she could hear and faintly see his jeans being pushed down his legs. "It's dark as hell tonight, we can barely see a thing, we have a blanket to put over us and you can sleep way over there against the rock for all I care. But if you're smart, you'll strip."

He moved. She heard the slight scrunch of compressing sand, and then he was back, stretching out at full length on the blanket with a sigh.

"Comfy?" she asked with bite.

"You wouldn't believe."

Fuming, Christy thought the matter over, and to her irritation concluded that he was right. Removing her sandals, she cast a baleful look in his direction —

wasted, of course — and pulled her T-shirt over her head, then quickly shimmied out of her shorts. Her bra and panties were thin white nylon and were practically dry. No way was she coming out of those.

"I spread my clothes out over the rock. I think there's still a little room up there."

If he'd sounded smug, she would have chucked something — like one of her dirty sandals — at him. Lucky for him, he didn't.

"Thanks for the tip," she said with what dignity she could muster, and did as he suggested. The tide was coming in now, and the ocean was only a few yards away. Turning, she could see the foamy white line of the surf curling against the beach.

"You planning to join me any time soon?" His voice was dry.

"I'll be right back," she said, not wanting to get too far away from him but needing to take care of a sudden pressing personal need. That done, she took an extra minute to rinse off in the ocean. Under other conditions, she would have truly enjoyed the feel of the warm water surging around her feet.

"Feel better now?" he asked when she dropped to her knees at the edge of the blanket. He had spread the second one over himself, she discovered, and he flipped back an edge of it now to let her in.

She realized that he had been able to see her dark shape against the pale sand, and hoped fervently that that was all he'd been able to see.

"Mmm," she said, brushing sand from her feet.

Then she crawled up the blanket, careful not to touch Luke, which posed some small degree of difficulty as he seemed to be taking up way more than his fair share of space. She ended up lying down just about as close to the rock as she could get. Curling on her side with an arm beneath her head, tucking the blanket around herself, she discovered that she was actually almost comfortable.

"Want a drink?" he passed her a bottle of water.

"Thanks." She raised her head and chugged some, then screwed the lid back on and set it in the sand above her head. Then she settled down again.

"Night," he said.

"Night." Christy closed her eyes. But with the best will in the world, she couldn't help being aware of Luke lying just a foot or so away. She could hear him breathing.

She could hear the scrunch of sand when he moved, see the outline of his near-naked body. She could . . .

Put him out of her mind.

She tried listening to the soothing sounds of the surf, relaxing her muscles, doing her best to drift off. Exhausted as she was, though, she discovered that she was still too wired to sleep. She was scared of what might lurk in the dark on the other side of the rocks. Heck, she was scared of what might lurk in the dark on *this* side of the rocks. Her throat ached. Her stitched-together shoulder ached. Her legs ached.

And he was hogging the blanket.

She turned over, tugging the blanket with her.

He tugged back and the whole front of her body was suddenly exposed.

"Quit hogging the blanket," she whispered, pulling it back over herself.

Luke sighed and said, "So if we're not going to sleep, you want to go ahead and tell me what happened after we said good night in your cottage?"

Now *there* was a tactful way of describing how they'd parted.

"I left," Christy said a tad coldly.

"Why?"

"Because I was scared. Because I didn't want to be alone." *Because you turned me down.*

"Figures. You know, I kind of guessed those were the reasons you came on to me like you did."

Christy almost choked. "I did not . . ." Okay, call a spade a spade. "All right, so maybe I did come on to you. And maybe those were the reasons." *At least the primary reasons. In the beginning.*

"I don't think there's much maybe about it." Luke's voice was dry.

"Is that why you took off? Because you suspected I had 'ulterior motives'?" Christy tried to keep her voice light as comprehension dawned. Understanding the 'why' behind his behavior should lessen the humiliation factor, but that only worked as long as he didn't guess just how much his rejection had stung.

"Partly." He moved, and his hand brushed her leg. Christy hadn't realized that he was quite that close.

"Partly?" *Partly* was not an answer.

"Yeah, partly. So you left the cottage under your own steam, right? Heading for where?"

"The Silver Lake Inn."

"Then what?"

Christy told him the whole story.

When she finished, ending up with how, when she'd felt the stun gun press against her neck, she'd thought she was about to get her throat slit like Elizabeth Smolski, he swore under his breath. Whether she'd shifted positions or he had, Christy couldn't be sure, but she was now so close to him that, lying on her side, her bent elbow and knees brushed against him whenever either of them moved. If she hadn't been afraid he'd think she was coming on to him again, she probably would have moved closer yet. Having him near was comforting. Or something.

"So what you saw was a white pickup truck with some kind of writing on the passenger side door," Luke said in a reflective tone after a moment. "Was the writing in script or block letters?"

Christy frowned, trying to remember. "Script, I think," she said, surprising herself. "Although I couldn't begin to tell you what it said."

"One line or two?"

"Two." Christy surprised herself again by remembering.

"Any glimpse of a license plate?"

"No. It was too dark. And he never got in front of me."

"Did he say anything besides 'Hi, Christy'?"

"No."

"You're sure he's the same guy as before? Burly, between five-nine and six feet, dark complexion, dark eyes, probably dark hair?"

"Yes." Oh, yes. She was sure.

"That's good. We're getting somewhere with this. We've got a general description of the guy and placed him in a white pickup truck with something written in script on the passenger door. To begin with, there can't be that many people on Ocracoke who own a vehicle of that description."

"Maybe he doesn't live on Ocracoke. Maybe he's just visiting."

"Good point." Luke was silent for a moment. Christy got the impression that he was pondering the possibilities. Then he continued, in a slightly different tone, "Your theory is that the guy wants to kill you because you saw him on the beach right before he killed Elizabeth Smolski, right?"

"Why else would anyone want to kill me?" If her voice was faintly hollow, the softness with which she was speaking coupled with the pounding surf was enough to disguise it, she thought.

"You tell me."

"That has to be it," Christy said firmly. And never mind the other, and to her mind even stronger, possibility. To distract him, she added in a mock indignant tone, "You sure ask a lot of questions."

A beat passed.

"Hey, that's what us lawyers do."

"Actually, it's usually the police who ask all the questions. We lawyers just argue about the answers."

"Whatever." He dismissed her attempt at redirecting the conversation with a verbal wave of his hand. "Whoever he is, you realize that he's serious about wanting to kill you. You've had two close calls in three days."

"Don't remind me." Christy shivered. He must have felt her body quake, because he reached over to curl a hand around her arm. The warm strength of that hand was both comforting and compelling. She was discovering that she really, really liked men with big, square-palmed, long-fingered hands.

"Are you over being stupid yet?" he asked mildly. "Because if you are, come here."

He tugged on her arm, and, thoroughly

disarmed by the charming invitation, she abandoned all pride to scoot closer. He wrapped an arm around her, gathering her close. His body heat enveloped her, far more warming than the blanket. He was wearing boxer shorts, she discovered with interest, that were only faintly damp around the thighs. The rest of his body was dry, and warm, and naked.

Disturbingly naked.

Intoxicatingly naked.

A mature, intelligent woman, driven as a result of circumstance to lie in such close proximity to approximately two hundred pounds of seriously buff male, would no doubt be above entertaining carnal thoughts while enduring the experience.

Unfortunately, she was not that woman.

By the time they were settled comfortably, carnal thoughts were as thick in her head as ornaments on a Christmas tree. She did her best to suppress them, but with indifferent success. The rush and hiss of the surf coming in, the darkness of the sky and sea, made her feel as if they were marooned on their own little island. Her body heated everywhere they touched — and they touched practically everywhere. Her head was on his shoulder, both his arms were around her, and the blanket was tucked snugly around them, keeping the rising breeze at bay. Her breasts in their flimsy nylon covering were pressed tight against his side, and her smooth bare legs snuggled against the long, hair-roughened muscles of his. Her arm was draped across his chest, and her hand rested against the satiny smooth skin just below his left pec. It was all she could do to keep her fingers still.

If she moved her hand up just a little, she would find his nipple. If she moved her hand toward the center, she would encounter the wedge of hair in the middle of his chest. If she moved her hand down, way down . . .

Okay, cut it out.

Fantasizing about Luke was a really, really bad idea. Especially given the circumstances. Especially given the fact that he had already turned her down once tonight.

But maybe he'd changed his mind. After all, she was next door to naked, too, and he had to be as aware of her body as she was of his. Probably the warmth of her, the feel of her soft breasts pressing into his side, the slide of her leg against his, the location of her hand, was driving him nuts. Probably he was getting so turned on that any minute now he would bend his head and kiss her. Just remembering how hot his kisses were sent an anticipatory tingle shooting all the way down to her toes.

"Now isn't this better than you being way over there all by your lonesome fighting me for the blanket?" he asked in a low, growly voice.

Oh yeah.

"I've got to admit, this is better," she said, practically purring.

"Damn right it's better." There was no mistaking the satisfaction in his voice. His arms tightened fractionally around her. "Now if you're all settled, maybe we can finally get some sleep."

21

"Hmm. Right."

Not what she'd wanted to hear. Not what she'd expected to hear, either. But probably a smart idea. While she was trying to convince herself that being shot down for the second time in one night was actually a good thing, she unexpectedly fell asleep.

Something — a sound, a movement — woke her with a start what could have been minutes or hours later. Eyes wide, heart pounding, she stared into the darkness, not quite sure of where she was. There was an odd roaring in her ears. She was lying on something soft and she was wrapped in someone's arms — Michael?

No, not Michael. These arms were definitely more muscular. The body attached to them was longer and more muscular, too. And it was almost naked and had a triangle of short, coarse hair in the middle of its chest and radiated heat like a stove — Luke. At the realization she felt a ridiculous kind of warm glow. Then everything came back to her in a tidal wave of memory, and the warm glow vanished as she froze, listening intently. What had awakened her?

She didn't know.

But just considering the possibilities made her heart pound.

Don't panic. It was probably nothing.

Methodically she took inventory of her surroundings. There were only a few stars visible in the night sky. Luke was asleep. His breathing was deep and relaxed, and his chest rose and fell steadily beneath her head, which was pillowed on it, and her arm, which was stretched across it. The roaring in her ears was the tide coming in.

Christy listened for what felt like quite some time, but beyond that heard nothing except a single muffled *thud,* perhaps caused by a falling branch or some nocturnal animal in the nearby forest or maybe even a wandering turtle. She refused to allow herself to even consider the possibility that the sound might have been made by her attacker, or to wonder if he might be close by.

As Luke had pointed out, what were the chances that he could have followed them so far, through darkness and a forest straight out of *Green Mansions*? What were the chances that he would find *them*, instead of, say, the turtle watchers up the beach? And in any case, she did not have the feeling of dread, the prickly sense of lurking evil, that so far had pretty reliably signaled when he was near.

She must have been awakened by another nightmare — big surprise. Her whole life had devolved into one long bad dream, so it shouldn't be all that surprising if her sleep was no different.

Relax already, she told herself.

Unfortunately, focusing on how much she needed to sleep to build her endurance up for the trials and tribulations of the coming day proved to have the opposite effect. More wide awake than ever, she tried another tack: focusing on the man in whose arms she lay.

Being snuggled up against Luke was the next best thing to being clean and dry and safe back in her own bed, she decided. They were both as close to naked as they could get and still be minimally decent, and she was wrapped around him like yarn around a spindle. Everywhere they touched he felt warm and solid, and his skin was rough in interesting places with hair. His body was long and strong, his chest was wide and resilient, and the arms around her were corded with muscle. He smelled of salt — so, she was sure, did she — and essence of man, and she could hear the steady beat of his heart beneath her ear.

Okay, she was still awake.

Sharpening her focus, she concentrated on the contrast between the thicket of short hairs curling around her fingers and the satiny warmth of the skin beneath. The muscles underlying the skin were really impressively developed, and given the sedentary nature of his profession provided *de facto* evidence of what must be some pretty grueling workouts. His waist and hips were hard and narrow — with her stomach pressed tight up against his hipbone she knew this for sure — and his legs, which she tested by flexing her knee and moving her thigh along the one nearest her, were powerful, confirming her impression that he must be a pretty dedicated weekend warrior, at the very least.

Sliding her hand upward in what she assured herself was a purely reflexive gesture, she absorbed the firm nature of his pecs and the hard flatness of his nipple, and gave herself a little electric thrill in the process.

Fortunately, the thrill served as a wake-up call. Practically molesting the man in his sleep was not something she needed to be doing, she told herself sternly. *Sleeping* was what she needed to be doing.

Clenching her fist, she pulled her hand back close to her side, stilled her leg, closed her eyes, and waited for exhaustion to do its thing and overwhelm any lingering inappropriate thoughts. When exhaustion proved slow on the uptake, she set about trying to lull herself back to sleep.

She listened to the surf; she counted sheep; she deliberately isolated each muscle and relaxed it, starting at her feet and working her way up. By the time she reached her shoulders, rolling them discreetly around to ease the stiffness in her neck, she could feel the tension slowly draining from her body.

"Having trouble sleeping?" The husky murmur in her ear made her jump.

"Did I wake you up? I'm sorry," she said, although she wasn't. Since he was awake already, and she didn't have to worry about disturbing him any longer, she snuggled a little closer, although she was careful to keep her hands to herself. Warmth and human companionship were undoubtedly what she really needed in order to relax enough to go back to sleep.

"I wasn't asleep."

Christy went still with surprise. "You were."

She sensed rather than saw his smile. "Uh-uh."

She didn't know whether to believe him or not, but in case he was telling the truth she searched for a conversational gambit that would effectively distract him from any totally wrong thoughts he might be thinking.

"You know, you never did tell me," she said, remembering their earlier abortive conversation, "how you wound up in my trunk."

A beat passed.

"It's a long story," he said. "Probably we should save it for tomorrow."

"So give me the short version."

"Did I mention that I'm trying to sleep here?"

"If you tell me how you ended up in the trunk, I promise I won't say another word. Or move. Or anything."

Another beat.

"Fine," he said. "Here you go. The short version. After I left you, I went out to get kitty litter for Marvin. On the way back from the store, I saw your car. I wondered where you were going, and I worried that something might be wrong for you to be leaving your cottage so late, so I turned around and followed you. I didn't see the accident itself — I was too far back and it was raining, remember — but I saw your car smashed up when I drove past. I stopped, ran over to the wreck to see if you were okay, and got cracked over the head with something for my pains. Next thing I knew, I woke up with you beside me in the trunk."

Christy didn't say anything for a moment as guilt built up inside her. The hard truth was that Luke had ended up in that trunk solely because of her. That he'd been targeted by the killer solely because of her. That his life was in danger right now solely because of her.

That he was an innocent victim in all this.

"Oh my God," she said. "I'm so sorry. I'm so sorry I got you involved in this."

The arms around her tightened. "It's not exactly what I would call your fault."

Little did he know.

"Listen," she said earnestly, shifting position so that she could look at him, although of course she couldn't see much more than the faint gleam of his eyes. "When we're safe out of this, when I'm back in my cottage and you're back in yours, I want you to stay away from me. This isn't anything to do with you, really, and there's no point in you putting yourself in danger over it. If you're not with me, you'll be perfectly safe."

A beat passed.

"Christy," he said. "Are you by any chance *worried* about me?"

Her eyes narrowed. "Of course I'm worried about you. What's happening here isn't anything to do with you. If you get killed, it'll be all my fault."

"That's cute," he said. "No, that's sweet."

Cute? Sweet?

"What are you talking about? Did you listen to anything I just said? You need to stay away from me. The only reason you're in danger is because of me."

"Why don't you let me worry about me?"

"Because you don't understand." Urgency filled her voice.

"Then why don't you explain it to me?"

"Explain what? That there's somebody out there who keeps trying to kill me but who doesn't seem to be really picky about who else he kills if they get in his way?"

"A serial killer, right?"

"Maybe."

"Maybe?"

Christy bit her lip. His tone told her that her slip of the tongue had registered with him big-time. Now she'd made him wonder. The temptation to confide the whole terrifying story to him was almost overwhelming. She needed somebody to talk to, somebody to trust, somebody who might be able to bring a fresh perspective to the situation as well as offer a few suggestions on how she might survive.

She couldn't think of anybody better than Luke.

But if she told him the truth, then staying away from her wouldn't keep him out of danger. They'd be after him, too.

"There's something you're not telling me, isn't there? I've thought so from the beginning," he said.

Oh God, she'd been quiet for too long. Her silence had taken him a step beyond wonder to suspicion.

"I don't know what you're talking about."

It only occurred to her that she sounded way too wooden when his arms tightened and he rolled with her so that all of a sudden she was lying flat on her back with him leaning over her. She could feel the heat of him, the weight of one of his legs pinning hers down, the hard strength of the arm draped across her chest.

"You can trust me, you know." His voice was quiet. A hand brushed her cheekbone, smoothed the hair back from her face. "And anyway, I'm already caught up in this. Now that this guy has gone to the trouble of knocking me unconscious and stuffing me in your trunk, I'd say that it's a good bet that he's not going to just forget about me."

"If you stay away from me . . ." Christy began desperately.

"Not gonna happen."

She could feel his hand against the side of her neck now, caressing, gentling.

"Luke. . . ."

"Christy." His thumb feathered across the soft hollow beneath her ear. "Don't you think that since you got me into this you owe it to me to tell me the truth? It would be a lot easier to protect myself — and help you — if I knew what was really going on. Something tells me that you're not entirely convinced that this guy is a serial killer, are you?"

Christy took a deep, shaken breath. His

points were valid, but she was afraid — for herself, and for him.

"I — don't — know." She drew the words out slowly, in an agony of indecision about what to do. She wanted to tell him so badly. . . .

"Tell me, honey. Tell me the truth."

"You don't know anything about me," she whispered wretchedly. "You don't have any idea what you're asking. Believe me, this is something you'd really rather not know."

"Is it something to do with your ex-boyfriend?"

Christy drew in a sharp breath. She was breathing hard, and her eyes were wide in the dark. "What makes you think that?"

"What you've said about him. What you haven't said about him. Your reaction just now."

"Oh God." She'd given herself away.

"Whatever it is, we're in it together now. Whether you tell me the truth or not, I'm putting you on notice that I'm not going to be walking away."

"I want you to walk away. *Please* walk away."

"Not till you can walk away with me." She could make out the slow negative shake of his head. "Tell me about your ex-boyfriend, Christy. How is he connected with this? What is he, some kind of big man in the mob?"

"How could you know that?" Christy gasped, then heard, too late, the semi-jocular tone in which the question had been put and closed her eyes. He hadn't really been serious, but she'd answered his question in the affirmative anyway without even meaning to. Her words were an admission, and she knew it. He was so close with his guesses — how was it that he was so close with his guesses?

"I didn't, not really. But I do now. Come on, Christy, tell me the rest of it. I want to help you, honey, but you have to trust me before I can."

Christy took a deep breath and opened her eyes again. She couldn't resist any more. She needed someone in her corner too badly. She needed Luke in her corner too badly. "Have you ever heard of John DePalma?"

"Vaguely."

"He's head of the Masseria crime family in New Jersey."

"Ah. This is your ex-boyfriend?"

"His father." Christy hesitated, then reached up to touch Luke's face. He was propped on an elbow beside her, leaning over her, and her palm rested lightly against a bristly, hard-angled cheek. "Believe me, you're better off not hearing this."

"Like I said, you let me worry about me." He turned his mouth into her hand, brushing her palm with his lips. Christy felt the warm touch of his mouth clear down to her toes. "I take it your ex-boyfriend followed his pop into the family business?"

"Y-yes." She let her hand drop to his wide shoulder, then slide down to rest on his triceps. The muscle there was hard and strong. *He* was strong, and smart, a man a woman could depend on. A man she could depend on? The jury was still out on that, but she thought . . . hoped . . . so. "I didn't know it, though. I thought . . ."

Her voice trailed off. But if she was going to involve him, he had to know the truth. The truth about her as well as everything else. She began again.

"Look, my father was a mob soldier. He was shot dead when I was a little girl. Nothing was ever proved, but it was probably a hit. My mother's boyfriend is a capo in the Masseria family. My sister was married to a guy who was in the mob. We're a mob family, you understand? That's how I was raised. Half the people I grew up with were criminals, and still are. No big deal, okay? Not then, and not now. But I didn't want to live that way. So I stayed clear of all that as much as possible, went to school, became a lawyer. Well, lawyers are a dime a dozen, so when Michael DePalma, my ex-boyfriend, offered me a job right out of school at a really good salary I jumped at it. He's a lawyer with his own law firm, and I'd known who he was forever, although I didn't really get to know him personally until I went to work for him. But I thought he was like me, a kid from a mob family who didn't want that kind of life."

She paused to take a breath, wishing she could see his face more clearly so that she could read his reaction to what he was hearing. But on second thought, maybe it was better not to know until she'd gotten it all out.

"But you were wrong," Luke said.

Christy nodded.

"Oh, yeah, I was wrong. But I didn't know it until just about a week and a half ago." She swallowed. "This is the part you really don't want to know."

Her hand tightened on his arm. He trailed warm fingers down her cheekbone and into her hair in response.

"Yeah, I do. Come on, honey. Tell me the rest."

Christy wet her lips. "Franky — my sister Nicole's ex-husband — came to my apartment one night. I never did like him much, he was lousy to Nicole and the kids, but he was still kind of family and so I let him in. He was really agitated, begging me to help him, telling me that I was the only one who could. I asked him why, and he said it was because Michael — my Michael — had put out a contract on him because he had gambled away some money — a whole lot of money — he'd been supposed to turn over to the Family. He said if I talked to Michael for him I could make it all go away."

"So did you talk to Michael?"

Christy shook her head. "I didn't believe Franky at first. I started checking things out. I went through the computer files at work, I cross-checked bank statements and case logs and pending litigation and settlements, and I found some things that didn't add up. When I figured out what was going on, then I went to talk to Michael. He admitted everything."

"Admitted what, Christy?"

"That the firm was basically a sham. Oh,

we really did legal work, but it was a cover for the company's real business, which is money laundering. Apparently all the illegal profits the Masseria family collects for things like drugs and prostitution and illegal gun sales and cigarette smuggling and gambling and kickbacks and, well, just about anything illegal you can think of, get run through the law firm, where the money is disguised and recycled and parceled out in various ways until it's untraceable to its original source." She paused, grimacing. "Just so you're aware, knowing that much is enough to get you killed."

"I'll take my chances."

He didn't sound nearly worried enough to convince her that he really understood the danger she had just put him in. If *she'd* understood how dangerous such knowledge was when Franky had come knocking on her door, she never would have gone digging into those files. Heck, she never would have answered the door. She'd still be happy as a clam in her old life, doing the legal work she loved by day and being Michael's girl at night.

At the thought she frowned. Whatever else she regretted, she didn't regret losing Michael. The man she'd been in love with had never really existed. She'd never actually known the true Michael DePalma until the end — and when she had finally made his acquaintance he had both terrified and repulsed her.

Luke interrupted her thoughts. "So what happened after you confronted Michael?"

"We had a fight, and I broke it off with him. Then I went to visit my mother. That's what I always do when things go wrong in my life: go talk to my mother. But not far from her house, my Uncle Vince — that's my mother's boyfriend I told you about — had some goons pull me out of my car. They shoved me in his, in the backseat. Uncle Vince was waiting there for me, and he told me that if I told anyone what I knew, my mother and my sisters and I would be killed. Up until then, I had always l-liked Uncle Vince."

Her voice started to shake. Luke gave an incomprehensible mutter and gathered her into his arms. He was lying on his back now and she was almost on top of him, shivering like it was thirty degrees outside.

"That's not all," she said, holding herself away from him with both hands on his chest, determined to keep nothing back so that he would know exactly what he — what they were both — facing. "Uncle Vince took me to a warehouse. There was a meat locker in the back. He and the goons took me inside — I was so scared, Luke; I thought they might be going to go ahead and kill me right then — and Franky was in there. Just lying there on his stomach on the floor. He was naked. He was dead. Uncle Vince said — he said Franky had been hit by a car. And the goons laughed."

"Shit," Luke said, and this time when he pulled her close she let him, burrowing her head into the hollow between his shoulder and neck, wrapping her arms around his neck, holding onto him like he was the only solid thing in an unstable world. "Jesus Christ, Christy, did you tell anybody? Did you go to the police?"

"You still don't get it, do you?" She lifted her head. His face was so close that she could feel the scratch of his chin when he spoke, and the warm flutter of his breath against her cheek. "These people — they *own* the police. They own judges. They own prosecutors. They own people that you would never believe. If I tell — if they think I'm going to tell — I'll wind up like Franky. Or my mom will. Or my sisters. Or all of us. They won't think twice about killing us. That's why I think that the guy who's after me might be a h-hit man. I think he might have killed Elizabeth Smolski by mistake while he was coming after *me*."

All of a sudden she couldn't talk any more because her throat had closed up. She rested her head against him, greedy for his warmth, his comfort. Her cheek nestled into the crisp hair on his chest. Beneath it she could hear the steady beat of his heart.

"It's okay," Luke said quietly, his hand sliding around the back of her neck. "You don't have to be afraid any more. It'll be all right, I promise you."

Christy lifted her head again.

"I keep thinking, if I'd just done something different. If I'd *believed* Franky. . . . I didn't even like the little twerp, but I just can't seem to quit remembering how — how *pathetic* he looked lying there dead."

Her voice broke, and she could feel the hot rush of tears crowd her eyes.

"Hey," Luke said. "You're not crying, are you?"

"No." Christy blinked rapidly to push back the tears that she refused to shed. "What would be the use of that? Anyway, I never cry."

"You know what?" Luke's voice was even softer than before. "I've got a real thing for girls who never cry."

Then his hand tightened on her neck and he pulled her mouth down to his and kissed her.

22

His kiss was every bit as devastating as she remembered. All he had to do was touch his mouth to hers and heat exploded inside her like a supernova. Christy closed her eyes and wrapped her arms around his neck and kissed him back as if she'd die if she didn't.

His arms tightened around her and he shifted so that they were lying side by side with his hard-muscled triceps pillowing her head. Clad in nothing but his soft cotton underwear, his body seemed to burn hers everywhere they touched. Fingers tangling in the curls at his nape, she pressed her breasts to his chest, reveling in the heat of it, in the abrasion of his chest hair, in the firm resilience of the muscles there, in the contrast between his hard masculine contours and her softness.

The hot sweet fire they generated was enough to dry her eyes, to block out memories of Franky and Elizabeth Smolski and the danger she and Luke were in, to narrow her focus to one thing: Luke, and the way he made her feel.

"I love the way you kiss," she whispered when he broke off to slide his lips along her jaw, then pressed his open mouth to her neck. As the wet heat of it crawled over her skin she tilted her head back and abandoned herself to sensation. A rhythmic throbbing sprang to life deep inside her as his mouth traced the length of her collarbone and then moved down the upper slope of her breast, only to be blocked by the silken edge of her bra. His mouth burned there against the creamy softness of her skin for a long moment before sliding over the thin nylon and opening over the tip of her breast. Her body tightened instantly as the scalding wetness of his tongue sought out her nipple through the cloth, jolting her clear down to her toes. Drawing in a quick, hard breath, she melted, going absolutely boneless. From that instant it was all over: she was his, to do with as he would.

"You're beautiful." His voice was a husky whisper. His hand replaced his mouth on her breast as he lifted his head to kiss her. She returned his kiss wildly, burning for him, feeling as if every nerve ending she possessed had been set aflame. She arched up into that caressing hand, loving the heat of it, the friction as he rubbed her nipple through the still-warm dampness his mouth had left behind. Then even that flimsy barrier was too much and his hand slid inside her bra to find her bare skin. It was large enough to cover her completely and warm and hard enough to make her shudder. She ached as his palm flattened on her. Then his thumb found her nipple, and she gasped as he moved it deliberately back and forth over the sensitive nub.

"You remember earlier, when I said I wasn't going to jump your bones?" His voice was hoarse now, guttural, as his hand curved over her breast, gauging the shape and weight of it, caressing it, possessing it.

"Yes," she managed, scarcely able to draw breath.

"I lied."

That was her cue to object if she had a problem with what was happening, she knew, but objecting was the last thing she wanted to do. The tantalizing heat of his hand on her breast and the blatant masculinity of his body against hers were blowing her mind. The last time he had kissed her like this, she'd been desperate to keep him with her, to do whatever she had to do to persuade him to help her make it through the night. The fact that he'd managed to turn her on had been something extra, something surprising, a special bonus gift that had caught her unawares. But now there was no ulterior motive, nothing on her agenda at all except exploring what it was like to be with Luke. She wanted him so much that she was dizzy with it, and she knew that he wanted her too.

There was no mistaking that. Pressed tight against the whole long length of him as she was, she had irrefutable evidence of the strength of his desire. Everything about him was hard: his breathing, his muscles, his erection. In response, the throbbing inside her grew more urgent, causing her body to burn and quake. She snuggled even closer, sliding her hands over his back. The skin was warm and faintly damp and smooth. The muscles beneath were firm and resilient. As she ran her hands along the length of his spine, she felt his chest expand and heard a sound that made her think that he was sucking in his breath.

"I want you naked." He reached behind her to unfasten her bra even as he growled the words into her ear.

"Naked's good." She wanted to be naked. Wanted to be touched. Wanted him inside her.

Running his tongue around the tender swirls of her ear, nibbling her lobe until she was breathing fast and felt as light-headed as if she were on a starvation diet, he got the last hook undone and pulled her bra away from her body. Christy's heart pounded in triple time as she felt the silken straps slide down her arms, and then she let go of him for just long enough for him to take the thing off. When the fragile garment hit the sand behind her with the merest whisper, she was already too distracted to do more than note the sound in passing. Her hands were sliding up his chest, her palms registering the hard arousal of his nipples, her fingers exploring the firm contours of his pecs. She was sweeping her hands out along the muscled width of his shoulders with real appreciation for their size and strength when he refocused her attention in a hurry by bending his head to just brush her nipple with his lips.

Christy gave a tiny choked cry and her hands stilled.

"Luke. . . ."

"Hmm?"

But whatever she'd been going to say was lost as the scalding heat of his mouth closed over her bare breast.

"Oh," she said instead, in a surprised tone as the sheer pleasure of it made her shiver. She could feel her heart pounding, feel her blood racing, feel the urgent tightening between her thighs as he suckled her breast, nibbled it, licked it, gave it his full attention, then moved on to work his leisurely wiles on its twin. He took his time, and when finally his mouth found hers and he kissed her again, Christy could do nothing but kiss him back and quiver with sensation and thread her fingers into the curls at the back of his head. She didn't even realize that they'd shifted position so that she was once again lying on her back until he lifted his head.

"Do you have any idea how long I've been wanting to get you in bed?" His voice was thick and low, a dark, seductive murmur that wrapped around her like velvet.

"How long?" she whispered, quaking, then stiffened in anticipation as his hand left the breasts he'd been fondling to slide down over her navel, over her stomach. . . .

"Ever since the first time I saw you. You were running. . . ."

Christy caught her breath on a little gasp as his hand slipped inside her panties. It covered her, moved between her legs, and her body clenched.

"Oh God, Luke. . . ." Closing her eyes, she abandoned herself to sensation. Her heart was pounding so hard and she was breathing so fast that coherent thought was all but beyond her. She was wearing only her panties now, and the feel of the soft Polartec covering the firm sand beneath her back reminded her that they were outside, doing it on an open beach, and the thought was so erotic that she moaned. Her nails dug into the blanket and she arched her back, welcoming his touch, wanting it.

"You feel so hot down here. I knew you'd be hot down here."

He found the tiny bud that burned and quivered for attention. Christy sucked in her breath and squeezed her thighs around his hand, quaking, knowing that she was going to come if he didn't stop and trying not to, not yet, because what he was doing felt so good and she wanted more.

He slid two fingers inside her, pulled them out, then put them in again.

Christy cried out, and her hips rocked against that hard hand in an urgent plea for him not to stop.

"Easy," he said, and did it again, and again, until she thought she would die with the sheer goodness of it. It felt so wonderful, his hand was so big and hot and he knew just what to do with it, how to turn her on, what made her shiver, what made her pant.

"That is so good," she whispered, shaken, and he kissed her mouth and then her breast even as his fingers continued to work their magic on her.

"Luke. Stop. Please."

She closed her legs again at last, wanting him to stop, needing him to stop right then or she would explode into flames. He seemed to understand, because he lifted his head, and his hand stilled in its exquisite torture. Then it was gone, and she was left quivering, quaking, burning, weeping . . .

"Let's take your panties off."

He kissed her navel, pressed the hot wetness of his mouth against her belly, then hooked his fingers in her underwear and pulled them down her legs. By the time they were off Christy was so far gone with lust that she was breathing in erratic little bursts, arching her hips up to meet the truly enormous erection that she could feel bulging through the shorts he still wore, reaching for him with both hands.

"Luke."

"Hmm?" She heard the soft whisper of

her panties hitting the sand.

"I want you naked, too."

"In a minute."

His hands curled around her knees, then slid up the softness of her inner thighs, parting them. When Christy felt the brush of his chest hair against her thighs, she began to shake.

"Oh, no, I . . ." She clutched at his hair, knowing what was coming. This was something she wasn't comfortable with, Michael had never liked to do it and she really didn't like it anyway, and besides . . .

"Shh."

His bristly jaw scraped against the inside of her thighs and she felt him settle between them. Her fingers stilled . . .

Then his mouth found her. The sensation was so unbelievably erotic that she moaned. He kissed her there, his mouth and tongue burning hot against her. He'd done this before, that much was clear, he knew his way around a woman, and he made her gasp and squirm and quiver with pleasure. When he lifted his head at last, kissing his way up her stomach, her body was pulsing with tremors and her legs were twining around his and she wanted him more than she'd ever wanted anything in her life.

"Luke. Now. Please."

He kissed her mouth, and she tasted herself on his lips and went wild.

Reaching for him, barely able to see him in the darkness, she first encountered the smooth sides of his rib cage, then stroked his flat, washboard-hard belly, and finally slipped her hands inside his shorts. He was right there, swollen so big he reached almost to the waistband, hot and damp and clearly hungry for her. She touched him, her fingers sliding over him, then closed both hands around him. He was huge and hard and she wanted him inside her so much that she ached.

"Ah, Christy," he said, going perfectly still.

She tightened her grip, moving her hands in the age-old rhythm of man-pleasing, and he groaned, then groaned again and pulled away from her. Then he yanked at his shorts and she helped him and finally between them they got them off. When they were both naked he pushed her flat on her back and covered her, his thighs sliding between hers and opening them wide, his mouth finding her breasts.

Her hips came off the ground to meet him and her hands found and gripped the firm smooth contours of his butt as he touched her. His body was on fire, burning her, and she whimpered and squirmed in invitation.

"Jesus, I want you," he muttered in a rough whisper.

Then he pushed inside her, forcing her hips back down against the blanket, filling her with a burning hot satin over steel instrument that felt better to her than anything ever had in her life. Moaning with pleasure, Christy slid her hands up his back and rocked up against him, drawing him deeper still, on fire with the pure bliss of having his body joined to hers.

He withdrew, then thrust again, deep and slow. She dug her nails into his shoulders and wrapped her legs around his waist and gave a little mewling cry of pleasure.

"Oh God, if you do that again I'm going to. . . ." She broke off, panting. Even in extremis, as she very nearly was, she couldn't quite bring herself to say it out loud.

He said it for her, his voice a growl as he wrapped his arms around her and pressed hot kisses along the base of her neck.

"Come? Good. I want to make you come. I'm going to make you come."

Then he kissed her. Their tongues mated with greedy passion as he pressed her down into the blanket, filling her, taking her with slow, controlled movements that had her moaning and squirming beneath him. His hand slid between them, sliding over her stomach, seeking the heart of her, the quivering flashpoint that needed only one final touch for her to explode.

He touched her there, pressing and stroking, and she gasped and arched up off the ground, and came, in a shattering series of Technicolor explosions that drove her out of her head with passion, with pleasure, with need.

"Luke," she moaned. "Oh God, Luke, *Luke* . . ."

In answer he lost control, driving into her in fierce, deep thrusts that came so hard and so fast that she was caught up in the pounding rhythm all over again, until once more she quivered and shook and clung and came.

"Christy," he groaned at the end, and buried his mouth in the hollow between her neck and shoulder as he found his own release, grinding into her trembling body, convulsing over her, shuddering, and then, finally, going limp in her arms.

Afterward, they lay still for a long time, with him on his back and her sprawled on top of him. Her arms were looped loosely around his neck, and her head rested on his chest. He was warm and sweaty, re-laxed, breathing deeply. She thought he might be asleep.

Typical man, she thought with a touch of asperity, and opened her eyes. The clouds were gone. Overhead there was a sky full of stars.

Then he moved, instantly distracting her from the beauty of the glittering sky, sliding his hand up her back, bending his head down toward her. She panicked a little as she realized that he was awake after all, because she wasn't quite sure what she thought about what had happened be-tween them, about how to act or what to say. Something on the order of, *Hmm, that was some really good sex* just didn't seem to strike the right note.

But the time was at hand, because he was tightening his arms around her and his bristly chin was nuzzling her cheek. Oh God, was he already up for doing it again?

"There's someone walking around in the woods right behind us," he said in her ear. "Don't make a sound."

23

Okay, Luke reflected, so maybe being in his underwear wasn't going to stop him from doing anything he could do with his clothes on, but being naked was definitely having a dampening effect on his macho impulses. Kicking bad-guy butt with his yang flapping in the breeze wasn't exactly his idea of a good time. Especially since this guy seemed to like knives. Luke almost shuddered, and started groping around on the sand for his shorts.

Finding them, he started pulling them on.

Christy elbowed him in the ribs. "Maybe it's one of the turtle watchers," she whispered.

Maybe. But they'd been based a good distance away, and they hadn't shown any tendency to go wandering in the woods. If they were looking for Christy and him, they'd most likely walk along the edge of the beach.

If it wasn't a turtle watcher, that might not be a bad thing. This guy was starting to piss him off. When he'd spotted the bruise by Christy's eye, he'd realized that he'd had it up to his eyebrows with her being hurt. He hadn't meant it to happen, it shouldn't have happened, it was no part of his game plan at all, but this case had suddenly gotten way more personal than he'd ever intended. Not only did he want to nail Michael DePalma in the worst way, but now he also wanted to make him pay for the terror and emotional and physical trauma he'd caused Christy.

There was almost no doubt in his mind that Donnie Jr. was behind what was happening to her. And it was going to cost him. Before this was all over, before packing him off to prison, Luke meant to personally kick his butt, rub his nose in the dirt, and walk off with his girl.

My girl, now.

That was an unsettling thought, Luke realized as soon as it popped into his head, but he didn't have time to worry about the whys and wherefores of it just at the moment. He had his shorts on now, and he felt ready, willing and able to take on the world. If the bastard who'd attacked Christy was out there sniffing around, he was about to get a surprise.

Unless the guy had a gun, of course. Then all bets were off.

Discretion being the better part of valor, Luke settled back down on his stomach beside Christy and watched the woods for the telltale glimmer he'd seen before. There was still maybe an hour to go before dawn, and with the sea pounding behind them his ears were all but useless. Even now, with the faint light of the moon and stars, he couldn't see more than shadows — except, once again as it was apparently turned back on, the white beam of a flashlight moving over the ground not so very far away.

Way too close for comfort, in fact. Close enough so that he could see every detail of the tangled vines and tree trunks and sea grasses that mingled at the very edge of the beach as they were caught in the flashlight's beam.

Beside him, Christy gasped. The sound, which she immediately muffled, told him that she had spotted the same thing. He could feel her stiffness, feel the rapid rise and fall of her chest that told him she was breathing hard, feel fear emanating from her in waves.

"Hang tight," he whispered in her ear

before dropping a kiss on her cheek and shifting into a crouch, ready to do his manly, protect-the-woman, confront-the-bad-guy thing. She clutched at him, whispering something in an urgent tone, but he had little fear that she would complicate an already volatile situation by following him. After all, she was naked. He knew how that felt, and *she* was a girl. Even if she wanted to follow, by the time she located her clothes and got them on he would have this business over and done.

The flashlight was a little farther to the south now, tracing a kind of steady zigzag pattern that told him someone was searching for something with a really impressive degree of zeal. Keeping low, moving as quietly as he could over the firm sand, and then, when he reached the forest, wishing vainly that he'd taken the time to pull on his sneakers, Luke crept up on the searcher.

Calling on all his years of training, he slipped from tree trunk to tree trunk, meaning to make the take-down as quick and silent as possible. In front of him, close now, the flashlight was a dead giveaway as to the location of his target.

Luke could see him, a dark shape among the trees.

Gathering himself together, he sprang, grabbing the guy in a chokehold, clapping a hand over his mouth even as the guy tensed up for a fight.

"Don't make a sound," Luke growled in his ear. Then he let him go, grabbed his arm, and dragged him away out of earshot.

"What the hell?" Gary didn't sound any too pleased when finally they stopped. "You almost made me drop the global positioning device, and you know how expensive that thing was. You might want to send a damage report on it into headquarters, but I don't."

He brandished the dark rectangle he held in his left hand.

"Keep your voice down, will you? And douse the flashlight. Christy's over there under a bush. She's not stupid. If you just happen to stumble across us while we're hiding in the woods in the middle of the night, she's gonna want to know how and why."

"How and why's easy: when you didn't come back, I started getting nervous. I figured you must have gone with Christy in her car, but I couldn't get the homing device to come on-line. When it finally did, it was transmitting from a weird place, so I thought I better come check it out. I couldn't figure out what her car was doing in the middle of a forest."

"The bug's not in her car any more. It's in my pocket."

The pocket of his jeans, to be precise, which were lying at that moment across a rock, not that he meant to bring his lack of them to Gary's attention. Apparently tightening the screws that held the little plastic doohickey together, which he'd done in the trunk of Christy's car before they had jumped, had done the trick. He'd been hoping it would, and that Gary was astute enough to realize that something had gone wrong and come to their aid. Which was exactly how it had gone down. For all his quirks, Gary, Luke was coming to realize, was a good man to have at his back.

"So what happened?" Gary demanded in a hushed voice.

Luke gave him a quick, thumbnail sketch, leaving out the personal details which were none of Gary's business and ending with, "And then I saw you walking through the woods and here we are."

"How'd you know it was me?" Gary sounded mildly puzzled.

Luke grunted. "The shoes, man. When the flashlight hit shiny cordovan dress shoes, I knew. Nobody else I've ever met in my life would wear dress shoes to search a forest."

"For your information, I didn't know I was going to be hiking through a forest when I put them on," Gary said with dignity. "And anyway, I drove most of the way. There's a gravel road — well, it's mostly mud now — about a quarter mile to the west. That's where I parked the Explorer. I have to say, tracking you down was a lot easier when I was doing it in the truck."

"Yeah, well, you did good." Luke clapped him on the shoulder. "Even to the shoes. Otherwise I wouldn't have known it was you, would I? Now here's what I want you to do. . . ."

"You sure you want to handle it this way?" Gary sounded doubtful when Luke finished.

"Yeah. You stumbling across us would be one too many coincidences for Christy to swallow."

"Don't you think it would be easier at this point to just tell her the truth and try to get her to cooperate?"

Luke grimaced. He'd told so many tall tales now that the thought of Christy's reaction when she did finally learn the truth was starting to worry him.

"I'll think about it," he said. "In the

meantime, just do what I told you, okay?"

"You're the boss," Gary said. Luke couldn't see him shrug, but he felt it. "You want my .38?"

Luke thought about it for a moment. A gun would be insurance, but hiding it from Christy would be next to impossible. The chances of the bad guy finding them were small; the chances of Christy finding the gun were almost one hundred percent.

"Nah," he said.

"Oh, right," Gary said. "Those hands are lethal weapons and all that, right?"

"Something like that, anyway," Luke said. "This is the same guy who attacked her before. He's driving a white pickup truck with some kind of writing on the passenger side. Probably a commercial application of some kind. Last time I saw it, it was towing Christy's car, but he might well have dumped it somewhere by now. Keep an eye out for the truck, or her car along the road, and see what you can come up with on a white truck through the department of motor vehicles. It very well might not be registered locally, but it sure doesn't hurt to check."

"Will do."

"Great." Luke turned away. "Gotta go."

He'd been gone a good ten minutes.

Christy was probably scared to death by now, and he didn't like to think of Christy scared. If he'd been able to think of a better way to handle things, a way that didn't involve frightening Christy — or, exposing himself as a world-class liar — he would have taken it.

"Luke. One more thing."

Luke was already a couple of paces away when Gary's voice stopped him.

"What's that?"

"How come you're not wearing any clothes?"

"I've got on shorts, okay? Everything else got wet and I took them off to let them dry. They're hanging up drying as we speak."

"Oh, is that what happened?"

"Yeah, that's what happened. Any more questions?"

"Nope. None."

"Great. Then I'll see you in a couple of hours."

"Copy that," Gary said, and they went their separate ways.

Despite the fact that a few stars now twinkled overhead, it was still pitch-dark. Having taken Christy's measure by now, he was careful to whisper *It's me* as insurance against getting clobbered over the head with something as he approached the rocks.

"Luke?" she whispered.

"Yeah."

"Thank God, I've been worried out of my mind."

She launched herself at him, wrapping her arms around his neck, trembling all over and pressing as close to him as she could get. She was fully clad, damp, and the flashlight was, as he had suspected, ready for use as a weapon in her hand. If he hadn't identified himself, he had no doubt that he would now have one hell of a headache. He felt bad about the trembling and about her being afraid, he reflected as he took the flashlight from her, but other than that he could take this kind of greeting any time.

"I told you not to worry about me," he said in her ear as his arms closed around her and he bore her down on the blankets, where he proceeded to kiss her breathless. Between kisses, he explained how one of the turtle watchers had just happened to wander their way.

"We need to try to get out of here as soon as it's light," Christy whispered when he finished. She wasn't shaking any more, but despite the supposedly soporific effect of his kisses and the reassurance imparted by his explanation she was still clearly afraid.

Okay, he felt bad about it, but what could he do? Telling her the truth about who and what he was was the only thing he could think of that would make her feel safer, and he wasn't quite ready for that. He had a feeling that, if and when he finally did confess, the results weren't going to be pretty.

"We don't need to be in any hurry. With the turtle people nearby we're safe enough, and even if he's still out there, which I don't think he is, he'll be long gone by morning."

"Are you sure?"

"Yeah."

Oh, yeah. He was sure. Anyway, he already had a hand up under her shirt and he could think of a far better way to pass the time until Gary got things in place than tramping around through a swampy forest.

Like getting her naked again.

By the time the sky had lightened from black to gray and the first orange rays of the sun were just starting to creep over the horizon, they were both naked and Luke, personally, could have done with a nap. Doing the deed with Christy three times in one night on a starry beach was probably as close to sexual nirvana as he was ever going to get, but it was also exhausting, especially on no sleep.

"I can't believe I'm doing this," she murmured, lifting her head to look up at him some few minutes after they'd scaled the heights one last time, then collapsed in a limp tangle of blissed-out limbs.

"Can't believe you're doing what?"

He cocked an eyebrow at her. Lying flat on his back with her sprawled naked and sated on top of him, he discovered that he had a bird's-eye view of the round globes of her breasts pressing against his chest and gave himself up to enjoying it.

"Getting you involved in this. Making it with you like this."

So much for hearts and flowers. What had he expected, that she'd be declaring herself wildly in love with him after a single — though admittedly memorable — night?

"Shit happens," he said mildly. He slid a hand over her ass — she had a really great ass; it was round and firm and warm beneath his palm — then gave her a playful little spank. "We need to get going. Get up and get dressed."

"Mmm."

She rolled off him. For a man who had just had a whole lot of really great sex, he felt surprisingly unhappy, he realized. Pulling his clothes on, he moodily watched her dress. Naked and rosy with sex, with her breasts all round and flushed from his recent attentions and her ass round too and so hot it was all he could do to look and not touch, she made as erotic a picture as anything he had ever seen in his life.

By the time he zipped his clammy jeans, the task was difficult because he was once again well on his way to being at full mast.

Unfortunately, this fairly remarkable resurgence of his libido did nothing to cheer him up.

And at the thought that he was starting to find getting turned on a downer, he got even more depressed.

"I'm just going to take a little walk," he said, sounding grumpy even to his own ears, and headed off to the forest to answer nature's call.

24

The beast was being no help at all. He had searched the forest for as long as he dared, but with only his own senses to rely on, he'd come up empty. Unbelievably, she'd gotten away from him. It was almost like it was a judgment on him for being cocky. The next time he got the chance, he was going to kill her on the spot, and then make her disappear. Or not. The important thing was, corpses couldn't talk.

The thought that she could remember at any time, that he might even have already scared her into remembering, was starting to prey on his mind. This was the closest he'd ever come to panicking, but panicking was the worst thing he could do. If he stayed calm, if he took just the little extra time needed to take Christy out before he vanished, he could be comfortable again.

Then it would be *California, here I come.*

The cops might figure out what he'd done, but they wouldn't know who he was.

Or where he was.

Getting rid of her car was the first order of business. He had the spot all picked out. The only difference was that he'd planned to have Christy's body in it when the car bit the big one. Just abandoning it somewhere was not an option. There was too much evidence on it. Paint from his truck, for one. Maybe some of his hair or something they could use to get his DNA.

Not worth the risk. He disposed of the car, then bumped back up on the road. It was getting light out, and he needed to get home.

Terri would be waiting. She wouldn't be going to California with him, but she didn't know that yet. Maybe he would tell her later.

He smiled a little in anticipation. It was a bright spot in a dreary day.

His route took him past the ferry dock, and he chanced to get there just as the first ferry of the day was unloading. It was surprisingly full for the early hour, lots of cars, lots of people, and he shook his head at how popular Ocracoke was becoming.

Didn't people ever just stay home?

One thing about the dock: at this hour of the morning, they did a brisk business in coffee. And Krispy Kremes. He was a sucker for coffee and Krispy Kremes.

With all the confusion — workers waving cars off the ferry, people milling around getting gas, getting directions, getting breakfast — there was no reason in the world for him to stand out. Nipping in to grab a cup of Joe and a doughnut wouldn't be taking a risk. No one would notice him.

He parked the truck at the side of the lot and walked into the mini convenience store there. It was busy, and he had to stand in line behind people buying everything from coffee and doughnuts to allergy medicine to maps.

"Mornin'," he said when it was his turn, and placed his order.

"Sorry y'all had to wait," the clerk said as he handed over the bag and Styrofoam cup. A pimply adolescent, he clearly had no interest in his present customer. He kept taking covert glances at a little blond teenybopper with multiple body piercings and a tube top. Giving her a fast once-over himself, he took a pass: she wasn't his type.

"Busy for so early, aren't you?" he asked as he paid and waited for his change.

"Seems like. You wouldn't think so, would you? Not after what's in the paper."

"What's in the paper?" He accepted the bills and change the kid gave him and tucked them away in his shirt pocket.

"About the serial killer. It's on the front page of this morning's *USA Today*." The kid nodded toward a coin-operated newspaper stand just inside the door. "Ocracoke made the national news."

Simple pride laced his voice: the hometown team had done good.

"You don't say?" Managing a smile, turning away from the counter while the kid said *sorry y'all had to wait* to the next customer, he transferred the doughnut bag to the hand holding the coffee cup, and fished in his pocket for two quarters.

Sliding them into the slot, he opened the door and removed a paper. At first he saw nothing. Then he turned the paper over.

Liz's face smiled up at him from the lower right corner. Looking at it and the accompanying story, he felt his heart begin to pound.

25

"This way."

By the time they'd said good-bye and thanks to the turtle people and started heading back through the forest, it was full morning. Luke was still feeling out of sorts, but he did his best to lose his unexpected attack of angst as he caught Christy's hand and headed west. Having been told by Gary exactly where they were and how to get where he wanted to go, Luke was able to take a pass on doing things like following water back away from the sea and looking for moss growing on whatever side of the tree it supposedly grew on to find the way out.

"How do you know?"

True to her untrusting nature, Christy hung back, glancing all around. The sun didn't penetrate the canopy very easily, which meant that there was just enough light to enable them to see each other and their immediate surroundings. The gray trunks and low-hanging branches of loblolly pines surrounded them like an army of silent sentinels. A fine mist hung in the air.

"You mean besides my unerring sense of direction? The turtle guy told me to head this way." Luke jerked his thumb to the east.

That did it. With their hands linked, she trudged behind him as he broke a path through the undergrowth. He was bone-tired and so, he judged from her silence, was she. Everywhere he looked, steam rose from the ground in misty columns, glistening like spider silk as sun rays slanted through the canopy to find it. The morning chatter of birds and the whirr of the stirring insect population formed an exotic background chorus. The whole world smelled like his jeans: musty and damp.

"Do you think he's still out here looking for us?" Christy's voice was hushed.

"No. It's after eight, and there are too many people up and about. Even if he is, he's not going to find us. The forest is way too big."

"Unless we have really bad luck. Oh, wait, isn't that what we've been having?"

Glancing back at her, Luke saw that she

was looking slightly wilted and way too pale. Her white T-shirt was smudged and grass-stained, and it was still damp enough to give him a decent view of her nipples. Her shorts ended at mid-thigh, and below them her truly phenomenal legs were scratched and dirty. Beneath that fringe of choppy blond hair that he wasn't sure he was ever going to get used to, her big brown eyes flickered over their surroundings nervously. And, sure enough, the left one had a purple semicircle at its outer corner.

His gut tightened just from looking at it.

"You've got a black eye," he said.

She frowned and lifted a hand to the eye in question. He gritted his teeth against the urge to turn around and press his lips to that damaged eye, and forged on.

"So tell me about your former boyfriend," he said over his shoulder. The question was intended to remind himself of his true reason for being in her life as much as it was to milk her for more information. The way he felt at the moment, information could pretty much go hang. "Michael, wasn't it?"

"There's not much to tell." He could hear the glimmer of a smile enter her voice as she continued: "By the way, just so you know, you're heaps better in bed."

That stopped him.

"Oh, yeah?" He turned around, tilted her chin up, and looked down at her. Choppy blond hair, black eye, dirty face and all, she was the most gorgeous woman he had ever seen in his life. That, he realized, was not good. In fact, it was shaping up to be a problem of major proportions — but recognizing it for what it was didn't stop him from dropping a quick hard kiss on her mouth.

"Yeah," she said, smiling up at him when he lifted his head.

He kissed her again, just for good measure, this time lingering a little over the softness of her lips. As they resumed their trek, he couldn't help but notice that his spirits were at least fractionally lighter than before.

Whatever else might be wrong with their relationship, the chemistry was definitely right.

"You think he's behind this? Michael?" He threw over his shoulder, doing his best to keep his eye on the ball.

A beat passed.

"Maybe." Christy said, her fingers tightening on his. Then, "Probably."

"Maybe you should ask him. Can you

get in touch with him some way?"

"I tried calling him at his private number. He didn't answer, and he hasn't called me back."

"He could be out of town. He could even have followed you here to Ocracoke."

Luke felt the sudden tremor in Christy's fingers and wanted to kick himself for putting the idea in her head. It frightened her, that much was clear. Hell, in her shoes he'd be frightened, too.

"You don't have to be afraid any more, you know," he said, his tone a little rough around the edges as his hand tightened protectively around hers. "I'll keep you safe."

The derisive sound she made was a classic male self-esteem deflator.

"You can't. How can you? You're a lawyer. They're the mob. I appreciate the sentiment, but if we're going to get out of this alive you need to get real."

It was getting harder and harder to remember that as far as she was concerned he wasn't his usual tough-guy-in-charge. "Okay, right."

"I shouldn't have told you," she said, clearly filled with remorse.

"You did the right thing to tell me." His voice was firm.

"If they kill you because of me, I'll never forgive myself."

"I'm actually pretty hard to kill."

"They kill people all the time, you know. It doesn't mean anything to them."

She was trying her best to warn him, and she sounded so earnest and so sweet and so genuinely worried about him that he couldn't help himself: he turned around and kissed her again. She wrapped her arms around his neck and kissed him back a little desperately. It was some few minutes before he summoned the strength of will to set her back on her own two feet and lead the way to the road.

It was a gravel track just about wide enough for a single car to squeeze through. As Gary had said, the last few nights of rain had basically reduced it to mud. The ruts on either side were a running series of mud puddles. The middle was squishy rock, but it was high ground and undergrowth free.

"Oh my God. A road," Christy gasped when she emerged behind him through the vegetation and saw it.

"Can you believe it," Luke said, towing her down the middle. Okay, so his acting powers were wearing thin. He was hungry, he needed coffee like a mosquito needs blood, and he was practically out on his feet. And what was happening between him and Christy was nothing he wanted to think about until he had the benefit of at least one solid night's sleep.

"Shouldn't we keep to the side, you know, over in the trees?" A glance back told him that Christy was glancing apprehensively behind her. "What if he's somewhere on the road?"

"We'll hear him coming." Since the truth was that they hadn't seen hide nor hair of the guy since about fifteen minutes after bailing out of Christy's trunk, Luke calculated that the chances were way slim that he'd be coming along that particular mud track at that particular moment. There was always bad luck, of course, but unlike Christy's his world view tended toward the optimistic.

"How far do you think we have to go?"

"A ways." Actually, not that far at all, although of course he couldn't tell Christy that. Gary would have left their transportation somewhere fairly close by.

After about ten minutes of walking, he spotted it: a nubby tire sticking unobtrusively — although not so unobtrusively that he'd walk right past it — out from beneath a bush that crowded the side of the road.

Luckily for his Academy Award aspirations, Christy spotted it about the same time he did.

"Luke, look!" Tugging on his hand, she pointed.

"I see."

Even before he pulled it out from beneath the bush, Luke knew what it was: a dirt bike, a small, all-terrain motorcycle, as per request. As transportation went, it wasn't fancy, but it would do the job. And it wasn't elaborate enough that its discovery would rouse Christy's suspicions.

"Do you think it works?" Christy stared raptly at it.

"Let's see." Swinging a leg over it, he kick-started it. After three pumps, the engine roared to life.

"Thank you, God," Christy said devoutly, casting her eyes heavenward. Luke nearly smiled: *thank you, Gary* was more like it. Then she fixed those big brown eyes on him and frowned a little. "Do you think anyone would mind if we borrowed it?"

He couldn't help it. He had to tease her a little.

"I don't know," he said gravely. "Some people might consider that stealing."

"We'll bring it back."

"Yeah," he said, capitulating because she

was chewing her lower lip and that did bad things to his peace of mind. "We will. Hop on."

She did, locking her arms around his waist. With her snuggled up tight behind him, they headed off down the track.

The seat was small, the road was bumpy, and the ride was of necessity stop and go. As the sun continued its climb across the sky, mosquitoes and flies and biting gnats came out in swarms. In theory, their forward motion should have kept the worst of the predators away from them. In practice, it didn't. Since keeping the bike on the uneven surface required both hands, Luke had to forgo all but the occasional swat. And since keeping her butt from bouncing off the back end of the seat required both hands, Christy was in pretty much the same boat.

By the time they jolted out onto I-12, the two-lane highway that traversed the island, a good hour had passed and, among other things, Luke basically itched all over. The specter of poison ivy was rearing its ugly head, and the only thing that appealed to him more than the prospect of a hot shower was the thought of coffee and a hot shower.

"Hang on," he yelled. As Christy's arms

tightened around him he goosed the throttle. The results were less than spectacular. The bike's top speed was probably sixty miles an hour, and with Christy perched precariously behind him he was able to do about a third of that. The traffic was sporadic as the Hatteras ferry, which connected with I-12 at its northern tip, disgorged its load of tourists and their vehicles in waves. Cars overtook them, occasionally honked and went on by, with everyone pretty much headed in the same direction: south, toward Ocracoke Village.

"You want to stop by the sheriff's office on our way through and tell them what happened?" Luke yelled over the roar of the engine when they paused at a light at the edge of the village.

"No! I want to take a shower before I even think about talking to anyone!"

That was so in line with Luke's own thinking that he didn't say anything else. Calling more attention to himself with the local fuzz was not something he wanted to do. Number one, if the sheriff's department decided to do a really thorough check on him, they just might discover that Luke Randolph, Atlanta lawyer, didn't exist. And number two, whoever was trying to kill Christy had no idea that he'd been in that trunk with her, and it would be better for all concerned if it stayed that way.

The problem was, unless he could think of some way to persuade her otherwise, Christy was going to tell the sheriff's department the entire story as she knew it.

Luke pondered the dilemma as they putt-putted down Front Road and around the harbor toward the beach. This part of the island was clogged with traffic of various descriptions. It said something about the motley nature of the vehicles that they blended right in. No one appeared to pay the least attention to a Honda 250cc trail bike with two very dirty people on deck as it roared through the picturesque town.

Christy's arms tightened around his waist as they turned a corner and her cottage came into view. It was nearly noon, the sky was blue, the sun was bright, and last night's torrential rain was forgotten. They passed his cottage, then pulled into Christy's driveway. Mrs. Castellano, her attention apparently attracted by the noise of the engine, looked up from her front yard, where she was, as usual, tending her flowers as well as the goings-on in the neighborhood. Luke gave her a wave. She waved back, and turned her attention to

431

her garden again.

"The garage door opener is in my car," Christy yelled as he stopped in front of her garage. Luke nodded, and cut the engine.

The sudden silence was deafening.

"But I have a spare key to the cottage tucked inside that flowerpot," Christy whispered as she climbed off the back.

"You're coming in with me, right?" she asked warily as he swung off behind her and put the kickstand down. Luke swept her with a glance: she basically looked like she'd been through a wind tunnel. Her hair stood out around her head like dandelion fluff, bits of leaves and other debris clung to her clothes, and one of the straps that secured her sandals flapped loose. Her eye was indeed black, her face was brown with grime, and to add insult to injury her nose was sunburned to a rosy pink.

Dirty and disheveled as she was, she made his heart skip a beat.

"Honey, you couldn't lose me if you tried," he said, gruff because what was happening to him was so not a good thing. Christy went over to a big pink begonia in a clay pot, dug around in the dirt and produced the key. As he followed her into the cottage, he realized Gary was watching, which didn't exactly do much for his comfort level, but the alternative — which was taking her with him to his cottage — was so fraught with peril that it wasn't really an alternative at all. All she had to do was open the door to the third bedroom and the shit would hit the fan. Just thinking about it made Luke wince.

Ignoring Gary, Luke did a quick search of the cottage for Christy's benefit, then followed her into the master bedroom. And shut the door.

And thanked God that he hadn't thought it necessary to plant a camera in the bedrooms.

An hour later, fresh from the long, hot shower he'd shared with Christy, Luke padded through the bedroom with a towel hitched around his waist, on his way to transfer his clothes from the washer, where hopefully they had finished their cycle, to the dryer. Christy, likewise wrapped in a towel, was standing in front of the bathroom mirror carefully blow-drying her hair. She'd shampooed it at least three times that he knew of. Along with leaves and pine needles and other debris, she'd found a couple of dead insects caught in the tangled strands, and her horrified reaction had made it clear: she was not a fan of bugs.

Luke smiled faintly at the memory as he left the bedroom. He hadn't gone more than two steps along the hall when the door to the second bathroom opened without warning. Every muscle in his body tensed. He stopped short, shifting instantly into kick-ass warrior mode. Who the hell — ?

"Christy?" A female voice asked, and a girl of about twenty stepped into the hall just a few paces in front of him. She was a flaming redhead, a real looker, with big hair, big eyes, big boobs, and a tanned, toned body stuffed into an orange bikini the size of a postage stamp.

She stopped dead in turn. Her eyes widened and swept over him, then returned to his face.

"Yo," she said, sounding both surprised and interested. "Did you come with the cottage?"

26

After the shower came food, and then as soon as she could she was going to collapse somewhere. With that agenda in mind, Christy headed toward the kitchen, only to stop dead in her tracks the instant she left the bedroom for the hall.

The bikini-clad redhead ogling Luke looked past him and spotted her.

"Christy?" She sounded doubtful.

"Angie!" All else was forgotten in a burst of welcome. Beaming, Christy rushed past Luke to hug her youngest sister, who returned her hug fiercely.

After a moment, Angie pulled back to look at her. "Oh my God, what have you done to your hair?"

Christy fingered it self-consciously. "I got it cut. I went blonde. It's a long story. Does it look awful?"

Angie grimaced. "Not *awful*."

"Yeah, I thought so," Christy said, resigned, reading between the lines with no difficulty whatsoever. The thing about sisters was, they could pretty much be counted on to tell you the truth whether you wanted to hear it or not. No big deal. After all this was over she'd go back to her natural color and let her hair grow out. If she lived long enough, of course.

"Actually, it's kind of sexy," Angie said thoughtfully, surveying her from head to toe. "Just not you."

"Are you saying I'm not sexy?" Christy planted her fists on her hips and narrowed her eyes at her sister.

Angie grinned at her. The truth was, Angie, with her teased-up hair, heavily applied makeup and wardrobe that ran to spandex shorts, miniskirts and skimpy tops with necklines down to there, was the only one of them who truly qualified as sexy; Nicole, now in frazzled mommy mode, was a has-been; and Christy, with her normally unexciting blunt cut and lawyer clothes, was pretty much the conservative never-was of the bunch. They all knew it, and were content in their various roles, even if from time to time each of them had been known to try to make a sister over in her own image.

"You're smart," Angie said loyally. "That's better."

Christy recollected how unlikely it was that Angie should be standing there in front of her. "What are you *doing* here?"

"I got laid off, and Mom was worried about you being down here all alone. She thought you might be in a funk or something about breaking up with Michael. So she said I should come down here and keep you company. I said, good idea. So here I am."

Angie's gaze flicked past Christy to Luke, who was standing in the background watching them with a slightly bemused expression. His arms were crossed over his chest, which, Christy realized, was bare, like most of the rest of him. Only then did she recall that, like herself, he was clad only in a towel.

Christy felt her cheeks start to grow warm.

Angie grinned wickedly at her. "I guess Mom was wrong. I guess you're not in a funk over Michael, after all."

"This is Luke," Christy said, feeling absurdly self-conscious. "Luke, this is my sister Angie."

"We met," Luke said, a little dryly.

Angie looked at him again and her grin broadened. "I thought he might have come with the cottage, but he said he didn't."

"He's staying next door," Christy said in a dampening tone.

Angie cut her a droll look. "It's nice to know the neighbors are friendly."

A shriek of laughter from the direction of the living room caused Christy's head to swivel in that direction.

"Uh, I brought a couple of friends with me," Angie said. "I thought we could make sort of a party out of it. We let ourselves in with the key Mom gave me. You were taking a shower when we got here." Her gaze flicked to Luke again and she grinned. "Or something."

"Okay," Luke said. "I'll just go see if I can't scare up some clothes. Nice to meet you, Angie."

"You too."

He retreated toward the bedroom and closed the door. Angie's grin turned on Christy.

"I think I scared him off," she said.

"Angie . . ." Christy didn't know whether to laugh or groan. One thing was sure, Angie and her friends couldn't stay. And she couldn't tell her sister the truth about why not, either. Or at least, not the whole truth.

"Look, I'm sorry if I'm raining on your parade by showing up like this. How was I supposed to know you were down here shacked up with some guy?"

"I'm not down here shacked up with some guy."

"Oh yeah? He looked like a guy to me. Hey, you don't have to be embarrassed. I don't blame you one bit. He's a total hottie."

"Angie —"

"Is it really all over between you and Michael?"

"Yeah," Christy said, there being no confusion at all on that point. "It is."

"Glad I didn't get around to buying the bridesmaid's dress, then. But Nicole did. She's gonna be pissed if it's off for real."

Christy sighed. "I'll pay her back." Then she gathered herself together. "Look, you and your friends can't stay."

"Angie, come here! You gotta see this!" a girl shrieked, and Christy realized that, rather than coming from the living room, Angie's friends were on the patio.

"Be right there," Angie called back. Then she looked at Christy again. "Hey, you can screw anybody you want to. I don't care. Amber and Maxine don't care either. All we want to do is soak up some sun and have a good time."

"You're gonna miss it!" the same girl

warned from the patio. Christy assumed that it was either Amber or Maxine.

"Yeah, okay, I'm coming," Angie called. She looked at Christy. "We'll stay out of your way, okay? And I'll tell everybody hands off Mr. Studly Neighbor. And I won't say a word about him to Mom."

"Angie, no." But her sister was already heading toward the patio, and Christy was left to talk to her waggling butt. Which, except for a tangerine-colored string around her waist, was bare. True to type, Angie was wearing a thong.

Christy rolled her eyes skyward.

Okay, Angie and company had to be gotten rid of before her sister could get caught up in this, too. Christy was going to get dressed, then go out there and tell them all about the serial killer.

If that didn't do the trick, nothing would.

She headed for her bedroom.

"Your sister's cute." Luke was standing at the foot of the bed hitching a pair of sweatpants up around his waist. Christy did a double take. She knew those sweatpants. They were baggy and gray and she usually wore them when she did the laundry. On Luke, they looked like leggings. High-water leggings. Kind of ridiculous, except they did a nice job of out-lining his package. And, she saw as she walked past him, his tush.

"Believe me, the feeling's mutual. She thinks you're a total hottie." Christy opened the closet door and rummaged through the clothes she had left.

"What can I say? Except she's got good taste."

Pulling a pair of jeans and a white eyelet-trimmed sleeveless blouse out of the closet, Christy turned and gave him a you-are-so-not-funny look. He grinned at her. Bleary-eyed and sporting a nice collection of random scratches, bruises and bites, he was still hunky enough to stop a suscep-tible woman's breath, she acknowledged. His shoulders were wide, his chest and arms were impressively muscled, and the wedge of dark brown hair in the middle of his chest was just thick enough to be mas-culine without going the full gorilla. His drying hair waved back from his face to end in a tangle of ringlets around his neck. His deep blue eyes were gorgeous even when they weren't all crinkled around the edges and smiling at her, as they were just at that moment. He was buff and bronzed and blond, and in her opinion that beat tall, dark, and handsome hands down any day.

"I can't believe she's here," Christy said, opening the dresser drawer in search of undies. "I'm not going to let her stay."

"She looks like she's got a mind of her own to me."

"I'm going to tell her about the serial killer. But not about the rest of it. I can't let her get caught up in this." Having found what she needed, she closed the drawer and turned. "I wish I hadn't gotten you caught up in this."

"Honey, believe me, I can take care of myself." He walked toward her, half smiling, and cupped her face in his hands. He looked down at her for a moment, his expression inscrutable. "And by the way, just for the record, I think you're sexy as hell."

Then he kissed her, a slow, deep kiss that sent heat shooting clear down to her toes. Christy closed her eyes, dropped her clothes, clutched at his forearms and kissed him back. She was so tired, she was groggy and so empty she could eat grass, and terrified and injured and achy all over to boot, and he could still make her want him. Bad.

This guy could rock my world.

The thought surprised her. It rattled her. She wasn't sure she liked the implications. Unlike Angie, who went through boyfriends the way a person with allergies goes through tissues, she'd always been the faithful type. Michael had been her most serious relationship. She'd been in love with Michael — at least, with the man she'd thought he was. She had been going to marry Michael.

But Michael had never made her feel like this.

The thought made her eyes pop open.

Luke must have felt her stiffen, because he lifted his head.

"Something wrong?" he asked, frowning down at her.

"No," she said, feeling a little spurt of panic in case he should somehow be able to read her thoughts in her eyes. "Nothing's wrong." Then she recovered a small measure of her composure, along with her sense of humor. "Unless you count being attacked with a hatchet, run off the road, knocked out by a stun gun, stuffed in a trunk, forced to run for my life and knowing the guy who did it is still out there wanting to kill me as something wrong."

"No," Luke said gravely. "I don't count that."

Christy laughed.

Luke didn't. Instead he smiled a little and watched her with an odd expression in his eyes, then ran his thumb over her cheek.

"You should laugh more," he said. "Shows your dimples."

An explosion of loud cheers sounded from outside. He glanced at the door, then back at her.

"Never a dull moment," he said, and his hands dropped away from her face.

Christy grimaced. "You know, I used to think that was a good thing."

Luke grinned, then watched with his arms crossed over his chest as she bent to gather up her clothes.

"I'm going to run next door and get some clothes and do a few things, and then I'll be back," he said when she straightened. "One advantage to having your sister and her friends here is that I don't think you have to worry about anybody trying to break in while I'm gone."

That was true. Actually, having Angie and her friends around would be comforting if she hadn't been so worried about somebody going after them as well as, or instead of, herself.

"You okay with that?" he asked.

"I'll be fine. Don't worry."

"That sounds like my line." Then his brow creased as something appeared to occur to him. "Oh, and you probably want to hold off on calling the sheriff till I get back. It'd be easier if we talked to him together."

She nodded.

He kissed her again, quick and hard, then left. Getting dressed, Christy heard the burst of loud greetings that, she assumed, met him as he stepped through the patio door, and smiled. Knowing Angie, she and her friends were giving him a hard time. Luke would be lucky to escape with his life — to say nothing of her pants.

Gary grinned at him from his post in Command Central as Luke walked into the cottage. Already smarting from the gauntlet of knowing looks, smirks, giggles, and ribald comments that he'd had to navigate to escape Christy's cottage, Luke returned that grin with a level stare.

"You got something to say to me?" he asked challengingly.

"Nope." Gary shook his head, then chuckled. "Except, nice ass."

Since that was a repeat of a comment one of Angie's friends had called after him as he'd headed down the beach path, Luke shot Gary a quelling look and continued on toward his bedroom without comment.

He opened the door a little cautiously. No foul smell greeted him. A glance at his bed reassured him. Fresh blankets. No cat crap.

How was he going to persuade Christy to leave him out of the report she made to the cops?

Honey, you know, it just makes me look like a total wimp if I admit some bozo was able to knock me over the head and stuff me in your trunk. So why don't we just leave that part out?

Oh, yeah, like that didn't sound suspicious. Casting around for another angle, Luke shed Christy's too-tight sweats in favor of a pair of jeans and an ancient Seventy-sixers jersey, and padded barefoot back down the hall to raid the refrigerator and make some decent coffee. The instant crap he'd cadged from Christy's larder before showering had basically tasted like mud, and its caffeine content wouldn't have kept a fly awake. On his way past Command Central, he paused, his attention caught by an image on the central monitor. Two of the girls were still out on the patio, he saw at a glance, but Christy's sister stood in the open doorway with her back to the camera. The view was, to say the least, distracting.

"Somebody ought to tell her that thongs aren't allowed on this beach," Gary muttered.

"Yeah," Luke said, perusing the close-up with lazy attention. "You go for it. Thanks for cleaning up the cat crap, by the way."

"I didn't have much choice. It was stinking up the whole house."

Christy walked into the frame. She was wearing faded jeans and a kind of frilly white top, and her feet were bare. She looked cool and slim and so lovely that she took his breath away. It bothered him to realize that he would rather look at her when she was covered from her neck to her ankles than at her hot and nearly naked sister.

There was something fundamentally wrong with that.

"Oh my God, what happened to your eye?" Angie shrieked, sounding like she was right in the room with them as she turned and, thanks to the light pouring through the open patio door, apparently saw Christy's shiner for the first time.

"I was in a car accident. Last night. Angie —"

"That's a relief. I was afraid you were going to say the hunk did it," one of the girls on the patio said, as they craned their necks to look back at Christy. Both were late teens, early twenties, bottle blondes in teeny bikinis with big hair cascading around slim shoulders and enough makeup to paint the cottage twice over. Their boobs were bigger even than Angie's, nice brown cantaloup-sized hooters that, under other conditions, would have caught Luke's eye for longer than the couple of seconds he accorded them. They'd managed to scrounge up two lounge chairs from somewhere and were draped across them soaking up the sun.

"Yeah," said the other. "Wouldn't you know it? It's always the good-looking guys."

"It was the air bag," Christy said.

"Oh, by the way, this is Amber. This is Maxine." Angie made the introductions while Christy moved up to stand beside her in the doorway. Luke found himself assessing two mighty fine asses: one all but buck naked, the other doing its bit to fill out a pair of faded jeans.

The jeans won again. Shit.

"Hey, Christy." Amber and Maxine chorused in unison. "Thanks for letting us come."

"Hey," Christy said, sounding faintly uncomfortable. "Uh, look —"

"Your boyfriend is the bomb," one of them — Luke had no idea whether it was Amber or Maxine — told her with a grin. "You get tired of him, you let me know."

"Or me," the other said.

Gary smirked and cast a razzing glance up at Luke.

"He said he's renting the cottage next door," the first one added. "What I want to know is, are there any more at home like him?"

Amber and Maxine both burst into laughter.

"There's your cue, buddy," Luke said. "They're here, they're hot, and they're horny. Go for it."

Gary grimaced. "Yeah, right. Anyway, Christy's more my type. Maybe I should go after her instead."

Luke almost said something on the order of *do it and die* when he realized he was being teased.

"Whatever floats your boat," he said, feigning indifference, and straightened away from the doorjamb to pad toward the kitchen.

"We got anything to eat?" he called over his shoulder.

"Leftover lasagna. Pasta salad. We would have some nice cold slices of steak teriyaki, but, oh, wait, the cat you brought home ate the steak." Gary abandoned Command Central to follow him into the kitchen.

"Christy brought the cat, not me." Luke opened a cabinet and slid his fingers around the blue Maxwell House can. Just the sight of it made his brain cells perk up.

"It was your fault."

"Could you give the cat obsession a rest, please?" Luke dumped coffee and water into the coffeemaker and turned it on.

"Sure. Fine." Settling himself on a barstool, Gary didn't say anything for a minute or so while Luke opened the refrigerator and rummaged around. Then, in a carefully neutral tone, he asked, "Dirt bike work out?"

"Yeah. You did good." Luke wasn't in the mood for leftover lasagna or pasta salad. He settled on plain old bologna, set it on the counter, and reached for the bread. "You get anything on the white truck?"

"Twelve registered here in Ocracoke. Over three hundred in the Outer Banks. More if you go inland."

"Great. Ah well, I guess we start checking each and every one out."

"Already doing it," Gary said, watching as Luke slathered mustard on bread. "I don't see how you can eat that stuff."

"I'm hungry." Luke slapped the sandwich together.

Gary made a sound under his breath that basically condemned bologna sandwiches to an outer circle of hell and abandoned the subject.

"Christy wasn't suspicious when you two just happened to stumble across a dirt bike way out there in the middle of nowhere?"

"Nah." Luke bit into his sandwich. The smell of coffee was beginning to permeate the air. His eyes half-closed in anticipation, Luke realized that, like many a seeker of truth in the past, he had accidentally stumbled upon the way: the on-ramp to the nirvana highway was reached via bologna sandwiches and coffee. "Anyway, I think by that time she was too tired to be suspicious."

"You get anything good out of her?" As Luke paused in the act of devouring his sandwich to fix Gary with a look, Gary apparently realized how that sounded. "Information, I mean," he clarified hurriedly.

"Some." Luke took another bite, and turned his attention to the coffee. It was almost ready. "Franky Hill's dead. They killed him, and showed her the body. She's been scared out of her mind ever since."

"I knew it," Gary said with satisfaction. "You gonna bring her in now?"

Luke chewed and pondered. He'd been asking himself the same question for the last few hours, and not coming up with any answers that didn't involve major helpings of shit hitting the fan. "Yeah, well, I'm thinking about it."

"It seems to me —" Gary began, only to be interrupted by a quick knock on the patio door. Luke's head swiveled toward the sound. Gary's head swiveled toward the sound.

Christy, with the feline Mike Tyson glowering in her arms, gave a little wave through the glass and slid the patio door open.

Luke almost choked on his bologna. Swallowing, he put the remainder of the sandwich down fast.

"Marvin had a bird trapped on the other side of my fence," Christy said, stepping inside and closing the door behind her, presumably so that the poor misunderstood kitty couldn't get out. That done, she let the cat jump to the carpet. After one hunted glance around, it bounded for the hall and disappeared. "When Amber heard it chirping and tried to save it, he scratched her. So I caught him and brought him over. I really don't think you ought to be letting him outside. It seems to make him nervous."

If Luke hadn't been so horrified himself, he would have laughed at the look on Gary's face. Coming face-to-face with the Antichrist couldn't have provoked a more appalled expression.

"Thanks for bringing him home," Luke said, walking toward her. The key was to get Christy out of the house fast, before the cat had time to vent its frustration on his bed.

"Yeah," Gary said.

"No problem." Christy slid her hands into the back pockets of her jeans and glanced past Luke toward the kitchen counter. "Do I smell coffee?"

"You know, I've been thinking," Luke said, sliding a hand around her elbow as a prelude to turning her around and escorting her out the door and back across the sand. "Maybe I should help you tell your sister and her friends about the serial killer."

"I already tried." Christy's expression turned glum as she looked up at him. "Know what they said? Amber said '*Whoa*' and Maxine said '*Ooo, that gives me chills.*' Then Angie said '*What are the chances?*'

And then they all three decided that a free week at the beach was worth the risk."

She sounded so disgusted that Luke had to smile.

"Let's see if I —" he began, only to break off as shrieks of laughter filled the air. Shrieks of female laughter. Realizing that it was coming from the third bedroom with a thrill of pure horror, Luke reached for the handle of the patio door.

"Hey, forget it. He belongs to my sister." Angie's voice rose above the laughter, clear as a bell.

Christy froze as she heard it. Her head spun almost as fast as Linda Blair's in *The Exorcist*. Luckily, a full 360-degree turn was not required. For an instant, a hideous instant, she stared at the open door of the third bedroom. Then, with a single awful look that encompassed both Luke and Gary, she jerked her arm from Luke's hold and, to the accompaniment of more raucous female laughter, rushed toward the door of Command Central.

27

For a long moment Christy stood there with her mouth open, absolutely unable to believe her eyes. Among a whole plethora of other electronic equipment, there were three computer monitors set up in the room. One showed a view of the outside front of her house as seen from, say, the woods across the street, complete with a couple on bicycles who were apparently just at that moment riding past. The second pictured her house from the rear, panning from one side to the other from a distance of about a hundred feet, with the pinkie-sized figures of her sister and her sister's friends sunbathing on the patio as the centerpiece. The third view obviously originated from inside the house. It was framed by an image of her open patio door. Beyond it, she could clearly see — and hear — Angie and her two friends in screen-filling close-up.

For a moment all she could do was stare while her mind went through an entire theme park's worth of spins and loops. Then she turned her head to find Luke right behind her, grimacing. Beyond him stood Gary, who couldn't have looked any more horrified if he'd just swallowed a live grenade.

There was no doubt about their guilt. It was written all over their faces.

"What are you two, a couple of perverts?" she gasped as memories of certain articles she had read about men who get their kicks bugging the homes of neighborhood women filled her head. Then she turned on her heel and pushed the flat of both hands against Luke's chest to move him out of her path. "Get out of my way. I'm calling the sheriff."

"Christy, no." Luke staggered back a step, but managed to grab her around the waist when she would have stomped past. "Wait. Stop. I can't let you do that."

"What do you mean, you can't let me do that? You can't stop me from doing that, you sick, disgusting . . . *pervert.*"

"Christy . . ."

"Don't you *Christy* me."

But despite her struggles he wasn't letting go, and all of a sudden it occurred to her that she might have inadvertently stumbled across a secret that he and Gary really, truly didn't want anyone to know. That might, in fact, put her in danger. Voyeurs went to prison, didn't they? Heart leaping, juiced by a jolt of pure adrenaline, she reverted to the scrappy little girl who'd had to fend for herself and her sisters in Pleasantville and elbowed Luke hard in the stomach.

"Oomph." Caught by surprise, Luke groaned and doubled over.

"Sicko!" Christy flung at him as she tore herself out of his slackened hold and fled toward the patio door and safety. Once outside, she planned to scream like a siren all the way home as she ran to lock herself in her house and call the sheriff.

"Get her, Gary!"

Gary, clearly appalled at the turn events had taken, stood valiantly between her and the patio door, his eyes as big as pizzas, his mouth agape, waving his hands back and forth in a clear — and futile — effort to ward her off.

"Not perverts . . . not perverts," he kept repeating in a kind of anguished chant. In well-pressed khaki slacks and a pale blue polo shirt that did absolutely nothing for his thin frame, with his glasses slightly askew and his red hair parted on the side and brushed shiny, he looked about as formidable as Sponge Bob Squarepants.

Christy didn't even slow down.

"Move." She strong-armed past him like a running back with the ball, making it through with laughable ease. Grabbing for the patio door handle, she jerked the door open —

"Jesus, Christy, hang on a minute! Stop!" Luke came leaping after her, hooking an arm around her waist and dragging her back away from the door. "Gary, get the door!"

Knowing Angie and her friends were outside and not so far away, Christy shrieked like a howler monkey at the same moment Gary dove for the door. He slammed it shut and locked it, then he stood with his back to it, his gaze glued to her face, his expression alarmed and stupefied, as if he had just realized that, against his will, he was probably going to wind up involved in a murder. Meanwhile, Luke, strong and steady, clearly the man who was going to have to do the actual physical job of silencing her, reeled her back toward him like a fish on a line.

Oh God, had she really trusted him? Had she really thought that she might, just might, be starting to fall in love with him? How bad a judge of men was she anyway?

Like the worst ever, apparently: first a mobster, now a pervert.

"Now just calm down —" Luke locked both arms around her waist while she strained with every ounce of strength she possessed toward the door.

"Calm down my ass! I'll show you calm down!" With the thought of how he had spied on her for impetus, she twisted in his arms and aimed a roundhouse punch for his nose. He jerked his head out of harm's way just in the nick of time, and her fist slammed harmlessly into the air beyond his shoulder. But she kneed him, hard, even if his thigh shifted at the last minute to block the worst of the blow.

"*Ow! Shit!* Damn it, Christy, chill out!" It was a yelp. Then he whirled her around, clamped his arms around her, and picked her clear up off the floor. Kicking and screaming, trying and failing to block his progress by pushing against the walls with her bare feet, she was carried out of the living room and down the hall.

"Watch the monitors and make sure none of those damned girls comes looking for her." Luke grunted over his shoulder to Gary as they reached the doorway to the master bedroom. Christy tried to grab onto the jamb but she couldn't get a grip, and Luke already had her inside the room. It was a near duplicate of her own, Christy saw at a glance as he lugged her over to the bed and then dropped her on it. She screamed, bounced, and rolled toward the floor; he hit the bed beside her and yanked her back.

"Let me go!" Shrieking, she turned on him, only to have him grab her wrists and pin them to the bed over her head before she could land so much as a single blow. She kicked at him, and he heaved himself on top of her. The sudden weight of his big body stilled her legs and crushed her into the mattress.

"Now just hang on a minute. . . ." His tone was that of a patient man being sorely tried.

"Pervert!" Shrieking the word, she bucked like a demented bronco. Luke, on top of her, barely even bounced.

"Jesus Christ, Christy, would you just —"

Sucking in every atom of air she could, she tried a different tack: she screamed right in his face.

Wincing, Luke transferred both wrists to one hand and clamped the other over her mouth, stifling her in full blast.

Feeling like a bottle that had just been corked, staring surprised at him over that muffling hand, Christy realized with a little thrill of frightened disbelief that she was well and truly trapped. Had Angie heard her screams? Had anyone? Heart thudding, blood racing, Christy faced up to the fact that the chances that she had been heard were remote. She had to assume that she was on her own.

"Cripes, Luke, don't hurt her," Gary said from the doorway, sounding alarmed.

"I'm not going to hurt her." Luke looked disgusted. "Of course I'm not going to hurt her. What do you think I am, anyway? But we can't just let her go running down the beach screaming that she just escaped from a couple of psychos, either." He focused on Christy, who was glaring at him. "Will you just please let me explain? Please?"

If there was an explanation that didn't involve some kind of weird proclivity on his part, she was all ears.

She gave a curt nod.

"That's my girl," he soothed, cautiously lifting his hand from her mouth. "Honey, I know this looks bad, but —"

That *honey* hit home. Appalled, she remembered the tender feelings she'd been experiencing toward him, the warmth, the lust . . .

"Oh my God, I slept with a fricking pervert," she gasped.

"Not pervert," Gary said from the doorway. "FBI."

FBI?

Luke's head dropped against her shoulder so that she could no longer see his face. That gesture as much as anything told the story. Knowing that she was physically safe should have been a relief, but she couldn't quite get her mind around how such a thing could be. Her heart continued to thud and her blood to race, and to make matters worse she was suddenly finding it difficult to catch her breath.

"FBI?" she asked blankly.

With Luke's head out of the way, she could see Gary in the doorway. He nodded glumly at her.

"FBI?" This time it was uttered in an awful tone.

Luke's head came up. He met her gaze. His expression was both pained and rueful.

"Yeah," he said.

It took another moment for her mind to fully grasp the hideous truth.

"You *creep*," she gasped.

"FBI," Gary corrected urgently from the doorway.

Luke's head dropped again.

"Gary, man, go watch the monitors, would you please?" His voice was faintly muffled by her shoulder. Christy could once again see Gary over Luke's broad back. "The only thing that could possibly make this any better is if we got another surprise visitor."

Gary made an apologetic face at her. If Christy had had a free hand available, she would have flipped him the bird.

"And shut the door," Luke added.

Gary nodded, and complied.

At the sound of the door being closed, Luke's head came up again. For a moment neither he nor Christy said anything as their gazes met and held. She lay stiff as a board beneath him, registering his bronzed handsomeness, his dark gold curls, his intense blue eyes as if she were seeing them for the first time.

"My God," she said slowly, as their entire association scrolled like a fast-forwarded movie through her head, "it's all been a lie."

"Not everything," he said, but she cut him off ruthlessly.

"You're not a lawyer from Atlanta." It was a statement rather than a question.

"No." His tone was apologetic.

"You're not here on vacation."

"No."

"You and Gary didn't get a week off and the use of this beach house from your employer."

He shook his head.

"I don't believe this. What are you doing here?" She drew in a sharp breath as suddenly everything began to come together in her mind. "You're here *spying* on me."

He grimaced. "We've had you under surveillance. Christy —"

"No." Her voice was sharp. "I want to work this out for myself. That first night — you were on my patio." Something black leaped onto the dresser, catching her gaze, startling her until she saw what it was: Marvin. He crouched there, tail lashing, glaring at them. A thought occurred to her, and her eyes widened as her gaze shifted back to Luke. "Marvin — is he even your cat? He's not, is he? You were *lying*."

Luke's jaw tightened. "He's a stray."

"I don't believe this. What were you doing on my patio?" Suddenly she tensed. "You didn't have anything to do with what happened to Elizabeth Smolski, did you?"

"Jesus God, Christy, you know me better than that."

Christy looked at him, then slowly shook

her head. "I don't know you better than that. I don't know you at all. Is Luke Randolph even your name?"

He sighed. "Luke Rand. I'm a Special Agent with the Philadelphia office of the FBI."

Philadelphia. Christy didn't say it aloud. She couldn't. She could barely breathe, let alone speak. His weight suddenly felt as if it were crushing her lungs. The sense of betrayal she felt was making her sick to her stomach.

"Could you get off me, please?" she asked in a tight little voice.

His eyes flickered over her face. "Sure. As long as you stay put. We need to talk here."

"So talk." Her tone was less than friendly, but he released her wrists and rolled off her, although he kept a careful hand splayed across her stomach. Just in case, she guessed, she should try to bolt.

Not that she had any intention of going anywhere just yet. She wanted — no, she *needed* — to hear exactly how big a fool she had been.

"Philadelphia," she said, her arms moving down until they were pressed flat beside her. Beneath her fingers she could feel the velvety texture of the velour blanket that covered the bed. "Exactly how long have you been watching me?"

He was lying on his side next to her, his head propped on one hand. She could feel the warm solidity of him against her arm, her side. Meeting his gaze, Christy felt pain twist in her heart like a small, cold knife. *It had all been a lie . . .*

"We've been aware of you ever since you went to work at DePalma and Lowery."

"Oh my God." Her stomach clenched. Her fists clenched. "Two years. I don't believe this."

His lips tightened. "You, personally, have only been under surveillance since you came to Ocracoke. Before that we were watching the law firm and the Masseria family in general, and Michael DePalma in particular."

"You followed me down to Ocracoke." The true scope of the situation was becoming clear to her in spurts. It was as if her mind could only absorb so much betrayal at once.

"We didn't exactly follow you. We're looking for Michael DePalma. We thought he might contact you here."

"Michael's still in Philadelphia." Her voice went very small on the last two words. "Isn't he?"

Luke shook his head. "A sealed indictment was issued for him last week. Before he could be picked up, he disappeared. We have evidence that suggests he may be here on Ocracoke. You wouldn't happen to have any idea exactly where, would you?"

"No."

He gave a little shrug. "Just thought I'd ask."

"What was he indicted for?" If her voice got any tighter it would squeak.

"Money laundering. Racketeering. Wire fraud. And soliciting the murders of two witnesses who can put him away for a minimum of twenty years, both of whom have been taken into custody for their own safety."

Oh God. Michael had solicited murders. She'd suspected that he was capable of that; now her suspicions were confirmed.

"Did he know? That he was going to be indicted, I mean?" Those last few weeks, she'd seen no sign of tension in Michael, no indication that anything was amiss. They'd been happy — at least, she'd been happy. Until Franky . . .

"It was supposed to be a secret proceeding. Obviously he got wind of it when the indictment was actually handed down, or he wouldn't have disappeared."

A moment passed.

"You've been pumping me for information about him, haven't you?" Light dawned in an unholy burst. "You've been trying to sweet-talk me into giving you information to help you find Michael."

Luke's jaw hardened fractionally. That was all it took: Christy knew it was true without him having to say a word. Recalling various exchanges, her eyes widened.

"That first night — what were you doing on my patio that first night?" Her stomach felt like it was being squeezed in a vise. Her gaze was riveted to his.

"Bugging your house."

"Bugging my house." Christy took a deep breath. She hadn't realized how tightly her fists were clenched until she deliberately relaxed them. "I thought at the time that it was odd that you could hear me screaming. These houses are practically soundproof. You heard me over your little audio/video system, didn't you?"

He looked grim. "You're damned lucky I did. I saved your life, remember?"

"Oh yeah, I remember." What Christy remembered was that it was then that she had first started to trust him. What a fool she'd been! "Didn't you make some kind of joke about being Johnny-on-the-spot that night?"

He had the grace to wince. "Christy —"

"Wait." She held up her hand. "Let me just get this whole thing straight in my mind before you start trying to sweet-talk me again. The lighthouse was next. You didn't follow me because you wanted to ask me out to dinner. You were keeping me under surveillance because you thought I might be meeting Michael. Weren't you?"

"Michael or somebody who could lead us to Michael."

"You know, I think I'm starting to see some light here. When I kissed you on my patio, it was night and the curtains were shut. A camera wouldn't have been able to see us. You were all over me like a bad rash. Then as soon as we got inside, you lost interest. That wasn't because you were afraid I was using you, was it? It was because my house is bugged, right?"

"I did not lose interest. Are you kidding me? I had to practically hobble home."

"But you turned me down even though I did everything but beg you to stay."

His face could have been carved from stone. "Staying would have been unprofessional."

"Unprofessional." Christy drew the word

out. The betrayal thing was really starting to sink in, and her temper was beginning to heat. "Uh-huh."

"You need to try to understand —" he began, frowning. His hand slid across her stomach.

"Oh, I do understand." Did she ever. She understood so much that her body hummed with tension; her eyes blazed up at him. "You romanced me to try to weasel information out of me. You kissed me to try to weasel information out of me. You *screwed* me to try to weasel information out of me. Where I come from, that doesn't make you a professional. It makes you a *jerk*."

"Just for the record, I did not romance you and kiss you and screw you to get information." His hand tightened on her hipbone. He leaned over her, his mouth grave, his eyes warm and apologetic and, yes, sensuous. "I did it because I wanted to. Because I couldn't help myself. Because you're the most beautiful woman I've ever seen in my life. Because every time I'm anywhere near you I get hot."

For a moment, as she met his gaze, her breathing suspended. For a moment, as she met his gaze, her bones seemed to melt and her heart did a funny little tap dance in her chest. For a moment, as she met his gaze, she believed.

But only for a moment. Unfortunately for him, she'd been down this route before.

"Don't you dare try to sweet-talk me anymore!" Outraged, she sat up and shoved the lying weasel hard with both hands when he grabbed at her. Caught off guard, he toppled onto his back, then with a yelp slid off the side of the bed. He hit the floor with a thud, and for the space of a heartbeat Christy blinked in surprise at the place where he had been.

Then she shot off the bed like a rock out of a slingshot and bolted for the door.

"Goddamn it, Christy, come back here!" he roared, already scrambling up.

"In your dreams, asshole."

Yanking open the door, she pelted for the great outdoors. At the precise same moment, Gary leaped out of the third bedroom yelling, "Incoming! Incoming! Incoming!"

28

"Help!" Christy shrieked at the top of her lungs as Luke grabbed her. Finding Gary square in her path had delayed her just enough to allow Luke to catch up. With a hand over her mouth and an arm clamped around her chest that, not coincidentally, also served to pinion her arms, he dragged her back toward his bedroom. Christy squirmed like a worm on a hook, but she couldn't break free.

"Her sister's coming," Gary said urgently to Luke over Christy's muffled cries. "What are we going to do?"

"Stall her. Talk about the weather. Exchange recipes. Hell, I don't know. Improvise."

"What do I tell her if she wants to see Christy?"

"Tell her we can't be disturbed. Tell her we're having a nooner."

With that Luke heaved her kicking and squirming back over the threshold, shouldered the door shut, then dragged her on past the bed into the bathroom and shut that door, too. It was dark as pitch in the small space until he managed to turn the light on with his elbow. Blinking, Christy saw that the bathroom was the twin of her own, right down to the fifties' tile and pedestal sink. Hauling her a little farther in, he managed to turn the water on in the sink, presumably to drown out any sounds she might make.

Like the muffled threats that were being garbled by his hand.

It was abundantly clear that she wasn't going anywhere. Christy quit struggling as she acknowledged that, giving the threats a rest, going still in his arms, hoping to lull him into a false sense of complacency. She was going to give Angie a few minutes, enough time to where she judged Gary might be talking to her, maybe even, if she was really lucky, with the patio door open, and then she was going to bite Luke's muffling hand like a rabid dog.

And scream for all she was worth.

He was watching her in the mirror above the sink, she discovered as she glimpsed their reflections. His broad shoulders dwarfed her own slender ones, and his hair gleamed with the dull gold of an old coin under the overhead light. With his hand over her mouth and his tall body curved around hers, he looked like a particularly sexy mugger caught in the act of overpowering his victim. The only problem with that scenario was that she, the muggee, did not look properly frightened. Instead, she looked furious.

Which was exactly what she was.

And that was a good thing, because it kept the hurt that lurked beneath the anger at bay. Everything had been a *lie.* . . .

Their gazes met in the mirror. Christy narrowed her eyes at him.

He sighed.

"Look, I'm going to take my hand off your mouth. If you scream, if your sister hears you, I'm going to have to tell her who I am and then she's going to be involved in this whether you like it or not. Is that what you want?"

Christy stared at him through the mirror as his words took form and substance in her mind. *My God.* She hadn't thought that far ahead, and if she'd carried out her plan the outcome would have been disastrous. If she screamed and Angie heard, Angie would come running. Getting Angie involved in this was the very last thing she wanted to do.

He must have read her reaction in her eyes.

"She's your sister. Whether you scream or not is up to you."

Watching her through the mirror, Luke slowly lifted his hand away from her mouth. It was clear that he wasn't quite sure what she would do. She could feel his tension, feel the heat of him, feel the accelerated rise and fall of his chest, feel the way his weight was balanced on the balls of his feet in case he should have to take action. His body was muscled and strong against her back and his arms were hard around her. He wasn't holding her tightly enough to hurt her, not at all, but she wasn't going anywhere anytime soon and she was left in no doubt about just how very strong he was. As she had thought before, those sissy curls and celestial eyes were downright misleading.

Just like the rest of him. She would never, in her wildest dreams, have guessed her laid-back surfer dude was a Fed.

More fool she.

"Go to hell," she said very pleasantly to his reflection.

His mouth went wry. "Jesus, Christy, give me a break here. I'm sorry, okay?"

"Not okay. And get your hands off me."

"Fine. Be as bitchy as you want." He let her go and stepped back, though, Christy noticed as she turned to face him, he was careful to stay between her and the door. Sliding his hands into the front pockets of his jeans, he rocked back on his heels. "For the record, though, this thing that's happening between us — it doesn't have anything to do with me trying to get information out of you."

Christy's brows twitched together ominously. "There is no 'thing' happening between us. Not now, not ever."

His eyes flicked over her face, and he sighed. "Do you think you could just listen to me for a minute?"

"Oh, absolutely," Christy folded her arms over her chest and glared at him. "Go ahead. Tell me a few more lies."

His lips tightened impatiently. "Okay, yes, I lied. I admit it. You tell me what else I was supposed to do. Walk right up and introduce myself? Not gonna happen. I'm an FBI agent, for God's sake, and I had you under surveillance. And let's not forget why: because you were down here acting as a bagman for the mob."

"Are you trying to say that it's all *my* fault that you lied to me?" She was outraged all over again.

"Damn it, Christy, what I'm saying is that I was just doing my job."

"Oh, that's original! Did you think that up all by yourself? That excuse is so old and so lame that we don't even try to use it in court anymore. 'I was just doing my job' doesn't cut it, not with me or anybody else."

He sighed again. "Look, it's not like I set out to lie to you. You were never even supposed to see me. If you hadn't caught me on your patio, you never would have known you were under surveillance. The only way you were supposed to know I was here is if I arrested you."

Christy felt her heart skip a beat. This was a possibility that she'd never considered. "Arrested me?"

"Yeah, arrested you. If we didn't find DePalma by watching you, the next step would have been to arrest you and charge you with a crime. That works real well as leverage. To avoid going to jail, people will generally make a deal to tell everything they know."

As she thought that one over, Christy started to fume.

"So, *are* you going to arrest me? Oh, wait, you don't need to, do you? You already found out everything you wanted to know by sleeping with me."

"Damn it, Christy —" He reached for her, but she took a quick step backward, dodging his hands. Anger was morphing into rage inside her, and this, she realized, was a good thing: she was now so mad that it completely blocked the pain of finding out he'd been using her all along.

"Don't touch me. Don't you ever touch me again."

Luke's expression turned suddenly grim. "You're determined to make me the bad guy here, aren't you? Okay, fine. I'm the bad guy. But just for the record, I made it with you because I wanted to and because you wanted to and for no other reason. And just for the record again, this surveillance thing has worked out as much to your advantage as mine: I may have gotten a little information out of it, but basically I've spent most of my time saving your ass."

"Oh, really?" Christy narrowed her eyes at him. "Did I forget to say thanks? Well, pardon me. My manners must be slipping." She took a deep breath. She was mad as hell, but she was working to get it under control. She had to summon up enough calm from somewhere to face Angie and the others in a few minutes without giving anything away. Which would take some acting: Angie knew her pretty darn well. "While we're putting things on the record here, let me just say that I think you're a lying jackass, and if you ever come near me again I'll cut off your dick and stuff it down your throat." She smiled at him, a quick, angry faux smile that was really more a baring of her teeth.

"Now you've gone and done it: my knees are shaking." Luke was smiling a little, and Christy realized, to her absolute fury, that he found her amusing.

"Are you *laughing?*" she asked.

"No. Absolutely not. Perish the thought." The smile vanished from his lips, but not from his eyes. He came toward her, caught her elbows, and pulled her into his arms.

"You're beautiful, you know that? I'm crazy about you. Lying was a mistake, I should never have done it, and I'll never do it again. Forgive me. Please."

Holding her gaze, he bent his head, clearly meaning to kiss her. Unwillingly fascinated, she watched his eyes as his head descended toward her. His lids drooped and the bright blue depths dark-ened until they were mere rings around his pupils. Beneath the lurking smile, his eyes went almost tender. . . .

The tenderness she thought she saw — to say nothing of the *I'm crazy about you* part of what he'd said — almost softened her up. Until she remembered that the dirty dog lied as easily as he breathed.

"When hell freezes over."

Infuriated all over again by her near-weakening, she punched him in the gut and, while he was still bending over sucking air, whisked herself around him and out the bathroom door.

"Wait. Stop. Hold it right there."

Okay, so she hadn't punched him hard, and he had a gut like iron. Next time he tried to kiss her, she would put some real muscle behind it.

"Get away from me, creep," she said, running for the bedroom door.

He caught her around the waist and spun her away from the door. She ended up with her back against the bedroom wall, her hands pinned beside her head, and all two hundred solid pounds of him pressing into her, holding her in place. The muscled resilience of his chest flattened her breasts, the hardness of his pelvis pinned her nether regions, and the solid strength of his legs lodged on either side of hers, rendering her all but immobile. To her annoyance, she discovered that the front of her was suddenly so hot that she positively welcomed the cool plaster at her back.

"Did I mention that you turn me on?" he said, looking down at her, still with that faint smile.

She gave him an evil look. Under the circumstances, the fact that the feeling was mutual in no way endeared him to her.

"Did I mention that I think you're better in bed than Michael?" Her tone was sugar sweet.

His eyes flickered, and his lids drooped a little, giving him a sexy, slumbrous look that made her want to do him and kill him at one and the same time.

"Yeah, I seem to recall something about that."

Kill him won in a landslide. "I lied."

"You did not."

The complacence in his voice made her grit her teeth. Only the thought of Angie possibly being within earshot kept her from ratcheting the encounter up a couple of hundred notches — like, with a quick upward jerk of her knee. Under the circumstances, though, she knew she needed to do her best to keep things low-key. Angie was the one who would suffer most if she lost it. She could not let Angie get involved in this.

Luke was watching her. She glared at him.

"You're not ready to forgive me yet, are you?" he asked with a sigh.

"Believe me, there's no 'yet' in this."

"Fine. Be mad. I'll still be crazy about you when you're over it."

"You can give the bullshit a rest. It's not working anymore."

"I mean it."

"Uh-huh. You want to let me go now?"

"You gonna go for my privates with a knife?" An infuriating half-smile still lurked around his mouth. Sexy little crinkles surrounded his eyes.

"I don't have one." Unfortunately.

"Then I guess I'm safe enough for now."

He eased himself off her, and positioned himself between her and the bedroom door. As she watched, he crossed his arms over his chest and negligently leaned one broad shoulder against the painted wooden panel.

As in, *you're not going anywhere.*

"Could you move away from the door?" In the interests of not making a scene, she kept the request polite.

"In a minute. Now that the game's

changed, there are a few ground rules I think we need to discuss. Number one, you don't leave my side."

"Oh, yes, I do. Like right now. Would you move, please?"

Luke's jaw hardened.

"Honey, I hate to break this to you, but this isn't up for debate: from here on out you're going to do exactly what I tell you."

Her determination to keep things low-key was being severely tested. "Like hell."

He studied her.

"You know, if you won't cooperate, I have a couple of choices here: I can take you into protective custody, or I can arrest you."

She realized that his eyes held an expression she'd never seen in them before. They were hard, determined, ruthless. Here was the truth at last, she realized: what he was, first and foremost, was a cop on the job. And she was part of that job.

"No. Oh no." Christy went cold as the full, hideous implications of his identity burst upon her with a vengeance. Uncle Vince had made it clear: the penalty for going to the authorities was death. Of course, in this case the authorities had come to her rather than the other way around, but she didn't think anybody was going to be in a mood to appreciate the distinction when they found out. Budding panic sharpened her voice. "You don't realize what you've done, do you? If they find out who you are, if they even think I'm cooperating with the FBI, they'll kill me."

His lips compressed. "In case it's escaped your notice, somebody seems to be doing his best to kill you anyway."

"It might not be the mob. It might be that serial killer they wrote about in the paper."

"Is that what you really think?"

Christy took a deep breath. "I don't know. Oh God, I don't know."

"I don't know either, but I'm working as hard as I can to find out. In the meantime, you're going to stay glued to my side until I can make arrangements to get you out of here."

"Get me out of here? What do you mean, get me out of here? I can't leave. Oh, wait, I forgot you don't know. I didn't tell you, did I? Uncle Vince sent me down here to deliver a briefcase to the Crosswinds Hotel. I don't know what was in it but that's why I was on the beach that first night. The deal was, if I did that for them, they'd let me alone. Then that phone call I got at the lighthouse — it was the same man who told me where to take the briefcase. He told me I'd be getting another delivery soon and to wait for it. I assume they'll want me to take whatever it is somewhere. I can't go anywhere until I've done it."

"Hey, I've been watching you, remember? I know every move you've made since you've been here. And I've heard every phone call you've made or received, too. So yeah, I know what's going on. And to hell with it. Much as I'd like to use you as bait to catch DePalma, this is getting too damned dangerous. You're not waiting around for somebody to take another crack at you. I'm going to make arrangements for protective custody, which should take maybe a few hours to set up, and then you're out of here."

"Luke." Christy took a deep breath. "Like I said before, you've got to get real. If there's a hit out on me, they'll keep trying until they get me no matter how long it takes, no matter where I am. I grew up with these people; I know how it works. The FBI can't keep me safe forever. You can't keep me safe forever."

It was true, and she knew it, and he knew it. She could tell by the look in his eyes.

"If it is them, if I just do this one last job for them, then maybe they'll leave me and my family alone."

Luke's mouth tightened. "Given what you know? Not a chance."

Christy looked at him, remembered Franky, and faced the hideous truth.

"Yeah," she said, and grimaced. "So now it's my turn to get real."

His eyes were grim. "I can get you into the Federal Witness Protection Program. A whole new identity, a new life."

She didn't want a new identity. She didn't want a new life.

"What about Mom? And Angie? And Nicole and the kids? Can you get them all into the Federal Witness Protection Program, too?"

The look on his face answered her question: No.

"I didn't think so." Not that it really mattered. Her entire family had *lives:* friends, jobs, school, social activities. A huge extended family that popped in and out of the picture like a revolving door. They were all entwined with each other, entwined in Jersey, a sprawling, brawling, undoubtedly dysfunctional but nevertheless devoted clan that was part of the wallpaper of all of their lives. Christy's heart bled at the thought of leaving that world forever; Angie, Nicole, and her mother would have to be dragged kicking and screaming away.

Only the problem wasn't going to arise: even if she were to make that choice for herself, her mother and sisters would have to be left behind.

Not happening.

"Okay," she said, thinking aloud. "If the guy trying to kill me is a hit man, even if you catch him it won't be enough. They'll just keep trying. I'll never be safe as long as I'm anywhere where they can find me. So the way I see it, I basically have two choices here: I can leave my family and everything I love behind and spend the rest of my life looking over my shoulder in some kind of protective custody, or I can stay right here and fight back. If you catch Michael, if he's facing charges that carry a significant amount of time, he'll tell everything he knows. He'll take the entire Masseria family down with him before he spends something like twenty years in jail."

"Yeah." Luke's eyes were opaque now. It was impossible to tell what he was thinking. "That's my take on him, too."

Christy's stomach clenched. Tightening

her arms around herself, she tried to ward off the cold that seemed to be seeping into her every pore. Taking on the Masseria family was something that she really, really did not want to do. "If the Masseria family goes down, I'm off the hook. I become the least of their problems."

"Christy . . ." He knew where this was going. She could tell by his tone.

Christy's heart pounded. Her mouth was dry. She had to wet her lips before she could speak. "Your plan was to use me to capture Michael. I don't see any reason to change it. We wait for the delivery, whatever it is, and then the phone call, and then I take the package to wherever they tell me to take it. Then you follow the package to Michael."

"No. Oh no. And there's no 'we' in this. There's me, federal agent. And there's you, protected witness, soon to be whisked out of harm's way."

"You can't whisk me out of harm's way, and you know it. Anyway, this is *your* plan. You came up with it. The only difference is that now I'm in on it."

"Yeah, well, since I came up with that plan, things have changed."

"What's changed?" It was a challenge.

His brow creased and he looked at her

steadily. "I've changed. You've changed."

"How?"

"You want to know how?" His lips tightened. "This is how."

Then his shoulders came away from the door in what was almost a lunge and he pulled her into his arms and kissed her, his lips hard and sure as they closed over her mouth.

For a moment, a weak moment, Christy didn't resist. Taken by surprise, her instincts took over and she melted against him, intoxicated by the heat of his mouth, by the hunger of it, by her own response. Closing her eyes, she kissed him back, wrapping her arms around his neck, pressing up against him, feeling fire shoot clear down to her toes.

Then she remembered that this was another one of those men she didn't really know. Luke Randolph, the lawyer who had made her laugh in the midst of her own personal hell week, the guy in whose arms she had felt safe, the man who could make her so hot that it embarrassed her even to think about it, did not exist. This was Luke Rand, FBI.

She'd had enough of falling in love with an illusion. Been there, done that. It wasn't going to happen twice.

Pulling her mouth from his, she tore herself out of his arms. Heavy-lidded with desire, he simply watched as she backed away.

"That's why," he said quietly.

Christy took a deep, shaken breath. For a moment they simply stared at each other. Her stupid, yearning body longed to step back into his arms. Her stupid, yearning heart longed to take a chance on love one more time.

Fortunately, she had a cool and sensible if momentarily passion-fogged brain, and it had just about enough wattage left to say *no way.*

"Christy —" He reached for her again.

"No," she said sharply, stepping back. "Luke Randolph, the nice lawyer I was sleeping with, doesn't exist. *You* I don't know. I'll help you catch Michael, and you'll keep me alive. That's as far as our new relationship goes."

29

By the time she and Luke left his bedroom some ten minutes later, they had come to a slightly uneasy accord. Basically, as long as things didn't get too hairy (Luke's word), she would carry on as before, with one modification: every step she took, he planned to be right behind her. Considering the alternative (a solo encounter with the psycho killer), she had no problem with that, as long as the relationship remained strictly business. The one stipulation of his that she didn't like was that he could pull her out at will; the one stipulation of hers that he didn't like was no sex. But neither was a deal breaker, and the bargain was struck. Christy figured that if and when the time came his stipulation would be subject to further negotiation; and she suspected that he felt the same about hers.

Fat chance.

The door to Pandora's box — i.e., the telltale third bedroom — was firmly closed, Christy saw as she passed it, and not a sound could be heard from it. Angie, still in her orange bikini, was seated at the table with Gary, picking at what looked like the remains of a blueberry muffin. Both had cups of coffee in front of them and were chatting away companionably.

"Hey." Angie greeted her with a big shit-eating grin. Her opinion as to what had been occupying her sister's attention was clear. Gary shot Christy a nervous look. Christy just managed to hold back on glaring at him. As far as lying was concerned, Gary wasn't a whole lot more innocent than Luke; he'd been part of the conspiracy, too.

Although, of course, Gary hadn't sweet-talked her into bed. That earned him extra bonus points toward a partial dispensation, as far as she was concerned.

"Hey," Christy said in return, feeling ridiculously self-conscious, especially when Angie's glance flicked beyond her to Luke, who had followed her in. What with one thing and another, they both looked a little disheveled, she knew. And tired. Definitely tired. Well, she felt tired, and she was sure it showed. Luke looked tired. His eyes were bloodshot and the tiny lines around them were more pronounced than usual.

They both looked like they had just finished up on a long and strenuous nooner, in fact.

At the thought, Christy felt her cheeks heat.

"Coffee," Luke said, and made a beeline for the kitchen.

"What are you doing here?" Directing the question to Angie, Christy pulled a chair out and dropped into it.

"What with the serial killer and all, when you didn't come right back I got worried." Angie's lurking grin spoke volumes.

There was a clatter, and a yelp from Luke, who was in the kitchen by this time. "What the — ? Why is there a bowl of milk on the floor? With — is that my sandwich cut up in it?"

Gary looked at Luke. "When Angie got here, Marvin was having one of his little fits because we were out of cat food. She suggested the milk, then mixed the sandwich in with it because I was getting ready to throw it away. He was eating it when you and Christy came in." His glance slid to Angie. "Probably Luke should have left him home in a kennel. He's been really nervous since we got here."

Christy practically had to bite her lip to keep from yelling *bullshit* at the top of her lungs. What did the FBI do, teach a master class in how to keep a straight face while telling outrageous lies?

"Where'd he run off to?" Now in the act of pouring himself a cup of coffee, Luke frowned as he looked back down the hall.

"Probably your bedroom. You know how he loves your bedroom," Gary said.

"I think it is so incredibly sweet that you have a cat. Most men go for dogs." Angie smiled at Luke. Christy knew her sister. If Angie hadn't thought Christy had prior dibs, she would have put some major-league eyelash and boob movement into it. But sisterly loyalty was strong, so Angie accompanied that smile with a single torso-twisting squirm.

Of course, a squirm when you're wearing a bikini that looked a lot like three Doritos on strings was eye-popping enough.

"Luke's like that. He's just a real sweet guy," Christy said, cutting him a look to see if he was noticing Angie. He caught her eye and smiled sardonically at her.

"You want cream and sugar in your coffee?" he asked her.

Actually, she liked her cream and sugar with a little coffee in them, but she wasn't about to tell him that.

"One teaspoon of sugar."

Now Angie was giving her a look. Angie, of course, knew how she liked her coffee. Christy made a face at her sister.

"How about something to eat? You want a bologna sandwich?" Luke asked.

"Go for the muffins," Gary advised with a shudder.

"Yeah, they're really great." Angie grinned at Gary. "You guys are the bomb. You're like the perfect couple. One of you has a cat, the other can cook."

"I'll have a muffin," Christy said to Luke, then added a quick thanks when he put the steaming cup and a muffin in a saucer in front of her before sitting down himself with coffee and some sort of sandwich.

"Besides being worried about the serial killer, I came over here to tell you some deputy called. He said they found your purse."

Christy sat bolt upright. "What?" It would have been an exclamation, except that it came out through a mouthful of muffin.

"Your purse. They found it. He said he'd bring it by about four, if that was all right. I said sure." Her eyes gleamed. "He sounded hot."

Christy's eyes cut to the clock on the

kitchen wall. It was nearly three-thirty.

"Did you get his name?" Luke asked. Having already finished his sandwich, he was slouched back in his chair, putting down coffee like he needed it.

"I don't remember, but he said he was headed this way anyway to visit his aunt, so that's why he didn't mind bringing it by."

Gordie Castellano. Christy felt her throat close up, and almost choked on her muffin. Her eyes shot to Luke, who was frowning now as he chugged coffee. His eyes met hers over the rim of the cup.

"So what's the deal about you losing your purse?" Angie asked, looking from one to the other of them.

"Remember I told you how the serial killer attacked me and put me in the trunk of my car? My purse was in the car."

"Oh my God." Angie's gaze cut to Luke. "I heard all about that. I am so glad you were there to save her."

Luke took another swallow of coffee.

"Yeah," he said in a slightly sour tone. "So am I." He glanced at Christy. "You know, when you're telling everybody what happened, I kind of wish you'd leave me out of it. It's embarrassing to admit that some guy managed to clobber me over the head and stuff me into a car trunk."

Angie looked at him wide-eyed. "You shouldn't be embarrassed about that. That could happen to anybody. Anyway, in the end you practically saved Christy's life. You should be proud and shout it from the rooftops."

"Yeah, well." Luke downed another swallow of coffee and looked at Christy over the rim of his cup.

"Fine," she said. Then, to Angie, with a shrug, "It's a man thing."

"I appreciate it," Luke said to Christy.

Angie looked at Christy. "So what did the cops say? Do they really think a serial killer's after you?"

"Actually, I haven't called the sheriff's department yet," Christy said. Exhaustion was setting in with a vengeance, and she couldn't summon up enough energy to get all worked up at the memory of the previous night. Terror would have to wait until she got a decent night's sleep. "This will save me from having to. I'll just make a report to whoever shows up. Then I guess I'd better call the insurance company about my car."

Marvin slunk into view, emerging from the hall. Both Luke's and Gary's eyes fastened on him, following him fixedly as he crossed the living room and disappeared into the kitchen. Then they looked at each other.

"We're still out of litter," Gary said to Luke.

Luke's face tightened. "Maybe you should just let him out."

"No," Christy and Angie said in unison. The Petrino women might be different in many ways, but they were cat lovers all.

"If you don't want to run to the store right now, you could scoop up some sand for him," Angie suggested. "Or if you have some newspaper, you could just tear it up and put it in his litter box."

"Or any box," Christy put in dryly.

Luke and Gary exchanged glances.

"I'm beat," Luke said plaintively.

Gary's lips thinned, but he got up, presumably to do what he could to round up a litter box.

Having finished her coffee, Christy forced herself to her feet. Sitting down had been a mistake, she realized. She was so tired she was light-headed. Her ears were ringing, and her legs felt weak.

"You don't look so good," Angie observed.

Thanks, Ange.

"Probably we should go back to our cottage. We don't want to miss the deputy," Christy said.

Both Angie and Luke stood up, although Angie displayed considerably more energy.

"Gary, I'm going over to Christy's. Hold down the fort," Luke called to the absent Gary as they trooped toward the sliding glass door.

"And don't let Marvin out," Christy added, giving Luke a pointed look.

"Yeah," he said, then called to Gary with a marked lack of enthusiasm. "Don't let Marvin out."

They were almost to the other cottage when Angie, who'd been chattering the whole way although Christy, being now too tired to focus, had missed most of what she'd said, turned to Luke.

"Are you still going to be here Sunday?" Since Luke was the last person in line, Angie had to raise her voice to be heard over the rush of ocean and the sounds of the happy vacationers who were crowding the beach below the dunes. " 'Cause if you are, we'll probably be having a little birthday party for Christy." She threw Christy a teasing glance. "I won't tell you how old she's going to be."

"Twenty-eight," Christy said sourly.

Luke grinned at her.

"Oh, by the way." Angie cast another glance Christy's way. "When he heard I was coming down here, Uncle Vince asked me to bring your birthday present with me. I don't know what it is, but it's all wrapped up in a big box and it's heavy. He said you shouldn't open it until Sunday."

First chance he got, Luke hightailed it back to his cottage with Christy's birthday present in his arms. He had almost no doubt that this was the delivery she'd been told to expect. Amori had either stage-managed Angie's little beach vacation by suggesting to Christy's mother that it might be a good idea, or he had taken advantage of the ladies' own concern for a hurting family member to get the package to Christy in as unobtrusive a manner as possible. That Christy had been told not to open it before Sunday — her birthday — told him something else: whatever was going down was going to happen before then.

"That certainly went well," Gary said to him in a dry voice as Luke stepped in through the patio door. Gary was seated in Command Central with the door open. Luke could hardly look at that open door without wincing.

"Yeah." So well he just wanted to stand up and shout, Luke reflected glumly. He was nuts about a girl who was, at the moment, a great deal less than nuts about him; he was having second thoughts about the wisdom of letting her stay in harm's way; and the thought of the alternative — her being swallowed up by the Witness Protection Program, never to be seen again — was too damned depressing to think about.

"She mad?" Gary asked.

Luke set the gaily wrapped box down on the table rather gingerly. He didn't think it was very likely, but given the way things had been going lately it was always possible that the thing contained a bomb.

"She's not happy. But she's going to cooperate, help us nail Donnie Jr."

"I almost crapped my pants when she saw those monitors."

"Yeah." *Oh yeah.* "You might want to keep that door shut from now on."

"Hey, I knew you were coming. I saw you sneaking out through the garage with somebody's present in your arms. Until then, it was shut. I just opened the door so I could ask you what's up with that."

Luke was studying the package from all angles. "Amori sent this down with Angie.

It's for Christy. Supposedly her birthday present. Her birthday's Sunday, by the way."

"Holy shit," Gary said, and stood up.

Luke looked at him. "Whoa. Stay put. You're on the monitor, remember. What's happening with Christy?"

"She's sitting with Angie, and they're both talking to Gordie Castellano. He's getting out a notebook to take Christy's statement." Gary was leaning out the door watching him.

"Where are the Barbie twins?"

Gary glanced at the monitor. "Hanging over the kitchen counter listening."

"Okay. Keep an eye on things." Christy should be safe enough for the short time it was going to take him to check out the package. "Where's the camera?"

"Kitchen drawer beside the silverware."

Luke retrieved it and took half a dozen pictures of the package. That was the easy part. Now he had to get the package open without tearing the wrappings noticeably. When he was finished checking it out, it was going to have to be wrapped up again so that it looked like it had never been touched.

A muffled yowl reminded him of another one of his problems.

"Where's the damned cat?" Wrapping presents was not really his forte. Unwrapping one was proving not to be any easier. Getting an elaborate bow and some tinsel and a bunch of sparkly tissue off one without tearing or breaking anything seemed to be beyond him, he discovered as he worked to unknot the ribbon.

"I locked him in your bathroom. With a plate of chopped up bologna, a bowl of water, and strips of newspaper in a box. I don't see why we don't just let him out."

"Because Christy said not to. Because he'll just end up on her patio again, and that'll piss her off, and she's pissed enough at me as it is."

"I told you we should have brought her in sooner." Gary watched his efforts with his head cocked to one side.

"Yeah, well, hindsight's a beautiful thing."

"No offense, but you suck at that. You want to watch the monitors for a minute and let me try?"

"Yeah. Good thought." He and Gary changed places. Instead of trying to unknot the damned ribbon, Gary simply slid the whole thing off to the side, bow, tinsel and all. Luke was impressed.

"Nice job," Luke said as Gary carefully

ran a knife under one piece of tape and then, by some process Luke knew he would never be able to duplicate if he lived a hundred years, slipped the box — it was silver, shiny, clearly from an expensive store — out of the paper, which was still neatly taped together except for the one opened side.

"I've had practice. I used to open my Christmas presents while my mom was at work, then put them back together again so that she never knew. You want to open this?"

Luke took a quick glance at the monitor. Christy was still talking to Castellano. With three other girls in the room, and perimeter sensors in place that would let out a beep anytime somebody passed from the inside to the outside of the house, or vice versa, she should be safe enough.

"Yeah." He and Gary changed places again.

Grimacing a little — it was still not beyond the realm of possibility that the thing might be a bomb — Luke braced himself and lifted the lid off the box. Lots of tissue paper inside. Parting it cautiously, he spied a pink satin box. Frowning, he lifted it out. A jewelry box: girly, lots of satin and lace.

Not what he'd expected.

"Open it," Gary said, and Luke did. A tinkly tune filled the air as a tiny ballerina twirled in front of a mirror in the lid.

A small blue satin bag tucked into the open space in front of the ballerina drew his eyes. Luke lifted it out — it was full, but not particularly heavy — and opened the drawstring top.

The sight that greeted him made his heart skip a beat.

"What? What?" Gary demanded, apparently in response to Luke's expression.

Luke poured the contents of the bag into his hand.

"Diamonds," he said, looking up at Gary. "Probably more than a million dollars' worth. They're small enough to be carried in a pocket and they don't show up on airport metal detectors. Bingo: Donnie Jr.'s here, these are for him, and he's planning to leave the country."

By the time the package was put back together again, the bag had been outfitted with its own minuscule tracking device.

They'd lost track of the last delivery. This time there was more at stake. Luke wasn't taking any chances on something getting screwed up.

Angie and Christy sat on the patio

watching the sky slowly darken from lavender to deep purple. Sea oats swayed in the salt-smelling breeze that blew in from the ocean; waves rolled shoreward in undulating white lines. With Gary, still in khakis and that blue polo shirt, roped into the role of bodyguard, Maxine and Amber were on the beach, which was slowly emptying of people. As Christy watched, the girls picked up their towels and shook them out, Gary unwound from his chin-on-knees huddle in the sand, and the three of them started heading back toward the cottage. Luke was in the living room behind them stretched out on the couch, watching sports on TV. With the patio door closed, he couldn't hear them but he could see them through the glass. As annoying as it was to have to acknowledge it, she was glad he was there.

With the onset of night, not even exhaustion was enough to keep her stomach from tying itself in knots, or her heart from skipping a beat each time a shadow moved. Talking to Castellano had been bad enough; seeing him with her purse had made her go all light-headed. They had only his word for it that a passerby had found it near the ferry and turned it in. She had no reason — other than her quivering sixth sense — to disbelieve him. But, as Luke had pointed out when she had whispered her suspicions to him, if it was in Castellano's possession because he was the man who had attacked her, would he have been brazen — to say nothing of stupid — enough to bring it back to her? She didn't know; she was too tired and too confused to calculate the odds. Then Luke had told her about the diamonds, and the knowledge that the delivery had been made had cranked her anxiety level up about a thousand degrees. The phone call she dreaded could come anytime now — like tonight. Thus it was no surprise that as darkness fell fear crept over her as inexorably as night crept over the beach. There was no escaping it, no doing anything about it. It just had to be lived through until morning came again.

"So, does Luke sleep here or what?" Angie asked in a low voice.

"Why do you want to know?" Christy countered, shooting her sister a look. Angie was lying on the chaise longue, where she had been sprawled ever since they'd finished the carry-out pizza that was dinner. Christy was sitting up in a hard plastic chair. If she got too comfortable, she was afraid she would fall asleep.

"That serial killer thing is starting to creep me out. A man spending the night in the house would probably be a good thing."

"At a guess, I'd say he's spending the night." Just not in her bed. Although she couldn't tell Angie that.

"You got hot and heavy with him pretty fast, didn't you?"

Christy cut her a glance. "What, you don't like him?"

"I like him. What's not to like? He's gorgeous, he's nice, he's got a cat. He looks like he'd be the bomb in bed."

"So what's your problem?"

"No problem. Shacking up with him so soon after you broke up with Michael just doesn't seem like something you'd do."

"It's been kind of intense down here. And like you said, he's the bomb in bed."

"Nice distraction." Angie grinned knowingly at her. Christy changed the subject.

"How's Mom?"

"She's okay. She's been spending a lot of time with Nicole. That shit Franky is six months behind on his child support, and now nobody seems to know where he is."

A cold little finger of dread slid down Christy's spine. *She* knew where he was. Or at least, she knew what had become of him. But telling her family would put them at risk. Franky would just have to turn up — or not — in his own good time.

"Franky's crapola," she said. She was sorry — a little — that he was dead, but being dead didn't change the truth.

"Yeah."

If there was one thing the sisters agreed on, it was Franky.

"You know, knowing there's a serial killer around kinda ruins the beach," Amber said as she, Maxine, and Gary reached them.

"And the guys," Maxine chimed in. "I couldn't even get into the hunky ones because I started thinking anyone of them might be him."

"Except for Gary here." Amber ruffled Gary's hair. His eyes went wide. Christy had to smile. He looked like a deer that had just heard gunshots in the distance.

"Not that you're not welcome or anything, but if I were you guys I'd head back home. A serial killer is nothing to mess with." Christy stood up, brushing sand off her jeans.

"We decided we're not going to mess with the guys," Maxine said. "We're just going to work on our tans."

"Except for Gary here." Amber gave

Gary a big, flirtatious smile and headed for the door, tracking sand across the patio as she went. Gary shot Christy an imploring look. She smiled mockingly at him.

The wages of sin are . . . Maxine and Amber.

"Luke's spending the night," Angie informed her friends in a comforting tone as she, too, stood up.

"Lucky you." Maxine rolled her eyes around to Christy. "Just looking at him makes me hot."

"Everything makes you hot," Angie said in disgust. "And you keep your hands off. He belongs to my sister."

"What about Gary?" Amber asked. "Is he spending the night, too?"

"Uh — not enough room," Gary croaked, looking hunted.

"Oh, too bad." Amber reached the patio door first and slid it open. The TV blared.

"— suspect that a serial killer is stalking the Outer Banks. A federal-state task force is being assembled to track down the man, who is described as a Caucasian male, five feet nine to six feet, with a dark complexion and a husky build. The description was provided by an unidentified woman who survived an attack by the man authorities are calling the Beachcomber."

"Oh my God," Angie gasped. "Christy, it's on TV! That witness — it has to be you!"

They were all crowded around the TV now, watching with mouths agape. It was the ten o'clock news, Christy realized, and by the time the segment concluded with a brief interview of a bathing-suit-clad woman standing on a beach in Nags Head, she was sick to her stomach.

"We've all been looking over our shoulders," the woman said into the camera. "We're just absolutely terrified."

Then the shot blinked away, and the anchor's face filled the screen. "In other news . . ."

"Did anybody lock the patio door?" Maxine squeaked.

Angie stepped over to it and locked it, then pulled the curtain, blocking out the night.

Christy took a deep breath. The news continued, but she didn't register so much as a word of it. There was a hard arm circling her waist, she realized after a few moments. She didn't need to glance around to know it belonged to Luke. He was supporting her weight as she leaned back against him. He must have stepped up behind her while she was watching the report. Even as she'd leaned on him, she hadn't even realized he was there.

"Does this suck or what?" Amber wailed. "First time I've been to a beach since spring break my senior year of high school, and what happens? It's got a serial killer!"

"You know, maybe we should go back home," Maxine said unhappily.

"Good idea," Gary said.

"Ready to call it a night?" Luke whispered in Christy's ear while the others debated the advantages of going versus staying. She was still leaning against him, breathing too fast, her legs as wobbly as rubber bands.

She nodded.

"You okay, Christy?" Angie surfaced from the argument to ask. Christy realized from Angie's expression that she must be looking as pale as she felt.

"I'm fine."

"She's practically out on her feet," Luke said, his arm still snug around her middle. "So am I. We're going to bed."

"And I'm heading out." Gary moved toward the patio door. "See you guys tomorrow."

He lifted a hand in farewell and was gone despite the chorus of protests.

"I told you you were coming on too

strong," Maxine said to Amber as Angie moved to relock the patio door. "Now you scared him off. And we *need* him."

"He's cute." Amber defended herself. "Geeky, but cute."

"Is that all you guys think about — sex?" With the curtain now closed behind her, Angie turned to regard her friends with disgust.

"No," Amber said.

"Sometimes I think about winning the lottery," Maxine added.

"Okay, we're going to say good night now." Luke's glance encompassed Maxine and Amber as well as Angie. "If you ladies stay inside the house with the doors locked, you shouldn't have anything to worry about. You need me, all you have to do is give a shout."

The three girls were still arguing animatedly as Christy, with Luke right behind her, headed off to bed.

30

"Just so you know, you're not sleeping with me," Christy said in a low voice as the bedroom door closed behind them. She was so tired her vision was blurry and so anxious that her heart was sneaking in strange little double beats every now and again, but she wasn't giving an inch in that regard. Her emotions were still too raw and the state of her heart still too uncertain where he was concerned. The only thing she could be sure she felt toward him was anger. Fortunately, under the circumstances, anger worked. Back militantly straight, she moved toward the small chest that held the oversized T-shirt she planned to sleep in specifically in his honor. With him as her roommate for the night, her usual sleeping attire was definitely out.

"Honey, I hate to burst your bubble but you don't have anything to worry about here. I'm going into a coma the minute my head hits a pillow."

A glance over her shoulder showed that he was standing just inside the door with his arms crossed over his chest.

"Your head's going to have to hit a pillow on the floor."

"You want me to sleep on the floor? Fine. Throw me a pillow and a blanket, and I'll sleep on the floor."

Christy pulled the requested objects from the bed, bundled them up, and thrust them into his arms as she passed him on her way to the bathroom. When she came back, with her face freshly scrubbed and her teeth Pepsodent clean, he was sprawled flat on his back on the carpet with the blanket covering him to his armpits and his head resting on the pillow. From the broad bare shoulders above the blanket, she assumed he'd stripped down to his underwear. At least, she hoped he was still wearing his underwear.

The thought of Luke sleeping in her room in or out of his underwear was enough to send an electric little thrill shooting along her nerve endings, but she ignored it. Clearly her body was not yet up to speed on the fact that he was a lying snake.

A quick visual sweep of the bedroom located his clothes piled in the chair in the corner. Jeans and shirt, socks, with sneakers beside the chair. Christy frowned, and looked more closely. Protruding from beneath the shirt was a black nylon — she crossed the room and lifted the shirt to be sure — shoulder holster. Complete with a businesslike black gun.

Her stomach lurched. Her heart skipped a beat. Staring down at the thing, Christy dropped the shirt back down over it and told herself that experiencing such a reaction was stupid. Of course he had a gun; he was an FBI agent, for heaven's sake. The only reason she hadn't seen it before now was because the dirty dog had been deliberately hiding it from her — along with his true identity.

Her own gun, along with her purse and its contents, was now in the hands of the sheriff's department. After hearing her story, Castellano had carted everything away as evidence; his only concession had been to let her keep the contents of her wallet: cash, driver's license, and credit cards, and only because she had pleaded with him and her wallet didn't appear to have been touched.

Probably she should be glad to know that she and Luke weren't going into danger unarmed.

She was glad, sort of, and yet she wasn't. Guns scared her. The idea of Luke as an FBI agent scared her more. And the reason it scared her so was something she hated to acknowledge even to herself: knowing that he had lied about everything didn't just make her so mad she could spit. It hurt.

Way too much for what she felt for him to be characterized as mere sexual attraction.

Earlier he'd said he was crazy about her; whether she believed him or not, the sad truth was that *she* was crazy about *him*.

But she wasn't going to think about that. Especially not tonight, when she was so tired nothing made sense.

What she was going to do was go to bed.

Skirting Luke, she cast his long, blanket-covered form a narrow-eyed glance. If having deceived her was causing him pain, he was doing a great job of hiding it. His eyes were closed, his hands were folded across his chest, and his breathing was deep and regular. He looked asleep.

Her lips compressed. At least he was between her bed and the door.

Christy eyed him more closely. He really did look asleep. If he was going into a coma, as he'd claimed, he wasn't going to be much protection if the psycho killer decided to pay her a return visit. Unless, of course, the guy tripped over him and knocked himself out.

Knowing that she wasn't going to be able to sleep a wink, Christy headed for the dresser and began wrestling it into place in front of the door.

"What the hell are you doing?"

Glancing around, Christy discovered that Luke's eyes were open a slit.

"What does it look like? Barricading the door."

"What, you don't trust me to keep you safe?"

"No."

With that bit of brutal honesty, she went back to work on the dresser, expecting that at any moment the task would be made easier by the addition of his strength to hers. It didn't happen. He didn't move. By the time the dresser was finally in place, he appeared to be asleep again.

Huffing and puffing now with exertion, feeling a bit of a glow despite the air-conditioning, she cast him a less-than-friendly look, walked around him, and climbed into bed. And turned out the light.

And heard a snore. And another. And another.

Okay, at least while he was snoring she

knew he was there and alive.

Despite her exhaustion, sleep didn't seem to be in any hurry to claim her. She was too wired, too anxious, on edge waiting for the doorknob to turn, or the phone to ring —

"Oh my God!" She sat bolt upright in bed.

"What? What?" She couldn't see him, but from the tension in his voice she wouldn't have been surprised to learn that he'd sat bolt upright on the floor.

"What if the phone rings, and Angie or Amber or Maxine answers it?"

"Jeez Louise, you scared the crap out of me." She heard sounds that made her think he was lying back down. "Go back to sleep. I fixed it."

"You fixed what?"

"The phone."

"You fixed the phone? What do you mean, you fixed the phone?"

"The house line only rings through to your bedroom. The other phone's on a different line now."

"When did you do that?"

"While you and your sister were yakking on the patio."

"How did you do that?"

"Hey, that's what us federal agents do,

all right? Would you please go back to sleep?"

Christy's lips thinned. Fine. He wanted to sleep, that much was clear. Well, so did she. She took deep breaths, and concentrated on relaxing her muscles. First her feet, then her calves . . . Another terrifying thought surfaced through the maelstrom that was swirling through her brain, and her eyes popped open.

"If you're in here, I may be safe, but what's preventing that guy from doing something to Angie, or Amber, or Maxine?"

A beat passed. She heard him sigh.

"Do you have this much trouble sleeping every night?"

"No, listen, this is important. If this guy is a hit man, and he can't get to me, he might go after one of them, especially Angie, to teach me a lesson." The thought made her heart pound. "Or if he should happen to be a serial killer, he might not be picky. He might take one of them just because they're easier to get to than me."

"This house has more security around it than the White House. After you got attacked that first night, I wired the place. The cameras are only the tip of the iceberg. There are motion detectors, perimeter alarms, the works. Nobody's getting in, nobody's going out, without us knowing about it. Now quit worrying and go to sleep."

"Okay. Sorry. Good night."

He grunted. It couldn't have been more than a minute later until he was snoring again.

Christy lay there and listened. In, out. In, out. A strong, steady rhythm. She was counting noisy inhalations like sheep when she fell asleep.

It was approximately eleven minutes till seven the following morning. The sky was robin's egg blue, the sun was climbing the sky, and the tide was out. A few hardy joggers trotted over the sand; an old man with a bucket and a small rake waded in the surf, digging for crabs; three kids played tag with the surging foam. Unlike these hardy folks, Luke was not yet in tune with the day. The night had passed as uneventfully as a night spent on a floor could pass. Which was to say, nobody screamed, the phone didn't ring, the door didn't get kicked in. He'd gotten just enough sleep to make him coherent but cranky. After a couple of hours in which he'd basically passed out, he'd tried every position under the sun in an attempt to get comfortable, and finally had given it up. His back hurt, his neck was stiff, and he needed a shower, a shave and coffee, not necessarily in that order. Christy was out like a rock, curled up in her bed with the covers pulled up around her ears, soft little snores fluttering past parted pink lips.

He considered crawling into bed with her, considered stretching his back out on her soft mattress, considered juicing himself awake by planting a good-morning kiss on her soft lips.

Then he considered how pissed she would be, and opted for a quick visit to his cottage instead.

"You're not gonna believe this!"

Gary, still in his too-neat-to-be-believed pajamas, bounced out of Command Central like a rubber ball when Luke stepped through the patio door. Luke eyed him dourly. Nobody should have that much energy so early in the morning.

"What?"

"I figured out the numbers. Well, the computer did."

"What?" Luke's gaze focused on him.

"The numbers. On the newspaper pages. In the briefcase Christy put in that Maxima the first night. It was right there in front of us the whole time. Nothing but the page numbers. It's a post office box and the combination to it."

Luke's pulse leaped. He was suddenly wide awake. "You're shitting me."

"Nope. I even know where the post office is: right across the Sound in New Bern."

"Let me see."

Luke followed Gary into Command Central, took a quick glance at the monitors to make sure all was right with the cottage next door, and then looked down at the computer printout Gary tapped with a proud forefinger.

"Look, this is the number of the post office, this is the number of the post office box, and this is the combination."

"Jeez Louise." Now that Luke saw it in black and white in front of him, it looked simple. Way too simple for the amount of man and computer power it had taken to figure it out. He frowned down at the paper for a moment, drumming his fingers on the thick glass covering the vanity top. "They must be using the P.O. box as a drop box. It might have been just a one-time deal, something put in there for Donnie, Jr. to pick up, but it may still be active. If it's a public post office there'll be hundreds of fingerprints, so that probably won't tell us much. I'll call Boyce and see if he can arrange to have a stakeout set up. We need to know who rented the box. Of course, whoever it was probably used a fake name."

"Got it right here." Gary tapped another piece of paper.

"You the man, Gary," Luke said, looking at the paper. Anthony B. Newton, with an address in New Bern. No one he had ever heard of, but then he hadn't expected it to be. He picked up the papers, then headed for the kitchen to put on a pot of coffee and call Boyce.

By the time he finished his call, he was on his second cup of coffee and his third muffin.

"How're the ladies?" he asked Gary as he paused in the doorway of Command Central on the way to his bedroom.

"Nothing's stirring. They're all still asleep."

"You get any sleep?"

"Yeah. I've got the system rigged so that if it's breached this baby" — Gary tapped what looked to Luke like a plastic box — "goes off like a four-alarm fire. Rip Van Winkle couldn't sleep through it. 'Course, during the day I turn the volume down."

"Good plan."

"Did you get things set up with Boyce?"

"Yeah. He's gonna get somebody on it pronto. You know, we've got a problem."

"What's that?"

"If Donnie Jr.'s here and thinking about approaching Christy, he's sure as hell not going to do it with that gaggle of girls around her."

Gary leaned back against the vanity, crossed his arms over his chest, and looked at him suspiciously. "So?"

"So until we can figure out a way to get rid of them, I want you to draw off the girls. Escort them to the beach. Show them around the island. That kind of thing."

"Oh no. No way. You got the wrong guy for that. I'm an FBI agent, not a baby-sitter. Besides, who's going to do the computer stuff? Log the phone calls? Man the monitors?"

"During the day, as long as I'm with Christy, there's nothing that has to be watched in real time," Luke said. "Anyway, I don't think anything's going to happen during the day, except maybe, if we get real lucky, Donnie Jr. or one of his flunkies coming up to Christy on the beach or somewhere. At night is when I need you here keeping on top of the monitors."

"What about the checks I'm running on

the owners of those white trucks? What about the criminal records check I'm running on just about everybody on the damned island? What about the hotel records checks, the RV lot checks, the campground checks?"

"Come on, Gary. I need you, man. We'll work the other stuff in."

Gary scowled at him. "You know what? Sometimes I hate my fricking job."

Luke laughed, clapped him on the shoulder, and went to take a shower. When he opened the bathroom door, he was greeted by a god-awful stench and the sight of the damned cat crouched like the Sphinx's evil twin on the closed toilet lid. Under the sink was a litter box, which, he determined after a single wincing glance at it, accounted for the smell. A bowl of dry cat food — Gary must have made it to the store last night — and a bowl of water were pushed against the far wall.

Until that moment he'd forgotten all about the animal.

It lashed its tail and narrowed its eyes at him. From its reaction, Luke had a sneaking suspicion that it hadn't forgotten him.

The thought of letting it escape into the wild was so tempting that he very nearly did it.

But then sanity returned. Christy was already plenty mad at him. Getting back in her good graces was going to be hard enough without losing the damned cat. Besides, he was pretty sure that even if he let it out, it wasn't going far. It would just turn up again in the vicinity of her patio like a bad penny.

Shit. Eyeing it distrustfully, Luke moved inside the bathroom and closed the door. Then he did a fast shave and shower.

When he stepped out of the shower, the stench had been taken to a whole new level. A wary glance told him that the cat was no longer sitting on the toilet. Instead it was sitting in its litter box. Or maybe hunched was a better word.

It was taking a dump.

"You are *foul*," he said to it, snatching up a towel and heading for the door. From the smug look in its eyes as it watched him, Luke had the feeling that he'd just been given the cat equivalent of the bird.

31

"This waiting is the pits."

Christy was on the beach, lying on a towel spread out on the firm white sand, having no fun at all as she watched dozens of giddy vacationers, who looked like they were having the time of their lives, play in the surf. She, personally, was not having the time of her life. It was late afternoon two days after Angie had arrived with the diamonds, and so far absolutely nothing worth talking about had happened.

Except that she had adopted poor, man-hating Marvin, and she had not had sex with Luke.

"You mean you're not having fun?" Luke's voice was a low, amused rumble in her ear, courtesy of the earpiece he had outfitted her with. He was sprawled on his own towel about thirty feet behind her, hopefully lost to the casual observer in the crowd that packed the beach. It was Thursday, which meant that the sand was more crowded than usual as locals who'd managed to wangle three-day weekends flocked to the ocean to let off steam. The serial killer who was supposedly stalking this and other area beaches was now national news, but if his existence had caused anyone to stay home Christy, for one, couldn't tell.

"You know, this doesn't seem to be working," she groused, looking straight ahead as per instructions. "And I'm tired of being the bait."

She was lying on her side with her head propped on her hand, wearing a solid-black one-piece bathing suit that Luke had selected for her because it was best suited to conceal a wire. The wire was tucked down between her breasts, and picked up everything she said and everything that was said to her. Unfortunately, so far the only thing that had been said to her was *oops, sorry* by a little kid who'd kicked sand on her as he'd run past her toward the waves.

"Relax and enjoy the view," Luke recommended.

"You know what? I've been lying here looking at this ocean for two hours. Waves come in, waves go out. People go in, people come out. That's pretty much the view."

"Okay, you've got a point. Lucky for me, though, the view's a lot better from my location."

"You're right behind me."

"Yeah, but I see hills and valleys. Curves. Lots of tanned skin. The most gorgeous legs I've ever seen in my life. A sexy ass that makes me want to —"

"Okay," she said, rolling onto her stomach to intentionally send static through the mike. "Give it a rest or I'm out of here."

"Hey, that hurt my ear."

"Serves you right."

"You gonna make me sleep on the floor again tonight?"

"Oh yeah. You can count on it."

"You're a hard, unforgiving woman, Christy Petrino."

"And you're a lying —"

"Excuse me, can you tell me which way the Crosswinds Hotel is?" A woman holding a little girl by the hand stopped in front of Christy to ask. In her modest bathing suit, Christy supposed she looked like the kind of mature, level-headed adult who might know.

"That way," she said, and pointed. The woman thanked her and continued on, clutching her little girl's hand as they picked their way among the sunbathers that lay thick as fallen leaves in autumn on the beach.

"I'm broiling here," Christy complained. "My sunblock feels like it quit working about an hour back. Can't I even go wade in the ocean?"

"One splash and you'll fry the wire. Besides, I'd have to go with you and somebody might notice that we're together."

"I hate to be the one to break this to you, but I don't think anybody's watching."

"You might be right. Then again, you might not be. I don't know about you, but if it's possible to catch DePalma because he sees you on the beach and comes over to talk rather than waiting to try until you're making a middle-of-the-night delivery of the diamonds, I pick the beach."

Since he put it that way, so did she. Just the thought of the had-to-be-coming-soon phone call was enough to make her forehead prickle with cold sweat, which, come to think of it, wasn't all that unwelcome given the heat.

"So talk to me. Tell me why you think Marvin hates you." Christy rolled back onto her side, adjusted her sunglasses, and resumed her former position, head propped on hand. In one of their nightly chats — her anxiety level hadn't declined notably, which meant she still had trouble falling asleep — Luke had confessed the truth about Marvin's origins. He'd also admitted to having the poor cat locked in his bathroom. Christy had rescued him first thing the next morning, and he was now readjusting to domesticated life in her cottage.

"I don't know why the damn cat hates me. I just know that he does."

"What, are you the pet psychic now? How do you know?"

"He takes a dump every time he sets eyes on me."

Christy laughed.

"It's the truth. I swear it on my grandmother's life."

Christy laughed again. "Do you even have a grandmother?"

"Sure I have a grandmother. I also have a mother and a younger brother."

"No father?"

"He died right after I got out of the Marines. That would be ten years ago."

Christy knew what losing a father felt like. "I'm sorry."

"Yeah."

A beat passed.

"So you were in the Marines? Really?"

"What do you mean, *really?* Yes, really. Just for the record, I haven't told you a single lie since . . ." His voice trailed off as if he were trying to remember.

"Since I caught you in all those lies?" Christy filled in sweetly.

"Yeah, about that long," he said.

"Okay, you were in the Marines," Christy said. "Then what did you do?"

"I finished college. Then I went to law school."

Christy sucked in her breath. It was all she could do not to turn around and glare at him. "You lying *scum*. . . ."

"No, I really did. Emory University. Then I joined the FBI."

"Is that the truth?" she asked suspiciously.

"Honey, I have to tell you, your lack of trust wounds me, it truly does."

Christy's grunt expressed her opinion of that.

"Where are your mother and brother now? Are you close to them? Do you see them very often?"

"My mother's a teacher. She still lives in Atlanta, in the house I grew up in — see there, I really am a lawyer from Atlanta, I didn't lie as much as you think — and I see her when I can, holidays, special occasions, weekends here and there. Yeah, we're pretty close. My brother is thirty — I'm thirty-two, by the way — and he's a dentist. We're close enough where every time I get around him he wants to look at my teeth. By the time Christmas is over, I usually feel like a fricking horse."

Christy laughed.

"You know what? Your laugh is almost as sexy as your legs."

"That's it," Christy said, rolling onto her stomach again. "I'm out of here."

"My ear," he groaned. Then, as she got to her feet and reached for her towel, "No, wait, I take it back. Your laugh *is* as sexy as your legs. And that's saying something, because your legs are really, really sexy."

Christy could see him now, stretched out on the sand behind her, one arm propping up his head, a teasing half-smile curving his lips. He was wearing faded blue swim trunks and Ray-Bans and that was it, and he looked so gorgeous that he stopped her breath. He was a veritable beach god, all gold hair and bronzed skin and rippling muscles, and she got a severe attack of lust just from looking at him. It was getting increasingly harder to keep the fact that he was a lying jerk firmly fixed in the forefront of her mind, but at the moment, if she was in danger of forgetting, all she had to do was feel the hard plastic of the wire between her breasts. He'd been dealing in illusion since she met him, and his beach godness was an illusion, too. A very good illusion, a sexy, mouth-watering, good-enough-to-eat illusion — and she wasn't surprised to discover two college-age girls on towels behind him ogling him while they rubbed lotion on their legs — but still just an illusion.

The truth was that he had been hard at work ever since she'd first laid eyes on him, and despite appearances he was hard at work now. The laid-back hunk was kind of his wolf-in-sheep's-clothing disguise. Underneath he was a federal agent prepared to do whatever it took to get the job done.

Including using her. For all his sweet talk, the fact was that to him, bottom line, she was the means to an end.

Unless she wanted to wind up with a broken heart, it would behoove her to remember that.

"Looking good, babe," he said in her ear as she walked past him.

Her lips compressed, and it was all she could do not to make like the bullies with the ninety-pound weakling and kick sand in his face.

By the time Christy reached the cottage she was feeling positively grumpy. She knew that Luke was a discreet distance behind her, watching her every move, but still she couldn't shake the prickly nervousness that had been her constant companion for days. She found herself jumping at every sudden sound or unexpected flutter of movement, and the sensation of being watched was so strong that she could feel it like a touch against her skin. Of course, she *was* being watched, between Luke and the cameras he had set up she was being watched pretty much twenty-four/seven so the feedback her sixth sense was giving her was necessarily muddied. But the knowledge that Michael was out there somewhere, that his goons were out there somewhere, that someone who wanted her dead and had already tried twice to kill her was out there somewhere, kept her constantly on edge.

The fact that she had fallen hard for a man who might very well walk out of her life as soon as he got through saving it was simply the icing on the cake.

As she reached for the patio door handle she happened to glance through the glass, and stopped dead. The sight that met her gaze drove everything else from her mind. Angie and her friends had gone shopping with Gary as glum-faced escort right before Christy had made her reluctant trek to the beach. Now they were back. Gary perched wide-eyed on a barstool in the kitchen with a sheet around his shoulders. While Angie and Amber hovered around, Maxine was taking a flashing pair of silver scissors to his hair. Fine red hairs fell on the sheet like snow in a blizzard.

Christy's jaw dropped.

"Oh my God," she said, and pulled the patio door open.

"What's up?" Luke's voice rasped in her ear.

"You're not going to believe this."

"Shit."

Popping the earpiece from her ear, turning the wire off, Christy stepped inside and closed the door after her. Gary's eyes met hers in a mute plea for help. It took her a minute to realize that he wasn't wearing his glasses.

"What are you doing?" she asked, looking beyond him at Maxine.

"Giving Gary a whole new look," Amber said, looking around.

"It's a makeover," Maxine explained as

the scissors continued to go *snip-snip* around Gary's head. "You know, like those extreme makeovers on TV."

"You should see his new clothes," Angie put in.

"Oh my God," Christy said again, as it became clear that Gary had already lost at least half of the previously thick thatch on his head. Her eyes met Gary's. "Did you volunteer or were you drafted?"

"A little of both." He gave her a strained-looking smile.

"Oh Gary," Christy said in helpless sympathy. He was a lying jerk, too, but not nearly as big a lying jerk as Luke, and in that moment she truly felt for him. It was clear that he was in the hands of forces too powerful for him to control.

"It's okay," he said, with the air of one who was determined to be brave to the end.

"You bet your booties it's okay." Maxine, still snipping, sounded insulted. "I'll have you know I'm a professional hairdresser. You'd pay sixty bucks for this cut at home."

The patio door slid open. Christy's eyes cut around to discover Luke, panting and perspiring, in the opening. Sunglasses in hand, he was wearing only his trunks with his shirt and towel slung over his shoulder, and his eyes had a haunted look as they fastened on her.

"Maxine's giving Gary a haircut," she explained.

Luke's chest heaved. Then his mouth clamped shut. Christy met his fulminating look with innocent surprise, then grinned, realizing that he had raced all the way up from the beach because he'd thought she was in danger. The taut skin around his eyes crinkled as he narrowed them dangerously at her.

"I was surprised, too," she said.

"Hey, Luke," Gary said feebly.

Luke's eyes cut to Gary. He stared at him for a moment, then began to grin.

Maxine put the scissors down. "Amber, hand me some of the gel," she said.

Amber passed it over. Maxine squirted some out, rubbing it on her hands.

"It's a makeover," Angie told Luke as Maxine stepped in front of Gary and ran her hands through his hair.

Luke stepped inside and closed the door.

"Voilà!" Maxine exclaimed, and pulled the sheet away from Gary with the air of a magician pulling a rabbit out of a hat. She stepped to one side, and Gary, looking dazed, stood up.

Except for the blaring TV, there was a moment of profound silence.

Gary's hair was short and mussed, standing straight up all over his head in the newest fashionable style. He was wearing chunky leather sandals, baggy khaki shorts that reached past his knees, and a bright blue Hawaiian shirt over a loose-fitting navy T-shirt that said Coors. He looked good. He looked cool. He definitely did not look like Gary.

"Unbelievable," Amber said, clearly impressed.

"Way to go, Maxine," Angie added.

"You really think so?" Gary looked both pleased and uncertain. His eyes sought out Christy and beyond her, Luke.

"You look great, Gary." Christy meant it. He wasn't a hunk by any means; no amount of haircutting and clothes buying could change him into a babe magnet like Luke, but the geekiness was definitely gone. Gary could now go walking out with Amber and Maxine on each arm and have them look like they belonged there.

Luke was grinning as he looked Gary over from head to toe.

"Looking good, man," he said.

Gary started to say something, but the *beep-beep-beep* from the TV that signified a breaking news bulletin interrupted. All eyes cut toward it.

A reporter stood in front of a modest frame house that had been roped off with yellow crime scene tape. In the background, police and other official types could be seen moving about.

"We've just been informed that authorities believe they may have found the serial killer who has been terrorizing women throughout the Outer Banks. Called to a residence in Nags Head by a neighbor who reported hearing gunshots in the wee hours of the morning, police stumbled upon a scene that one officer described as being straight out of a horror movie. The male suspect, whose identity police have not yet made public, has apparently committed suicide inside the residence. The remains of at least five victims have been recovered so far. Police believe there may be more. Authorities are working now to confirm the identity of the victims, but clothing and other personal effects found with the bodies have led authorities to tentatively identify them as some of the missing women previously identified as probable victims of the man known as the Beachcomber."

32

"*Yes!*" Maxine gave a punched-fist salute when cameras cut away to another story.

"Now aren't you glad we didn't go home?" Amber crowed.

"Christy? Are you okay?" Angie asked quietly, moving to stand beside her, nudging her arm. Christy realized that she had been staring at the TV transfixed. Her heart pounded, her knees had gone weak, and she was feeling distinctly light-headed. Was it possible . . . ? Could the man who had attacked her really be dead?

It seemed impossible. It seemed too good to be true.

"Christy?" Angie prompted.

Christy glanced at her sister, and realized that Angie was looking concerned.

"Yeah, sure, of course I'm okay. That's good news," she said, and summoned up what she hoped was a reassuring smile.

Angie's attention was distracted just then by Maxine whooping, "*Par*-ty!"

Christy's gaze swung around to Luke. He was still standing right inside the door. Their eyes met, and he crossed the room to stand right behind her. She felt his arm slide around her waist, and was glad of its presence. Leaning back against him, thankful for his solid strength, she absorbed the damp heat of his skin against hers, the soft springiness of the hairs on his chest, the firmness of his muscles and the hardness of the arm around her waist, the way a thirsty plant soaks up water. She needed him right now, she realized. Needed his presence, needed his support, needed his shared knowledge of what was at stake.

"Par-ty! Par-ty! Par-ty!" Maxine and Amber were doing a kind of celebratory war dance, chanting and shaking their assets as they went. For today's shopping expedition, they'd put on microminis, tube tops, and high-heeled wedgie sandals, and their progress around the room could best be described as a jiggle-fest. Marvin, who'd apparently been hiding beneath the couch, took fright at their antics and shot down the hall and out of sight.

"Okay, guys, cool out. You're scaring Marvin," Angie yelled at her friends, and at the same time signaled time-out with both hands in case they couldn't hear her above the noise they were making.

"Who cares about Marvin? They're scaring *me*," Gary muttered. He was standing beside her now, Christy discovered at a glance, and she was still so unused to his new nongeeky persona that she had to look a second time to make sure it was him.

"We need to celebrate." Maxine had stopped chanting, but she was still moving, grooving to a beat that only she — and maybe Amber, who was also grooving — could hear. Christy watched them for a moment: two big-haired, big-busted Jersey girls in tiny clothes. It was enough to make her nostalgic for home.

"Let's go out to eat," Amber said, dancing toward Gary and hooking her arm through his. Christy could feel Gary crowding closer to her in a useless attempt at evasion. "Then maybe we'll hit a few nightclubs. I feel like having a *par*-ty."

Amber echoed, "Yeah, *par*-ty."

Christy braced herself for the resumption of the chant.

"This is Ocracoke," Angie said dampeningly. "I don't think they have nightclubs."

Maxine made a dismissive gesture. "So we'll hit some bars. This place has bars, doesn't it? I've been dying for a margarita ever since I got here."

"Yeah, that serial killer had us spooked to the point where we were afraid to go out at night," Amber chimed in. "Now we can *par*-ty."

Maxine took it up. "Yeah, *par*-ty."

"Sounds like a plan," Luke said, with the air of a man who was most concerned with heading a head-ringing chant off at the pass. "Gary, man, why don't you take these ladies out on the town?"

"What about you?" Gary almost wailed as he was tugged into an impromptu shuffle with Amber. Christy watched Gary being danced around the room like a woeful rag doll and had to smile.

"You want to go?" Luke asked in her ear.

She shook her head. Call her a pessimist, but she was having trouble believing that the most urgent of her problems could be solved so easily. Either the authorities had made a mistake and the serial killer wasn't dead, or the serial killer was dead and it wasn't going to matter for her, personally, because the guy who was after her was a hit man. In her world, that was how things tended to work out.

"We're going to take a pass," Luke said, loud enough so that everyone could hear.

"You want me to stay with you?" Angie

asked her in a low tone. "You kind of look like you don't feel so good."

Christy shook her head. "It just gives me the shivers to think about that guy, is all," she said.

"I bet." Angie looked sympathetic. Then she glanced up at Luke. "You take care of her, hear?"

Angie's tone was fierce. Her question, Christy realized, was the equivalent of her stamping Luke with her seal of approval. On the whole, Angie, who'd grown up in an entirely female household, didn't have a lot of faith in men. The question indicated faith that Luke both could and would do as she asked, and was thus a compliment of the highest order. Not that Luke realized he was being complimented, of course; he didn't know enough about how Angie's psyche worked to see beyond the tough expression.

She couldn't see Luke's expression, but his arm tightened fractionally around her waist. "Don't worry, I will."

"Go have fun," Christy encouraged her.

Only as Angie nodded and headed down the hall to primp for a few minutes did Christy realize that she'd folded her arms on top of Luke's as she'd spoken. The knowledge so unsettled her that she missed the opening salvo of Gary's urgent protest to Luke, delivered in a near whisper as Amber and Maxine hurried after Angie.

"I'm going to go take a shower and change," Christy said, and freed herself from Luke's grip. Even though he was still talking with Gary, she could feel his eyes on her as she padded down the hall.

She deliberately took her time in the shower, refusing to allow a single unpleasant thought to enter her head, enjoying the steamy heat of the water hitting her face, breathing deeply of the mango-scented shampoo. When she finally got out, wrapped herself in a towel and padded into her bedroom, it was to find Marvin stretched out on her bed. He blinked sleepily at her as she scratched him behind an ear, and promptly went back to sleep. He might have a problem with men and noise, but it was hard to fault him for that. At different times she'd had problems with both herself.

When Christy padded barefoot back into the living room, she was wearing a pair of white capris she had borrowed from Angie's closet — her own wardrobe having been sadly depleted by the loss of her suitcase — and a hot pink T. Her lips were slicked with a smidgen of sheer pink gloss.

Other than that she wore no makeup, and when she thought about that it was kind of disconcerting. With Michael, she'd always been careful to wear full war paint, tastefully applied but definitely there; he had made no bones about liking her to look good, and to know that she had made an effort for him. With Luke, making an effort had never even crossed her mind. The nature of their relationship combined with the circumstances had made worrying about what she looked like the least important item on the agenda. It occurred to her that with Luke she was more free to be herself than she had ever been with Michael.

The thought was vaguely unsettling.

He was in the kitchen rummaging around in the refrigerator, and Christy perched on a barstool at the breakfast counter to watch. With the TV off now and no one else in the cottage, the lack of commotion was soothing.

"Hungry?" he asked over his shoulder. He was still wearing his blue trunks, she saw, and he'd pulled on his T-shirt, which was a faded and shapeless gray and which, if her memory served her correctly, had some sort of sports team logo on the front.

"Don't tell me you cook, too," she said,

idly admiring the taut and muscular rear that did such a superb job of turning that ancient pair of swim trunks into a thing of beauty.

"Sure I cook. Want to watch? There's some leftover pizza in here. How about I pop it in the microwave?"

Christy laughed, and felt some of the tension that had gripped her ease. For the first time since the TV broadcast she felt almost normal.

"Sounds good."

"Great." He pulled a pizza box and a bowl out of the refrigerator, set the bowl on the counter, lifted some pizza slices out of the box and put them on a plate, then put the plate into the microwave. "There's salad, too." He waved a hand at the bowl.

"I can hardly wait." A thought gripped her, and she frowned. "Um, do you have someone who usually does your cooking for you?"

Mouth curving, he turned, leaned back against the counter and folded his arms.

"FBI agents don't get paid enough to hire a cook. At least, this one doesn't."

Christy gave him a look. He knew perfectly well what she was getting at. "I meant like a girlfriend. Or, um, a wife."

"Honey, don't you think it's a little late

in our relationship for you to be asking me if I'm married?" There was a little thread of amusement running through his voice.

"Just answer the question, will you?"

"No. Not married, and never have been. My last serious relationship broke up a little over two years ago, when my girlfriend got a job in Texas and wanted me to go with her."

The microwave pinged. Luke turned, pulled the plate out, and closed the door. A few minutes later they were sitting at the table chatting companionably over pizza and salad. With the curtain open, the view was breathtaking. It was after seven, and the sunlight had taken on a mellow golden quality that rinsed everything in warm, glowing hues. The ocean rolled in, a deep, marine blue, and the sky was a near cloudless azure. The beach was still crowded, but not quite as crowded as earlier. Closer at hand, the house's shadow was just beginning to creep past the patio toward the dunes.

"So what do you think the chances are that this guy they were talking about on TV is the same guy who attacked me?" Christy asked, finally broaching the subject that had been preying on her mind as they carried their dishes to the kitchen.

"I don't know." Luke took her plate from her, put it into the dishwasher with his own, and turned to look at her. "The Bureau is certainly involved by now, even if it wasn't there at the house at the beginning, so I'll be able to get information as it comes in. By tomorrow we may know more. Right now, it's safer to assume there's still somebody out there who wants to kill you."

Christy made a face, and turned away to walk over to the patio door. "That's what I thought, too," she said, staring out. "God, I wish this was over with."

"Hey." He came up behind her and wrapped his arms around her waist. Christy stood unmoving for a moment as her heart speeded up and her breathing quickened. It was such a comfort to lean back against him, such a comfort to have his arms around her, such a comfort to know that whatever happened she was no longer alone. He smelled of soap and, faintly, of suntan lotion, and she found she loved the smell. Held against him like this, she could feel how tall he was, how strong and broad and solid, and she loved the way he felt. Then he bent his head, nuzzling her neck with his mouth, and she loved everything about that, too, from the firm moist heat of his mouth to the scratchiness of his bristly chin.

Her eyes drooped, her bones melted, and her hands slid along the hard warmth of the arms at her waist. Then she remembered that he was going to be in her life for probably no more than another few days; she remembered the lies he had told, and who and what he really was; and she remembered, most of all, that a broken heart was something she really did not need.

"We had a deal," she said, tamping firmly down on her own impulse to turn in his arms and lock her hands behind his neck and kiss him. "Remember the ground rules? No sex."

She pushed at the arms holding her, and, somewhat to her surprise, he let her go. Folding her arms, she turned to watch him as he dropped onto the couch. He slouched back, stretching one arm along the cushioned back, and looked at her out of eyes gone dark in the shadowy room.

"I remember the first time I ever saw you," he said, and she nodded.

"On the patio. You said you were looking for Marvin." Her voice was dry.

He shook his head. "Nah. The first time I ever saw you was long before that. I've been watching DePalma for a while, remember. It was about two years ago, in the fall. I remember, because when you got out of DePalma's car and walked into this restaurant with him leaves were blowing from a big oak tree near the sidewalk and one got caught in your hair. It must have gotten tangled in there some way or another, because it took you a minute to get it out. DePalma tried to help you and you looked up at him and laughed. You know you get dimples when you laugh? That was the first time I saw them, and they blew me away. I thought you were beautiful, and I thought DePalma didn't deserve to have a girl as beautiful as you laughing up at him like that. When you came out of the restaurant with him, he kissed your hand."

Christy drew a deep breath. There was a brooding quality to his tone that clutched at her heart.

"I remember that," she said softly. "I'd just negotiated a big contract for a client, and Michael took me out to lunch to celebrate."

"I remember how much I didn't like watching him kiss your hand. Looking back now, I think, on some subconscious level, I might have been wishing you were mine."

Christy felt her heart skip a beat. There

was no mistaking the heat in his eyes.

"There you go, trying to sweet-talk me again." She was trying to keep her emotions on an even keel, to remember why getting any further involved with him was a really, really bad idea. "Just so you know, it's not going to work."

His mouth curved wryly. "I'm opening my heart to you here, and all you can do is be suspicious." He shook his head. "Honey, did it ever occur to you that maybe we're falling in love?"

Christy's eyes widened and her head came up as though at a blow. He was watching her, still sitting in that negligent attitude on the couch, a golden beach god in swim trunks and a ratty T-shirt, and just looking at him made her stomach clench and her blood heat and her heart turn over. For a moment they simply stared at each other while heat seemed to sizzle in the air between them.

"No. Oh no." It couldn't be true. She didn't want it to be true. The thought that it might be true terrified her.

"Think about it," he said, very calmly, and then he leaned forward and caught her hand and pulled her down on the couch with him and kissed her.

33

At the touch of his mouth on hers she was lost. He kissed her gently, tenderly, his lips molding themselves to hers with exquisite care. Christy slid her hands over his broad shoulders and around his neck and kissed him back as if she'd die if she didn't, pushing her tongue inside his mouth, loving the warm, faintly spicy taste of him. Pressing her body against his, she reveled in the feel of him against her, in the unyielding firmness of his chest against her breasts, in the sturdy strength of his neck, in the crispness of the curls at his nape. As her fingers threaded through them he made a slight, harsh sound and pulled her across his lap, twisting a little with her so that her head was pillowed on his hard arm. Then his lips turned hard as they slanted across hers, taking control of the kiss, making her quiver and burn. His hand found her breast. . . .

Just as waves of heat threatened to swamp her, Christy thought of something, and pulled her mouth from his.

"Wait, Luke, no," she said, breathless, pushing at his shoulders. He lifted his head to look down at her. His eyes were ablaze.

"Christy . . ." His jaw was clenched, she saw, and his voice was hoarse.

"The cameras." It was capitulation, and they both knew it. There was nothing else she could do. She was so hot for him she was melting inside. She saw his eyes go all dark and dangerous, and she sucked in her breath.

"Damn the cameras," he said through his teeth, but he scooped her up and got to his feet with her in his arms and started walking with her toward the bedroom. Christy clung to him, pressing short, sweet kisses in a line along his jaw, her lips brushing against the firm, warm skin with its faint bristles, her teeth finding his earlobe and nibbling at it playfully.

"I love the way you taste," she whispered, and ran her lips down the throbbing cord at the side of his throat.

"God, I want you," he said, his voice thick. "I think I've wanted you for years."

"Luke . . ." But whatever she was going to say was lost forever as he put her down on the bed. It was still made, and the bedspread smelled faintly of something vaguely floral as she sank into it, pulling him down on top of her, loving the fact that he was heavy, that he was pressing her deep into the mattress, that his body was hard, that his arms were trembling with need.

"Look what you do to me. I think the last time my arms shook like this I was about sixteen," he said with the faintest touch of rueful humor, and then his mouth, hot and wet and hungry, took hers again. His hand found her breast, tightened over it, squeezed. She gasped into his mouth and slid her hands up his back under his shirt, pushing it up, trying to push it off.

"I want you naked," she pulled her mouth from his to repeat the words he'd once said to her.

His mouth curved.

"Naked's good," he said, his eyes hot, and sat up to pull his shirt over his head. Christy lay where he had left her, her nails digging into the bedspread as she watched him hook his thumbs in his waistband and slide his trunks down his legs. She had just a moment to admire the sheer golden splendor of him, the bronzed skin and firm muscles, the wide shoulders and narrow hips and powerful legs. Her fascinated gaze was focused on the hard evidence of his desire for her, huge and swollen as it jutted out from his body, when he reached for her, unfastening her pants with quick efficiency and pulling them and her panties down her legs in a single quick movement. Christy kicked to help him get them off, and was sitting up to pull her T-shirt over her head when he pulled it off for her, then reached around behind her back to unfasten her bra. When that came off he dropped it to the floor, then stood for a moment looking down at her. She was sitting in the middle of the bed, leaning back on her hands, naked, and as his gaze swept her she felt a rush of desire so intense that she shivered.

"Now look who's shaking," he said, his eyes hot and tender at the same time. Then he came down on top of her, pushing her into the mattress, his body hard and urgent as he found her mouth with his.

Christy met his kiss with her own, sliding her tongue inside his mouth, wrapping her arms around his neck, parting her legs for him. His legs slid between hers at the same time as his hand found her breast, and her need for him was suddenly so strong that she was reaching for him with both hands, on fire for him, melting, her bones turning to liquid as she guided him to her.

"Christy . . ." He tried to pull back, tried to slow it down, to make it last, but she couldn't wait, she needed him inside her, she was so hungry for him, so ready for him that her hips were coming up off the bed in a wordless plea.

"Now. Please."

He groaned and surrendered, pushing inside her, his body thick and hard and scalding hot, and suddenly she was coming, crying out, clinging to him, and he was thrusting deep and hard and fast, taking her with a fierceness that was exactly what she wanted, what she craved.

"Luke, Luke, *Luke*," she cried at the end, straining up against him.

"Christy," he groaned in answer, and buried himself inside her one last time, holding himself there as he found his own release.

Then it was over, and Christy simply lay there, drained, breathing hard, feeling the hot heavy warmth of him lying atop her with every nerve ending she possessed.

"You fucking whore." The voice came out of nowhere, out of her worst nightmare, paralyzing, terrifying, freezing her in place while an instantaneous explosion of cold sweat poured over her.

Michael.

Even as she put a name to the voice Luke moved, thrusting her away from him so that she fell off the far side of the bed, diving in the opposite direction himself while men shouted and gunshots exploded: *boom, boom, boom!*

Luke yelped and there was a heavy thud like a body hitting the floor and Christy couldn't see, couldn't get up, because the bedspread had come off the bed with her and it was heavy and she was tangled in it.

"Luke," she screamed, arms and legs flailing, finally managing to get to her knees and look across the bed, across the room, at Luke lying facedown on the carpet while Michael, flanked by two other men, stood over him with a gun.

"Michael, no!" Christy cried, and would have scrambled to her feet except the cover was heavy, way too heavy to allow her to move that easily. She was tangled in it. Realizing that it was all that kept her from being naked in front of Michael, in front of the strangers with him, she quit trying to lose it and instead clamped one arm across her bosom to hold it in place as she tried again to get to her feet.

Michael looked around at her. His face

could have been carved from stone. He wasn't as tall as Luke but he was handsome in a dark Italian way, with short black hair that was thinning on top, a hawkish nose and square jaw, and eyes so dark they were almost black. Those eyes snapped with fury as they ran over her, and she realized with a little thrill of terror that his pride had been outraged, that to his way of thinking he had caught her, his woman, his property, in flagrante delicto with another man.

"You fucking whore," he said to her. Then, to his men, "Keep him covered," as he stepped away from Luke and came around the bed toward her.

"Michael," she said, trying to think of some way out, some way to reason with him, to save herself and Luke because this was bad, Michael meant to kill them, she could see it in the taut fury with which he moved, in the jut of his jaw, in his eyes. Gary was gone and there was no one manning the monitors and they were caught, trapped, at Michael's mercy, his to do with as he would. He walked right up to her and slapped her in the face, slapped her so hard that she fell back, one hand flying to her face where her cheek burned and throbbed and stung.

"You want your diamonds?" Luke asked. His voice sounded strained, but Christy was so glad to hear it she barely noticed until she was on her knees again and looking across the bed toward him. He was sitting up, one hand pressed to his thigh, and she saw bright red blood oozing between his fingers. Oh God, he'd been shot.

"Damned right I want my diamonds," Michael said, pivoting to face Luke. His gun was pointed down now, but it didn't matter because the other two men had their weapons trained on Luke. Like Michael, they were wearing dark dress slacks and pale short-sleeved shirts, but unlike him they were nondescript goon types, one dark-haired, the other bald. "Where are my diamonds?" Michael asked Luke.

Christy tried again to get to her feet, bringing the cover up with her. It was still impossibly heavy, but a barely audible snarl and the faintest of movements beneath the tangled folds made her freeze. Marvin . . .

"Let Christy go and I'll give them to you."

Michael laughed. It was a chilling sound that made Christy's blood run cold. It told her as plainly as if he'd said it aloud that he was going to kill her as soon as he got what he wanted: the diamonds.

Oh, why, why, why hadn't they stayed on guard?

"You want me to shoot him in the knee, boss?" the bald goon asked, and Christy gasped. She recognized that voice: the man on the phone. Her heart slammed against her chest, and she went cold all over as her gaze swept him. Stocky, about five-ten, dark-complected. Bald, but he could have worn a cap. Was this her attacker? It was possible; probable . . .

"Hey, little girl," he said, glancing over at her in response to her gasp, and waggled his fingers at her. As she met those dark eyes, Christy went light-headed with terror. For an instant the room seemed to spin.

"I'm not playing games here. I want my diamonds." Michael turned and leveled his gun at Christy. Staring down the mouth of that pistol, she knew despair. She had tried so hard to live, worked so hard to live, done everything she could to live, and she was going to die anyway. It wasn't fair.

Marvin growled again, and pressed against her leg. She could feel his warm slick fur just above her knee.

"Oh God, Michael, please. Please don't hurt me." Cowering, Christy bent double, her hands clasped together pleadingly as she abased herself on the carpet, her eyes huge and teary as they fastened on Michael's face. "I'll do anything. Please. Please."

"Give me my fucking diamonds." It was a furious growl. Christy knew the signs: Michael was losing his cool. Once the slide started, it didn't take him long. A few more minutes, and he'd be raging mad — and she and Luke would die.

"I'll get them. Just don't hurt me. Please."

Breathless with eagerness to get him what he wanted and thus, possibly, save her own life, Christy got clumsily to her feet, clutching the bedspread around her, trying to juggle the tangled folds so that she had her hands on what she needed when she needed it.

"Hurry up."

Clearly not considering her a threat, Michael's gaze swept back to Luke. Christy took advantage of his momentary lack of attention to fire her weapon: Marvin. She released her grip on the bedspread and hurled the cat toward Michael. Marvin hit the target, and Michael screamed and dropped his gun.

As Christy dove after it, from the corner

of her eye she watched Michael and Marvin engage in an epic battle complete with curses, shouts, and yowls. Nearer the door, Luke was in motion, too, lashing out with his feet and hands, sending guns somersaulting through the air and bringing the goons crashing to the floor. Beyond Luke, there was a flurry of movement in the hall.

"Freeze, assholes," Gary yelled, bursting through the bedroom door, new hairstyle, baggy shorts and all, and assuming combat stance, knees bent, both hands clasping his gun. "FBI!"

Except for Marvin, who leaped from Michael's shoulder to go tearing past Gary, everyone froze.

Michael put his hands in the air, his eyes gleaming savagely.

Christy more or less slithered back to where she had dropped the bedspread and wrapped it around herself before her knees gave out and she collapsed in a boneless heap beside the bed. Luke, naked, blood running down his leg, got rather gingerly to his feet and grabbed a gun.

"Get up," he barked at the goons, who were still on the floor. Then, as they scrambled to their feet, "Get your hands up and get against the wall."

As Michael and the goons complied,

Gary glanced around and scooped up the remaining gun. Then he handed Luke his trunks.

Half an hour later, what seemed like half of Ocracoke packed the cottage. It was still early, not quite ten o'clock and just getting full dark, and the neighbors were out in force, drawn by the flashing lights of the police cars and ambulance in front of the house. Sheriff Schultz and various assorted deputies, including Gordie Castellano, were on the scene, taking statements, getting photographs, gathering evidence. Aaron Steinberg was there, practically salivating over the prospect of another huge story for his little paper. Amber and Maxine followed Gary around like overly exuberant puppies. Angie stuck close to Christy. Michael and the goons had just been taken away by FBI agents in the area to work on the serial killer task force, which had not yet been disbanded. Luke was sitting on the couch having his leg looked at by paramedics and arguing about whether or not he needed to go to the hospital. Christy, fully dressed again, was curled in a chair near Luke. Her cheeks were still faintly pink from the statements she'd had to give. Explaining exactly what she and Luke had been doing to be taken so unawares by Michael and his goons hadn't been easy.

In fact, she'd taken a leaf from Luke's book and lied.

"Just bandage it up and I'll get it looked at tomorrow," Luke was saying impatiently to the paramedic prodding his thigh. Luke was dressed again, too, in trunks and T-shirt, and his pants leg had been pushed up to allow access to the wound, which was just above his knee. It wasn't much more than a flesh wound, just a thumb-sized gouge taken out of his flesh by a bullet that had gone on to bury itself in the floor, and thanks to some first aid it had quit bleeding, but the flesh around it had swollen up pretty significantly and the paramedic wanted to take him, at the very least, to the clinic.

"You probably could use a couple of stitches," Christy told him with a lurking smile. He glanced up, met her gaze, and his mouth curved. The paramedic stood up just then to confer with his partner, and Luke leaned toward her.

"Just so you know, that's going to be one of my all-time favorite memories: Michael DePalma being taken down by a naked woman with a cat."

"Hush," Christy said, glancing around in alarm. Of course, there was no hiding anything from Gary, Angie, Amber, and Maxine, who had been discouraged by the long wait at their restaurant of choice and had decided to let Gary make dinner instead. Christy wasn't sure exactly how much they'd witnessed — Angie just grinned at her when she asked — but Gary at least had seen enough to come rushing to their rescue.

"How's your face?" Eyes darkening, Luke lifted a gentle hand to the cheek Michael had slapped.

"It's fine." Actually, it was still just a little tender, but she didn't see any reason to tell him that. She smiled at him. "Hey, we did it. We got Michael. It's all over."

His lips quirked. "Afraid I'm going to have to wait and jump around all excited-like tomorrow."

Christy laughed.

"If you're sure you don't want to go to the clinic, we can just bandage it up for tonight." The paramedic was back, crouching down in front of Luke, opening his kit.

"I'm sure," Luke said firmly. As the paramedic starting unrolling gauze, Christy stood up and moved toward the patio door to get out of the way.

The curtain was still open, and through the window she could see the dark gleam of the ocean as the tide washed in. The pale quarter moon was just starting its journey across the sky, and Christy could see its reflection in the water. For a moment she stood there, looking out at the beauty of the night, listening to the goings-on behind her with half an ear, as the tension began to slowly creep out of her body.

As she had told Luke, it was over. She could get on with her life now. She was unemployed, but getting another job shouldn't be that difficult. She was no longer part of a couple — no, she took that back. A smile touched her lips as she caught a glimpse of Luke's reflection in the glass. She was part of a new couple. She thought. She hoped.

Luke had asked her if she thought they were falling in love.

Just considering the possibility made her feel warm and fuzzy all over.

A movement on the patio made her frown. She looked more closely, trying to see past the reflections in the glass. A pair of bright gold eyes turned her way, gleaming in the moonlight.

Marvin: in all the confusion, he'd managed to get out.

Sighing, Christy slid the door open and stepped outside.

The warm sea breeze caressed her face as she crept down the fence in pursuit of Marvin, who was clearly hunting again. It smelled of brine, and was heavy in a way that warned of rain. There would probably be a storm before morning.

"Marvin." She could see him. He was at the edge of the dunes now, but she stopped at the end of the patio, suddenly nervous. Although she had left the door open behind her and could faintly hear voices through it, the living room seemed very far away.

She heard a crunch, as of a footstep, and a little frisson of fear ran down her spine. Looking sharply in the direction from which the sound had come, she tensed as adrenaline flooded her system. Her fight or flight response, having been subjected to one heck of a good workout lately, was primed and ready.

"Is that you, Christy?" Mrs. Castellano came around the corner of the fence, hobbling on her cane.

"Oh, hi, Mrs. Castellano," Christy said, relaxing.

"Your mama called," Mrs. Castellano said as she got closer. "She wonders why you haven't been calling her."

Christy was just opening her mouth to reply when Mrs. Castellano slid a hand around her arm. She looked down at that rough hand in surprise — and felt something hard thrust into her neck.

Pain stabbed into her body like a knife. With no more than a single gasp, she collapsed into darkness.

34

She was being rocked, gently rocked, sweetly rocked, not to sleep but to wakefulness. Stubbornly Christy clung to the retreating shadows, not wanting to relinquish blessed oblivion. On some subconscious level she knew that being aware was bad. . . .

Clang. The sound of metal against metal was sharp enough to startle her eyes open. For a few merciful seconds her vision remained blurry, but then it cleared. What she saw turned her blood to ice. She was in a cell, pinned in by iron bars on three sides, lying on a wooden floor. Everything was moving, in the gentle rocking motion she remembered from her dream. A boat, she realized with a clawing sense of panic. She was on a boat. Locked in a cell on a boat.

"Can you hear me?" The urgent whisper came from her left. Christy glanced around, tried to sit up. Something clattered when she moved her leg. Looking down, she felt a thrill of horror as she saw the shackle around her ankle. It was attached to a chain that ran to a loop in the wall.

Oh my God. This had to be a nightmare. It was supposed to be all over. She was supposed to be safe.

"Hey." The whisper was sharper. The voice was rough, scratchy. "We don't have much time. What's your name?"

This time Christy's gaze traveled far enough to find the occupant of the cell next to hers. The light was dim and shadowy, provided by a single fixture swaying from the ceiling. But she was able to discern matted dark hair not much longer than her own; a small form wrapped in a tattered blue blanket; a thin, pale face and dark, hopeless-looking eyes.

"Christy." Even her voice sounded strange. Thin, otherworldly.

"I'm Terri. You have to help me figure out a way to get out of here. He's going to kill us."

A little electric shock of terror sliced through the fog that still shrouded Christy's brain.

"Wh-who?"

"I don't know his name. He's a psychopath. He makes us call him *master.*"

"Us? Are there more?"

"Oh God, no." Terri's voice broke. "Liz — Liz got away. I don't know what happened to her. She said she'd send help. But it's been a long time. . . ."

Her voice trailed off into heavy breathing that wasn't quite sobs.

A lightbulb went on in Christy's brain. "Liz? Terri?" She took a deep breath, trying to clear the last of the cobwebs away, trying to think. "Elizabeth Smolski? Terri Miller?"

Terri clutched the bars separating their cells with a clawlike hand. "Yes. *Yes.* How do you know our names?"

"People are looking for you. You've been reported missing. They think you're the victim of a serial killer." Horror rocketed through her. Her voice shook. "Oh my God, this guy's the serial killer."

"Do you have anything on you we could use to try to pick these locks? A bobby pin, maybe? Or a barrette?"

"No." Christy's mind raced to try to find a way out. "Liz got away. How did she do it?"

Terri sucked in a ragged breath. "She was missing some of the bones in her foot. From an accident. She could squeeze it real small. She kept working at it, and one day she was able to squeeze it out of the shackle. By then she was real thin, thin enough where she could slip between the bars. So she did. But she couldn't get me out. And she was afraid to stay. It was night, and we were out on the water, and he had gone ashore. She leaped over-board." Terri paused, and Christy could hear her breathing. "I know she didn't make it. If she'd made it, she'd have sent help."

Christy didn't have the heart to tell her what had happened to Liz.

"That's why you're in that cell. He never used to put us next to each other. But he can't figure out how Liz got out, and I keep acting like I don't know. He thinks there's some kind of escape hatch in that other cell." She gave the merest hint of a rusty-sounding laugh.

"Have you tried screaming?" Christy asked urgently. "What happens when you scream?"

"It doesn't do any good." Terri sounded exhausted now. "Nobody comes."

The boat swayed, and Christy heard a creak, as if a door had opened. The sounds were small, innocuous in and of them-selves, and yet they were scaring her to death.

There was no mistaking the sounds of footsteps coming down the stairs.

"Here he comes," Terri warned in a terrified squeak, and scuttled away from the adjoining bars to huddle back against the wall.

Christy heard a faint rattling. Dread ricocheted through her as she realized that the sound was coming from Terri's chain. Terri was so frightened she was shaking.

Christy's heart lodged in her throat as the footsteps reached the bottom. She couldn't see anything more of him than a shadow — a bulky, dark shadow. Heart pounding, chest heaving, she stared at that shadow as it turned toward her.

Then she saw who it was, and she was so stunned she could do nothing but stare. Her breathing suspended. Her mind went blank. Her heart skipped a beat.

"Hi, Christy," Mrs. Castellano said in that weird high-pitched voice that had chased Christy through her nightmares. Then as Christy gaped at her she reached up and pulled off her wig.

A warm breath of wind caressed his face, and Luke looked up from having his leg wrapped to discover the patio door open. He frowned, and glanced around the room. There were people here, there, and everywhere, but no sign of Christy.

He felt the sudden tension in his shoulders. Glancing around again, he spotted Angie talking to Gordie Castellano.

"Angie." When she looked his way he beckoned. When she was near he asked, "Have you seen Christy?"

Angie shook her head, and glanced around, too. "She was right here." Her gaze riveted on the open patio door, and she frowned. "Did she go outside?"

"I don't know. The door's open." Impatiently he pulled his leg away from the paramedic, who was making a procedure out of securing the gauze with tape.

Angie was already at the door. "I'll just check."

"Wait for me." Luke didn't know why, but he was starting to get a bad feeling about this. A real bad feeling. Following Angie, he stepped out through the door and glanced around the partially lit patio and into the darkness beyond. No Christy. Nothing except Marvin, crouched under a chair.

"Come here, Marvin." Angie scooped him up. Luke wasted a second to marvel at the attraction that nasty-tempered animal held for the sisters Petrino, then dismissed the cat from his mind.

"What are you two doing out here?" Maxine stepped out onto the patio.

"Have you seen Christy?" Luke and Angie asked in practically the same breath.

"No." Maxine looked from one to the other of them. "Why? Have you lost her?"

"It's not funny, Maxine," Angie said in a sharp voice.

"Sorry." Maxine stepped back inside the door and bellowed to the crowd in general. "Has anybody here seen Christy?"

"She was out on the patio," Aaron Steinberg volunteered. "Talking to Mrs. Castellano."

"Oh my God," Christy whispered, as Mrs. Castellano peeled latex wrinkles from each cheek. Then she straightened, squaring her shoulders, and all of a sudden she seemed much taller and not at all frail.

Mrs. Castellano — whoever this person was — smiled at her, a slow smile of anticipation. The boat rocked, the lantern swung, and light hit her full in the face.

"Uncle Sally," Christy gasped. It had been years — eighteen years — but his face suddenly appeared in her mind's eye as clearly as if she had seen it yesterday.

The smile broadened. "I thought you would remember," he said with satisfaction. "In fact, I knew you would. You always were a smart little girl."

"But . . . I thought you were dead — it was a hit — I always thought of it as payback for what you did to my father." Christy's voice started shaking on the last words.

"What makes you think I did anything to your father?"

Christy felt as if an iron band was constricting her chest. It was hard to breathe, to talk. All she could do was stare at this nightmare out of her past — and remember.

"I know you did it. I know you did it. I always knew. I came out of the house and he was lying there on the driveway with a gun beside him. When I went to him, I picked it up. It was still warm, and I could smell it — it had just been fired. He'd just come out of the house; he'd just been talking to me. *There was no reason.* I heard a car start up in the street. I looked up, and I saw you in the driver's seat. I saw you as clearly as I'm seeing you now."

"Yeah," Uncle Sally said. "And I saw you."

"My mother was afraid. She kept telling

me I was mistaken. She kept telling me I saw nothing."

"Your mother's a smart woman."

"They killed you. Why didn't you die? You should have died." Christy's voice grew high-pitched with hysteria. "I thought you died."

"See, I got a thing about that," Uncle Sally said, reaching for the lock on her cell. Christy saw that he had a key in his hand, and terror ricocheted along her nerve endings. "I don't like the whole idea of dying. Now, killing, that's a different story. I like killing. I'm especially going to like killing *you*."

"Sweet Jesus," Gordie Castellano whispered, but Luke heard, and his head whipped around so fast his vision blurred. One look at Castellano's paling face told Luke that something was badly awry.

"You know something," he said, moving toward Castellano. His throbbing leg didn't even slow him down. Castellano looked at him, and Luke saw fear and confusion in his eyes. Every instinct he possessed went on red alert, and he snarled, looming over Castellano, backing him up against the wall. *"Tell me."*

Castellano sucked in a ragged breath.

"Christy's in danger. Whatever you know, *tell me.*"

"I kept telling him she wasn't a threat. What would a little girl remember, I kept asking him. But he was obsessed. Just nuts with it. He thought she saw him. When he hit Joe Petrino. He was just sure of it. He kept following her around, ever since she got here. I told him, you're gonna make her remember you. But he said, she already does."

"Who?" Luke demanded. *"Who?"*

"Aunt Rosa," he said. "Only she's not Aunt Rosa. She — he's my cousin Sally, Salvatore Castellano. He was kind of nuts, you know, got carried away with things, killing people he was only supposed to rough up, that sort of thing. A real loose cannon. So they hit him, only he didn't die but he had to hide. Aunt Rosa hid him in her basement for fifteen years. Every once in a while he'd come out at night, but that's all. He was going nuts from the confinement. He wanted to see the sun. So when Aunt Rosa died, he got a guy to help him look like her, and he moved down here. Like she retired to the beach, see?"

"Where would he take her?"

"Christ, I don't know. Wait. His boat. He's got a houseboat called the *Lorelei*.

See, he gets tired of being Aunt Rosa sometimes, so he goes down to this boat and he can be a guy again. He even got a little business going with the marina where the boat is, a boat launching service." Castellano's voice thickened. "I know I shouldn't have helped him, but he's *family*, for God's sake. And I didn't think he was doing any harm."

Luke was so scared now he was practically jumping out of his skin. "Where is it? The boat?"

Castellano told him.

In the cell beside Christy, Terri started keening. The high-pitched wailing sound was like terror given voice, and it made the hair stand up on the back of Christy's neck. Uncle Sally looked around sharply.

"Shut that noise up!" He banged on the bars. Terri choked the sound off instantly, but it was too late. His attention turned to her.

"You wanna go first? Sure, you can go first. It doesn't make no difference, I'm gonna do you both anyway. I'm going to California. The Beachcomber is going to California."

His voice was starting to go high-pitched, and Christy's heart speeded up until it felt like it would pound clear through her chest. That high-pitched voice — that was the voice he had used both times he had attacked her. It must be a sign that he was getting psyched up to kill. . . .

"But they found the Beachcomber," she said loudly, hoping to throw him off, hoping to keep him relatively sane for as long as possible. She would have been missed by now, she calculated, and they'd be looking for her. Searching frantically for her. Luke. Angie.

How could they possibly know where she was?

Don't think about that, she told herself fiercely. *You need to stay calm. You need to stay cool.*

"It was on the news," she continued as he stopped and glanced back at her. "The Beachcomber killed himself. They found him, along with the remains of some of his victims, in a house in Nags Head."

Uncle Sally made a *tch*-ing sound. "They're stupid," he said. "I set that up. The guy was a pervert named Andrew Madden. Used to go around peeping in windows. I just took some of my girls over there — their remains, that is — planted some evidence, made it look like a suicide.

They may figure it out — that damned DNA shit stinks — but they may not. Even if they do, by that time I'll be long gone." He headed back toward Christy again. "And I won't ever have to worry about you anymore."

He stopped in front of the door to her cell, and slid the key into the lock.

As she heard it go home, Christy trembled with fear.

Terri began to keen again.

By the time they reached the rickety old dock that Castellano directed them to, Luke was sweating buckets. He was sick with fear, light-headed with it, crazed at the idea that somehow they'd got it wrong, that he'd be too late, that Christy would be dead.

Even the thought of it made him feel like he was going to pass out.

Please, God, let her be all right.

He wasn't a praying man, but he was praying now, praying like he'd never prayed for anything in his life as he raced along the dock with the others — Gary, Castellano, Sheriff Schultz, the deputies — pounding after him. It was at the end of the dock, the only boat there, a ramshackle old houseboat that looked about as seaworthy as a tank. He checked himself as he reached it, afraid to leap aboard, afraid of making it pitch, of alerting Castellano to the fact of his presence.

Stepping lightly onto the deck, making a shushing gesture to the people behind him, he saw faint glimmers of light around the edges of a door. Creeping toward it, he turned the knob, eased it open, and started cautiously down the stairs, gun held stiffly at his side.

Christy screamed. The sound was muffled, distant, but so loaded with terror that it pierced the air like a blade.

Terror grabbed him by the throat, and he took the rest of those stairs in great leaps. There was another door at the bottom, and he opened that, too, not bothering to be cautious but flinging it open, and the scream hit him in the face.

Sweating, panting, he leaped down the stairs.

And saw Christy. She was bent back over a table with the bastard leaning over her tying her hands down, while she kicked and twisted and screamed and did everything she possibly could to fight for her life.

"Freeze, FBI!" he yelled.

Christy shrieked. The bastard looked

around, grabbed a handful of her hair, and lifted a knife. The crazily swinging light caught the blade, making it gleam shiny silver.

Luke dropped him with a single shot as the cavalry came thundering down the stairs after him.

Then his leg gave out and he had to sit down.

35

Just after noon the following day, Luke opened his eyes, glanced at the glowing numbers on the bedside clock, and groaned. Loaded with painkillers administered when his leg had been cleaned and stitched up the night before, he had fallen into bed shortly before five a.m. and immediately passed out. That meant he'd had — what? — something in the nature of seven hours of sleep. Then it occurred to him that he was alone: Christy was gone. He rolled onto his back to make sure, and a stab of pain in his thigh made him wince. It also brought a flood of memories with it.

With the rescue complete and Gary for an escort, Christy and Terri Miller had been taken immediately to the clinic to be checked over. Starved and traumatized but with no life-threatening injuries, Terri had been helicoptered to a hospital on the mainland, where she was to be reunited with her overjoyed parents sometime today. Except for assorted bumps, bruises, and scrapes, and a whole heck of a lot of wear and tear on her nerves, Christy had been pronounced fine. Having stayed on the *Lorelei* long enough to debrief the agents from the serial killer task force who had arrived to take over, he had arrived at the clinic just as Christy was being released. Christy had stayed with him while his leg was treated, and then, since he'd been woozy as hell, she and Gary had driven him back to her cottage and put him to bed. He'd gone out like a light, but he retained the distinct impression of her warm body having been curled at his side while he slept.

She was gone now. He was alone in her bed in the shadowy bedroom with the door firmly shut.

Residual fear caused his heart to skip a beat. He had to deliberately remind himself that it was all over: she was safe. There was nothing in the world to stop him from closing his eyes and going back to sleep.

Yeah, right.

"Christy!" He had to get up and find her.

His bandaged thigh ached like a sore tooth, but he managed to pull on his trunks and hobble into the living area, where sunlight poured in through the patio doors. Except for dancing dust motes and a smug-looking Marvin, the cottage was deserted.

Where was everybody?

Marvin went to the patio doors and meowed.

Don't tempt me, cat, he thought, as he joined him in front of the glass. Looking out, he saw that the sky was a beautiful, cloudless azure. The sea was a frothy indigo. And the sand sparkled like white sugar beneath a butterscotch candy sun. Happy vacationers crowded the beach, sunning and playing. More happy vacationers romped in the surf. And at least one happy vacationer soared high in the sky, dangling from a parasail being towed by a boat bouncing over the waves.

For no particular reason, his eyes were drawn to a bodacious blond babe in an itty-bitty black bikini standing with her back to him, waving at someone he couldn't see. A bodacious blond babe with a booty-licious ass.

Christy. *That's* why he'd felt that magnetic pull. Edging Marvin aside with his foot, Luke managed to get outside while keeping the cat in, and limped down the path toward the beach.

She was standing barefoot on the sand just beyond the dunes, watching as her sister, the Barbie twins, and Gary paddled out to sea on brightly colored polyurethane floats. She must have sensed his presence just as he'd sensed hers, because as he came up behind her she looked around.

"Hi," he said.

"How are you feeling?" she asked, her eyes running over him from head to toe.

"Never better."

She grinned at him like she knew that he was lying through his teeth.

Luke felt his mouth curve at her.

For someone who had just survived a harrowing ordeal, she was looking mighty fine, he thought. Eyeing her appreciatively, Luke decided that he had a previously unrecognized jones for women with choppy blond hair and purplish rings around their eyes and the faintest of bruises on their cheeks.

Or maybe just a jones for Christy.

"You ready to make the most of your last few days at the beach?" he asked.

Christy made a face at him. "To tell you the truth, I think I've had about enough of the beach for a while."

"Me, too," Luke said. "I'm kind of thinking about packing up and heading

590

back to Philly. Want a ride?"

"Can I bring Marvin?"

Luke narrowed his eyes at her. Wasn't that the way life worked? A fly for every ointment. "Sure. But I'm putting both of you on notice: if he takes a dump in my car, he's hitchhiking the rest of the way home."

Christy laughed.

Watching, Luke felt his heart swell exactly like the Grinch's when he woke up to the meaning of Christmas Day.

"You had a chance to think about that falling-in-love thing yet?" he asked.

"Yeah, I've had a chance to think about it."

"Well?"

"I'm for it," she said, and, being careful not to jostle his injured leg, she stepped right up to him and wrapped her arms around his neck.

Then she kissed him.

And when she was done kissing him, her fingers found his, and they walked hand in hand off the beach.

The employees of Thorndike Press hope you have enjoyed this Large Print book. All our Thorndike and Wheeler Large Print titles are designed for easy reading, and all our books are made to last. Other Thorndike Press Large Print books are available at your library, through selected bookstores, or directly from us.

For information about titles, please call:

(800) 223-1244

or visit our Web site at:

www.gale.com/thorndike
www.gale.com/wheeler

To share your comments, please write:

Publisher
Thorndike Press
295 Kennedy Memorial Drive
Waterville, ME   04901

DATE DUE

GAYLORD			PRINTED IN U.S.A.